CAROLINE BOND was born in Scarborough and studied English at Oxford University before working as a market researcher for 25 years. She has an MA in Creative Writing from Leeds Trinity University, and lives in Leeds with her husband and three children.

The Second Child

Caroline Bond

CORVUS

First published in trade paperback in Great Britain in 2018 by Corvus,
an imprint of Atlantic Books Ltd.

This edition published in 2018 by Corvus.

3 5 7 9 10 8 6 4 2

A CIP catalogue record for this book is
available from the British Library.

Paperback ISBN: 978 1 78649 336 1
E-Book ISBN: 978 1 78649 337 8

Printed and bound in Great Britain by
CPI Group (UK) Ltd, Croydon CR0 4YY
Corvus
An Imprint of Atlantic Books Ltd
Ormond House
26–27 Boswell Street
London
WC1N 3JZ

www.corvus-books.co.uk

In memory of
Frances Anne Bond
who was a reader,
a good writer
and a very good mum.

1

The Results

SARAH

OUR DESTINATION is a nondescript waiting room located in the far corner of the hospital. A cul-de-sac tucked far away from the normal, noisy traffic of the wards and clinics. It's an appropriate location. The genetics department rarely sees patients; for us they've made an exception.

There's no one around to welcome us, just a series of blank doors facing onto a small waiting area. There are windows, but they're too high up to see out of. Two flickery fluorescent tubes make up for the lack of natural daylight. There's a water dispenser and a single row of grubby, wipe-clean vinyl chairs. They're empty. No one else is in our predicament.

We're early for our appointment, desperate for an end to the hiatus of the past ten days, but now we're here I'm gripped by the desire to run away. I can't settle. I pace. Nine steps to the wall and turn. Nine steps and turn.

Phil is immobile. He sits, hunched forward, staring at his shoes, utterly still and unreachable. It's his way of coping. He's trying to protect himself from what's happening, but he can't. He hasn't looked me squarely in the face for days, but I've caught his oblique glances when I've been busy doing something or when he thought I was reading or sleeping. I've seen his confusion and hurt and, beneath that, his doubts – doubts that I've been unable to assuage. How can I explain the inexplicable? How can I defend myself against an accusation that he can't bring himself to level against me? Instead of talking things through, sharing our fears, we've retreated into our respective corners and waited for today, and for the results.

Nine steps and turn.

Phil keeps his head bowed as if he's praying, but I know he's not; the only faith he has is 'us' and that's been called into question. Besides, it's not prayer that's going to save our marriage, it's science.

The scuffed door with the black name-plaque, outside which we wait, is closed. On the other side of the door is *Mr Stephen Berill. PhD, CSU Lead Clinician, Department of Clinical Genetics*. Mr Berill knows our future because he has looked into our past. He knows and we do not. So we must wait. We must bear the corrosive ignorance for a few minutes more.

Nine steps and turn.

The distant sounds of the hospital leak around the corner.

Phil does not look up.

Nine steps and turn.

At last the door opens and a smart woman in her fifties emerges. Her voice booms around the spartan waiting room. 'Good morning. Maria Tharby. We spoke on the phone.' She extends her hand, first to me, then to Phil. Brisk, smiling. 'Please, come through.' Like obedient children we follow her into the room. 'Stephen. Mr and Mrs Rudak are here.' A tall man steps out from behind his desk. His hand is papery-dry in mine. He says 'hello' in a soft Scottish voice, then falls silent, letting the woman do all the talking, and she is still talking. 'I know this must seem unnecessarily pedantic, but could I just check: you have brought the documents with you, haven't you?'

I nod. For a second her sparkly tone falters. 'I'm sorry, but may I see them.'

'Yes, sorry, of course.' I fumble the envelope out of my bag and pass it to her.

'Please, take a seat.' We do as instructed and she talks some more. 'As I explained on the phone, I'm afraid I have to repeat the identity checks again today. Overkill, I know, but the data-protection guidelines – as you can imagine… in the circumstances…' She flutters her hand through the air as if to sum up the complexity of it all, but when her eyes meet the blankness of mine she subsides back to her task. She pulls our documents out of the envelope and begins to go through them. 'Passports *and* birth certificates, excellent. If you can bear with me, just a moment, while I take down the details, then I promise we'll get under way.'

Phil and I have no choice but to sit there while she laboriously records whatever it is she needs to record onto her set of official forms. She starts with Lauren's passport, cracking open the cover and turning to the photo pages at the back. Lauren, at ten, round-faced and unsmiling. The main colour image is as clear as my memory, the duplicate image, on the facing page, faded and recessive, like a child from the past. I hold myself still as the silty anxiety in my stomach churns.

'You'll be needing a new one for her soon.' Ms Tharby chatters away as she transcribes the dates and serial numbers. 'And her birth certificate… Ah, here it is. Oh…' She separates the sheets of paper with a moistened fingertip. 'You seem to have brought your son's along as well. I've no need for his, thank you.' She hands it back to me. 'Now, just yourself and Philip's details, and we'll be finished.' Phil stares at her, in disbelief. I stare past her, at Mr Berill. He has gone back to work, immune to Ms Tharby's brittle prattle and to our presence: glasses on, head down, his attention totally focused on the lab report on the desk in front of him. In his hands Mr Berill holds the fragile skeins that bind our family together. I watch him, unable to discern our fate.

PHIL

The administrator woman seems incapable of shutting up. On and on she rambles. I stare at her and concentrate on thinking... nothing. It's more difficult than it sounds. It's been a struggle to keep control of the tight coil of possibilities that has been wedged in my gut for the past ten days, but somehow I've managed it. The alternative is unbearable. Sarah and I do not lie to each other, we have never lied to each other; she would not lie to me, not about this. So that's what I've chosen to think – nothing, because nothing is far less frightening than the alternative. I resolutely refuse to start chasing nightmares until we know, for definite, what the tests say. It's hard work. I focus on the pressure in my spine and wait for the bloody woman to shut up.

'All done,' she eventually trills, gathering together her forms with officious zeal. She glances at the consultant, transferring the power to him, then withdraws to a chair at the back of the room. Her job done. We turn our attention to Mr Berill. He removes his glasses and composes himself. When he finally speaks his voice is low and calm. 'First of all, I want to apologise for the length of time this has taken, it must have been very difficult for you. It was a consequence of the initial problems in obtaining your daughter's samples and the resultant delay in them coming through to the lab. Our sincere apologies for that. Thank you for your patience. We also wanted to be absolutely confident in our reading of the results.'

'And are you?' Sarah asks.

'Yes.' He slides his finger under the top cover of the file and flips it open. 'The results have been checked, very thoroughly, and we've run a number of extra screens, above the usual PCR and RFLP approaches, due to the result.' Sarah edges forward on her seat. I stare at his downturned face, wanting to shake the answer out of him. 'We were obviously tasked to establish Lauren's paternity, but I'm afraid we were unable to do that.' Sarah makes an inarticulate noise. I taste ash in my mouth. 'What we've found is very unexpected.' He hesitates and picks up his glasses again, twisting the frame between his fingers. 'The tests... all the tests we ran... confirm, unequivocally, that Lauren is not your biological child.'

'That can't be!' Defiance from Sarah, absolute defiance.

The nightmares I've kept buried scream free. Sarah lied.

'Please, Mrs Rudak, you must hear me out.' Mr Berill has to raise his voice to overcome Sarah's furious denials.

'But it's not true. I—'

He cuts her off. 'Mrs Rudak! Please! It's very important that you *both* hear me out.' He waits for silence, and in the gap I start to mourn. He begins speaking again, insistent, slow, clear words. 'What I mean is: she is neither your child, Phil, nor is she yours, Sarah. Lauren shares no DNA with *either* of you.' One beat, two beats. The blood still flows through my heart, oxygen must still be reaching my brain, for his soft, educated, authoritative voice still gets through. 'You both scored zero per cent on "probability of parentage".' He waits, letting what he's just said seep in. 'We've already looked into a possible chimera situation, but we've discounted that.' I concentrate very hard on listening to one word after another. 'I'm sorry, but to clarify: the test results categorically confirm that Lauren is not your biological daughter.' He looks from me to Sarah. 'I'm so very sorry. I can only try to imagine the shock you must be feeling.'

It feels like a car crash. I ricochet from one soul-jarring impact headlong into another, leaving me stupid with shock. 'What're you talking about? How can she not be ours? I don't get it.'

The woman lamely chips in, 'We appreciate that this must be a dreadful shock.'

'No, I don't get it. How is that possible?' My voice is shaking.

Mr Berill draws a deep breath. 'That I don't know; all I can do today is go through the results with you.' He gestures at the papers in the file. 'I can explain the processes we've used, but I'm afraid the conclusive finding is that Lauren is not your biological child.' The sound of Sarah's chair being pushed back draws our attention. She curls forward in her seat and wraps her arms around her knees, a tight curve of misery. 'Mrs Rudak, are you all right?' Mr Berill makes a move to come out from behind his desk, but I stop him.

Sarah is my wife. Sarah did not lie. Sarah has never lied to me. I kneel down beside her and tentatively place my hand on her back. 'Sarah?' I need her to come back to me. I need to tell her that I'm so sorry I ever doubted her. I need to get through to her, to comfort her. I need her. But she doesn't unlock. I keep my hand there, touching her, pressing my fingers gently into the soft fabric of her jumper, trying to reach her. Eventually I feel her lean her weight back into me as she unfurls upright to face him and, in a voice that sounds unnaturally normal, she says, 'Are you telling me we have another daughter out there somewhere?'

And we crash and ricochet again.

2

Like Normal

SARAH

AN HOUR and a half later we're home. It's like waking abruptly from a nightmare, disorientating and disconcerting. My body's still coursing with adrenaline, making me feel trapped and breathless, and yet we are resolutely back in the world of the mundane. Phil opens the porch door and moves aside to let me through, and for a split second I'm struck by the urge to step backwards, not forwards, but one of us has to break the seal on the house. We're being ridiculous. This is our home. It's the same, slightly over-stuffed mid-terrace with the chipped-paint front door that we stepped out of this morning. There's the same pile of shoes in the porch and the same tangle of jackets on the newel post. There's still only one slice of the bread left in the bread bin, the thick crusty end that no one will eat, not even as toast; and I still need to go shopping, take the washing out of the machine, change Lauren's bed and check my emails. But it's the very normality of it that's the problem. The house hasn't changed, but we have. Phil puts his hand to the small of my back and the contact propels me forward. We step inside. He pauses in the middle of the hallway, the keys in his hand.

'Tea?' I ask.

He looks at me, taking far too long to respond. 'No.'

'Okay.'

'What time is it?'

'Just after two p.m.' I know what he's asking. He's calculating how long we have until Lauren arrives home. It's not long. We have exactly two hours and fifteen minutes before our daughter – who they say is not our daughter – returns. I reach out and take the keys from him and dump them in the bowl on the side. We stand, stranded, in the hall.

'Sarah?' He reaches out and pulls me to him and we cling to each other, wordlessly, for a few seconds. It's me that breaks us apart.

'Come on.' He follows me through to the kitchen and waits while I unlock the back door. I shove it open with my hip, it always sticks, and we step out into the garden, leaving the pressure of the house behind.

It's a relief to be outside after the stale, closed-off atmosphere in the hospital. We sit on the bench and breathe fresh, soft air into our lungs. A cloud of midges swirls in the sunlight threading through the branches of the apple tree and somewhere, a few gardens over, a radio cuts the quiet. The burn in my throat eventually eases enough for me to speak. This isn't about me and Phil any more, we'll heal; this is about us, as a family. We have to start thinking about James and Lauren. 'I don't think we should say anything yet. Not until we've had time to… think.'

Phil nods, but after a second he says, 'But it's going to kick off. From what that woman said, an army of bloody professionals is going to descend on us, now that they've confirmed she's not ours.' He sees me flinch.

'She is ours.'

'I know, but… legally.'

'Phil, don't. I can't bear to think like that. I know what the biology says, but that doesn't change Lauren being our daughter.'

He shifts around to face me. 'So what do we do? We can't just pretend that everything is normal.'

'Can't we?'

We fall silent, thinking about the impossibility of the next few hours, the next few days, the rest of our lives. The pain returns and the fear, but not the panic, because I know we can survive this, navigate a way through it, as long as we're together, counterbalancing each other, keeping each other in shape. We've had twenty years of this yin and yang: his pragmatism framing my emotion, his impulsiveness balanced by my caution... both of us always, ultimately, brought together by what's best for the kids. And that's precisely what I think we need to do now: what's 'best' for them. We have to absorb the shock and dilute its power, before we unleash it inside our family. 'Just for tonight. Please, Phil. Besides, what are we going to say?'

Phil leans back and tilts his face up to the sky. The radio contributes something loud, rappy and completely inappropriate to the moment as he thinks. 'Okay... until we know how we're going to handle it, we'll say nothing, but tomorrow...'

'I know.' The enormity of it is overwhelming. It's also hard to countenance sitting in our small, sheltered back garden.

'Are you okay?' He takes my hand and holds it lightly. I can feel his pulse through his fingertips.

I nod; it's an obvious but necessary lie. We both look back at our solid, slightly scruffy house. Everything appears so calm and ordinary. Eventually I say, 'I need to get something in for tea.' And with that, we pick up the worn-smooth threads of our daily routines.

We are both fully back in role by the time James thumps into the house after college. I'm prepping veg for our evening meal and

Phil's working on his laptop. James heads straight to the bread bin, now replenished with a toastie loaf and a pack of bagels. 'Can I have two?' He's already ripping open the packet. 'Oh, hi.' This to his dad, a rare sight this early in the day. 'Why are you here?'

'I live here, remember? Pay the bills, drive you to stuff, clean your footie boots.' James pulls his 'you're *so* not funny' face. 'I'm just working from home for a change. Stick one in for me, will you, mate?' We missed lunch and Phil, like James, can only last a couple of hours between feeds. 'College okay?'

'Uh-huh.' James isn't a fan of words when noises will do. Conversation disposed of, Phil goes back to his emails, James slathers butter on his bagels, and I slice peppers and mushrooms, and what looks like normality reigns as the clock ticks towards 4.15 p.m.

She's late back, only a few minutes, but it feels like longer. Phil and I go out to meet her from the bus. We watch silently as it reverses alongside the kerb. Graham, the driver, clambers out. He acknowledges our presence with his usual, slightly shy 'hello' and a hitch of his council regulation trousers. Phil and I stand side by side on the pavement like sentinels as Graham opens up the doors, clambers aboard and sets about undoing all the straps and buckles that secure Lauren's wheelchair. He chats to her as he kneels at her side, working free the anchors. I notice how careful he is as he lifts the last strap over her head, making sure it doesn't touch her face. 'There you go, sweetheart. You've got the full welcome committee today.' Graham always chats to Lauren, despite knowing full well that he will never get a reply. He reverses her chair onto the lift and lets Lauren push the down-button on the control panel, which is, as he's told me twenty times before, *strictly against council health-and-safety guidelines, but who's gonna tell 'em*. They ride down the four feet slowly and regally. My pulse races. 'There you go.' He eases her chair carefully up the kerb and Phil takes the handles. 'She's been good as gold, as always. See you in the morning.' One more trouser hitch and Graham turns back towards the bus. He has three more kids to drop off before his shift is over for the day.

We take her inside and then...

Then it's just like normal. Lauren hands me her hat, I unbuckle her and she slides herself out of her wheelchair, then crawls to 'her spot' on the floor in the lounge and signs for her iPad, and for something to eat. Phil brings her the iPad, but I sign, as I always do, that she must wait for her tea. The room fills with the sound of her pre-school programmes. She is content to be home. Just like normal.

And so it's the routine that saves us, the necessary, boring, repetitive routine of family life. Phil and I steer clear of anything that touches on the future and stick to immediate concerns, the usual, pressing issues of whose turn it is to stack the dishwasher; how it's possible that I can hear the freezer door opening and ice cream being stealthily removed, despite being three rooms away; and why it's not a good idea to leave the back door wide open, as next door's cat will always end up on our kitchen counter, eating butter from the dish. The mundane rituals go some way to soothing the shock.

At 8.30 p.m. I take Lauren up to bed, leaving the boys free to switch the TV straight over to the football match that they're 'missing'. She's as compliant as ever, 'helping me' as much as she can. She knows the routine. As I pull her T-shirt over her head, I catch sight of the bruise in the soft, chubby crease of her arm where they drew the blood samples. Her skin bruises easily and deeply, and the area around the puncture wound is still a sickly yellowy-green. I whisper, 'Sorry' and stroke her arm, and for a second she studies me as if she's trying to fathom the connection between her skin and my words, but of course she can't. She settles into bed and I switch off the light, and in a heartbeat the momentum that's been keeping me going all day judders to a stop. I push aside a pile of clothes and sit on the chair in the corner of her room, feeling hollowed out. Lauren wriggles around for a few moments getting herself comfortable, but soon settles, lying on her side, facing me. Her eyes blink open and shut. She's asleep within five minutes, tucked safely within the fold of our family, dreaming her untroubled dreams.

I study her face. It's a face that I've washed and dried all her life. I'm as familiar with her body as I am with my own. She needs me now as much as she did when she was a baby. But as I sit in her darkening bedroom, I know that I'm looking at her differently. In the arch of her eyebrows and in the deep cleft above her lips, in the colour of her hair – always a shade darker than Phil's or mine – and in the paleness of her skin, I'm searching for evidence of her otherness. It feels like madness.

When they said there was a problem with the initial blood test, I assumed the worst. Or I thought I did. I assumed it was another problem linked to her condition. I braced myself for a new curve ball, thrown hard and low at us by her faulty genes. Something degenerative? Her kidneys? Something they'd missed, despite all the years of medical prodding and probing? Then came Phil's unspoken doubts, his overplayed indifference, while the worm of distrust ate away at him from inside. But this new blow has nothing to do with Lauren's disability, or anything to do with Phil or me. It is bigger than her and us. Lauren is not ours.

She begins to snore softly and I struggle to comprehend the truth of it. This child, the child we've spent fourteen years loving and caring for, who has grown but will never grow up, this child is not our daughter. Somewhere out there she has another mother, oblivious as yet, living her life, assuming her reality is just that: real. And wherever that mother is, there is another child, my birth daughter.

I cry quietly so as not to wake her.

3

Sleepless

PHIL

I DON'T remember going to sleep, but when I jerk awake it's dark, that middle-of-the-night silvery dark that confirms there's hours to go until dawn. I sense Sarah beside me silent and, I hope, asleep.

I go to the loo and piss noisily in the grey, moonlit bathroom. Lauren's snores are loud enough to be heard above the crash of my pee. Our house is small. There's no escaping each other, even if you want to. I can't face going back to bed, so I go in to check on her, like I have a thousand times before.

Her bedroom is stuffy. She's lying flat on her back with the duvet pulled up over her head. I ease it off her face gently so that she can breathe more easily, then I slide down and sit on the carpet, my back resting against the cold mirror on the wardrobe door. I'm aware of how stupid and melodramatic I'm being, prowling around the house in the early hours of the morning. I know I'm encouraging the anger that is churning in my gut, feeding it the oxygen that it needs to grow. But I can't be calm. I don't feel calm. All evening trying to pretend that everything is okay, when inside I'm raging. I'm furious with them – at the bloody hospital, at the whole sodding medical profession – every contact we've ever had with them has been bad and now this. I can't conceive of how it was possible that they gave us the wrong child. How?

And I'm mad at myself, because on one level this chaos is of my own making. If I hadn't gone to the paediatric appointment in the first place, if I hadn't been clueless about the details in Lauren's file, if I hadn't queried her blood group just to prove that I was interested and involved, I wouldn't have stirred up this whole mess and this wouldn't be happening. We would've walked out of that room none the wiser and life would've gone on as normal.

This is happening because I was trying to prove to Sarah, and to myself, that I am a good husband and a good dad. No irony there.

A month or so ago Sarah was pissed off with me. There'd been the usual accumulation of things that I'd missed, forgotten about or, the real killer, never realised needing doing, sorting, booking or cancelling in the first place. She'd been circling the growing pile of grievances all week, dive-bombing in on something different every morning, usually just as I was about to set off for work, but on that Friday evening, with James round at Harry's, Lauren upstairs asleep and most of a bottle of red demolished, she swooped. 'You have no idea, have you? Go on, which appointment is it on Thursday?'

I hit *mute* on the TV remote. Guess-or-confess time. 'I'm sorry, I don't know. She has a physio appointment coming up, but that's not until the end of the month, is it?' I heard the uncertainty in my voice.

'That's on the twenty-fifth.'

'Sarah, please just tell me.' Nothing. 'I'm sorry, but Lauren has a lot of appointments. I can't remember them all.'

She bashed down her glass. 'Yes, she does. It must be nice *not* having to bother with the petty details of them.' Her face was flushed, mottled pink by wine, anger and tiredness.

'I know it's been a bit full-on this past month or so.' This was obviously the wrong thing to say.

'Full-on? You haven't a clue. Every damn appointment, all the phone calls, all the sorting out – it doesn't just happen, you know.'

'I do know. And I appreciate how much you do; you're brilliant at keeping on top of it all.' And she was, and I meant what I was saying.

'I don't want your appreciation.' Her irritation was fierce. 'I want you to be more involved. I want it to be *you* having to repeat, over and over again, her medical history, chase social workers, sit there while they mess with her, drive around panicking that you're going to be late, trying to find somewhere to park.' She was barely drawing breath. The escalation of this particular argument was familiar and the end result was the same. I ploughed on, trying to make amends, letting Sarah vent her frustrations until she finally ran out of steam and got upset. It was a rerun of a conversation we seemed to be having with worrying regularity.

In bed, an hour or so later, the tension slowly eased and she let me hug her. The dark, and our double bed, coming to our aid.

On the Monday evening I made sure to be home on time from work and, instead of bringing flowers, which I'd misjudged before and seen rammed into vases with as much force as the preceding argument, I told Sarah that I'd booked the following Thursday after-noon off, so that I could pick Lauren up from school and take her to the appointment with the paediatrician.

Which is what I did. I took my daughter to the most routine of her appointments for her general health check, to help share the burden with my wife.

And Sarah was right. The parking provision was crap. A delivery van and a taxi were hunkered in the two designated disabled spots, engines running, their drivers avoiding eye contact. There was nowhere close enough or big enough to park the van, so we ended up on a meter, which gave us precisely seventy minutes to get in and out of the appointment. I was sweaty and in a mood by the time we crashed into the waiting room, fifteen minutes late. We needn't have bothered rushing. There were three other families already there, two of them, as it turned out, also booked to see Ms Langford. I tried to amuse Lauren by showing her the pictures in the magazines, but the reading material in the clinic seemed to consist of a series of specialist engineering mags, a few copies of *Reader's Digest* and three ripped-beyond-reading pop-up books. One of the other mums took pity on me and passed over a couple of her daughter's picture books. At least Lauren was quiet and relatively content, only registering her profound boredom by gently rocking her head, poking me in the arm every two minutes and signing for her tea.

One of the boys waiting with his parents had some form of autism. He bounced on his chair and flapped his hands hard against his ears, making a low keening sound that grew loud and then soft for no apparent reason. His parents tried unsuccessfully to distract him when the noise grew too insistent. I smiled each time the volume crept up, pretending it wasn't getting on my nerves and everybody else's. The other little boy looked 'normal', apart from being small and having a slightly misshapen head. The book-lending mum had a daughter in a wheelchair who looked very poorly indeed. A tube ran across her face and into her nose, and her frail legs were encased in some sort of metal frame. I went back to showing Lauren *The Three Little Pigs* and avoiding eye contact with of any of the other parents. If Sarah had been there, it would've been different. Conversation would have sparked and flourished, running back and forth along that wavelength that most mothers seem to be on, especially the mothers of kids with a problem.

The wait dragged on, and Lauren's boredom thickened and made her restless. I remembered Ms Langford from the early days.

Experienced, kind, very thorough, which was great when you were in with her, but not while you were waiting. The small boy went in next, followed soon afterwards by the autistic lad. They must have been seeing another consultant. The mum with the poorly daughter also turned out to be before us, which confirmed in my mind that we were buggered, as there was no way *that* was going to be a short conversation. I could see the meter ticking over into penalty as we sat there, trapped. Sarah's desire to include me in the realities of Lauren's appointments was working.

By the time our turn ground around, Lauren was past it, banging her head in protest. She tried to jam her hands in the spokes of her wheelchair when she realised that we were heading *into* another room, not outside. Ms Langford stood up to greet us, shook my hand, then crouched down to say 'hi' to Lauren, who refused to respond. 'Sorry,' I said, 'she's a bit tired from school and all the waiting around.'

To her credit, Ms Langford smiled ruefully. 'Yes, I'm sorry you've had such a long wait. Sometimes there are some complex issues.' We both paused and I thought about the frail blonde child with her attentive, resolute mother. 'Please, take a seat.' Lauren, as if suddenly completely au fait with what was about to occur, flicked off her wheelchair brakes, spun her chair around and wheeled herself a couple of feet away from us, back turned, as good an impression of a teenage strop as you were ever going to get. Ms Langford laughed. 'Good to see she has a mind of her own. What is Lauren now – fourteen?'

'Very nearly fifteen.'

'And well, I see?'

'Yes, apart from the usual stuff.'

'But her glaucoma is under control, and I gather there are no immediate plans regarding further leg surgery?' She started looking through the notes on the top layer of Lauren's huge file, nodding as if in approval, which somehow irritated me. It was as if there was a league table for problems and, in that context, Lauren had got off lightly.

'Well, the surgery was hardly a success; we're not putting her through anything like that ever again,' I bit back.

Ms Langford read on, telling me about the events of the past year – our year – then asked about Lauren's eating and her weight. By the time we were onto the questions about her school and her social life, both she and I knew we were going through the motions, heading into the home straight. A loud snore from Lauren startled us both. Her head lolled at an uncomfortable angle. She was obviously fast asleep, her back still turned.

'Does she do that often? Sleep during the day?'

I was past politeness. 'Only when she's bored.'

Ms Langford, the consummate professional, didn't take the bait. She continued rifling through Lauren's file. 'Oh, I see you had a couple of appointments with Mr Belmont?' She peered at me over her reading glasses, waiting.

'We did?' It was a question that could've meant anything, including 'Did we?' I had no recollection of a Mr Belmont. I had no idea what she was talking about.

'Her sleep apnoea?' Ms Langford was quizzing me, but I was still coming up short. Sarah, of course, would've known immediately what the appointments were for. Ms Langford skim-read more of the notes and I sat there like a chump, listening to Lauren's snoring. 'I see you did an oxygen saturation trace, and they took bloods to check for anaemia and to look at her thyroid function.' She read on: the results presumably.

'And the results were?' I had to ask, whatever my ignorance would seem to indicate about my involvement with Lauren and the state of my relationship with my wife.

'Reasonable on her oxygen levels and' – she flipped over to the next sheet – 'her blood work showed a slightly lower-than-average white blood-cell count, but nothing to indicate a need for treatment. Would you like to see the test results?'

To which, though I was tired, Lauren was fast asleep and the van was no doubt ticketed, I of course said, 'Yes.'

She slid the sheets of paper across the desk and I glanced down at them. Ms Langford explained, to my idiot eyes, the peaks and troughs of the trace. 'It's like a polygraph, only measuring oxygen levels rather than body temperature. But there seems to have been no real cause for concern and, as you'll see overleaf, the blood tests didn't indicate a problem, either, which is why I'm a little puzzled about her nodding off. Is she doing it a lot?'

At this, she turned to look at Lauren. I forced myself to skim-read the information; after all this was about my daughter's health, not about Sarah and me bickering. At the top of the page I noticed that it gave Lauren's blood group, then a series of figures with percentages.

'*Is* she doing it a lot?'

'No, not a lot.' I didn't look up from the page. 'I think it's just been a long week at school.'

'Well, let's just keep an eye on it for the time being.'

Blood group: A Positive.

Ms Langford started to wrap it up. 'I suggest we see you again in twelve months' time. Obviously, if there's anything that troubles you or your wife in the interim, you've got my number; you can always call and we can get you in to see me more quickly.' I kept staring at the sheet of paper. 'Mr Rudak, was there something else?'

I nearly left it. I very nearly left it alone and took Lauren home. 'Yes, could I just ask… we've never been told Lauren's blood group before. It says here that she's A positive.'

'Yes?'

'Well, when we met with the genetics team, when Lauren was a baby, when she was first diagnosed, they said that RTS isn't inherited, that it was just a glitch, not from either of us? They tested us both for some kind of chromosome markers, but there was nothing.'

'Yes. I know families can find it hard to accept, but many conditions, including Rubinstein–Taybi, are naturally occurring.' She was looking at me, waiting for an actual question.

'But Lauren would inherit her blood type from us?'

'Well, yes, after a fashion.'

'How do you mean… after a fashion?'

Ms Langford returned to her desk. 'It's somewhat complicated by factors called antigens and antibodies, the Rh factor that you might have heard people mention?' I neither nodded nor said no. 'A child is a blend of its biological parents, when it comes to their blood.'

'So you can say what a child's blood group will be, if you know the parents'?'

'You really need the grandparents as well, but I can assure you, an individual's blood group isn't relevant to RTS. Mr Rudak?' Lauren, as if sensing the tension in the room, stirred and shifted position with a deep, noisy breath. We both watched, waiting to see if she would wake or settle. Sleep claimed her again.

And that's when I could've just left it, should've just left it. But I didn't. 'So how come, if I'm O and Sarah is O negative, Lauren is A positive?'

Lauren catches her breath, rolls over and the snoring stops. I clamber to my feet, feeling the stiffness in my joints like an old man. It's still dark, hours to go until dawn. If I'd just left it, we could've carried on as normal, but if I had, we'd never have known about our other daughter.

20

4

Disclosure

SARAH

ON FRIDAY morning Lauren sets off for school, Phil for work and James for college. All as normal. The house is empty by quarter past eight.

The first phone call comes at 9.05 a.m. There are six others before lunchtime.

By the second call I'm prepared. I'm armed with a notepad and a pen, and an alertness that is purely defensive. I make notes, check the correct spelling of everyone's names and the precise format of their email addresses. I'm calm and cooperative and organised. I aim for, and assume I'm making, the correct impression. I'm fully aware that these people have power over what happens next.

The callers are all, initially, hesitant and very courteous. They introduce themselves and their official roles in our 'case'. They each explain the different processes they have been tasked to initiate. I agree to all their requests for information, confirm that we will participate in something called 'full disclosure', though I have no idea what this entails, and agree dates for various meetings with various people. Everyone who disturbs my morning, and my peace, is professional and considerate and implacable. One of the last people to get in touch is a woman called Mrs Winter; she's from the social-care team. Mrs Winter is the most hesitant, the most polite and the most worrying of them all. I have to strain to hear her, as she quietly explains the situation in terms of our new status as Lauren's 'recognised guardians'; we are no longer legally her parents. Mrs Winter is at pains to stress how central our relationship with Lauren is, and will be, *in any, and all, decisions, now and in the future*; the parentheses do little to reassure me. She whispers on in my ear about 'the process' and the need to ensure that everything possible is done to protect and promote Lauren's well-being, and that of the other child. She also explains that she has been tasked with preparing information for the 'birth family'. It takes me a moment to grasp what she means by this. She ends the call by quietly insisting on a home visit at the earliest possible date. I politely tell her that the earliest we can do is a week on Wednesday, as we already have appointments booked with the enquiry team and a legal advocate. She sighs, as if deeply disturbed by how long she must wait to meet us. 'Well, if that's the earliest you can manage, it'll have to be Wednesday.' She wishes me a good day, without any sense of irony.

The insidious creep of strangers into the security and sanctity of our family has begun.

I'm still sitting blankly with the phone in my hand when it rings again, making my heart thud. 'Hi.' The informality throws me. 'Hi? Sarah?' I don't respond. 'It's Ali.'

'Hi.'

'I was just checking you're still okay for the weekend.'

'Right.'

'So? Are we still on?' I can't think about moving furniture for my sister in the middle of all this. 'Look, if it's a problem, just say.' The spikiness in her voice is ill-disguised. Coming on top of the litany of calls I've received this morning, it punctures my already-frayed patience.

'It's not that.'

But Ali has already stopped listening. 'Look, I'm at work. I'll text you.' And she hangs up.

The rest of the afternoon is a write-off. I can't settle to anything and, though I try numerous times, I can't reach Phil. In desperation I call his office, but they say he's on a site visit out in the middle of nowhere. 'Somewhere up beyond Halifax, with the sheep and the hunchbacks,' Matt unhelpfully and unfunnily adds. So I roam around the house, moving from room to room in a restless, point-less dance while I shift silently through some of the small, simple, devastating phrases that I plan to use when we speak to James.

'There's nothing wrong with Lauren.' That's our opening gambit. James looks from me to Phil, clearly confused as to why he's been summoned downstairs for 'a talk'. It's Friday evening; he should be lying on his bed playing *FIFA* or faffing with his hair. I plough on. 'What I mean is, Dad and I had an appointment at the hospital yesterday, about Lauren. That's why Dad was at home when you got back. It's thrown up something we weren't expecting.' How's that for an understatement. 'It's not to do with her health, not this time.'

'Okay.'

I look at James's half-man/half-boy face and it strikes me how much he's grown up while we've been looking the other way. At seventeen, he can't remember a time without Lauren, his life has been dominated by her and her needs, yet here I am about to smash the simple but fundamental basis of his relationship with his sister... that she *is* his sister.

'The appointment was with the genetics team.' I can hear the waver in my voice.

He still isn't really paying attention. I can see his eyes flicking to his phone. He's so used to us having appointments with one special-ist or another that he isn't expecting this to be any different. 'Okay.'

'They needed to look into a result they got back on a blood test they did.' Once I say it, I can never unsay it. 'It...' I dry.

James pushes himself upright, his nonchalance finally replaced by attentiveness. 'And?' He may be used to stuff happening with his sister, but he's not used to hearing fear and uncertainty from us.

'It's okay. Well, it isn't. It's a shock... what they've found. But we'll be okay. I promise we'll be okay. We'll work it out.'

'Sarah, just tell him,' Phil prompts.

'The blood test showed that Lauren isn't ours. Not biologically.' There, it's said and it can't be unsaid.

James blinks, twice, and pushes his fringe out of his eyes 'What?'

Phil steps in. 'Somehow there was a mix-up at the hospital when she was born. They think it happened when she was in the nursery. We were given the wrong baby to bring home. They're starting an investigation.'

'Fuck!' James immediately looks at me. 'Sorry.' He knows I hate him swearing.

Phil responds. 'Yeah. To be honest, "Fuck" just about sums it up.' He smiles at our son and I feel a tug of grief that I can't communicate with him as naturally as Phil does. I love James ferociously, he is my piece of joy in the world and I would do anything to protect him, but I don't always know how to talk to him.

'It sounds like something out of a film.' James looks puzzled more than anything else.

Phil takes over from me. 'I know. But I'm afraid it's not. We're telling you because you have a right to know and, well, there's going to be quite a lot of people who are going to have to get involved. Social workers' – his face betrays his feelings about more social workers poking into our lives – 'and the court and the hospital. They're obviously trying to track down the other family. The other baby. Your biological sister.' I admire Phil's clarity, his commitment to punching home the truth of the situation, leaving no doubt about the implications. James shuffles about on his chair.

I leap in. 'It's okay to not know what to say. We don't, really.'

James's first question, when it comes, surprises me. Of all the things he could be worried about or not understand or say, he asks, 'Does Auntie Ali know?'

'Ali? No, not yet. We've not told anyone yet, apart from you.'

Then he surprises me again. 'I think we should tell her.' It's not like James to have a firm opinion about anything, never mind express it so forcefully.

'Yes, we will.'

'When?'

'This weekend.' I don't understand why my sister is his priority in all this.

'Can I tell her?' He actually reaches for his phone as if contemplating the call there and then.

'No, I will, when she comes over tomorrow. I'll speak to her then. Okay?' He nods, but seems disappointed. We gabble on, offering him reassurances that I'm not sure we'll be able to deliver on. 'We promise to tell you everything. Let you know what's going on. Nothing will happen immediately; well, nothing that should impact directly on you or Lauren.' God knows what may happen in the future. 'You can talk to us – ask us anything. You know that, don't you?'

'Yeah.' But he doesn't ask anything else. He shuffles about some more in his seat, stretching his legs out and flexing his huge feet. There's a hole in one of his socks and his big toe is poking through the shredded cotton. He studies his feet, and Phil and I study him, trying to gauge his reaction. 'So, is it still okay for me to go round to Ryan's, like I was gonna?'

'Course.' Phil hands him his 'Get Out of Jail pass'. 'Back by ten-thirty p.m., though.'

''Kay.' And James slides out of his seat and away from our scrutiny.

5

A Family Photo

SARAH

AFTER JAMES leaves, the evening stretches out ahead of us like a challenge. For the want of anything better to do, I go and search out a bottle of wine in the kitchen. I screw off the cap. Phil sits at the table, silent.

'That went as well as it could, I suppose?' I can hear the plea for reassurance in my voice.

'Um.' He doesn't turn his head as he responds.

I pour the wine, spilling some in the process. 'We're going to have to keep a close eye on him, though. You know how he bottles things up.' The wine soaks into the kitchen towel as I wipe the splashes off the base of the first glass. I pour a second. 'Phil?'

'I heard you. I agree.' But he's still staring off into the middle distance. It isn't difficult to see where James gets his diffidence from.

As I carry the glasses across to the table I realise what he's looking at: it's the digital photo frame that Ali gave us. It sits on the side, unnoticed most of the time, the images so familiar that they've become wallpaper. I place the glasses down carefully, fearful of disturbing Phil's thoughts, and we watch in silence. The past and the present parade before our eyes on a random, seemingly endless spool: a shot of Ali, in her peroxide phase, with a chubby-faced, pre-school James, playing car crashes on the hideous old carpet we used to have in the lounge; a rare photo of Phil and I all dressed up for a night out, from years back; Lauren, at eleven, fit to burst with excitement, hugging Mickey Mouse in Florida. Just as I feel a smile of recognition start to form at the memory, the image shifts again and there it is: a shot of me in the hospital just after Lauren was born. It shows the ghost of a new mum, propped up in bed, attached to a drip, with a tiny baby bundle on her lap. Me and my new daughter. I look at Phil, but he doesn't react, he doesn't even blink. He stares without a flicker of emotion on his face. When I glance back at the frame, the image has disappeared, replaced by a recent photo of the four of us lined up on the sofa: the classic happy-family snap.

'Phil…?' My voice finally triggers a reaction in him, but not the one I was hoping for.

He pushes his glass of wine away. 'Would you mind if I went for a run?'

'What, now?'

'Yeah. I'm sorry. I just feel I need to *do* something. Get out of the house, just for a bit.' He must see the hurt on my face. 'It's not you. It's just all this. I promise I won't be long. We can sit and have a drink together when I get back. Talk about stuff then.'

There is no possible answer other than 'Okay'. As soon as I say it, he gets to his feet with exactly the same look of relief on his face as James had, five minutes earlier. Once the front door slams shut behind him, I stand up and bring the frame over to the table with me. I want it close so that I can see every tiny detail, every expression captured within each frozen moment, and I sit and wait for the photo to reappear.

Phil took the picture on the day she was born. I know that, but I don't really *remember* him taking it because, in truth, I remember hardly anything about Lauren's birth, or the days afterwards. I've never really wanted to before, not until now. It's such a patchwork of half-memories, a blur of pain and panic followed by sleep, but buried somewhere in those muddy, confused echoes there could be a clue to how and when the baby I struggled so hard to deliver got replaced by another baby, who became our child.

As I wait I try and summon up what I can. It's not much. I can remember our excitement when my waters broke, and our giddy confidence at the beginning. We naively thought that because this was our second child, it was going to be easier. We had it all mapped out in our minds: a quick labour, a few hours in hospital and then us bringing our new baby daughter home to our son; our perfect little family complete. We were so wrong. Nothing went to plan. My labour was stop–start from the beginning, a lot of pain but very little progress. 'Nothing to worry about,' the harassed midwives kept saying, 'walk around, keep moving. Baby will come when it's good and ready.' So that's what I did all day, with Phil, on the ward, then all night, alone, around an empty TV lounge; endless, anxious loops, with my hands cradling my belly. But the following morning there was still nothing to show for it, so they induced me, using chemicals to achieve what nature hadn't. And it worked. It was like a switch being thrown. I went into immediate, full-blown labour. It was a storm of pain and pressure. The only still-point amid the roar was Phil, talking to me, anchoring me, trying to keep me safe. It went on for hours. More drugs were administered, this time to try and dull the pain, but they didn't work. I felt like I was being ripped apart. Then at last, almost unbelievably, there was a final body-rending push, then relief. Then nothing.

She was born.

I didn't hold her. I didn't even look at her.

And afterwards, after they'd patched me up and sent me back to the ward, I wanted her gone. I just wanted to rest and recover from the shock of her birth. I remember how much I resented the midwife forcing me to feed her that first day, how the sensation of her being held against my breast left me drained, and how all I wanted to do was slide down under the sheet and go back to sleep. And that's what I did. I rejected her. I rolled over, turned my back on her and left them with no choice but to take her away.

A photo of me holding a tiny Lauren fades up on the frame: three months old, tiny, fluff-haired, asleep on my lap. Then, as if in mockery, the very next photo is the one from the hospital again. As it slides in front of me and away, as impermanent as everything else in my life right now, I allow the possibility that I never held the child I gave birth to in my arms crash down on me, heavy and hard.

The absurd cruelty of it leaves me breathless.

PHIL

I set off fast, way too fast, and within minutes the burn in my throat and the tightness in my chest remind me that I'm no longer young and fit, but I push on, hard up the hill, my breathing growing more ragged and laboured with each step. I want nothing more than to get away from the house and the ambush of memories. At the top I deliberately cross over and take the path that leads down onto the ring road, committing myself to the long loop round. The physical punishment is a welcome distraction. All my energy goes into forcing my feet to lift, my arms to drive and my lungs to respond. For about ten minutes it is pure pain and exertion, but as my body acclimatises and I find my rhythm, my heart rate steadies and my breathing starts to keep pace with my stride.

People say that you forget the trauma of birth, but that's crap.

29

I remember every awful moment of when Lauren was born, all the noise and blood and pain and, above all, the overpowering feeling of utter, abject helplessness. The sense of loneliness that settled on me as Sarah retreated deeper and deeper inside herself, searching for the reserves to cope. I remember the sheets soaked in blood and the journey down to the delivery suite. I can picture, as if it was yesterday, the crush of people in the lift and how I had to let go of Sarah's hand as they wheeled her out into the corridor. There was a split second when I just stood there and the possibility of simply not moving, of letting the doors grind shut and properly separating me from her, occurred to me, even appealed to me.

Then there was the battle of the following hours, a fight that Sarah's body raged through alone, with me pinned on the sidelines. The staff remained impassive. They resisted any involvement with Sarah as a person, but by then she had been reduced to something quite inarticulate and basic.

By midday there was still no baby, but I truly no longer cared. I just wanted it to stop, any which way; it needed to stop. But it didn't, it went on and on and on, until the old nurse came in and saved us. She went straight to Sarah, bent low over the bed and spoke clearly and loudly to her and, indirectly, to the rest of us. 'Right. I'm sure you've had enough of this. We need to get this baby out. And we will. Soon. We're going to move you up the bed. Then you're going to push as hard as you can, when I tell you to, for twenty seconds at a time, and I promise you this baby will be out and this will be over.' She directed everyone, brooking no dissent. They hoisted Sarah up the bed, more blood, but there was a momentum about this nurse that spread around the room and this somehow got through to Sarah. For the first time in hours she focused outwards. 'Good girl. You keep looking at me. When the next contraction comes, use it. Work with it. Push down. Dad, get ready.' Sarah took a deep breath and started pushing. She gripped onto the edges of the bed. I put my hand on the back of her neck, just to keep contact with her. 'Good. Keep going. Keep pushing. Good girl. That's it. Harder. Push down.'

Sarah stopped. Then the next contraction hit, then the next.

'Good, nearly. Good. Harder, keep going, Sarah. Push, push, all the way. Just one more, Sarah. Even harder this time. Yes. Yes. That's it. Good girl.' Sarah slumped back. There was a flurry of activity at the other end of the bed. I bent my head against her sweaty hair. Ice-cold relief sluiced through my insides. It had stopped.

Then through the voices of the nurses a wail rose. 'Dad?' I was summoned to pay attention. They lifted up a bloodied, waxy baby. 'A healthy little girl.' But my attention was back on Sarah. The pain had let go of her body, but what was left was absolute stillness.

An unnatural stillness.

'Sarah!'

One of the nurses brushed past me and strapped a cuff on her arm. The mood in the room shifted. There was a new type of urgency. The older nurse barked instructions. 'Dad. Listen to me. Sarah's lost a lot of blood and her blood pressure is dropping. She needs to be looked at by the consultant. We're going to transfer her now. We'll take good care of her, but we need to do it now.' They pulled the sides of the bed up and started pushing Sarah out of the room. 'You stay here. We'll come and fetch you.' They thrust the bundled-up baby into my arms. The door banged shut behind them as they took Sarah away.

They tricked me into staying.

I glanced down and saw a tiny, scrunched-up red face, creamy smears on its forehead and around its nostrils. My daughter. The young nurse who was the only one left in the room smiled nervously. 'Congratulations. Five pounds four ounces. She's small, but perfectly formed.' I passed the bundle back to her and ran out into the empty corridor.

*

I can't run any further. My pace slows to a jog, then a walk, then to a complete stop. My legs, my lungs, my heart are just too tired. The baby Sarah gave birth to was our daughter, but she was not Lauren. I gulp for air, hands braced on my knees, head down, trying hard to get myself under control. For a few seconds I have no idea where I am. A car drives past, slowly, and the occupants stare at me, curious, concerned... suspicious. I force myself to set off again, but the effort I have to make simply to move is phenomenal. Suddenly I want desperately to be with Sarah. What the fuck am I doing miles from home! I start to plod along the road, heading back, one foot in front of the other, feeling a level of fatigue that bears no relation-ship to the distance I've covered. I wish I had my phone with me so that I could ring her. I wish I could pick up the pace and get home quicker. I wish I had some money and could get on a bloody bus, but I haven't any of these things, I just have my memories.

If I thought the birth was bad, the aftermath was almost worse.

It took a frantic half-hour of running along corridors before I finally found the right operating theatre. They told me that Sarah had to be given a general anaesthetic and a blood transfusion and that she... *was being stitched back up.* I sat on a plastic chair in the waiting room with the other, grey-faced people and stewed with frustration and anxiety. It took eleven door swings before they summoned me into Recovery.

Recovery was a series of separate bays, each containing an inert form and a load of machinery. The room was filled with the regular blip-blip of the monitors, the hiss of oxygen and the murmur of nurses trying to rouse their patients. Sarah was in the end bay. The Recovery nurse was stroking her hair, speaking softly to her.

After what felt like an eternity, Sarah's eyes fluttered open and she focused on me. Her face was very pale, her hair a tangle, but she was calm. She looked more like Sarah again, but a drained and spent version of Sarah. I held her hand, careful not to knock the plastic tube inserted in it. Her eyes closed again briefly, then opened.

'Phil. Where's the baby?'

'She's fine. Healthy. No problems. They're looking after her,' I reassured her. Sarah closed her eyes and drifted back to sleep.

The painful truth is that I had no idea where our baby was at that point.

The next forty-eight hours were grim. Sarah had a very high temperature that they just couldn't get down. They said it was her body fighting the blood loss and the exhaustion. We were put in a side room, away from everyone else. It freaked me out that Sarah was so immobile and absent. They brought the baby in on the first day, but Sarah really struggled. She fed her, with the nurses' help, but that was all she could manage. She was too unwell. That's when they suggested that the baby should spend a few days in the nursery.

At the time we were glad that she was being well cared for.

In my defence, I didn't know what to do with a newborn. After James's birth Sarah had introduced me to our son, willing into existence a bond between us. From day one, she taught me how to love and handle him. They came as a unit, a physical, flesh-bonded block of mother and son, with a small space left open for me to start growing into being James's dad. This was completely different. Sarah simply wasn't well enough to handle me, or the baby.

So there really was no other option but for her to go into the nursery.

Day two brought another blood transfusion, another shot at getting Sarah sorted out. And finally, on day three, she did start to improve. During the course of the morning, the Sarah I knew started to come back. She ate something, she got up very slowly and she managed a shower. By teatime they'd booted us out of the side room and back onto the ward.

That's when they brought Lauren back to Sarah for good.

Or at least that's when they brought us a baby that we assumed was our daughter.

The following day, to my shock, they discharged us.

But even that wasn't straightforward. There was some cock-up with Sarah's medicines that had to be put right, and I hadn't adjusted the car seat enough for a newborn. One of the other mums was there, thankfully. She helped by holding Lauren while I struggled with the straps. And then at last it was all sorted. We left the ward and headed home.

Thank God!

I round the corner and see our house, lights blazing, curtains open. The relief is enormous.

6

Saturday

PHIL

THE FIRST thing I hear when I open the front door is, incongruously, laughter, followed by a series of thuds and bangs coming from upstairs. Ali. The last thing I need right now is Sarah's sister. The light-fitting rattles overhead and I hear James yell, 'Not fair', followed by a load of shouting. I take the shopping through to the kitchen and dump it on the side. There's another crash. Sarah follows me in with Lauren. We both glance up at the ceiling.

'James is right – she has a right to know, after all she's done for us, for Lauren.' Sarah is spookily close to telepathic sometimes, or perhaps she just has an extra-sensitive antenna when it comes to the mutual reservations that Ali and I have about each other.

'Yeah.' I pull frozen peas and ice cream out of the bags.

'She's been around for all of it.'

I move on to the fresh stuff: apples, broccoli and, for some reason, sprouts. No one likes sprouts, apart from Alan, so Sarah must be planning a visit from her dad. Another conversation we seem not to have had. 'I wasn't disagreeing.'

Without looking at me, Sarah responds, 'You were, in your head.

I'll sort Lauren, then I'll speak to her. Do you want to be there?'

'Not really.'

With the shopping put away and Lauren settled in the lounge, Sarah takes a deep breath and heads upstairs. I hear the 'Hi' and the sudden drop-off in the wrestling, then nothing. She must have pulled the door closed behind her. Lauren pats the floor next to her and I take up my position. I get an old-fashioned look when I click off the kids' TV in favour of the golf. She signs 'More', meaning more of her stuff, and I sign 'Later', meaning 'No – time for my stuff'. We watch golf together in companionable silence, only for half an hour, I mentally promise, an equitable compromise. As I sit on the carpet, watching multicoloured millionaires hitting a small ball around the testing eighteen holes of the Open, the memory of the first time I was alone with Lauren, the night she came home from hospital, comes unbidden into my head: that first slim thread of a bond that has thickened and twisted and knotted itself around my heart ever since.

After the trauma of her birth, it was like coming through an airlock back into a safer, kinder, familiar sanctuary. James was a complete giddy kipper having his mum back, resisting Sarah's hugs in favour of chattering her through the amazingly complicated parking system that he and Ali had constructed in the front room, using every book from the bookcase. Ali said a brief 'hello' and thankfully took the hint and left fairly quickly. James gradually slowed down. He feasted on boiled egg and soldiers, as we didn't have much in the cupboards, then he had a cuddle with Sarah and eventually he crashed out asleep. Sarah, after much nagging, went up to bed soon after. Feeding Lauren hadn't gone well.

I sat in the lounge, the lamp on low, the TV murmuring in the background: the US PGA Tour, sunshine and long strolls up immaculate fairways. We were finally together under one roof, safe and sound, everything calm. Lauren was in her carrycot on the floor, sleeping, I wrongly assumed. As I came back in with a coffee, I saw that she was actually awake, lying there peacefully, eyes blinking. I sat on the carpet beside her cot, my back against the sofa, sipping coffee, easing back into the comfort of home. It was time for me to say 'hello' properly to my daughter.

I put my coffee down and, with warm hands, I carefully lifted her out of her cot and laid her on my knees, supporting her floppy little body. She was small – small all over. James was a strong, bouncing baby from day one, a bit of a bruiser really; in contrast, Lauren was all in proportion, but she had bird bones, delicate and feather-light. Her little body felt loose inside her Babygro. It was much too big for her; Sarah had had to roll up the cuffs to free her clenched little fists. She flinched as she lay on my knee, her arms jerking outwards, her eyes wide in shock. I remembered those early-days jerks and tremors. James did it as well: physical aftershocks from the birth, or so the midwife said.

She had blue eyes, dark-fringed, not like Sarah's at all. I vaguely remembered something about all white babies having blue eyes – could that be true? It didn't really matter. I gently stroked my clumsy fingers across her scalp with its covering of tufty, soft, almost black hair and, as I did so, I noticed a dark-pink flush on Lauren's forehead; it was as if someone had pressed their thumb against the skin, leaving an impression. I kissed her gently, marvelling that she was here and home with us. After three holes of golf, her eyes closed and she drifted back to sleep. I finished my coffee while she slept lightly on my knee.

My negotiated 'half hour' of golf is nowhere near up when Lauren pokes me in the ribs. The manicured greens of golf give way to the lurid AstroTurf of Teletubbyland. Such are the compromises of family life.

When I walk into his room James has his head wedged against the wall and Ali is sitting on his back, demanding he admit defeat. Seventeen and thirty-five years old respectively and they still play like ten-year-olds. Ali has always loved playing rough. I hated it when we were growing up. I'd try to escape whenever she challenged me to any sort of contest, but she'd chase me round the house, demanding I join in, relentless and combative. I'd usually go crying to Mum the minute it got too physical. In James, Ali has finally found a willing accomplice.

The roughhousing started when he was tiny. It was Ali who taught him how to do headstands when he was three, and back-flips on the trampoline at five. It's down to her that James developed the 'best' Chinese-burns technique of any kid at junior school and that he can now beat most fully-grown men at arm-wrestling; apparently it's something to do with where you put your elbow. The scar on his thigh is courtesy of Ali convincing him, when he was eight, that of course he would be fine going another branch higher in the apple tree, and the only broken bone he's ever had happened during a game of beach cricket that got out of hand when Ali was bowling.

James 'taps out' and she rolls off his back. They both look up at me, faces flushed. 'Oh, hi.' Neither of them is the slightest bit embarrassed.

'Hi.' I respond. With a heavy heart I pull the door closed behind me, putting paid to their fun.

Twenty minutes later Ali is still shaking her head in disbelief – and who can blame her? She seems unaware that as soon as I started talking, she reached out and took hold of James's hand and she has yet to let it go; the physical closeness between them goes much deeper than headlocks and endless games of 'knuckles'.

'So what happens now?' she asks.

'They're trying to work out who the other family are. When they're sure, we'll be notified. Then there'll be more blood tests and then… then, I suppose we'll meet them.'

'Shit!… Sorry.' She puts her hand to her mouth like a child, casting me as the parent. Then, in the new world of topsy-turvy reactions that we seem to be inhabiting, her next question is, 'How's Phil coping with it?'

'He's okay. He's cross with the hospital, of course.'

'Cross? I'm guessing that's a bit of an understatement,' she says and she shakes her head again.

7

Mementos

SARAH

THERE IS no rhythm to the following days. It's a staccato stagger of the normal routine, interspersed with long periods of waiting, punctuated by unpredictable phone calls. They ask a lot, but tell us very little. Jeremy Orr, the guy leading the investigation, informs me that they've found all the relevant staff rosters and they've started interviewing the people who are still working within the Trust. More hesitantly, he also tells me they've put together a definitive list of mothers and babies who were on the maternity unit at the same time as us, but he gives me no indication as to the possible time-scales or the likely success of their searches. I find myself holding my breath while doing the most mundane things. Phil and I orbit each other, mistiming our attempts to talk and misinterpreting each other's feelings. Since the weekend his quietness has taken on a tense, uptight quality; it's not so much sadness any more, it's more impatience. His anger at the hospital – in fact at the whole medical profession – is just below the surface of every conversation we have. I'm wary of stoking it. I choose my words very carefully when I update him on the lack of progress being made. I'm lonely without him and worried about the bitterness that's flooding through him; his usual tenderness is being drowned out by his silent rage.

As the days crawl by, the house becomes both my refuge and my cage; it's also, I realise, as the sun streams through the smeary windows, a damn mess. I decide to restore some order. I may have no control over anything important, but I can at least tackle the sticky fountain of rubbish overflowing the top of the kitchen bin and make some inroads into the wash basket. Once I get started it's almost cathartic. I throw bleach around in the kitchen and crash through the rooms with the Hoover, knocking paint off the skirting boards. With the downstairs done, I go up to tackle the bedrooms. I'm drawn first, as I always am, to Lauren's room, but when I step inside the energy of the past hour deserts me and I flop down on the bed. Everything in this room was chosen for her: the fairy lights that soothe her at bedtime, the soft toys she never cuddles, the picture books she hurls on the floor and the soft rug we change her on. It's a sanctuary created by us to keep her safe and snug. I lie down and watch the paper whales twirl on the mobile above her bed. The temptation to sleep tugs at me. I pull her duvet around me, breathing in her scent.

When I start awake, I don't know whether I've been asleep for two seconds or two hours. I'm lying on my side, cocooned inside her covers, feeling blunted and confused. This low down, the view is completely different. I can see the dusty corners of the room that my slapdash vacuuming never reaches, the clothes that have slipped off her chair and the clutter of odds and sods pushed under her chest of drawers: her sandals, the slippers she never wears, a box of toys? No. Not toys.

I'm awake now.

I scramble out of bed, reach under the chest of drawers and pull out the box.

It's thick with dust, put away fourteen years ago and never looked at since. I wipe away the accumulation of years of neglect, getting

41

my fingers filthy in the process. Heedless, I smear the mess on my jeans. It's Lauren's baby box. Dad bought it for us, an unusual and unexpected gift, not his type of thing at all. The cover design is twee: 'It's a Girl!' is emblazoned across the front in curly script and underneath the writing there's a cartoon of a bouncing baby with a cute topknot. The box is tied with a bow, once pink, now grey. I pull loose the ribbon and open the box.

Inside is a time capsule. The beginning of our daughter's life, our daughters' lives – the one that came home with us and the one I gave birth to. I lift the congratulations cards out onto the floor and carefully put aside the identity labels, the teddy and the newborn Babygro patterned with tiny pink puppies; and there, in the bottom of the box, is a small pile of photos. I look through them slowly. There are seven in total. There is the original of the photo on the digital frame and six others, taken by Ali when she came in to visit me. In these later photos the ghost mother is replaced by a more recognisable version of me.

I select the 'Ali' photo with the clearest shot of Lauren's face and the one taken on the first day and I put them side by side on the carpet. I kneel over and study them, my face lowered as close to the images as possible, looking *now* for what I didn't see *then*. Is it the same vulnerable little body or is she a touch longer in the second photo? Does a baby visibly grow or just unfurl in the first few days? Is it the same shock of dark hair? It looks fluffier in the later shot, but she'd have been bathed by then, wouldn't she? Not by me, by one of the nurses. Am I looking at the same small, fragile skull? Is it the same shape? Are the scrunched-up features the same? The nose? Is it flatter? Are they the same curled hands? I study the hands closely. In both photos their tiny fists are curled shut, hiding the fingers and the thumbs. With the weight of hindsight heavy on my back, I know that the little fists on the second photo hold tight the first clue to Lauren's disability.

The hard lump that lies buried beneath my ribs shifts.

I did not notice that they had swapped my baby.

I did not notice that there was something wrong with my baby.

How is that possible?

PHIL

When I get home from work Sarah is even more subdued than normal, if you can call the last month 'normal'. The whole house picks up on her mood; well… James does, he takes himself off to his room at the first opportunity and shuts his door. Through the ceiling we can hear him plucking away at his guitar. Things must be bad if it's driven him to practise. I'm guessing it's The Beatles' 'Let It Be', but I could be wrong.

Lauren is, as always, Lauren. Content. Unfazed. Unaffected by the storm raging around us, quietly insistent that we meet her needs, which are simple: *feed me, sit with me, sing to me, love me*. Sarah covers the first requirement, me the second and third, both of us the fourth. The same tag-team approach that's served us well in the past.

It's not until Lauren's settled asleep, I've showered and we think James has gone to bed that Sarah approaches me. She comes into the lounge clutching something in her hands. She sits alongside me on the sofa, a seat gap between us.

'I found these.' It's a handful of photos, old photos. Again the sense of our life as a minefield creeps up on me, but this time I know I can't run away from whatever it is we need to confront. Sarah passes the photos to me. 'They're from the hospital, after she was born.' I hold them carefully, a small pile of the past, and wait for her to tell me what she wants me to find in them. 'I was looking to see if we had photos of both of them.'

I know immediately what she means. 'Do we?'

'I think so.'

I deal the photos out onto the cushion between us. Seven in a row. She points. 'This was the day she was born.' She slides the photo apart from the others. 'And these were taken after she'd been in the nursery.'

It's like a peculiarly cruel version of 'Spot the difference'. I study the freeze-frame images of the baby... two babies? A froth of dark hair and a tiny squashed face. I can't separate them. We just assumed she was ours. Why would we not? Why would anyone not? I pick up the isolated first photo and hold it close to my face, seeing if I can squint the image clearer, trying to see the face of my actual daughter.

The heavy thud of James coming into the room jolts me back into the present. He stands over me like an outsized child in his tatty boxers and T-shirt. 'Why is Mum in the kitchen crying?'

I scoop the photos back into a pile. 'She's just a bit worn out with it all.' He casts me a look and strides out of the room.

I'm too slow. By the time I've put the photos away and gone to find and comfort Sarah, it's too late. I stop short in the doorway. Sarah is standing at the sink, with her back to me and next to her, with his arm wrapped around her shoulders, is James.

8

A Tiny Glitch

SARAH

MRS WINTER and her colleague are scheduled to arrive at nine o'clock. I see their car pull up just before eight-thirty. They sit outside waiting, while Phil and I drift from room to room, uncomfortable in our own home. We both jump when the doorbell rings.

We show them through to the lounge.

'Are you happy for us to get under way?' We nod. 'As we discussed on the phone, we've started pulling together all Lauren's medical notes, and the school has been very responsive in providing us with the relevant information regarding her education. Thank you for giving your permission for us to access her records. What we want to do today is put together a more detailed picture of Lauren, of her life with you, her development, the key milestones in her life, her family, her likes and dislikes, that kind of thing.' Neither Phil nor I say anything. The other woman sits poised, a notepad resting on her knee, the pages blank. 'I appreciate it sounds a little daunting, trying to sum up fourteen years, but to help we've drawn up some key questions to act as prompts. We thought it would make sense, if it's okay with you, to go back to the beginning, to when Lauren was a baby.' I know what's coming next. 'Perhaps we could start with her diagnosis?' The point at which she became disabled.

Phil looks at me, expecting me to launch into my well-worn fact file of 'life with Lauren', summing up our child in easily digestible chunks. I've spent a lot of time across the past fourteen years doing just that, bringing social workers, teachers, doctors, nurses and complete strangers up to speed on life with an RTS child, but this time I'm hesitant, this time the end recipient isn't some anonymous professional, it's Lauren's birth parents.

Mrs Winter looks perplexed. 'Are you happy to proceed? I can explain what we need in more detail if you feel...'

I rouse myself. 'No. Sorry. I was just thinking.' Thinking that my life is no longer my own, nor my family.

Phil says. 'Yeah, let's get started.' He wants this over with.

Mrs Winter begins. 'So, I gather the diagnosis was made when you were referred for Lauren's thumbs.'

I take a breath, look at Phil and start to tell her.

When Lauren was four months old the midwives decided there was something wrong. As her hands relaxed, it became clear that she had wonky thumbs. We thought they were cute, like she was giving a big thumbs-up to life, but the nurses at the clinic thought we should get them checked out. That's why we were referred to see someone called Mr Law, a paediatric surgeon. We went along, thinking the worst that could happen was that she might need some corrective surgery; we were wrong about that.

The waiting room was busy when we arrived, lots of couples and children and a strong undertow of anxiety. Eventually we were invited into one of the consultation rooms. There were two empty seats. Sitting on a swivel chair in front of a desk was a large man with a big face, and standing behind him, along the wall, were four or five other people, medical students we presumed, though they weren't introduced. The big man, Mr Law, wasn't wearing doctor's whites. He wore a tweed jacket, a bright-yellow shirt and a turquoise tie that went with neither.

Lauren was wrapped up warm in her all-in-one suit, strapped in her car seat, safe and sound and oblivious. Once we were settled, Mr Law asked some general questions about my pregnancy and the labour – all the same basic questions that I'd been asked before. He nodded and said, 'Shall we have a look then?' I unclipped Lauren and lifted her onto my lap. He came forward on his chair and took hold of one of her hands. He laid her little fist on his palm and studied her thumb, then he unfurled her fingers, like you would smooth out a paper curl. The minute he removed his fingers, Lauren's hand curled back up into a fist. He repeated the process twice. Then he took hold of her wrists and held up both her hands, comparing the bend in her thumbs. Held like that, in such an unnatural position, you could see how misshapen they were, each thumb making a right angle from the joint. Mr Law studied her thumbs. We all studied him studying her thumbs. It was quiet while he deliberated. He released her wrists and her little arms flopped back onto her lap. He pushed himself backwards in his chair. Still he didn't say anything. Then he unnerved me – he scooted forward again and took hold of her head in his big hands and studied her face. He was so close that I could see the scrape on his neck where he'd shaved. Suddenly he was brisk. 'Would you mind waiting outside for a moment? I want to get some information sent through. It shouldn't be long.' He pushed his chair away from us and we were dismissed.

We went and sat outside. The waiting room was even busier, and still more people seemed to be arriving. A woman with a little boy of about three, who was playing aeroplanes between the seats, looked at Lauren on my knee and smiled. I smiled back.

'Why do you think he sent us out?'

Phil shrugged. 'Don't know.'

'He wasn't giving much away, was he?'

'He's supposed to be one of the best surgeons.'

'I know.' Lauren squirmed and started to grizzle softly. 'She's getting hungry, maybe I should give her a feed?'

'Yeah, okay.'

'Phil!'

'What? Sorry. I just think we need to wait to see what he says; there's no point second-guessing what he's going to advise.'

I fed Lauren, then walked her up and down until she dozed off. She grew heavy in my arms as she went off to sleep. I eased her back into her car seat. While we waited, Phil and I made distracted attempts at day-to-day conversation, but it was hard. We drifted into silence and instead watched the comings and goings of the other families. In they went behind closed doors, then out again, like figures on a cuckoo clock; some emerged chatting and relaxed, presumably those at the end of their treatment, while others were silent, holding tight onto their children, in a rush to get away. Our door finally opened and one of the junior observers asked us to come back in.

Phil put Lauren's car seat on the floor between our chairs, out of sight of the phalanx of white coats. Mr Law began talking about her thumbs. I braced myself. 'Surgery will be advisable, probably desirable, given the acute angle at the joint; unfortunately, the distortion will only increase with age as her hands grow. Her pincer grasp will be affected in the medium term, adversely... I'm afraid. But before we look at the thumbs, I think it's important that we get you in to see the hospital geneticist. I'll call through and make an appointment for you. Get you to see the team as soon as possible.' I was confused about why a surgeon was suggesting that we see a geneticist, but Mr Law hadn't finished with us yet. 'I've seen thumbs like this once or twice before and it's characteristic of...' a muffled boom... *Characteristic.* That was the point at which Lauren's bendy little thumbs stopped being a personal quirk and became a marker of something far bigger. Then he said 'syndrome' – *something-or-other syndrome*. Each word detonated an explosion, one echoing thud after another. A syndrome could only mean something bad. This was something worse than her thumbs; this was something else altogether. At this point he seemed to be talking to the assembled students rather than to us. His chair was angled away, taking in his audience, allowing him to avoid eye contact with either Phil or me.

I glanced at Phil. His face was rigid, his body tense. In profile, I could see the tightness in his jaw. He refused my silent plea to look at me. Neither of us looked down at Lauren. Mr Law was still talking. 'But it isn't only the thumbs; the facial features are also very reminiscent of' – *something-something* – 'children: the narrow palate, the marking on her forehead and the excess of hair, they are the indicator traits of' – *something-stein*. 'That's what I wanted to check with a colleague while you waited outside. The genetics team will do all the necessary tests. I want to stress that it's really not my area, but I believe it's caused by a deletion on chromosome sixteen, a small glitch, it occurs soon after conception; but we'll need the lab work for a definitive diagnosis.' He reached for his pen, a fat, old-fashioned fountain pen, and dashed off a note, still avoiding eye contact with us. Then he seemed to address his acolytes again. 'We'd best get the ECG done straight away to establish heart health. That should be done today.' He held out the scribbled note towards us. After a long second, Phil reached forward to take it. 'It's a precaution. It's liable to be fine – any cardiac issues would probably have presented at birth.' Now there was something wrong with her heart. 'Do you have any questions?'

Of course I had questions, a cacophony of half-formed thoughts gushed through me. He looked from Phil to me, and back at Phil.

'But you think you can do something about her thumbs?' Phil seemed to have deleted the past ten minutes.

49

'Yes, but let's get everything else looked at properly first. I'll pencil in to see you in about three months' time.' I didn't even realise that we were finished. Mr Law rose from his chair and held out his hand. I watched Phil and him shake on it, like business colleagues. 'Ground floor, Clarendon block. They'll sort you out with the ECG. I'll ring ahead.' We were being dismissed. I almost expected him to say, 'Good luck', but he didn't. Phil bent down and picked up Lauren's car seat and I stood and followed him out of the room, too stunned to do anything else.

And that's how it began.

9

A Beautiful
Little Girl

PHIL

SARAH'S DETAILED recall of how we found out there was something wrong with Lauren knocks some of the indifference out of Mrs Winter. Her expression shifts subtly as Sarah talks, a dawning realisation perhaps that her 'unusual case' involves real people. Us. She listens carefully and doesn't interrupt with any questions. Why would she? My wife is fluent and accurate in her replaying of Lauren's diagnosis, so much so that it catches me off-guard. It's something that we don't talk about, because what's the point? It happened; and talking about it, comparing notes on how we felt and what we remember, isn't ever going to change that. I excuse myself and escape to the only place I know I'll be guaranteed some peace: the bathroom.

I sit on the side of the bath and listen to the burble of their voices coming up through the floor. We didn't realise it at the time, but when we left Mr Law's consulting room we were stepping on to a treadmill, one that has been moving beneath us ever since. There's no getting off, no way of changing direction, no resetting the speed or the destination – we go where Lauren's faulty DNA sends us. And again and again it has sent us into the clutches of the medical profession. Because that initial diagnosis was just the beginning.

After we'd been ejected from Mr Law's presence, Sarah and I joined all the other people swilling along the hallways of the hospital. I needed us to keep moving, away from his office, away from what he'd said. As we waited for the lift a smelly old guy, wearing a donkey jacket over his hospital gown, leant on his drip-stand and coughed, repeatedly. I moved Lauren to my other arm to get her away from the spray of germs. Sarah stood mutely beside me. We shuffled into the packed space. I rested Lauren's seat against the back wall and instinctively Sarah and I closed in around her, turning our backs on everyone else. She was still fast asleep. Unaware. As she should be. Our Lauren, the same little girl who went into that bloody room an hour ago. It didn't make sense. She'd had all the usual tests. Nothing wrong. An endless series of midwives had weighed and examined her; no one had said anything – just that she was a poor feeder. It didn't make sense. And even Mr Laws wasn't sure. He'd needed to speak to someone else. He was a surgeon, not a specialist. He could be wrong.

Sarah reached out and stroked Lauren's little fist, breaking my torrent of thoughts. She looked shell-shocked. I wanted to comfort her. 'It'll be all right. We'll cope with whatever it is.' Sarah nodded at me. 'What did he say it was called?' But the lift doors opened and we had to turn and rejoin the masses. We emerged from the lift back into the reception area. 'Rubinstein-something… I didn't get it. Did you?'

'No.' We were getting in people's way. 'Where are we supposed to go?' Sarah looked at me for direction.

'I don't know.'

'He wrote it down.'

Only then did I remember the note crushed in my hand. I put Lauren's car seat on the floor and uncrumpled the paper. People swerved past us. There was a scribble of loopy, blue-inked letters that I couldn't read. 'He said an ECG, so it must be the cardio unit, I suppose.'

It was the cardiology unit, a short walk around the corner into a high-tech, high-spec, white-light environment, where we were expected. There was no waiting around, no joining the ranks of the non-urgent outpatients sitting in the waiting area; we were taken straight through into a consulting room and asked to wait a few moments. The door shut. The quiet that filled the room was sharp and brittle. I couldn't break it.

Sarah could. 'What do you think they'll actually do to her? The tests?'

'I don't know. He said it was just a precaution. She's been fine. She'll be fine. We'd have known, if there was something wrong.'

Sarah didn't respond. She bent and unclipped Lauren from her seat and held her up against her chest, stroking her back. It was the position we always held her in to soothe her when she was upset or fractious, but Lauren wasn't crying. I wasn't even sure she was awake. The only bit of her that was visible was her head, a halo of tufty dark hair that brushed against Sarah's cheek. I felt a wave of loneliness. I wanted that embrace, I wanted to hold her close to me and protect her, but I sat empty-handed.

A young woman came in and explained the test to us with the minimum of jargon and in a reassuringly calm voice. She stressed how important it was that we tried to remain relaxed. 'It's important that she doesn't pick up your stress. We want her as happy as possible, so that we can get a clear read.' My body was unable to follow her directions as a knot of anxiety formed in my chest. She explained that they were going to connect a series of monitors to Lauren and take measurements of her heart rate, blood flow and oxygen saturation levels. 'Nothing invasive at all. Do you want to bring her through now?' No, I didn't, but Sarah had already stood up and was following the nurse.

The room we were led into was small and bright and very warm. There were a lot of machines and cables and, incongruously, a corner unit set up with a baby-changing mat patterned with faded cartoon rabbits and a box of wipes. 'Can you strip her down to her nappy, please?' The knot tightened. Sarah started taking off Lauren's clothes. Lauren lay placidly on the mat, blinking up at the bright light. 'If you could just lift her onto here. Thank you. Now it's just a case of attaching lots of these little tabs. They don't hurt.' The woman set to work, placing what looked like sticking plasters with press-studs across Lauren's chest and tummy. 'What a good girl you are.' And she was. She lay there quite content, pushing her little legs out occasionally, but not making a sound. Then the technician or nurse, or whatever she was, clipped all the wires into place and connected them up to the machines. 'We need to run the trace for ten minutes, ideally. It's sometimes hard with babies, but you're being a little sweetheart, aren't you?' She lightly stroked Lauren's hair. 'If you could just step back a little bit, Dad. Thank you. Sorry. I just have to make sure it's as clear a trace as we can manage.' I left Lauren's side and handed her over to the calm woman. Sarah and I edged back against the wall, while Lauren lay, wired to the machines, her little belly rising and falling contentedly with each breath.

A syndrome. No, we came to talk to a surgeon about corrective surgery for her thumbs. Nothing else. Two hours later, Lauren was pinned to a table with wires and machines, with a woman studying reams of computer printout. Her heart was being tested.

No.

Mr Law had seen something we hadn't. He'd exposed her to this, then dismissed us.

Lauren lay on the table, unconcerned. Her nappy bagged around her little legs and her arms waved. We'd grown used to her wonky thumbs, we loved her thick hair and her downy neck, her blushed forehead was just *her*, but he'd said they were signs. He'd taken her away from us, with his big hands, and he'd given her back flawed.

I took hold of Sarah's hand and we stood patiently, pathetically by, while Lauren was tested.

'That's it. All finished.' The woman switched everything off. Only when she started to peel off the tabs did Lauren finally protest. I scooped her up and soothed her, before carefully easing her flailing limbs back into her Babygro, relieved to get her away from the machines.

Sarah asked the question. 'Can you say whether everything is all right?'

The technician hesitated. 'The consultant will need to look at the results... but it all seems normal, from the readings we've got today. You'll be sent an appointment to see Mr Oxhey – he'll talk you through it all in detail.'

'But... her heart?' asked Sarah.

'Seems to be working fine.'

'So everything looks normal?' Sarah again.

'As far as I can see from these tests, yes. You're free to take her home now.'

'Thank you,' Sarah and I said in unison.

We gathered our stuff together. I carried Lauren, not wanting to put her back into her car seat. I needed the weight and the warmth of her. The technician collected her printouts and walked to the door with us. 'You were an absolute sweetheart, weren't you?' She lightly touched Lauren's head. 'Good luck with everything, she's a beautiful little girl.' We rejoined the sway of people, and the knot in my chest loosened enough for me to breathe again.

Two further tests, two long weeks of waiting and two curiously impersonal appointments later, the Rubinstein–Taybi diagnosis was confirmed and the knot pulled tight for good.

10

RTS

PHIL

I'D HOPED to have dodged some of the questioning, but when I come back downstairs it appears they've waited for me. Sarah is making small talk, trying hard to introduce the air of a coffee morning to this invasion of our family and our privacy. A spasm of irritation passes through me. No matter what the circumstances, Sarah always wants things to be nice. Well, they aren't.

'Can we get on with this? I have to get to work by ten-thirty a.m.' My brusqueness squashes flat the fake bonhomie.

Mrs Winter responds by a return to 'professional mode'. 'I gather Rubinstein-Taybi syndrome is quite rare.'

'Yes.'

'Were the doctors able to give you much of an indication as to what the impact was going to be on Lauren's development?'

'No,' I snap.

Sarah has obviously had enough of me not playing nice. 'They told us as much as they could but, like most conditions, it's hard to predict and it's very variable. Phil and I agreed, when Lauren was diagnosed, not to research it too much. We were warned that a lot of the online information was very general and could be quite... unhelpful.'

'So you didn't really know what to expect – longer-term.'

'No, not really.' This time it's Sarah who's not playing with a straight bat, because we did find out about RTS. Sarah made sure of that, with the disastrous trip to that bloody awful RTS family event. We exchange a look, but both keep our mouths shut, because what right has this woman to know any of this? She's only here because they need to put this damn profile together. She's not really interested in us. She's here for the other family – the family that has got our daughter. And why should they have a neat, fully annotated handbook to life with a disabled child, when we didn't?

'What else do you need to know?' I ask, aiming to move the conversation on, to its end. Sarah shoots me a warning glance, but Mrs Winter ignores my impatience. She looks down at her long list of questions and ploughs on, absorbing my resistance.

Over the next hour we relate the key events in Lauren's life: her development, her surgeries, her curtailed life and her simple pleasures. My answers would fit on the back of a fag packet, while Sarah's help to fill page after page of the silent woman's book, a steady stream of thin words onto thin sheets of paper; 10.30 a.m. comes and goes, but Mrs Winter still isn't finished. 'Now, it would be helpful if you could tell us a little bit about the impact Lauren's disability's had on yourselves, and the wider family.'

Enough.

I stand up. 'I have to go.' Sarah looks at me with a mixture of shock and irritation. 'I've got a meeting. Surely you've got enough to be going on with.' And without waiting for a response, I walk out of the room.

I'm uncharacteristically grateful for my thirty-minute drive to work; it gives me time for the anger that seems ever-present within me these days to subside. What's happened is bad enough – the not-knowing is driving me mad – but raking everything up is making it worse. Life with Lauren has required us to keep focused on the here and now: no expectations, no looking back, that's how we've coped, at least that's how I've coped; yet since the DNA result, all everyone wants us to do is hack into the past. It's ripping our life apart.

I change gear and pull onto the dual carriageway, nipping in front of a grey BMW that's steaming up the inside. The driver, a woman wearing huge sunglasses, gives me an irritated flash of her headlights. I accelerate away from her. If only it were as easy to escape the past.

After we got Lauren's diagnosis I stuck my head in the sand, but Sarah set off on a mission to find out anything and everything she could. This included getting in touch with a charity for families with RTS kids. Over the months she exchanged emails with some of the other mothers, and she read everything they sent her about the 'condition' – some of it aloud to me. But it was her 'thing'. I didn't want to think about Lauren having 'a condition', of her being like other kids. All I wanted to do was to act like everything was normal and, in wishing, make it true. So when Sarah mooted the idea of going to the RTS get-together, I was lukewarm, to say the least. What 'sold' it to me, in the end, was the thought of a weekend at the seaside. If it'd been in Stoke, we'd never have gone. Three nights in a specially discounted family chalet on the coast, with meals included, and free activities for the kids. I reckoned I could just about manage that. Besides, once James got wind of it, there was no way we weren't going.

It began well enough: the sun was out, the roads weren't too busy and, as we turned into the entrance to the park, early on the Friday evening, the bunting was fluttering brightly. We could even see glimpses of the actual sea between the pebble-dashed chalets. The scream of seagulls and the smell of frying chips nailed 'Welcome to the seaside' pretty well.

At the reception desk a slack-faced teenager told us our chalet number, gave us a key attached to a fob the size of a grapefruit and handed me a plastic bag with the camp logo on it: a surf-dude bear riding the waves on a fluorescent yellow surfboard, more west-coast California than east-coast Yorkshire. The bag turned out to contain our bedding. When they described the facilities as 'self-catering', they obviously weren't joking. As we were leaving the girl called us back. 'I'm supposed to give you this.' It was an A4 envelope, heavy with content. I shoved it in the bag.

The chalet, when we eventually found it, was a small box with a flat roof and a clear view, not of the dancing waves, but of the main roundabout and the laundry block. James rushed up the path gleefully. Inside it was tiny, with narrow doors, a low ceiling and a selection of space-saving fold-up furniture, none of which fitted. The brown blinds lent a dusty gloom to the overall depressing effect.

Two trips to the car later and the chalet was chock-full of our crap, including the travel cot, which fitted fine in every other bedroom we'd ever slept in, but had magically grown to the size of the Isle of Wight on our trip over. It simply would not 'go' in our room and, as none of the furniture moved in the *sitting, additional sleeping, eating and cooking area*, it wouldn't fit in there, either. We folded it back up and agreed to sort it out later. Which, I guessed, would mean Lauren sleeping in the double with Sarah, and me having to squash myself in alongside James on the sofa bed.

James was bored by the time we'd got everything in, and he started whingeing. He wanted the beach and something to eat and a wee – all immediately. I sympathised. The tiny shower room with the mould-speckled decor fulfilled his need to pee, and a bag of Wotsits staved off his hunger, but the beach would have to wait. Sarah had ominously opened our welcome pack and was looking at the itinerary. 'There's a "meet and greet" starting in the restaurant soon, shall we head over?' Thinking only about food and the possibility of a beer, I agreed.

The restaurant was more of a canteen. Huge and loud. Strung along one wall were the serving counters, each lit by the coppery glow of the overhead food warmers. There were already queues building up. Large families with small children criss-crossed the room bearing trays of gravy-covered chips and pizza slices. James's eyes widened in delight as a mum came past with a tray laden with ice-cream sundaes and chips. But Sarah was walking away from the food counters. 'We're over here, look.' Right down at the far end of the room an area had been cordoned off, and behind the rope sat a separate group of people. The RTS families. I suddenly wanted to pretend we were just there on holiday and go and sit with the 'normal' folk.

'You go over. I'll get James something to eat.' Sarah started to protest, but I interrupted her. 'If we don't feed him now, he'll have a meltdown. We'll be over in a few minutes. Come on, bud. Let's see what they've got.'

Pizza and chips, ice cream smothered in chocolate sauce and Coke for James, Dutch courage for me, and red wine in a plastic tumbler for Sarah. We were all sorted.

In the time we'd been queuing, the RTS corral had filled up. It was chaotic: people fetching food, talking, others greeting each other like long-lost family members, and a few, like James and me, standing on the periphery looking lost. I eventually spotted Sarah and Lauren through the throng. They were sitting with a couple and their son, a little boy of about Lauren's age. I steered James towards their table, nodded a hello and settled him down with his mountain of food.

Sarah did the introductions. 'This is Phil and our son, James.'

The chap stood up and shook hands. 'Carl.' He indicated his partner. 'Alexis, and this is Harry.' The little boy had both his arms in casts, exactly the same as Lauren had had, after the surgery on her hands. Fingertip to armpit encased in plaster, the same awkward, rigid bend in the middle. I remembered the problems we'd had finding anything wide enough to fit over the clumpy casts. Carl must have seen me looking. 'Another two weeks and they're coming off, thank God. Your wife was just telling us about how Lauren got on, when they cut the casts off.'

I smiled at him, recalling the shocking smell of her skin and the deep, red seam of the scars that ran up her 'straightened' and 'repaired' thumbs. 'Yeah, she coped fine, really. It just took a while to get her using her hands again.' I became aware of James demanding my attention.

'Daddy, Daddy. I can't do my pizza.' He was hacking ineffectually at it with a plastic knife.

'It's okay, mate, use your fingers.'

Sarah began filling out my response, with timings, physio details, advice and empathy, a useful version of what it had been like, but one softened by some careful omissions. I pulled up a chair, took a deep drink of my beer and started to take in our surroundings.

Lauren and Harry sat side by side in their buggies. Two un-related children from opposite ends of the country, different parents, completely different backgrounds and biology, and yet so many similarities. They had the same slanty eyes and the same pointy nose, the same-shaped mouths, the same dark eyebrows and same dark hair. Again the anger rippled through me. I didn't want my child to look like other people's children, I wanted her to look like me. And when I forced myself to look beyond Lauren and Harry, I started to see all the other RTS kids. I saw the same features replicated, time and time again, across thin faces and chubby faces, across boys and girls, across babies and teenagers, and it struck me, like a punch in the stomach, that we were sitting in a room full of strangers that all looked like my daughter.

Yeah, it would be fair to say that the trip to the seaside brought me up to speed on the impact of RTS, so abruptly that it hurt.

11

Pandora's Box

SARAH

WHEN I told Mrs Winter that we made a pact after Lauren was diagnosed, I was telling the truth. Phil and I did, initially, agree not to go digging up anything and everything on RTS, but I didn't honour our agreement. The first opportunity I got, I went straight onto Google and opened up Pandora's box. The litany of statistics and facts was overwhelming, but also brutally informative:

What is Rubinstein–Taybi syndrome?

Rubinstein–Taybi syndrome is a condition characterised by short stature, moderate to severe intellectual disability, distinctive facial features and broad, often malformed thumbs and first toes. Additional features of the disorder can include eye abnormalities, heart and kidney defects, dental problems and obesity. People with this condition have an increased risk of developing non-cancerous and cancerous tumours.

How common is Rubinstein–Taybi syndrome?

This condition is uncommon; it occurs in an estimated 1 in 100,000 to 125,000 newborns.

What are the genetic changes related to Rubinstein–Taybi syndrome?
Mutations in the CREBBP gene are responsible for some cases of
Rubinstein–Taybi syndrome. The CREBBP gene provides instruc-
tions...

The technicalities were too much for me to grasp, but the rest of
it was painfully clear. I was swamped by the detail. 'Kidney defects',
'mobility problems', 'obesity', 'tumours'; no one had said anything
about cancer. There were reams of text about the carnage that RTS
caused. And Phil was right. I regretted it. I wanted to unread all the
problems, I didn't want to know about what might be and what was
statistically possible or probable, I wanted the protection of ignorance.

But that first foray into the facts was just the beginning, because
as Lauren grew and her disabilities emerged, I realised that I didn't
have a choice, because if I was going do my best for Lauren, I had to
know. Ignorance wasn't an option.

Which is why, when Lauren was two, I dragged us all to the RTS
get-together. I foolishly thought I was prepared for it, that it might
be good to meet real families rather than just wading through the
facts. But it wasn't what I was expecting. No, that's not right, it
was what I was expecting. It was supportive and informative and
friendly, like being welcomed into a family, but almost as soon as
we arrived I realised... it was a family that I didn't want to belong to.

With each child we encountered, my sense of claustrophobia
built. I was okay with the babies and the toddlers, but the older
children and the teenagers bothered me. They were a window
onto a future that I didn't want to look through. In the play barn
on the first morning an older couple, with their teenage daughter
trailing in their wake, came and sat with me and Lauren. Phil was
climbing through tubes and careering down slides with James at
the time. Without any preamble they asked, briefly, about Lauren,
then launched into the history of the struggles they'd had with their

daughter: schooling difficulties, funding and provision fights with their local authority, behaviour problems handled badly by teachers. They even went into intimate details about their daughter's 'difficult-to-deal-with' puberty, and all the while their daughter sat and stared at me, passive and unheeding. When a sweaty James and a dishevelled Phil reappeared, I made our apologies, saying that we needed to go outside to let James cool down – any excuse to get away from the weight of the burden that the couple so desperately wanted to share.

Outside it was a lovely day, blue sky, high clouds. The normal business of having a good holiday was going on all around us. There was a steady stream of kids, wrapped in towels with ratty wet hair, coming out of the pool, and there was a game of Crown Green Bowls under way. As we headed to the playground we walked past an elderly couple on a bench who were sharing a bag of freshly cooked doughnuts between them, sugar coating their lips. An amazing vanilla smell rose from the greasy bag. As soon as we reached the play area, James made for the curly slide, shouting, 'Watch me, Mummy, watch me!'

With James off climbing, we fell silent. Seagulls and squealing kids filled the void. I felt a long way from home, trapped in a situation of my own making. Beyond the playground there was a flimsy wire fence and, a hundred yards beyond that, the cliff edge and the sea, a piece of site-planning that beggared belief. The signs made it abundantly clear that 'Children are the responsibility of their parents AT ALL TIMES'. Ashamed as I was, I knew I couldn't face another two days of it.

'Phil?'

'Yeah.'

'Would you mind if we went home early?'

He turned and looked at me. 'No, of course not. But why? I thought you wanted to be here.'

'I did. But I'm… I'm finding it a bit…' He didn't make me finish my sentence. Didn't even reproach me for dragging us all there in the first place.

'Yeah, I know what you mean. A bit full-on?'

'Yep. They're nice people, really nice people, but that's all we have in common – the RTS – and it's all anyone ever talks about, and I understand that, but…'

'Hey, no need to convince me. One more night in that sodding chalet would've finished me off anyway.' And he put his arm round me and hugged me close.

'MUMMY!' James ran up to us, his face a fierce pink from exertion and indignation. 'You promised you'd watch and you never did!'

'Sorry. I will, this time. Show Mummy how high it is.'

'You have to watch PROPERLY this time!'

'We will, I promise.'

And he raced off across the grass.

We watched him climb the tower, the wide expanse of blue sea in the background throwing his bright-yellow T-shirt into relief. He reached the top, checked we were looking, then came hurtling down, bumping against the sides of the slide as he careered around the bends. At the bottom he shot off the end onto the scuffed earth with a spine-jarring bump. I stepped forward, ready to run over and help him up, but he jumped up immediately, waving like a demented thing, and shouted, 'Again! Again! Watch me do it again.' And so we did.

12

Family Values

SARAH

I DON'T tell Phil that Mrs Winter is coming back. There's no point, not after his performance. He was rude. She's only doing her job.

There's also a part of me that doesn't want Phil involved. I know he hates having to talk about Lauren, he always has done, but I'm discovering that I don't. It's the first time anyone has ever asked what life with Lauren is like and has really wanted an answer. And it feels good to be able to get past the bald facts and dates and to talk honestly; and the more I talk, the more I want to say and the more I remember. The irony is that it's precisely this that's forcing me and Phil apart. He doesn't want to reflect on Lauren's disability, he never has done. For him, we went there, tried it, declined the T-shirt.

For her second visit, Mrs Winter arrives just before 2 p.m. with the same mousy woman in tow, the one who took the notes last time. They settle in their places and Mrs Winter glances down at her list. The silent woman smooths open a brand-new notepad, uncaps a pen and sits poised, ready, and we pick up right where we left off, with me not quite telling the truth.

'As I said last time, we've never really felt the need to get that involved with support groups and suchlike. We've tried as much as possible just to carry on as normal.'

'But given Lauren's level of disability, it must have had an impact on your lives, on your career?' A career. Hell, how long is it since I thought about myself as having a career? 'I gather you're a linguist.' I silently thank Mrs Winter for her use of the present tense.

'I did Spanish and French for my degree. I worked for a pharmaceutical company when James was small; we had offices in Paris and Madrid, there was a fair bit of travel.' The silent woman glances up for a second, as if surprised that I had a life quite so exotic. It's not the first time I've seen someone disconcerted to realise that I once had a life that wasn't defined and dominated by having a disabled child. 'Phil really did the lion's share of the early childcare with James – he's a very hands-on dad – but the balance shifted when we had Lauren. I went part-time to start with. We needed at least one steady income, and I needed – had to be – at home.'

'You miss it.' It's not a question.

'I still do some freelance translation work. It keeps my hand in and it's flexible.' But a laptop on a kitchen table and a local-government report on the transport infrastructure in the Rhône Valley isn't a lunchtime stroll across the Pont Neuf with colleagues so cool that even I felt some of their style rubbing off on me.

'And Phil's job?'

'He works for a utility company. We're lucky, it's a very secure job.'

'And do you have much support, from your families or from friends?'

'My mum died before we were married. My dad's always been there for us, but the person who's the biggest help has been my sister, Ali.' Saying it out loud makes me realise how much it's true.

'And Phil's family?'

'They're not in the picture. Never have been. His dad died last

November, but they're weren't close, and his mum has lived in Spain for years.' And it would make no difference if she lived round the corner; she's not grandma material, which is no surprise, given that she wasn't mother material, either. Mrs Winter is looking at me quizzically and I sense her putting another minus in Phil's column, assuming his poor performance as a son influences his performance as a dad. She's wrong, because Phil is, without question, a man who loves and values his family, precisely because he grew up in one that was so inadequate. 'Phil's a very good dad. He loves having kids. Family is important to him, very important.' I'm pleased to see the woman make a note.

Mrs Winter merely nods and moves on. 'You seem to cope very well.'

'Thank you,' I say politely. Of course we cope – sometimes well, sometimes barely – what other option is there?

'And James? How's he dealt with it all?'

This one is easy to answer. 'He's been fab. Always has been. He just rolls with it. That's his nature. He's probably missed out a bit. It's inevitable, because no matter how hard you try, there's never enough time, and things are more complicated with Lauren, especially now she's older. But he's fine. I'm... we're very proud of him.'

'We would like to have a word with him, if that's okay? The sibling perspective? We were hoping maybe to speak to him today? If he's back in time.'

'Oh, okay.' It hadn't occurred to me that they'd want to speak to James.

'And Lauren. We must, of course, meet the young lady herself.'

Mrs Winter gets both her wishes. I'm just signing off the notes from our session when James comes home and heads, as always, straight to the kitchen. I interrupt him just as reaches for the biscuit tin. 'They'd like a word with you.'

'Me? Why?'

'As her big brother.' He shrugs and, with obvious ill ease, goes through to the front room, four chocolate digestives clamped in his fist. Someone shuts the door. Five minutes... ten, fifteen, twenty. Against every expectation, James must be talking to Mrs Winter, but about what? He's still not out by the time Lauren arrives home. Their cosy chat finally breaks up as I wheel her in through the front door. James flips Lauren's hat off onto the floor, drops a swift kiss on the top of her head, then bounds upstairs out of range.

Mrs Winter steps forward, looking awkward, as everyone always does when they meet Lauren for the first time. 'Hello, Lauren. How was your day at school?' A reasonable question, but she seems to expect an actual answer.

The last fifteen minutes of the visit are excruciating, as Mrs Winter makes a concerted effort to engage with a mortally unresponsive Lauren. I admire her efforts, I really do, it shows commitment and a degree of preparation, but no matter how many smiley-face charts and symbol cards Mrs Winter draws out of her bag, she will not get an answer to... *what makes Lauren happy, what makes her sad and what makes her feel safe?* Nor can Lauren... *say how she feels about what is currently going on.* At last Mrs Winter admits defeat and gets up from the floor.

I think we're finished – but not quite.

Mrs Winter addresses the silent woman. 'Hannah, it's fine if you want to get off now.' 'Hannah' gathers together her stuff and slides out, self-effacing to the end. To be honest, I'd forgotten that she was still sitting there. Mrs Winter walks through to the hall with me. 'Thank you. I appreciate that this whole process must be quite onerous for you and your family, but it is necessary. When they're found, the other family, they'll go through an identical process. They'll have to provide the same access to medical and school records, and suchlike. And of course someone will talk to them about the more general details of the other young lady's life, just as we've done. That way, before you meet, you'll at least have an insight into each other.' She shakes my hand. 'And it was good to meet Lauren and James.' On the doorstep she pauses. 'He is, as you said, a fine young man.'

It takes three lots of shouting and a trip upstairs to get the 'fine young man' down for dinner. There are times when I want to rip his headphones off and hurl them out of the window. He ambles down and pulls up a chair. 'Sorry. I didn't hear ya.'

'I guessed.' He and Phil set about dispatching the meal as if it's some sort of eating time-trial. I sit alongside Lauren and help her, choosing my moment to bring up the subject of Mrs Winter. I decide sooner rather than later. 'Mrs Winter came back today with a last few questions.'

Phil pauses. 'Did she?'

'Yeah. She wanted to meet Lauren. And she spoke to James.'

At this, Phil puts down his knife and fork. 'About what?' Phil looks at me and I look at James. No one fills in the gap.

'What *did* you talk about?' I ask.

James ploughs through his lasagne. 'Just stuff.'

'Such as?'

'Just stuff. Lauren. You guys.'

'And?' Phil is as curious as I am.

'That's all really.' It's on the tip of my tongue to ask James why it took the best part of an hour to say 'just stuff', but I know that kind of pressure is never going to yield results, so I keep my counsel. He mops up the last of the béchamel sauce with a lump of bread and shoves his plate away, sated, at least for the next forty-five minutes. 'Oh, and I told them about when we went to Florida.' That throws both of us.

'The trip to Disney? Why on earth did you tell them about that?' Phil asks.

'I dunno… cos it was great.' James pushes back his chair. 'Thanks, Mum, I'll do the dishwasher later.' And he beats his retreat.

PHIL

So… when asked what it's like having a severely disabled sister, my son chose to talk about the one and only time we flew halfway around the world to spend money we didn't really have, on a holiday we couldn't really afford. I'm proud of him. I bet she was fishing for signs of neglect, expecting him to tell her all about how ignored and jealous and frustrated he feels. Well, tough. James is as loved as Lauren, and he knows it, and growing up with her hasn't been one long trauma that has left him with psychological problems. Go stuff that in your report, Mrs Winter!

And he was right about the holiday. It was great. Two weeks, in Florida, at Easter, peak season, peak prices, peak crowds.

It started at Manchester airport and went from there.

There were heaps of dirty snow piled on the side of the M62 as we drove over. It was March and still bitterly cold. As the doors slid open to the Departure Lounge a wall of noise, heat and human traffic hit us. The queues for the check-in desks were long; they doubled back on themselves, creating a mesh of irritated, suitcase-anchored people. Deep-breath time. I was about to plunge in to try and find our queue, when out of the sea of people emerged a tiny woman in a red uniform with a name-badge. She smiled brightly with her shiny red lips and invited us to follow her.

What happened next set the tone of the rest of the holiday.

She guided us towards the correct check-in desk, but instead of directing us to join the back of the queue, she unclipped one of the barrier ropes and waved us through, securing the rope behind us. The waiting passengers watched as we were escorted to the front. After a firm hand gesture to the couple next in line, she beckoned us forward, indifferent to the man's silent but obvious indignation. I didn't look behind us as we stepped up and checked in. When I explained to James that we were getting priority because Lauren was disabled, he grinned like the Cheshire cat. Suzanne – she of 'shiny red efficiency' – then steered us towards Security, where we were directed into the empty business class channel. This shamelessly, and very visibly, bypassed all the other passengers who were standing patiently and sullenly in the long, snaking line. James was bug-eyed with glee as we sailed past them.

And so it continued for the rest of the trip. We were first onto the plane, first to be offered a welcome drink. They were lovely throughout the flight, making a fuss of James as much as Lauren. And when we landed at Orlando they couldn't have been more helpful. The transfer was straightforward. The apartment at the resort was big and spacious. Everything went so smoothly. And the parks! The Magic of Disney. Never mind flying elephants and wizards; it was the facilities, the accessibility, the special consideration that we were shown that were the real revelation. Everywhere we went we were treated with politeness and enthusiasm. It was evangelical... and I loved it, my cynicism swept away on a tide of goodwill and good service. Spiderman, wave pools, monster ice creams, fireworks, flat surfaces, adapted trains, singing princesses, talking trees, clean changing rooms, polar bears, sunshine, cold beers and frozen margaritas, tired kids and a happy wife. It was a glorious, fantastic, happy, cripplingly expensive two weeks. A once-in-a-lifetime holiday... a lifetime ago.

Sarah has been clearing the table while I've been wandering around the sunlit theme parks of the past. As she piles cutlery onto a plate, she pushes her hair away from her forehead with the back of her hand, a gesture that is so familiar it reminds me of how rarely I properly look at her any more. Under the harsh light in the kitchen I can see how tired she is. I stand up and reach out to take the plates from her, which seems to startle her. We have a brief, bizarre tug of war before she relinquishes them: 'Let me finish off.' She sits back down heavily, and absent-mindedly pushes crumbs across the tabletop with her fingers while I tidy up. Neither of us mentions the return visit of Mrs Winter, my utter ignorance of it, or the sucking of our children into this unstoppable exposé of our lives.

Her silent unhappiness is tangible and it troubles me. I dry my hands on a tea towel for longer than necessary, searching for something to say to make it better, but there's nothing. We are in limbo. Instead I step behind her and tentatively rest my hands on her shoulders, attempting to gauge whether she wants my inadequate, inarticulate comfort. After a second she leans back, connecting with my touch. I press my fingertips into the base of her neck, trying to ease tension that's locked inside her body, but beneath her soft skin the muscles are rigid and unyielding. I knead at the knots in her neck and she tilts her head back further, letting it rest against me, her eyes closed. In those few moments the house echoes our family back to us: Lauren's endless TV, James's music and the silence between me and my wife.

13

The Concert

SARAH

PHIL AND I agree that the concert is important. James insists that it's not. 'I'm only playing backing on a few of the numbers. Not many of the sixth-form parents are going. It's not a big deal.' He's toasting four slices of bread for a pre-tea snack as we have this debate, his back to me.

'But we want to come and support you.'

'There's no need. It's mainly singing.'

'James?'

'You really don't have to bother, not with everything else that's going on at the minute.'

'We'd like to,' I say firmly. Phil and I have agreed that we must make more of an effort with James. We need to do something to prove we're still thinking about him, that we're still interested in what's going on in his life.

James reaches for the peanut butter. 'Okay. But I warn you, Dad'll be bored.'

*

On the night of the concert we arrive with all the other parents, most of us ill at ease at being back in school, with the Head doing the rounds. Phil and I lurk near the far wall, safely out of his orbit. We clutch our plastic cups of weak tea and study the frankly disturbing artwork on display; there seems to be a bias towards broken-necked girls with waterfall hair and big tear-filled eyes. Some of the kids are running front of house, selling late tickets and trying to flog cheap biscuits and crisps. They're not getting many takers. There's an air of slight hysteria in the foyer, a curious blend of parental discomfort and student excitement. The sudden appearance of a handful of teenage girls in black leotards and glittery green face paint ups the atmosphere even further. At last the theatre doors open and we troop in and take our places. Phil's knees press against the seat in front of him as he studies the programme morosely. 'This is going to be two and a half hours of our lives that we're never getting back. Oh, good, it looks like there's a lot of dancing.' I ignore him.

PHIL

The concert is, as expected, painful. Endless renditions of warbling pop ballads, fake emotion from teenage divas basted in fake tan. When James isn't on the stage I drift off, alternating between worrying and sitting blankly, letting the off-key noise roll over me. When he is performing I ignore everyone else and focus on him. He keeps his head dipped low over his guitar, concentrating hard on his playing. He resolutely avoids looking at the audience or at his fellow performers. Even at the end of his numbers he barely raises his head to acknowledge the polite applause from the parents and the screeching of the kids in the auditorium. The most excruciating point comes when James has to back a duet performed by a tall blond lad, who is obviously very popular, judging by the catcalls, and a strikingly pretty black girl. His discomfort is visible in the hunch of his shoulders. I told Sarah we shouldn't have insisted on coming. But if I thought the singing was bad, the dancing is worse. It consists of a group of barely clad girls writhing on the floor and striking disturbing poses. It feels wrong to look, and rude to look away.

It's a relief to make it to the interval. Sarah says she's going to ring home to check on Lauren. I'm desperate to stretch my cramped legs, so I leave her to it. The scrum around the refreshment stand and the confusion of faces I don't recognise propels me outside – yet another moment when I wish I smoked. I wander around aimlessly, enjoying the quiet. What I assume are tiny birds, but on a second glance turn out to be bats, flit around in the settling dusk. Behind me the school radiates light. On my second stroll along one of the paths I realise that I can see into the classroom that the cast are using to get ready. It takes me a few seconds to register that I'm looking straight at James. He's sitting on one of the tables in the middle of a big group of kids, most of them girls, many of them leotard-clad. Despite the sea of teenage flesh surrounding him, the self-consciousness he showed onstage is gone. He's laughing and larking about, completely at ease. In fact he seems to be showing off. The stunning black girl from the duet is sitting very close to him. Something he says makes her laugh and she touches his arm. I turn back towards the school entrance with a sense of pride that has nothing to do with his musical talent.

SARAH

Ali says Lauren is fine, just coughing a bit, nothing to worry about. I slip my phone away into my bag and sit back on my uncomfortable plastic seat. The auditorium is nearly empty, apart from me, a few elderly couples who presumably didn't fancy tackling the slippy, polished stairs, and a hassled-looking music teacher, who is organising the sheet music for the second half. The buzz from the foyer is loud, but uninviting. I sit there, suspended from duty, relishing doing nothing. The music teacher clatters over a stand and curses under his breath, while the lighting crew runs through a series of psychedelic changes as the old couples and I sit quite contentedly in the luridly lit silence, waiting for the concert to start again.

Surprisingly Phil seems less bored in the second half, he claps in the right places, and actually looks at the stage rather than off into the middle distance. He turns and smiles at me when James is on: shared pride, a warm, simple, clean emotion. James does okay; he keeps his head bent low over his guitar, concentrating with the same intensity that he used to give to his toy cars when he was little. Now he's all legs and folded limbs, no longer a boy, but not yet a man, but what strikes me as forcibly as the change in James is the transformation of the girls. From their junior-school days together, I recognise quite a few of them: Amy and Lottie Pierce, Freya Harding, 'little' Samira, who is now big and sporting braces, and the very tall girl with glasses – Anya, Anna? They are all turning into young women, slim-hipped, full-busted, stunning in their tight black jeans, make-up and heels. There are probably other kids here that I should recognise, but don't, the 'morphing into teenagers' process having obliterated the children they used to be.

Suddenly, out of nowhere, a wave of darkness washes over me.

The stage is full of healthy, giddy, able teenagers, showing off their talents, and themselves, to an audience of equally able, giddy friends, just as they should, but as Lauren never will. The gulf between her heavy, unwieldy body and their normal young, voracious ones is stark. As they sing and dance, laugh and flirt, the blackout curtain that I keep closed on the life Lauren should be living tugs and parts, letting in the hurt. I glance at Phil. He's sitting forward concentrating on the show, happy and untroubled, but I've started on a train of thought I can't stop.

Lauren will never be a teenager, she will never share a secret with a friend, never wear a push-up bra and too much eyeliner, never dance, never stand in a spotlight, never be admired and applauded. She will never have a crush on a boy, never be kissed, never be loved by anyone other than us, because she will never really grow up. The act changes and the choir comes on and starts singing 'Let It Be' and I sit and spiral downwards, while everyone else claps and waves to their taken-for-granted, perfectly normal kids.

PHIL

I enjoy the second half of the show. Some of the kids are really quite talented. The choir in particular is really good, well rehearsed, 'on it'. In the way that even cheesy music has, the singing creeps up on me, sucking me in. It's as they're doing some Disney number, a song that I recognise but can't place, that a young woman steps forward to sing the lead solo. She's slim, with very straight brown hair, pale skin and high, sharp cheekbones. Compared to the self-consciousness of many of the other kids, she's very assured – and God, is she good. Her voice is clear and strong. As she sings, she looks out at the audience with utter composure. And that's when it hits me. Our other daughter could be like this: able, talented, glorious, full of potential. Until this moment the other child has been a distant figment, a character in a story that isn't really true, but as I watch the girl perform, I realise that she is real. That, at the end of this nightmare, there will be a real fourteen-year-old girl just like one of the kids on the stage in front of me. It's transfixing. For the first time since this chaos began, I begin to feel excitement, real 'fizzing in my gut' excitement, at the thought of coming face to face with this 'other daughter'.

SARAH

We have to wait for James at the end of the concert. He finally emerges from the inner recesses of the school, his guitar slung across his back, his hair quiffed to perfection, chatting animatedly to a bunch of girls: a modern-day James Dean. The moment he sees us, however, it's as if a switch has been thrown; he goes quiet and seems to fold back into himself, shrugging off our praises with acute embarrassment. He can't get us away from his friends fast enough. On the walk to the car, Phil makes it worse by winding him up about the girls, asking which one James thinks is the prettiest. In fact Phil is weirdly hyper, chattering on about the performance and messing about with a kind of mania that is in stark contrast to his mood at the beginning of the evening.

On the drive home he's equally erratic, heavy on the accelerator and late on the brake. There's no need, it's only a short drive and we're in no rush. As we come along the bottom road we find ourselves behind a bus. Phil slows down and then, without warning, swings the car out onto the wrong side of the road. Coming towards us, fast, is a van. I brace my hand against the dashboard. He jerks the wheel and pulls back in behind the bus, just in time.

'Phil!' My heart is pounding.

'What?'

'For God's sake, slow down.'

'It was fine.'

'It wasn't.'

'Look, are you driving?'

'No.'

'Well, can you back off then?'

We travel the last mile with the tension pulsing between us. James is silent.

When we get back home James heads straight up to his room, and Ali, sensing an atmosphere, leaves promptly. I go into the kitchen to get away from Phil, but for some reason he follows me. He leans against the cabinets, watching as I empty the dishwasher, and when I go to put a handful of cutlery away in the drawer it takes him a beat longer than necessary to move out of my way. I bristle with irritation. I turn and start extracting plates and bowls from the racks. Still he scrutinises me.

'What?' It comes out like a bark.

'Nothing.' His response is equally sharp.

'Then why are you standing there, watching me?' I want him to get out of my face.

He shrugs and moves across the kitchen, taking up a new position, slouched against the sink. I stack the bowls into an uneven pile, wincing at the sound of grating ceramic. When I take them to the cupboard, he's in my way again. Deliberately? Goading me? Why won't he just go away?

Instead he challenges me. 'Come on. Spit it out. I can tell you're in a mood about something.'

'I'm not,' I say, though it's obvious that I am.

'Yes, you are.' For a second we both glare at each other, holding back the torrent. Then it breaks loose.

'You could've killed us.'

'Don't be so dramatic. It was perfectly safe.' His words are clipped and precise. 'It's you. You're so wound up at the moment.'

'That's not surprising, is it? Anyway that doesn't change the fact that you were driving way like a bloody maniac.' I can feel the adrenaline still pumping through my bloodstream. We only just pulled back in in time.

'Forget the sodding trip home, will you?' He pushes himself away from the sink and comes towards me. 'That's not what this is about, is it?'

I shrug, unwilling to get into it with him, but he doesn't seem to want to let it go.

'You're not the only one struggling, you know. This isn't your own private nightmare.'

His words sting and something inside me rips, but instead of revealing hurt, what they expose is anger – a stewing, rolling reserve of stored-up resentment and bitterness. 'You think I'm enjoying this?'

His response is swift and sharp. 'No. Don't be ridiculous. But you're acting as if you own it. All of it. And you don't. You don't have a monopoly on finding this whole mess impossible and upsetting. You're not the only one who's struggling.'

I strike back at him without thinking. 'You didn't seem too upset tonight.'

There's a moment before he responds. His mouth sets in a tight, hard line. 'There it is. That's precisely what I mean.' He actually jabs a finger at me, speaking slowly and very clearly. 'It's not a fucking competition, Sarah.' The expletive bounces round the kitchen. We don't swear at each other, we never have, not until now. Phil doesn't seem to care that he's just stepped over one of our 'lines', he's too worked up, and he's not finished. 'Anyway, how would you know what I was feeling tonight?'

'Meaning?' I look at him, aware that, with the brakes off, we're hurtling into uncharted territory.

'Meaning... you never ask.'

'Ask what?'

'Ask me what *I'm* feeling, what's bothering me.'

Though I recognise that there's some truth in what he's just said, I can't stop the next attack. I strike at the heart of our marriage. 'That's because you never want to talk. You never have. You always dodge anything that's difficult or messy. You leave it to me to sort out. It's easier that way, isn't it, Phil? At least it is for you.' He looks at me, and in that moment I can see an utter absence of any love or affection or respect in his eyes.

He is angry. 'No, actually, it's not. It's bloody hard.' He waits for me to back down. I don't. He glares at me. 'Go on then, do you really want to know what I was feeling at the concert – do you?'

'Yes,' I say, although in that moment I'm not sure that I even care.

'What I was feeling was good. For the first time in ages I actually felt more than just okay. I was excited. I saw all those young girls up on the stage and I started thinking about our daughter. Our other daughter.' He ploughs on, indifferent to my reaction. 'And I started trying to imagine what she might be like. What she's going to look like. What she's going to think of us. That's what I was thinking about: our daughter. But do you know what, Sarah? I was too scared to say anything to you because I knew, I just knew, that if I told you, you'd do this!' He gestures despairingly.

'What do you mean, "this"?'

He doesn't even hesitate. 'I knew that you'd make it about you.'

It's as if he's punched me. It's such a cruel thing to say. All the fight goes out of me. I suddenly just want it to stop. I can't cope with him attacking me. With me attacking him. 'Please, Phil?' I look down, desperate to escape his anger, hoping that he'll hear in my voice the regret and the need for reconciliation. 'I'm sorry. I shouldn't have said what I did.' He's silent. I wait, praying he'll remember that we don't do this, hoping that he'll be able to haul himself back over the line.

But he can't.

'No, you shouldn't,' he snaps and, with that, he walks out of the room.

PHIL

I'm furious, so furious that I have to walk away from her.

I was on such a high after the concert, feeling hope for the first time since this whole nightmare began, and she has to go and wreck it, pulling me back down into her unhappiness. The cloud of misery that she wraps herself in is just too much.

I do know. I get it. It's shit. But it's shit for all of us. Not just her. She hugs it to her like a bloody child. All the meetings and phone calls and emails, I know it's a strain, but deep down I think she likes it. She likes the control it's giving her. She's loving being at the centre of it all, the wronged mother! But what about me? It's as bad for me. It's mashed up my head as much as hers. Yet I seem to be on the outside, looking in, just where she wants me.

And she bloody lied. She deliberately kept quiet about Mrs Winter coming back, because she wanted to keep me out of it. She made certain it was her take on things that got recorded. She was even iffy about poor old James getting a look-in. How is that acceptable?

And then, when we really got into it, she did what she always does – she blamed me. None of this is anyone's fault. That's the awful truth of it. It's just one monumental fuck-up. But oh no, wait a minute. Yes, it is. Somehow it's my fault... I'm the one who's not in touch with my feelings. I don't talk enough or, when I do, I say the wrong things! Because when she says she wants me to talk, she doesn't really. What she means is... she wants to hear me say what she wants to hear: her version of events, her version of emotions, the gospel according to Sarah. She has no idea what I keep to myself, what I protect her from, how I censor what I say, for fear of upsetting her. Exactly like tonight.

Doesn't she realise that I'm drowning here?

I can't keep paying for what I thought. I'm sorry. I really am, but what else was I supposed to think? It was the only logical conclusion. When a test says your child is not your child, there's only one assumption you can make. All that time with it eating at me, ripping at my insides: the thought of Sarah with someone else. It drove me crazy, but I kept it to myself. I kept the lid screwed tight precisely because I couldn't face hurting her. And for that she's punishing me.

I hear Sarah come into the hallway. She says, 'I'm going to bed. I'll see you up there,' quietly, almost nervously. And the bastard in me doesn't respond. I don't even turn my head. Her tread on the stairs is slow and heavy.

Jesus, what a mess!

How can anyone live normally with all this?

I hang my head, waiting for the surges of anger and guilt to subside, but when at last they do, I feel no better, just lonely and tired beyond belief.

Upstairs Sarah and I lie, back to back, together in the dark, miserable.

14

Lost and Found

SARAH

THREE DAYS later Jeremy Orr, from the investigation team, texts and asks if I'm free to talk. I call him back immediately. Without any preamble, he says they think they've found her. Life lurches forward, then shudders to another stop. He explains that the hospital has contacted the other family, but he advises that the next steps may take some time. 'As you can imagine, it isn't something you can just land on someone in one fell swoop. The team will give them time to absorb the news, before they ask about taking the blood samples and the DNA swabs. The timing of that will all depend on the reactions of the family.' As he tells me this, he keeps saying 'sorry', as if he's to blame. He rings off with repeated assurances that he'll keep us informed.

I sit and hold his news in my lap, where it rests, heavy and unwieldy. I need to ring Phil, but I don't. We're bruised from the fight, still struggling to be around each other, both of us sorely missing the rhythm that used to characterise our marriage.

In the past we've always drawn together when things have got tough, our differences making us stronger. It's been a balancing act that has wobbled as more weight has been added, but we've always managed to find equilibrium. Now it feels as if we're completely out of whack.

When we argued, the thing that shook me most was his fascination with our birth daughter. Our 'real' daughter. Which leaves Lauren as what?

When I eventually ring and tell him about Jeremy's phone call, I can hear it in his voice… excitement.

'So they think they've really found her?' He seems able to block out the thought that where she is, so is her family.

'Yes.'

'Did he tell you anything about her?'

'No. They need to verify things first, and that's going to take a while.'

'But not that long, surely. Once they know for definite, then it's in everyone's interests that we get on with it.'

'We may have to be patient. Jeremy said it could take weeks.' Phil makes a small, compressed noise: frustration? I try and steer him back to our immediate problems. 'Do you think we should say anything to James yet?' I want to root Phil back in the family we have, not the one he's creating in his head.

'Yeah. We promised we'd tell him everything.'

I risk disagreeing with him. 'But don't you think we should hold off until we know more?'

'No, I've just said I think we should tell him.'

'But—'

He cuts me off. 'Look, I can't get into this now, I can barely hear you anyway; we'll talk when I get home.'

But we don't. Because by the time Phil gets home, our worries about the future have been firmly shoved out of the way by a much more immediate concern.

I can't find James.

Thursday is a half-day at college for him, he's normally back by 1 p.m., but today there's no sign of him. No text, no voicemail, no note on the kitchen table, nothing. He just doesn't come home. At 2.30 p.m. I phone him to ask where he is, and it goes straight to voicemail. By 4 p.m. I'm beginning to worry. I phone Ryan, who claims that James said he might go into town to look for a birthday present for Lauren, which I know can't be true for four reasons: because James would've told me, because he's skint, because Lauren's birthday is weeks away and because he's never that organised. But while I know what he's not doing, I've no idea what he is doing. I try phoning and texting again – still nothing. It's so 'not him'; James wouldn't disappear without telling us, it's just not something he would do. By the time Phil walks through the door at 6 p.m. I've gone beyond worrying. Phil doesn't placate me with 'It'll be fine'; he's equally concerned. We hash over whether James said anything to either of us, but he didn't. We try his phone again and Phil leaves a message, to add to the four I've already left, but there's no response. In desperation, we even ring Ryan back and ask him to put the word out that we need James to get in touch with us. I no longer care about embarrassing him in front of his friends. At 8 p.m. we put Lauren to bed early, to give us more space to worry ourselves sick. There's still no sign of him. Something must be wrong. James wouldn't ignore us like this if everything was okay. I torment myself with graphic images of him on a hospital trolley, the victim of unprovoked violence or a horrific road accident. I try his phone again. Voicemail. When I look up, Phil has his jacket on.

'I'm going to go out and look for him.'

'Where?'

'Just around.'

'What, just driving around randomly?'

'Yes. Have you got any better ideas?' The edge in his voice is sharpened by anxiety.

'Well, no.'

'Right, well, it's worth a try then, isn't it?' He is heavy-handed as he pulls the door shut behind him. I feel trapped, alone in the house with Lauren, forced into a passive role while Phil gets to play 'action man'. The bitterness of the thought shocks me. Our son is missing and I've still got the time and energy for sniping. I prowl around from room to room, the telephone number for the police held tight in my hand. We haven't agreed how long I'm to leave it before I call them. This is the type of thing we should decide together.

I go up to James's room. It's the usual mess, the bed not even straightened, but I leave it be. He doesn't like me touching his stuff, disturbing his 'den', and I respect his right to some privacy, but in the circumstances I wonder if there are any clues, which if I knew what to look for, or where, might explain him behaving so out of character. Yet I resist opening his drawers and looking through his stuff. Am I scared of finding something I shouldn't, something about my lovely boy that would shock or disturb me? I don't know. I touch nothing. Disturb nothing. I can't cope with the thought that he might be hiding something – anything – from me, but I understand why he might.

I go back downstairs, the acid of worry building up in my stomach. It's gone 9 p.m. He's been 'missing' for nearly eight hours. Ryan texts and tells me that no one has seen him since college… but: Try not to worry too much. It's meant as a kindness, but his message only serves to confirm that something must have happened to James. My heart rate climbs. I nearly drop my phone when it rings.

It's Phil, sounding far away, ringing to tell me that he hasn't found him.

PHIL

It's better driving around the streets than pacing around the house. Better for me. I start with the local area, driving in a slowly expanding grid, with our house at the centre. But that yields nothing and is, I soon realise, pointless. Why would a seventeen-year-old lad hang around a suburban street? I switch tactics. I head for the takeaway joints and the local shops. On my travels I see a few groups of lads, indistinguishable in their hoodies and expensive trainers, but none of them are James. I hardly expect them to be. I don't associate my son with the street-roaming youth on display and yet, as time passes and the number of 'not James' that I see increases, it occurs to me how little I know about my son's social life. When he says he's going to Ryan's or Jim's, that's where I think he is, aspiring to be a musician or just messing about. But who knows? He could be going to pubs. He could be in town, in the bars. He could be smoking weed with his 'other mates', the ones we never get to meet. I pass another group who are lounging like a pride of skinny lions on the steps of the cenotaph. A mixed pack this time, with as many hair-tossing, midriff-flashing girls as sullen-faced boys. None of them are James. Has he got a girlfriend? The black girl at the concert? Is he with her? I wouldn't know. Besides, it's irrelevant. James has never not come home without telling us. Something must have happened.

I pull over and ring Sarah to tell her that I haven't found him, but that I'm going to keep looking.

SARAH

The rising panic feels like choking, but it's a quiet and slow process. By 10 p.m. I want to ring the police, but I don't, for fear of what they'll say. Phil is still out trawling the streets. Left alone, I find my brain stuck in overdrive. When my phone rings I fumble to accept the call.

It's Ali. 'He's here.' Relief floods through me. 'He turned up a few minutes ago. He's sorry.' I sit down abruptly.

'Is he all right?'

There is a fraction of a pause before she says, 'Yes. He's okay. He's not hurt.'

I'm too shaken to question her hesitation. 'I'll be there as soon as I can. I just need Phil to...' I trail off. Ali doesn't need to know the logistics.

'Okay.' She's about to hang up.

'Ali. Tell James I'm not mad with him. Tell him I'm just relieved that he's all right.'

'Okay.' The line goes dead.

I call Phil. I hear the same shaky relief in his voice that's in my heart, but I refuse point-blank to let him pick James up. The call goes from joyous to tense in seconds, but I'm adamant. 'He's at my sister's. I'm going. You have to come home, so that I can go and fetch him.'

'I don't see what difference it makes.'

'Phil. Please. Let's just get him home.'

I hear him draw breath for a fight, but he thinks better of it and retreats. 'Okay. I'll be ten minutes.'

I'm standing in the hall clutching my keys when he walks through the door.

The drive, which normally takes me thirty minutes, takes me half that. Ali opens the door to her flat and I smell it straight away, the acrid smell of vomit, overlaid but not overpowered by floral disinfectant. It's a stomach-turning combination. 'Oh God, sorry. I don't know what the hell he's playing at.'

Ali actually grins. 'Don't worry about it. We've all had a bad ex-perience or two with cheap vodka. The hall needed a mop anyway.' I know Ali is just trying to deflect my despair, but her good humour is so at odds with my mood that I can't find it in me to respond. As always, she reads me, but as always she chooses confrontation rather than conciliation. 'Hey, come on. He just had a bit too much and now he's paying for it. There's no need to chew him out about it. Let him sober up first. He's going to feel rotten, in more ways than one, in the morning.'

'Where is he?' I just want to see James for myself, get him back within my protection.

'Lying on the sofa in the lounge, with a blanket, a pint of cold water and a face like Eeyore.'

I go to open the lounge door. 'I'll get him out of your hair.'

But Ali rests her hand on my arm. 'Sarah. Wait a minute, just come into the kitchen for a sec.' I hesitate, but she tugs at my arm, insisting. 'He's fast asleep. Come on, please.' Reluctantly I follow her through to the lovely, sleek spotlit kitchen. Her partner, Jess, is sitting up at the counter, a mug of coffee at her elbow and a pile of school books in front of her.

'Oh, hi.' She slides off her stool and I register yet again how tall she is, even without her killer heels. I can't imagine Jess having too many discipline problems with her classes. 'I'll leave you to it.'

I feel bad all over again, disrupting their evening with the fallout from our problems and yet, as so often with Ali, my emotions are complicated. Feeling grateful, impatient and yet beholden to Ali is not a good combination, not after so many long hours of stress.

'Jess, there's no need. You're obviously working.'

She smiles. 'I was going for a bath before bed anyway.' As she passes she drops a kiss on my cheek, and the sudden kindness weak-ens my shredded resilience. Ali offers coffee, but I shake my head. I just want to get James, go home and pull the door shut behind us.

'Ali, I really think I should just get him home. Phil's been going nuts.'

'More than usual?' She taps her teaspoon loudly against the rim of her cup as she digs into my husband.

'Ali, not now. I'm really not in the mood.'

She makes a movement with her head that is not consent. 'I know you're gonna say it's none of my business.'

'So don't go there,' I warn her.

But she keeps talking. 'I know it's rough for you at the moment.' Rough – she has no idea. 'And I know it must be virtually impossible to know how to handle it, but—'

I cut her off. 'Ali, I appreciate you sorting James out, I really do, but you're right: you don't *know* how any of this feels. We're dealing with it as best we can.' I feel she's holding me hostage, while my son sleeps in the other room.

'Are you?' I'm surprised to hear a hard, challenging edge in her voice. 'Then why is James turning up on my doorstep, drunk as a skunk, crying?'

It's like she's slapped me. 'He was crying?' She goes quiet, clearly wishing she could snatch back her words. 'What was he crying about?' Silence. Ali has obviously betrayed a confidence by telling me he was upset. She studies me, weighing up her loyalties. She chooses James over me.

'You need to ask him yourself.' She turns away and unnecessarily straightens the pristine brushed-steel storage jars lined up on the counter. Her back speaks volumes. I know that pushing her will not yield any further information. Ali has a capacity for stonewalling that is ingrained, a defence mechanism hard learnt in her teens that lingers, even now that she's happy and out. I haven't the energy to battle against her resistance tonight, not on top of everything else. Besides, my concern isn't our sometimes rocky sisterly relationship, it's my son.

James was crying. James never cries. Hasn't since he was about seven. Ali doesn't turn round as I go to my son.

The lounge is as stylish as the kitchen, lit by lamps, comfortable in a tasteful, organised kind of way. Jess's flair is visible everywhere in the flat; it's certainly not Ali's doing. She's a mess merchant, never happier than when surrounded by stuff and chaos. How she and Jess navigate their very different approaches to domesticity I have no idea, but they obviously do. Tonight the designer-effect is marred by the leggy sprawl of my son, who is lying on the sofa covered in a faux-fur blanket, with a plastic bowl resting on his stomach. Ali was wrong. He's not asleep.

He props himself up on his elbow at the sound of me entering the room. He's very pale and his much-cherished and sculpted fringe is stuck to his forehead, making him look young and nerdy. 'Mum?' It's a small word, but it's enough to reveal that he's still very drunk. His gaze slides from me back to the floor and his head wobbles. It would be funny if it weren't so heartbreaking.

'Come on. Let's get you home and into bed. We can talk in the morning.' James shows no sign of hearing or understanding me. If I'm going to get him to move, it's going to be down to me. I push and prod him upright. He reacts in slow motion. 'Your shoes?' He swings his head from side to side; whether he's looking for his trainers or telling me he has no idea where they are, I'm not sure. I can't see them anywhere. I'm just about to give up and walk him down to the car in his grubby socks, when Ali appears in the doorway holding his Nikes aloft.

'I got the worst off.' She passes them to me and I bend down and cram his big, bony feet into his shoes. He lurches forward as I do it and crashes a heavy hand on my head to steady himself. Jesus, he is very, very drunk. Ali helps me drag him onto his feet, and between us we manoeuvre James out of the flat and into the lift. He sags between us as we travel down. His head dips and tilts, jerks up, then dips and tilts again, coming to rest on Ali's shoulder.

'Oh no you don't, mate. You can't nod off in here.' Ali and I heave him upright. His weight is astonishing. The blast of fresh air outside thankfully seems to wake him a little, and he walks virtually unaided to the car. The relief when I slam shut the passenger door is huge.

Ali stands back, her arms folded across her chest. 'Let me know how he is in the morning, will you?'

'Course I will.' She turns to head back inside. 'Ali, thank you.'

'Yeah.' She's gone by the time I've reversed the car out of the space.

15

Time to Stop It

SARAH

IN THE morning Phil goes into James's room, unnecessarily early. I'm just getting dressed and Lauren is still asleep.

'Morning!' I hear him pull open the curtains with brutal zest. There's a deep, rumbly, wordless response. 'That bad, eh? Here, I brought you a juice and some toast.' This time James manages an audible 'Thanks'. There's silence for a while, but Phil doesn't come out of his room. 'Fancy telling me what that was all about?' I hold my breath, straining to hear his reply.

'I dunno.'

For all of two seconds Phil contemplates this insight. 'Fair enough.' I can't believe he's going to accept that for an answer. More silence. I hear Phil's voice more clearly as he backs out of James's room. 'Well, I'm off to work. At least you chucked up round at Ali's rather than here; that was your one sensible decision of the evening. See you tonight.' And that's it.

Phil comes back into our room and takes a pair of shoes out from the bottom of the wardrobe. He sits down to put them on. I sit up in bed, feeling grainy and tired.

'Is that all you're going to say to him?' They're not the kindest first words for the day.

'For now. I really don't think we should hit him with anything else at the moment.' He ties the laces on the left shoe, then the right, always the same sequence.

'But it's so not like him.'

'I do know that. He is my son as well.'

'But we need to find out what made him drink half a bottle of vodka, on his own, on a college night, while wandering around God knows where, on his own. Anything could've happened.'

'But it didn't.' Phil straightens up and, although I catch the tension and the strain around his eyes, I persist.

'It's obviously affecting him far more than we realised. How the hell is he going to cope with what's going to happen next, if he's already struggling?' Phil merely sits on the bed, looking done in. 'Phil! I'm saying that we need to *do* something – it's got to be his way of telling us he's not coping with it all.'

Phil finally looks at me. 'I know, but he'll talk to us in his own good time. I think we should just back off. He's probably got a cracking headache and a mouth full of sawdust at the moment. We need to let him come round before we start ambushing him with questions and more stuff to deal with.'

'So you're just going to go off to work?' I can hear the disbelief in my voice and the anger.

'Yes.' Phil stands up and reaches for his jacket.

I clamber out bed. 'Leaving me to deal with it!'

We're back to our worst, trapped in our corners, snarling at each other because neither of us knows how to do anything different.

'Stop it! Will you both… just… STOP IT!' James's roar silences us both. I haven't heard James shout in years. Not in anger. He's standing on the landing, his hands clenched, shaking.

'Whoa!' Phil steps towards him and instinctively James raises his hand. The shock stills us all. 'James, it's okay.' James's arm drops by his side and his eyes blur with tears. 'Stop what?' Phil approaches him cautiously.

'Getting at each other. That's all you ever do nowadays.'

Phil steers him into our room and gently places his hands on James's shoulders, pressing him down onto our bed. 'James, take a breath. It's okay.'

James is too agitated to do that. I can see the emotion swirling within him. 'It isn't. You two, being horrid to each other, all the time, it's NOT okay!'

'It's just that we're both a bit stressed. That's all.' I nod along to Phil's reassurances.

James is still tensed up, flight and fight warring inside him. 'You said it'd be okay, you promised, but it isn't.'

I can see that Phil is as rattled as me by James's outburst. Our calm, laid-back boy seems to be unravelling before our eyes. 'But nothing's really changed. Not the important stuff, anyway.' Phil glances at me. *Yet*, I say in my head, but that's not helpful.

But James isn't in a state to be placated. 'Yes, it has. You've changed. Both of you.'

'How?' we ask, in unison.

He drags his hand across his face, angry and tearful, like a small child, his embarrassment making his distress even more painful, and I expect him to retreat into silence, but after a moment he says, 'You.' He gestures at Phil. 'You're mad all the time. Every tiny, little thing winds you up. It's like you're always looking to pick a fight. Mum's frightened of saying anything to you. We all are. And when you're not in a mood, you pretend that everything's fine, like nothing's happening, when really it's all shit. You're never just... normal.'

Phil looks about to argue with him, but stops himself.

'And me?' I prompt him. This has to come out. He blanches even paler and looks down. 'James?'

'You're always so sad. It's like you're not really here. I talk to you, and you look at me, but I can tell that you're not really listening. You've been like it before, but never this bad.' He rubs his eyes, scrubbing the tears away. Then he says. 'Sometimes I think neither of you would notice if I wasn't here.' To which, of course, the only possible reaction is sadness, followed swiftly by a deep regret about all the pressure we've loaded on James's shoulders, thinking that we were protecting him.

'Is this why you didn't come home?' I ask.

He looks from me to Phil, his face muscles working beneath his pale skin. 'It doesn't feel like home any more, not with you two fighting all the time.'

Phil and I sit on either side of him, both patting him ineffectually, saying 'Sorry' over and over again, but he needs more from us.

'It's going to be okay. I promise,' Phil says shakily.

James's response is fierce. 'How? Tell me how it's going to "magically" be okay?'

'Well… we'll do what we've always done: stick together, work it out.' Phil is floundering.

'Is that what "this" is then?' He gestures angrily at us both. 'You two "sticking together", "working it out"?' There's a sarcasm in his voice that I've never heard before. I can't bear to look at him, to see him struggling and so upset. I ache to put my arms round my son and hug him close, make it better, scale it down for him, but James is no longer a child and a cuddle is not going to be enough.

That's when he pushes Phil's hand away and asks, seriously, despairingly, 'What's going to happen to me and Lauren, if you don't love each other any more?'

After Lauren has gone to school, Phil calls into work and cries off. He makes James get dressed, then herds us all into the van for a 'mystery tour' – he refuses to say where. 'Where's the mystery in that!' He drives carefully. When we get stuck behind a caravan on one of the narrow lanes that climb out of the valley, he slows and waits until there's a long, clear stretch of road before overtaking. As he drives he keeps glancing in the mirror, checking on James, who's sitting in the back, earphones on, staring at nothing. I have no idea where we're going, but I'm glad we're together and we're going somewhere.

We take an unlikely-looking turn through one of the blackened stone villages above Halifax and keep climbing, twisting higher and higher. At last we crest the ridge, Phil indicates and pulls the van into a small lay-by. There, fronted by a scatter of plastic chairs and tables, is a burger van. I shoot Phil my 'really?' face; nearly an hour in the car for this.

'Trust me. Come on.' And so we obediently climb out. Phil orders for us: two number twos and a number six, with three teas. He chats away to the owner of the van as if he's a regular. The owner is, incongruously, a tiny Chinese woman. She and Phil appear to understand each other perfectly well, despite her speaking very little English. She has her hair scraped back into a bun that's so tight it seems to have stretched her face completely flat. She smiles shyly at me as she slides our orders across the serving hatch, two bacon butties and a breakfast special. The smell is amazing. Balancing our napkin-wrapped baps on top of our Styrofoam cups, we follow Phil around the side of the burger van. It's then that I realise why he's dragged us up here because, without any warning, a view opens out below us that is breathtaking. The Calder Valley has never looked so good. The bulky mass of Halifax hunkers in the bottom of the valley, fringed by the outlying villages and farmland. As the sides rise and steepen, the fields give way to scrubby moorland and the blackened, sharp sandstone of the Pennines. You can see for miles.

Phil turns and grins. 'God's own, and the best bacon sarnies outside your mother's kitchen.' We drag three chairs round onto the grass and sit, chewing and slurping and looking at the view. It's easy to see why Phil decided to bring us all the way up here. He knew we needed to escape from the house and the pressure that has been brewing within it for the past few weeks.

James eats steadily and slowly and some colour edges back into his cheeks. When he's finished, he balls up his napkin and wipes the grease off his chin and his fingers. 'Sorry.' His voice sounds less raw.

'You don't have to say sorry, mate. It's us who are sorry.'

'I mean for going AWOL. I'm sorry I worried you.' I reach out and touch his knee lightly. 'I just couldn't come home. The vodka was a stupid idea.'

'That we agree with. Getting pissed never helps.' Phil's voice is gentle.

'I need to ring Ali and Jess and apologise.'

'Yeah, you do, but not now. That'll wait.' Phil's tone grows serious. 'James, you've got to believe us: me and your mum, we're okay. We really are.' I look across James at Phil, and he must catch something in my expression because he corrects himself. 'But you're right, we haven't been treating each other very well. I'm not sure why.'

It's my turn. 'We've both been really knocked by what's happened and worried about what's going to happen, and I think…' I look to Phil for reassurance that I'm getting this right, 'I think we've been a bit lost in our own feelings and worries. We've not been thinking about you and Lauren enough. Especially you.'

'Or each other.' Phil looks at me and something buried but deep-rooted pushes back towards the surface. 'Me and your mum love each other, nothing is ever going to change that… At least, not if she realises that it's her turn to get another round in.' We both smile, willing James to accept Phil's weak joke for what it is – a peace offering and a promise to try harder.

When I come back with the teas and a couple of chocolate bars for the boys, they're both slouched in identical positions in their flimsy chairs facing the view, the sky high and cloud-filled above them, and I overhear Phil say, 'It was love at first sight. Well, it was for me; unfortunately, your mum was going out with a slimeball called Adam when I met her, but it didn't take her too long to realise the error of her ways. I had this technique, you see, of following her around, doing anything she wanted me to do, making myself indispensable. Of course you have no self-respect or dignity to speak of, but trust me, it works. Forget six-packs and rugged good looks; adoration, that's the way to go with women.'

I walk over to them, pass them their drinks and extra calories and take my seat. Talk of Phil's seduction technique ceases. Five seconds later the balmy calm is broken by a deep, satisfied burp. Phil apologises with a grin. I shake my head and laugh. 'How could I resist such charm?'

And, to my relief, James laughs too.

16

Safely Home

PHIL

THE DRIVE home is relaxed. James falls asleep within seconds, full of fat and fluids and, hopefully, some reassurance, they're the only antidotes we can offer him, and Sarah watches the scenery rather than the brake lights. It feels like we've patched up some wounds or at least stopped inflicting them on each other. At the junction at the bottom of the hill, as we wait to pull into the traffic, Sarah reaches up and rests her fingertips briefly on the back of my neck. It's the first time she's touched me in weeks.

'We are going to be okay, aren't we?' she asks.

'Yes. We are,' I reply. *Because I love you and always have done*, I add in my head. A space opens up and I pull out, and Sarah tilts her head back and closes her eyes, trusting me to get her and James home safely.

SARAH

The sun through the windows is warm and I feel drowsy. I feel relaxed for the first time in ages. I close my eyes. Phil drives smoothly, carefully, no sudden breaking or accelerating.

The temptation to drift off is strong, but even stronger is the echo of what Phil said to James, the simple statement that for him it was love at first sight. I reach out and touch the bare skin just above his collar.

It wasn't love at first sight for me. It wasn't even vague interest. I barely registered Phil at first, because when we met him I was in the midst of a full-on, all-consuming relationship with Adam, my dream boyfriend. Adam was a medic; good-looking, well educated, full of easy confidence. His failings – his chronic self-absorption, his total unreliability, his snide view of almost everything and everyone – didn't, at the time, seem too high a price to pay for such reflected glory. Phil shouldn't have stood a chance, and yet he did. He laid siege like an old-fashioned knight, with humour and generosity and cheap bunches of flowers, and with his sheer ebullient presence. And of course when Adam proved to be the shit he'd always been, Phil was there. As he has been ever since, steadfast, loyal and, above all, loving.

I keep my eyes closed and consciously conjure up memories of Phil, recalling his strengths and his forgotten kindnesses. I think about his quiet patience after Mum died, right at the beginning of our relationship, and his willingness to wait for me to realise what he was offering me. I remember how nervous and serious he was at our wedding, the awestruck joy on his face the first time he held James, and his unshakeable belief that being a good husband and a good dad are the mark of a man, not his bank balance or his golf handicap. And I think about his laugh, which has been silenced of late, his crappy jokes and his unwavering insistence that the glass is half-full, even when there's actually nothing left at all.

The sensation of swinging round the big roundabout on the route back into Leeds tells me that we're nearing home. I float back to the surface of the day, my mind easing slowly out of the past. I glance across at Phil, looking at him properly for the first time in months, possibly in years. He concentrates on the road, unaware of my scrutiny. It's hard to see the person you love the most, their sheer presence and predictability rubs them out, little by little, day after day, but sitting there in the car, I see Phil for what he is, the only person that I truly, completely trust.

We pull up outside our house and he switches off the engine. He turns and smiles at me. He seems in no rush to get out of the car. Neither am I.

'Just look at him.'

I release my seatbelt and twist round. James is lying across the back seat, fast asleep, a heap of relaxed limbs. I feel my heart stretch and expand. 'Do you think he's going to be okay?'

Phil looks at me steadily. 'I think he'll be fine, as long as we are.'

17

News

PHIL

AFTER FIVE long weeks of waiting we're finally called back into the hospital to be told who our daughter is.

As we walk into the room the overwhelming sense is of too many bodies, too close together, in too small a space. Everyone is introduced to us, but I relegate most of them to the edges of my consciousness; lawyers and social workers, they're irrelevant. I'm angry that Ms Tharby thought it appropriate for so many people to be present, but for Sarah's sake I keep my irritation to myself. All that matters is that we find out who she is and where she is, and today, finally, we're going to. Ms Tharby orchestrates the room, getting everyone into their allotted places. When she's satisfied with the seating arrangements she signals the start of the meeting, then she talks, ad nauseam. She keeps banging on about *reciprocity*. She seems to like this word, as she uses it two or three times, enunciating it very clearly as if she's proud of her grasp and articulation of the challenging situation we have found ourselves in. Another ripple of irritation courses through me, but it quickly fades, replaced by stronger emotions, curiosity and excitement.

On the table there is a slim, blue file. It's closed. This is the file that contains the details of our daughter – our biological daughter – and her parents.

SARAH

Ms Tharby's lips are painted a deep plum colour to match her suit. I watch her mouth spewing out words. Everyone else in the room is watching us. It still doesn't seem real, despite the presence of all these people; it's too much like a scene from a drama. I can't bear the weight of their expectation, their sharp faces and their blatant anticipation. It makes me want to slide out of my seat and crawl away from them. It's all wrong, the whole thing is all wrong. This shouldn't be some kind of bizarre spectator event.

On the table in front of Ms Tharby there's a file, the file that contains our daughter, the child I had and gave away.

Ms Tharby finally stops talking and reaches for the file. Once we look inside there can be no going back, our family will change for ever. Are we ready for that? I reach over and take hold of Phil's hand, seeking reassurance. He grips it tightly. No more uncertainty, no more wild imaginings and no more endless speculation. They have found her.

As I hold my breath and watch Ms Tharby push the file across the table towards us, I'm acutely aware that at this very moment, in another room, there's another couple and another file.

What must they be expecting, what must they be feeling and what will they do?

18

Another File

ANNE

I ARRIVE on my own. They show me through to a small side room. There's a table, four chairs and a glass wall, which looks out across an open-plan office. I take one of the empty chairs, my back to the glass. Across from me sits Andrew Brennan and a woman I've not seen before, presumably his boss. Andrew takes the lead, starting off with the usual pleasantries about my journey and the weather. The woman taps her fingers lightly and he moves on. He thanks me for my patience with the process. I barely listen. The file rests on the table in front of them, in front of her. I look at it and she puts her hand on top of it, proprietorial. The gesture propels him into less smooth waters. He tells me they've received a message saying that Nathan will not be attending the meeting today. Mr Brennan ends this statement with a question mark. I nod, confirming that yes, Nathan, my ex-husband, has no intention of 'attending', today... or any other day. He masks his shock at this lack of paternal involvement by talking about *a parallel process for ensuring that Mr Elkan has access to all the information that he may, in time—* The woman steps in.

'Ms Elkan, what we have here is the profile of your biological daughter and her family. As you are aware, we've been putting these profiles together over the past few weeks. I want to reassure you that the same questions have been asked of both families and the same background data has been collected. The disclosure process has been identical. Thank you for cooperating so fully, I appreciate that it can't have been easy.' She meets my eye, and I see kindness. 'I think it best if Andrew and I leave you alone to look at the file. There's a lot of information in here, an awful lot to take in.' Her hand still rests on top of it, as if she's reluctant to relinquish her hold over it. 'Take as much or as little time as you want to today. I'm around, should you have any immediate questions. Which I suspect you may. I'll call back in to see you in a little while. We'll obviously need to speak further, about the next steps, but that can wait. We are here to help in any way we can.' Finally she turns the file round and slides it towards me. She rises and they both leave. The door closes softly behind them.

There's a glass of water on the table and someone has left a top window ajar to let a little air into the room.

It's a thick file. I sit and stare at it. The life I should have had exists within its confines. I take a shaky sip of water and lift the cover.

The bombardment begins.

There are pages and pages of black-and-white type separated by coloured dividers. I don't know where to start, so I select a tab at random. A section falls open, *Medical Information*, and I find myself staring at a set of surgical notes and a sheaf of photocopied X-rays. The X-rays show a child's hands; the delicate bones float, ghostly white, against the black background, eight straight little fingers and two badly deformed little thumbs. I flip over the pages quickly and bury the image back in the file. The next section is some sort of timeline, a map of her life. The age spans are highlighted in bold – 0–2 years, 3–5 years, and so on and so on – an avalanche of words and dates, hospital stays, surgeries, school admissions, physio appointments. My eyes skim the dense text, unable to settle on one spot. Certain words seem to rise from the pages darker, bolder, more insistent than the rest... *special, complex, severe, limited, need, needs*. I turn whole sections of her life over, unwilling to dwell long enough to assimilate what I'm reading. Then I notice the tab marked *Photos*. I steel myself and lift away the weight of words.

I hear myself take a sharp, shallow breath as I look at my daughter for the first time in fourteen years.

I thought I'd prepared myself for this, but how could I?

The shock bludgeons me. I shift through the images slowly, hoping to blunt their power, but as I see her change from a baby to a child to a teenager, it only gets worse. I feel myself shrinking inside my skin, growing smaller and tighter, trying to retreat from the evidence in front of me. My daughter is not like other children. As I look at the photographs I don't notice the colour of her eyes or the shade of her hair, I'm not drawn by her smile or the shape of her face, I don't try and guess at her personality from her expression or judge her confidence by her stance. Because all I can see is the wheelchair, the heavy body and the blankness in her eyes.

All I can see is her disability.

19

The Journey

PHIL

IT'S ONE of those days when the normality of life seems weird, given what's about to happen. We have breakfast early; even James is up and awake. Tea, toast, Marmite. The 'same old same as', but not really, in fact, not at all. Sarah can't sit down; she's full of pent-up energy, shuttling up and downstairs, checking with me every two minutes that we've packed everything we need. We have. Our bags have been lined up in the hall since yesterday evening. When she disappears upstairs again to sort Lauren, I stand by the sink, a second mug of tea in my hand, listening to the traffic reports for any possible hold-ups; none are mentioned. It's almost like the morning of a holiday, there's the same nervous excitement, only this time magnified to a ridiculous level and underscored with huge anxiety. Today, in two hours and fourteen minutes, if the estimated journey time is correct, we will get to meet our daughter, and her family.

As the travel news segues into the sport, the back door bangs open, without a knock, and Ali steps into the kitchen. 'Hi.' Ali's participation in this is Sarah's idea. She's still worried about James. Sarah thinks that having Ali along for the ride will give him some back-up. I was reluctant, initially, but when they said that James couldn't be present at the first meeting, even I had to agree it made sense. Ali dumps her bag on the table. 'You okay?' Gruff affection, but affection nonetheless.

I nod and drain my tea. 'Yep. Time to get this show on the road.'

SARAH

Though I know I shouldn't hassle him, I can't stop myself. 'How much longer?'

'About twenty minutes, maybe half an hour if the traffic stays like this.' Phil switches lanes, thinking the outer queue is crawling along faster than the inner one. It's not. We're going to be late. How ludicrous is that? What sort of message will that send? What a terrible first impression. Late for the most important meeting of our lives.

'I'll ring them. Let them know we're stuck in traffic.' Phil nods and switches back into the inside lane, which promptly comes to a complete standstill. He rests his forehead on the steering wheel for a few seconds and takes deep breaths while I make the call. When I'm done, I swivel round in my seat, checking that they're all okay in the back. They seem to be. All three of them are contently plugged into their earphones, inured to their surroundings. Ali is asleep and James is drumming along to the silent rhythms filling his head, but I know that his nonchalance is an act. This morning he came and sat on Lauren's bed while I was getting her ready and asked me, again, to tell him how the day was going to pan out. I told him as much as I could – how everything was going to be done in stages, that he might not even get to meet her today – but it seemed that something specific was preying on his mind. Eventually, after much prompting, he finally said, 'What do you think I should say to her?

You know, when I do meet her.' Because of course there's no established etiquette for how you're supposed to speak to your teenage sister the first time you meet her. Between us, we came up with two or three safe questions that he could ask, which seemed to reassure him a little. It broke my heart that he actually put them into his phone so that he wouldn't forget them.

The traffic starts moving again, a tedious, brake-light-illuminated crawl. Between James and Ali sits Lauren. She's dozing, her head tipped to the side, mirroring Ali. Her eyelids droop and lift in slow motion as she alternates between sleep and consciousness. Her mouth is slack. She's utterly relaxed. I try to calm my breathing as I contemplate what Anne will think when she sees her. I know, because I'm not blind, that at first she will only see Lauren's disabilities.

Suddenly, stupidly, I decide that no matter how late we are, I must get Lauren changed. Phil looks at me as if I'm mad, but I insist, so he starts looking for somewhere that we can pull in. The only place we find is a petrol station where the facilities are woeful, but I'm gripped by an illogical compulsion to put Lauren in 'something nice'. This involves us dragging out all the bags, finding her suitcase, rooting through all her clothes and, finally, after much deliberation, deciding that her shorter blue trousers, her other pink sweatshirt and her trainers, not her boots, are what she should wear. The whole process is difficult, stress-inducing, time-consuming and utterly pointless, because when we finally set off again Lauren looks the same. But why wouldn't she? A change of clothes was never going to make a difference.

And now we are truly late.

20

A Slow Process

ANNE

THE SATNAV tells me there are two-point-three miles to our destination, four and half minutes remaining – not long enough. The volume of traffic squeezing through the tight grid of roads has slowed our progress. I don't mind; every instinct coursing through my body is urging me to swing the car around in a reckless U-turn and drive back home. Rosie has barely spoken to me since we set off. Her headphones went in before the car had even bumped off the end of the drive. Under two miles now. We are honing in on the council offices through a warren of tatty side streets, heading towards *the mutually convenient venue* that has been decided upon by our respective key workers. Our social worker, Jenny, is meeting us there. It's madness, but it's real and it's happening, now. After weeks of bureaucracy and the barrage of emails and letters, it is really happening, today. A Tesco's looms up ahead and, on impulse, I indicate and take the sliproad down onto the massive, grid-marked car park. That gets Rosie's attention. 'What're ya doing?' She rips one earbud out from beneath her cloak of hair. The car park isn't busy. There are acres of empty, white-lined tarmac, but I drive up and down the rows, unable to decide which slot to choose. 'We're gonna be late.' There it is, her pure, undiluted teenage indignation, unmoderated by any concept of how impossible this is for me as well as her. Callum's presence in the back of the car does nothing to curtail her tone.

My defence, as it has been for the past few weeks, for the past few years, is calmness. 'I need a drink. I'm just going to call in and grab a bottle of water. Do you want anything?'

'No.' Snap, like a rubber band hitting tender flesh.

'Callum, can I fetch you anything?'

'Yes, a water would be good. Thank you.' His studied politeness only serves to accentuate her lack of it.

I slide the car into a space and escape towards the startling brightness of the store. Though I hear the thud of the passenger door as I get out, I don't turn round.

The snack fridges are lined up near the entrance, stacked full of bottled water and juices. They're also stuffed full with all manner of chocolate bars and cream cakes. I stand and consider the comfort of empty calories. Rosie stews behind me. She breaks first. 'For God's sake, Mum, hurry up. We're gonna be late.'

I try and keep my voice level. 'Are you sure you don't want anything? You didn't have any breakfast.' This draws a petulant groan from her. I relent and head towards the tills, clutching two chilled bottles to my chest.

There are queues, long queues considering it's the middle of a Tuesday morning. Rosie is having none of it; she takes the water from me and heads into the self-check area, pausing only in her stabbing at the instructions on the screen when it asks for payment – my role, of course. She's forced to wait while I put my purse back into my bag.

'Why is *he* here?' This is the real reason for her fury.

'I want him here.'

We start back towards the car. 'It said… *a relative or a close family friend.*' Rosie has insisted on reading every letter and every piece of tortuous correspondence. She has been asserting her rights very forcefully since that first impossible conversation. 'Why couldn't Steph come, instead?'

'Steph can't get time off work that easily and, besides, Callum is a friend.' This is not strictly true, and we both know it. Rosie makes a dismissive sound and walks ahead of me, as eager to get going as I am to stay put. We can see Callum sitting in the back of the car as we cross the asphalt: suited, solid and briefed. The truth is that he's here for me because there was no one else I could ask. 'I want you to be polite to him, do you hear me, Rosie? It's really important that you try to be polite to everyone today, however, difficult it is. It's going to be hard for us all.' My answer is the slam of the car door. The slender leash I have around her slips further.

She wants to get there. She wants to meet them. She wants what's coming next.

When I first sat down to tell her there was, of course, a profound sense of shock, but straight away there was another emotion – it pulsed through her, stirring up dark sparks in her pale grey eyes. It took me a moment to grasp what it was, then I realised: it was excitement, a bubbling, brewing desire to meet her other parents, her real family. The same energy has been coursing through her ever since; it's a type of static that surrounds her, warding me off. And no matter how hard I try, I can't break through it to reach her, and that frightens me.

I click my seatbelt into place, check my mirrors unnecessarily and edge carefully out of the parking space. There is no more delaying. We complete the last one-point-nine miles in silence.

Our destination is a truly nondescript low-rise block of offices, with totally inadequate parking. I'm forced to reverse back out of the car park and leave the car on a side street. The building is as depressing on the inside as it looks from the outside. A half-hearted attempt has been made at modernity, but it has done little to mask the desperate purpose of the place. The reception area is trimmed in spotlights and there are two sickly-looking weeping figs standing guard on either side of the lifts. Every time the main doors open, a drift of papery leaves eddy and stir in the grubby grooves of the carpet.

Callum announces our arrival, his voice sounding wholly out of place. The receptionist has to check on her screen to verify that we are indeed supposed to be there, then check again as to where she's supposed to send us. There must be some kind of note or flag on her calendar, indicating that we're not the normal run-of-the-mill clients, because she suddenly flushes pink and flusters a call through to someone in a position of authority. We stand, awkwardly, an unlikely trinity, awaiting permission to enter.

After a short while a door opens and a lanyard-garlanded man hurries forward. 'So good to finally meet you' – hand outstretched – 'Daniel Brownlee, we spoke on the phone. Jenny's already upstairs.' He's anxious. 'Please, come through. We'll get you settled. The other' – tiny hesitation – 'party hasn't arrived yet. They rang, a slight delay. But come through. A reasonable trip?' And so he continues, a ramble of pleasantries as we are escorted into the lift, along a corridor and into a large side room, a room that seems strangely under-furnished. Perched on one of the seats is Ms Hill, our social worker. 'Can I fetch anyone a drink?' Mr Brownlee asks.

'No, thank you,' I reply.

'I'd like a coffee,' Rosie pipes up.

'Please!' I add, drawing a look.

He looks relieved to have an excuse to leave. We take our seats, facing each other across the expanse of durable carpet, and we wait... for Rosie's coffee and the arrival of my biological daughter, whichever comes first.

I hear the telltale *click, click, click*. That's what draws my attention. Callum doesn't notice. He's too engrossed in studying his soft, manicured hands. Family friend! What crap. Mum's hands dip into her handbag. I see her do a subtle, fake little cough, hiding whatever pill it is she's just popped, then she takes a ladylike sip of her water. It triggers a memory.

I must be about four years old. I'm playing on her big double bed with Dog, and she's getting ready to go out to one of her posh dos, putting on her face, the face that looks different from the one she really has. She glances at me every now and again through the dressing-table mirror as she darkens her eyebrows and reddens her lips. I'm bored, and being bored makes me brave. While she's distracted by the application of her cheekbones, I roll over and slide open the drawer on her side of the bed. There are two identical sides to the bed, but I know which is her side because Daddy used to have the other one, but all his things have been cleared away. Inside the drawer is Mum's stuff, and among her stuff are the brown bottles that I mustn't touch. I sneak one of them out. It's see-through, made of toffee-apple-coloured plastic, full of little white seeds that rattle like a rainmaker when I shake them. I like the sound, but I'm frightened that if I shake too loudly she'll find me and take the bottle off me, so I prise free the tucked-in bedcovers and wriggle underneath where it's hot and muffled. I can't see the seeds any more, but when I tilt the bottle I can still hear them patter and slide around inside. The thing that spoils the bottle is the white lid with the ridges around the edge. It feels clunky and ugly. I try to get it off, but although it turns round and round, *click, click, click*, it won't come off.

'Rosie!' The roof of my den is ripped off and a waft of her perfume hits me in the face. Flowery, sweet, overpowering. 'Give that to me, this instant.'

I do as I'm told.

I wonder if it's the same prescription today, after all these years, and I wonder if I shall do as I'm told.

21

The Meeting

ANNE

IT'S THE coffee and Mr Brownlee, *whom we really must call Daniel*, that arrive first. He's jittery, excited to be so close to the grand denouement. 'They're on their way up.' He can't sit down; the anticipation is too much for him.

Adrenaline floods, black and bitter, into my heart. I look across at Rosie. Her face is ashen. Suddenly she starts out of her chair, catapults across the room and crashes down onto the seat next to me. She sits right on the edge of the chair, jiggling her leg nervously. Her slim back and her soft pelt of hair are within touching distance. I clutch my handbag hard. I want to comfort my child, but can't bear the thought that she might recoil from my touch. Callum leans towards me, and for a second I ache for him to put his arm round me and hug me, but he merely whispers, 'Remember what we said.'

There are voices in the hallway. Daniel continues to ramble on about how we must take this first meeting slowly, not expect too much. The voices outside stop and there's a pause. The door swings open. Too far. It thuds into a chair and springs back half-shut.

SARAH

One moment the door is shut and the next it swings wide open. I have a momentary glimpse into the room. Anne Elkan: smart, straight-backed, stiff with tension; a man, expensively dressed; another man who is talking rapidly, some unknown woman and the girl: a cascade of dark hair and a pale, frightened face. Our daughter. Then the door swings back in our faces.

ANNE

The commotion of the door rebounding rattles the inertia inside me. We all stand up and brace ourselves, as if for an impact. Then it happens, they walk into the room and into our lives. I focus solely on Lauren. The photos and all the background information were a preparation, of sorts, but not enough. They push her into the room and manoeuvre her wheelchair into place. Of course, that's why they'd cleared the furniture out. Brakes on. We all stand there for a second, frozen by uncertainty, on our opposite sides of the room. Daniel steps into the void and makes the introductions. We shake hands and introduce ourselves. Even that seems too intimate, too soon. Sarah's hand is clammy, Phil's dry. Rosie hangs back, staying close to the wall. Daniel looks to me, prompting me to say, 'And this is Rosie.' My words force her to step forward. She keeps her arms clamped by her sides. Phil quickly drops his outstretched hand. Rosie nods, but nothing more. Then it's Sarah's turn to 'present' her child. She crouches down beside Lauren's wheelchair. 'And this, obviously, is Lauren.' She strokes the girl's face to get her attention; the response is a sound and a brief smile. Everyone looks at me. I step forward and try to squat like Sarah beside the chair; it brings me level with Lauren, so close that I can hear her breathing and look into her eyes. Her hands lie on her lap. I go to touch them, a way of 'saying' *hello*, but she suddenly becomes animated and pushes me away. It catches me off-guard and I stumble backwards briefly. Callum puts out a hand to steady me.

Sarah looks stricken. 'I'm so sorry. It's just strangers. She didn't mean anything by it. Did you, Lauren?' Lauren doesn't register this conversation, but looks past us both and signs something to her dad.

I recover my balance. 'No, of course. It's fine, it's completely understandable.' But even as I say it, I can feel tears in my eyes. I'm embarrassed by my weakness, undone by the strength of my emotions, but ironically it proves to be the best thing in the circumstances. My distress releases the lock on the room and we all shift positions, taking up different roles in the new dynamic. Sarah steps forward to comfort me. She takes hold of my arm and pulls me over to sit down beside her, Phil moves over to replace Sarah in attending to Lauren. Callum is freed to talk to Daniel about getting some drinks brought up, stage-managing the situation with his customary composure, and the two social workers go into a huddle. It's like we're learning the choreography for a complicated new dance. Sarah talks unevenly to me about the stress of it all and how... *we all need to take a breath*. Only Rosie stays locked and alone, marooned at the edge of the room where I cannot reach her.

Tea is brought: the English panacea. Daniel seems to realise he needs to navigate the whirlpool swirling around the room. 'I propose we all take a seat and I'll maybe kick things off with an introduction to the protocols. If that's okay with everyone?' We settle into a therapeutic circle of chairs and he starts to talk us through a recommended process for the situation, though even he has to admit to having never been involved in supporting families *in our unique situation*. Unwittingly, however, he's fulfilling a vital role, he's providing cover for us all to scrutinise each other.

I know I cannot look too long at Lauren, staring would be too cruel, so I start with Sarah. I do remember her, I recognise her features well enough: the grey eyes, the pretty, mobile mouth, a face quick to express emotion. Her lips are chapped and she keeps trying to catch and bite the flakes of skin. There's so much that jerks me back into the past. Daniel drones on, laying out the guidelines for our interaction. Sarah's hair is neglected, a scragged-back mess; she looks my age, maybe older, though I know she is younger by six years. She sits to one side of Lauren and I notice how often she reaches out to pat her daughter's sleeve or adjust the looping coil of the earphones as we talk, all unnecessary and unheeded gestures, for Lauren is oblivious, sitting quite still, listening to her music, no foot tapping to the rhythm – but then of course there isn't.

Lauren is overweight. Phil and Sarah are not. Phil is slim, he has cropped, dark hair with the grey just starting to show through, casually dressed. Him I don't remember, not in any detail. He's very attentive, but not to what Daniel is saying, or to Lauren's needs, or even to Sarah's flushed distress, but to Rosie. I notice how his eyes roam around the circle, but keep coming back to rest on her. She's his focus. Rosie herself sits, head tilted forward, shielding herself with her hair, a ball of pent-up energy, and in the midst of my messy, painful emotions I feel a flash of something hot and sharp and very clean: jealousy. I *will* Rosie to keep her defences up and keep him out.

Lauren is unavoidable. She draws my eyes precisely because she is more of an absence than a presence. We are all sitting tight-coiled, balancing on the edge of our chairs and our anxieties, wrapped in the barbed wire of our nerves, but Lauren is inert. Her stillness has a peculiar, flat quality. She's utterly indifferent to what's going on around her. She listens to her music, ignores the petting and fussing of her mother... Sarah... and looks at no one.

She looks profoundly disabled.

She is profoundly disabled.

The room is very hot.

PHIL

Rosie resists us all, head down, her hair a soft, impenetrable barrier. I stare at the crown of her head, her pale scalp visible between the dark swathes of her hair. Her hands twist and flip her phone, over and over, a restless, repetitive action. She has dark, painted nails that click and clack against her phone case, slender fingers, a slim plait of silver around each of her thumbs – her perfectly straight thumbs. Her legs are trembling, energy coursing through them. She looks poised to run. Suddenly she glances up for a second and I catch sight of her face. *Sarah*'s grey eyes stare back at me, full of challenge, and any uncertainty I had about the reality of the bizarre situation we are trapped in drops away. She dips her head again, cutting me off. Inadvertently I must have caught Daniel's eye. 'Sorry, Phil, did you want to say something?'

Everyone stares at me in anticipation, and I can't think of a damn thing to say. I look at Sarah, always the one with the words, but even she struggles. 'It's just so difficult to know where to start.' No one leaps in to contradict her, and my heart goes out to her as she ploughs on, trying to stitch some semblance of ordinary out of it all. 'It's too much to deal with at once, but I think that it's important that we... we... are kind to each other. That's all I can think for now, that we have to be kind to each other because it's very hard to know how else to start.'

Everyone's attention now shifts to Anne. It's her turn to step up to the plate, but she just reaches out and lightly presses the arm of the guy next to her, which triggers what sounds very much like a prepared speech. 'I couldn't agree more. I believe that this first meeting should be kept short, for everyone concerned. The stress you are all under is enormous and there's no rush, after all. Now you have made this vital, initial contact, there's plenty of time to' – a fraction of a hesitation – 'start the slow process of establishing new connections.' Smooth, calming, placatory.

We're all startled when Rosie spits out, 'Who asked you?' The dislike packed into those three words is intense.

Now Anne responds. 'Rosie, please!'

Daniel hesitates, then regroups. 'I can't reiterate strongly enough to everyone that this is a *process*. What you're feeling from one moment to the next could very well be – will in all likelihood be – extreme. There are bound to be some very intense, possibly confusing emotions. This has to be a safe place for everyone directly involved' – and here he looks pointedly at Anne's friend – 'to feel, explore and express those feelings and work through them. But Mr Hanson is right: there's no rush, there does need to be space. I propose a break of, say, fifteen minutes… and then we'll reconvene.'

Callum rises, takes Anne by the elbow and ushers her towards the door. Their social worker gathers together her bags and follows, but Rosie doesn't move. At the doorway Callum turns. 'Rosie?'

'I'm staying here.'

Anne starts to object, but again Callum takes charge. 'Very well, if Jenny could, perhaps, stay with you. We'll be back very soon.' He delicately pushes Anne from the room. Rosie ignores the awkward return of her nominated chaperone and, for the first time, looks at us properly. Her gaze swings back and forth from me and Sarah with a kind of startled panic. She does not include Lauren in her scrutiny.

She is beautiful, flawless. Our child. I cannot imagine what she must be thinking, looking at her parents for the first time in her life. I yearn to reach out and touch her, to still her jerking leg and her restless hands, but of course I can't. I have no rights.

ROSIE

'Can I take a picture?' My voice sounds way too loud, demanding and screechy, and I see her flinch, but he meets and holds my eye, smiling carefully. I just want their picture on my phone, and that's all I want. I don't want to talk to them, get to know them, tell them anything about me – I don't want any of that and if I don't want it, then no one can make me. I just want a picture.

'Yeah, sure, of us together?' His eagerness is almost pathetic.

'Yeah.' I click on the camera icon, but when I frame the shot, it's not what I wanted at all. I take the photo quickly, not caring if it's even lined up; who gives a shit if I chop off their heads or they're out of focus? Phil stands and starts digging in his pocket for his phone. I walk out before he can even ask, catching a glimpse of the raw disappointment on their stunned faces as I leave.

SARAH

Is she what I was expecting? I've no idea. I've not been able to imagine her, because, as much as we've pored over the contents of the file, I've struggled to connect the images and details in it with a real person. Yet here she is, real, darker, nervier, more tangible and more alien to me than I can comprehend.

She's so agitated that it's hard to look at her. It feels like I'm invading her space every time I so much as turn in her direction. She uses her hair and her body to ward everyone off. The only moment of contact comes when she refuses to leave with her mother when we take a break, preferring instead to stay back and take our photo. It's a chink of something, an admission of some degree of interest in us, but the minute Phil tries to reciprocate, she bolts. The mountain we have to climb feels even higher.

After the break the conversation continues to swoop and stagger around the room. I hear myself waffling rubbish and wish I could sound more in control, but coherence is beyond me. The whole experience is destabilising, it's like being drunk. Anne seems to be struggling as much as me. She is mute and wild-eyed. She sits rigidly, gripping her handbag as if it's her lifeline. The man with her keeps stepping in with suggestions and observations that she accepts without comment. I'm relieved when Anne quietly says that she's struggling with the heat and feels she may have a migraine coming on. This thankfully, effectively brings the session to a close, but not until we've agreed to meet again in the evening... if Mr Brownlee can find us an appropriate location. Mr Brownlee is ominously confident that he knows somewhere that will be 'perfect' for an early, informal meal, not too far away from either of our hotels.

At last everyone gets to their feet and the tenuous, distended web that we've painstakingly and inelegantly spun over the past couple of hours frays and pulls apart.

22

The Gallery

ROSIE

THE FIRST thing I do once we get to the hotel is lock my door and collapse on the bed. On my own, at last. I stretch, listening to my joints click and crack. Mum and Callum are talking in the room next door, or rather he's talking and Mum isn't, her favoured response at the moment. I flick on a music channel, some R & B crap, anything to drown out his droning, monotonous voice and her nothingness. My T-shirt stinks, a disgusting reminder of the sweat-inducing meeting. I feel tainted. I should shower, face the cold light of the en suite, but I can't. I can't be bothered to roll over, never mind haul myself into the bathroom and get undressed in front of the wall of mirrors. I reach for my phone and click on Gallery.

The photos I took, three in total, are all crap. My real mum and dad, and Mum's real daughter. What crap. The whole thing is crap. I turn up the volume, knowing full well it will irritate her, grate on her already shredded nerves. I feel so mad and messed up that I don't know what to do with myself.

I wanted their picture, not Lauren's. I can't show these to anyone, because she's slap-bang in the middle of all of them. The minute I asked, they crouched down either side of her wheelchair, their heads forming a tight little huddle, the perfect, imperfect family. A wave of rage slams through me. I consider hurling my phone at the wall or smashing it against the bedside table. I imagine the smashed screen, the flying bits of phone innards, all my contacts lobbed into thin air, but as quickly as my anger storms, it breaks and I'm left feeling flattened and wobbly, too choked by the pain in my throat to cry. The picture of the three of them stares back at me. I expand the image, using my fingertips to isolate and enlarge... first her face, then his. She looks knackered, but as I stroke away the tatty edges of the shitty little room, her bland clothes and her nothing hair, her features come into focus – my features come into focus. Sarah looks like me. I look like her. We have the same eyes, the same-shaped mouth. It's the weirdest feeling, like being on a ride that's making you feel really sick and disorientated, but that's exciting at the same time. Do I look like him? I can't see it. My dad. Not Nathan. This man. Someone completely different and new. The wave of not knowing how to feel smashes over me again. I pull Dog out of my bag and hold him against my cheek, feeling the softness of his synthetic fur against my skin. I close my eyes and breathe in the smell of him.

After an age, Callum's voice finally stops and I hear him leave Mum's room. I shut down the photos and step back into my other life, the one I've been living for the past fourteen years, thinking it was all there was. It's still going on as if nothing has changed. According to my messages, Lily and Kennedy are off shopping after school, Stacey has got some new footie boots, expensive ones, and Megan's new kitten is so cute she's just had to post another ten photos of it. Katie has messaged me saying she hopes it's going okay, and that she's there for me if I want to talk. And say what? There's a knock at the door. I ignore it. I lied to Katie and said I had a hospital appointment. I deliberately left it vague. I wonder how many people Katie's told about my mysterious day off school, and what the rumours are? Mum knocks at the door again, louder this time, loud enough to be heard above the music. I know she won't shout, not in a hotel corridor. I decide to leave Katie hanging. At the third knock I force myself off the bed, tuck Dog out of sight under my pillow and open the door.

'Could you turn it down, please?' I hit 'Off'. 'I said *down*, Rosie, you don't have to turn it off if you're watching it.' I climb back onto the bed, leaving her standing in the middle of the room. I see her eyes flick to the clothes spewing out of my bag onto the floor, but she stops herself from making a comment. She comes and sits on the edge of the bed, a gap of a few centimetres between us. Her perfume is strong and flowery, recently reapplied; nothing stops Mum looking her best. She smells good, I smell bad. She's obviously waiting for me to say something to reassure her. I don't oblige. After a moment she says, 'Are you all right? I know today was difficult – well, impossible – but it went as well as we could have expected, I suppose.' I have nothing to add. 'Rosie, please, darling. I don't know what's going on in your head.' I close my eyes. 'Rosie!' There's an edge to her voice now, she's getting pissed off with me, but she doesn't move. I can tell that she isn't going to go away until I say something.

'They seem nice.' There, make something of that. I've been brought up to be polite, so I'll be polite.

'Nice?'

'Yes, nice. They seem like a nice family.'

'Well, yes… on first meeting, but I meant more: how are you coping with it all?'

'I'm fine. I'm going for a shower in a minute.' I open my eyes quickly and catch her looking at me; she's frustrated, like always.

'Yes, good idea. It'll be good to freshen up.' She means sort myself out and stop being such a disgrace, in comparison to her. 'And you're sure you're okay about this meal, tonight. If it's too much,

I can ring and cancel, say I'm not feeling up to it, I'm sure they'd understand.' She twists her opal ring back into line on her finger and checks her nail polish. So we are definitely seeing them again, all of them this time. I can tell she wants to get out of it.

'No.' I sit up. 'Might as well get it over with. Is *he* coming tonight as well?'

'Yes, Callum is coming.' The tone warns me not to even bother putting up a fight.

I leave her sitting on the bed, cross to the bathroom and reach for the handle. 'Just keep him away from me.' She sighs and runs her nails down her skirt, smoothing out an invisible wrinkle. I want to shake her. The rage returns and I deliberately try to provoke her. I want her to hurt, like I'm hurting. 'And my brother and my aunt will definitely be there tonight, won't they?' 'Brother', 'aunt', 'grandfather', they're new words in my vocabulary. I've been trying them out over the last month, not just to see her flinch, but to get used to them meaning something.

'Yes,' she says faintly, as I pull the door shut.

Why I'm being such a bitch is beyond me. All I really want is a hug.

23

Table for Eight

SARAH

MR BROWNLEE has booked us in for dinner at a local restaurant. We're going early to avoid the crowds. I'm now convinced this is a bad idea. I imagine an echoing, nearly empty dining room, the scrape of knives on plates and the stutter of forced conversations. He stressed that he'd double-checked that the place was wheelchair-accessible; apparently *it even has a disabled toilet*. He seemed disappointed when we didn't express much enthusiasm or gratitude. I can't believe we thought it a good idea to try and meet again today. I feel bone-tired, papery-dry from being trapped in that room for so long, trying to acclimatise to the shock.

Getting back to our hotel room was such a relief.

Lauren is out of her chair, sitting, back braced, against the bed. She's content, flicking between YouTube clips on her iPad. It's the usual pre-school cacophony, an endless loop that never fails to delight and surprise her, even on the hundredth viewing. At home it's easier to ignore, but here the 'Dingle Dangle Scarecrow' is even more insistently sunny and saccharine than normal. I lie on the bed, within stroking distance of Lauren's happily bobbing head, my eyes closed and my shoes kicked off. Phil, James and Ali are sprawled on the other bed. It's Twenty Questions time – all of them completely valid, but no less tough to answer. 'What's she like? Who does she look like? What were her mum and dad like?'

'What do you mean he wasn't there?' Ali is shocked by his absence, but she doesn't know the backstory. We haven't discussed Nathan Elkan's increasingly firm rejection of every approach that has been made to involve him in the process. All we've had are a number of very formal, impersonal letters from his legal representatives. It has been made very clear that Mr Elkan wishes to waive any claim on Lauren. He is, and will remain, absent: that is the message.

I feel for Anne. His denial of her, their past and their child is brutal.

I can tell that Phil's patience is thinning and cracking with each question. Ali doesn't ask what the reaction to Lauren was, as always she's the unspoken presence, unignorable, but at the same time unmentioned. I reach out and stroke her hair. She briefly presses her head against my hand, recognising my affection in her usual distracted way.

James brings it all back down to reality. 'It's not somewhere posh tonight, is it?'

'You mean will they do chips?' Phil's relief at getting back on solid territory is obvious. 'I expect so.'

'Can I google it and see what they do for pudding?'

Phil nods. I can't work out whether James's mood is bravado or genuine okay-ness, but for now I'm just glad he's coping. He slides down on the floor next to Lauren and she reluctantly lets him pull up the menu for the restaurant. When the photos of banoffee pie and double chocolate cheesecake appear, her interest noticeably increases. Their heads dip together over the screen.

'Are you okay, Sarah?' Ali's concern pulls me back into their conversation.

'Yeah, nothing that a hot shower and a big glass of wine won't put right.' She holds my gaze for a fraction longer than necessary, then smiles so cautiously that I feel a sudden tilt towards losing it. Movement, momentum – it's the only solution. 'Honestly, I'm okay. Come on, let's get sorted.' I force myself off the bed. Somehow we have to keep going forward. Ali goes next door to change and call Jess, and I head into the bathroom.

Phil follows me. 'Keep an eye on your sister for a few minutes, mate.' James nods absent-mindedly, absorbed. Phil pulls the door shut. 'How are you holding up, really?'

'Okay.' He comes towards me and hugs me hard, pressing me into shape. 'I'm frightened about what happens next.' I know he doesn't want to think about what comes next: the decisions we have to make and, more horrifying, the decisions that Anne and Rosie will get to make. The thought makes me breathless, but Phil, as always, is resolutely staying in the here and now. We hold on to each other in the stark white bathroom.

Phil's voice bounces off the tiles. 'We go to dinner and stumble our way through it as best we can. We've done the worst bit. Nothing can be as bad as this morning. James'll be okay. We'll keep an eye on him. You were right, Ali being here will help.' He strokes my arms. We have both been trying harder, been kinder to each other, ever since the scare with James. 'And we'll be seeing Rosie again.' I see the brightening in his face at the thought of her. Some differences remain.

I wasn't thinking about James or Rosie. 'I meant after all this meet-and-greet stuff is over and done with. When we start talking properly about what's going to happen, what we're actually going to do.' At that, he lets his arms fall away and I feel the floor tilt beneath me.

'Let's just get through tonight, shall we?' And he kisses me and leaves.

In the shower I sponge hot water and cheap hotel shower gel across my shoulders, legs and stomach. The familiar silver-thread stretch marks pattern my belly, evidence of James and Rosie. My two birth children. Contrary to what I've always believed, Lauren never curled and unfurled inside me; she grew inside Anne. Lauren is her child, not mine. It was Rosie who began inside me. It's so hard to comprehend. The complexity of it is ridiculous. I don't see how we can go back and unravel the skeins of fourteen years of family. I stand and watch the suds swirl and drain away.

Rosie's self-possession in the meeting was unnerving. It was as if she was sealed off from us, by her upbringing, her confidence, her defiance and her normal fourteen-year-old teenage-ness. I'd under-estimated how different she would be from Lauren, how much older she'd seem and how able. I hadn't thought through that she'd have such independence and resistance, but I suppose we're used to the quiet, biddable dependency of Lauren. It was a shock to be faced with what a 'normal' teenage daughter looked, sounded and acted like. God only knows what the reverse was like for Anne.

I turn the water off and wrap myself in the stiff, unyielding towels. Time to go through the charade of happy, functional families once again.

ANNE

This time Rosie chooses the back of the car, so Callum gets to ride up front with me, though once again there's no conversation, civil or otherwise. The satnav spouts regular instructions into the silence, steering us decisively along a vaguely familiar dual carriageway and off into a faceless retail park. Another journey that I don't want to travel. The compulsion to deal with this is immense, but intolerable. I feel frozen. I can see everyone else struggling, but somehow they're managing it better than me. They're becoming themselves, starting to uncoil and relax back into something close to normal. They're not like me, the mannequin in the room. I heard my clipped, short responses to their questions. I saw how puzzled Sarah was by my polite reserve and the way she glanced between Rosie and me. I was conscious of the barrier that I was erecting. But I know if I relax I will lose control, and I simply can't do that. I'm dreading being with them all again.

Unfortunately, as promised, it's a short ride. Our destination this time is one of those pub-chain restaurants, big, mock and uninviting. The signage is plastered with huge photographs of oozing steaks and cream-piled puddings. I feel Callum stiffen in anticipation of microwaved veg and overcooked meat. Inside it's cavernous – empty tables as far as you can see. The only other customers are an elderly couple who sit at the far side of the restaurant, silhouetted against the fake mullioned windows, silently chewing through their meals. There's no sign of the Rudaks. The welcome lectern at the entrance is unmanned, so we hover aimlessly in the foyer until a barman spots us and shouts across, 'Just grab a table, anywhere you like. I'll get one of the girls out to you in a minute.' He goes back to unbagging change into a till. Rosie sets off across the room. She has showered and changed, as asked. She's wearing skinny jeans and a plain white T-shirt and trainers. She must have washed her hair, because it shines under the pub lights. I see the barman catch sight of her and stare openly as she weaves through the tables. She steps through an arch and out of sight.

'I'm really not sure that this "getting everyone together" again is a good idea,' Callum says.

'And how was I supposed to say "no"?'

He shrugs. 'It won't help.'

'Do you mean me or Rosie?'

'Well, that's my concern. The more exposure you have, the more difficult it's going to be, for both of you, but I was thinking, primarily, of Rosie. Given how emotional you say she is at the moment, meeting her brother and the aunt, so quickly after the first encounter with Sarah and Phil' – I notice his deferential avoidance of calling them her mum and dad – 'well, to my mind, it's ill-advised.'

'She's very nearly fifteen, Callum. In the current circumstances I suspect that even you might be struggling slightly. And, anyway, she wanted to meet them tonight. I could hardly refuse.' He holds his hands up, mea culpa, but I can see that he thinks I'm being weak, bowing to Rosie's demands. He has pointed out the risks to me, repeatedly and very firmly. He's focusing on the end result. To him, everything not directly pertaining to an agreed final outcome is just a quagmire to be waded through as directly and quickly as possible. But then that's Callum's forte: negotiating a lucrative route through life's messes, making sure that the mud doesn't stick to him or, more importantly, to his clients. For a moment I share Rosie's dislike of him, but not her distrust.

Rosie reappears and beckons us over.

Through the archway a long table has been laid for eight; there are two hand-scrawled RESERVED notes plonked at either end. Callum turns on his heel. 'I'll go and fetch us all a drink. Anne, a bottle of no-doubt-undrinkable red? Rosie, a cola?'

'A Diet Coke.'

The war of attrition wages on.

PHIL

I'm excited as well as anxious. I'm fascinated to see her again. Selfishly, I hope that Sarah will sit next to Anne, surely it's natural that they will want to talk to each other: two mothers together, a shared experience to reconstruct and digest. James will stick close to Ali, hide behind her barricades, which means that I should be able to sit next to Rosie. Anne's reserve and her reluctance even to look at Lauren during the meeting scratch at my conscience, but I push this into touch in favour of the anticipation of seeing Rosie again.

Our arrival at the pub is the usual Rudak shambles. We're late, again, flustered and apologetic. I get stuck with Callum, who massively overdoes the mine-host role, buying drinks for everyone and directing the seating places. My irritation with him mounts. At dinner I end up with Lauren to my left and Callum to my right, Ali and James form the buffer zone in the middle, and Rosie sits at the far end of the table flanked by Sarah and Anne. Instead of all the things I wanted to ask her, I hear myself making small talk about dietary preferences with a chronically bored Callum, while simultaneously trying to minimise the mess Lauren is making with her pasta. James barely looks up from his plate, eats a lot and talks mostly to Ali. Thankfully we aren't in the open section of the restaurant; what other diners would make of the family dynamic around our table is anyone's guess. We even look mismatched. There's a sheen and a smartness to Anne and Callum that suits neither the venue nor us. Ali's dyed-red, cropped hair swings back and forth between James and Sarah like a provocation.

It's obvious that Sarah and Anne aren't getting much beyond the stilted niceties of earlier in the day. Anne's face remains closed, her responses brief. I can tell from the agitation in Sarah's hands and her slightly raised voice that whatever conversation is taking place is an effort. Rosie sits trapped between them, concentrating on her phone. Mid-meal, Sarah catches me off-guard. 'Do you want to swap places, and I'll help Lauren?' To my shame, I decide that the suave platitudes of Callum are easier to cope with than the frozen distress that seems to be immobilising Anne.

'No, I'm fine.'

Sarah turns once again to Anne and asks her and Rosie about their home in St Albans. Somehow we make it to pudding, which only Ali and James order. Callum, who has steadily drunk most of the second bottle of wine, despite his evident disgust, decides on a Scotch to round off his stoic sojourn into pub cuisine. The arrival of James's house special, a brownie tower stack topped off with a frenzy of whipped cream, sets Ali and James off. They start giggling like little kids. The stiff responses of Anne, Callum and Rosie seem to increase their hysteria. I know it's the pressure getting to them both, but the laughing, snorting and digging around for extra-big chocolate chunks seems completely inappropriate.

It's at this moment that Lauren soils herself. The smell is unmistakable. 'Come on, chicken, let's go and get you changed.'

Callum makes a show of being solicitous, moving chairs out of the way.

Sarah rises from her seat. 'I'll come and help.' A sudden silence falls as we make our departure. James flushes red, recognising where we're heading and why. He looks down at the destroyed mess of his pudding.

The disabled loo is, as they often are, too small for two adults, the wheelchair and Lauren, so Sarah waits outside, shouting, 'Are you all right?' through the door at regular intervals. We are all right, but it's awkward. Lauren has to lie on the floor while I change her. There's nowhere within easy reach to put the wipes, so I balance them on the loo rim and, of course, knock them into the toilet, from where I have to retrieve them. 'Shit, shit, shit!' Lauren smiles at my outburst; any energetic communication is fine with her; swearing, shouting, even crying, it's all just part of the show.

Sarah, with her sixth sense for me cocking things up, asks again, 'Are you sure – you're all right in there?' I grunt a reply.

With Lauren clean, I heft her up onto the toilet seat. She's heavy.

It's a tough lift; how Sarah manages when she's on her own with her, I don't know. By the time I've managed to settle Lauren back into her chair, binned the nappy and the soggy pack of wipes and washed my hands, I'm feeling claustrophobic. I push the door open and we escape.

Sarah is waiting. 'Here, I'll take her. It's hard going, isn't it?'

'Yeah.' She means the meal, but 'hard' fairly accurately sums up the whole day. I try to be positive. 'Without Ali and James, it'd be worse.'

Sarah nods and strokes Lauren's hair. The thought of going back to the table is a grim one. Then, with her knack of reading me, Sarah offers me a gift. 'Why, don't you catch a breather? I'll take her back to the table and see if I can get the bill.'

'Thanks.' I lean across Lauren and kiss Sarah quickly on the cheek with a rush of love and gratitude for how perceptive she can be. 'I'll only be ten minutes; I'll just grab a bit of fresh air.'

'Okay; any more than ten, mind, and I'll be sending Ali out to round you up.' She heads back into the restaurant.

24

A Breath of Fresh Air

PHIL

OUTSIDE, IT'S a shock to realise that it's quite a nice evening. There's warmth in the air, as well as traffic noise and petrol fumes. There's a small garden to the side of the pub, so I walk round and through the wonky latched gate. Compared to the restaurant, the garden is busy, a mix of post-work, swift-pint drinkers and cheap-suited girls sharing bottles of wine. The tables in the weak sun are all occupied, that British desperation to catch a few rays after a day cooped up in an office or a van. I head for the empty tables in the shade, feeling conspicuous being on my own and without a drink in my hand, but it's a relief to be out in the fresh air. The clack of the gate a few minutes later draws my attention. Rosie steps into the garden and pauses, shielding her eyes from the sun as she scans the tables for somewhere to sit. Like a real dork, I raise my hand and wave. Whether she sees me or not, I'm not sure. Her attention is drawn to two girls gathering up their jackets and bags, ready to leave. She slips into the space left by them, immediately digs out her phone and starts scrolling through. I'm left sitting there in the shadows, watching her. I feel uncomfortable. It's as if I'm spying.

In pursuit of the fading sun a couple, three tables over, grab their glasses, up sticks and begin to move towards Rosie's table. She tenses, glances up and proceeds to stretch her long legs out along the bench, a non-verbal F— off, if ever I saw one. The couple think better of it and reroute, heading out of the garden and presumably inside the pub. Rosie keeps her bubble of isolation intact. I risk it and head over. 'Hi. Can *I* sit with you, just for a minute?'

'Okay.' But it's reluctant.

I sit opposite her. She doesn't shift, leaving me with her profile, her face dipped down towards her phone. Finally I've got some time with her, but she isn't going to make it easy for me. I don't know where to start. The silence is filled by a couple at the next table debating whether or not to call into the supermarket on the way home.

'You don't say much, do you?' Her tone is challenging.

'You mean, not as much as Sarah?' This is disloyal of me, but it raises the ghost of a smile. 'I'm not sure what to say right now.'

Rosie relaxes, slightly. 'It's proper weird, isn't it?' She flips her phone over in her hands a few times, then puts it on the table, a concession at last.

'Yeah, that's not a bad way of describing it.' A group of girls nearby bark with laughter at something, and in the distance a police siren rolls around and away. The garden settles back down into a scatter of alcohol-eased conversations and the sun slips a bit further. It's really quite cool, even in the sun. Rosie's only wearing a thin cotton T-shirt and jeans. I can see the hairs on her bare arm lift and prickle.

'Am I what you expected?' She strokes her long hair self-consciously and stares at her trainers, all her brusque certainty gone.

'We weren't expecting anything other than what we'd seen in the photos. We saw how pretty you were, but they're just pictures.'

'Yeah. People aren't always like what they look like on the outside, are they?'

'No, I suppose not. It's going to take time for us all to get to know each other. But that's okay.' The silence stretches between us.

'And what happens if you don't like what I'm like on the inside?' Her trainers are still the focus of every ounce of her concentration.

It's such an odd question that it stumps me. 'I can't see that being a problem, but either way, you're our daughter.' The strangeness of the word clunks in my mouth and I stagger on into a weak attempt at humour. 'So I suppose we'll just have to put up with you, however dark your soul is.' Her response is a non-committal shrug. She's slipping back inside her shell. I'm desperate to cling on to her. 'I wonder how they're getting on at the table. It was a bit of a grim meal, wasn't it?' Nothing. 'Don't be put off by the way Ali looks; she's good fun when you get to know her, if you can live with her idiosyncrasies. And James is just a bit overwhelmed by it all at the moment. He doesn't normally sit and shovel food into his face. Actually, come to think of it, that's precisely what he does.' I'm babbling.

'Mum's hating every minute of it.'

'She looks like she's finding it hard.'

'Who isn't?' The ferocity is back.

'It'll get easier, over time. We're really looking forward to getting to know you... and your mum. Rosie' – I realise it's the first time I've called her by her name – 'hang on in there. I can't begin to imagine how awful this is for you, and how confusing, especially not knowing the next bit, but we wouldn't ever do anything that you weren't okay with. And we really don't want to come between you and your mum.' She doesn't say anything, just wraps her arms around herself. 'It's getting cold sitting here,' I say. 'Do you want to go back inside?'

'Not specially.' Nearly half of the garden is in shadow now and more people are drifting inside or off home. She stays put, watching the departing drinkers. I go with my instincts and keep quiet, and the silence eases into something slightly more comfortable. One of the barmen comes out and starts collecting glasses, stacking them in a precarious tower against his chest. He reaches his limit and heads back inside. I'm just about to open my big mouth again and make a joke about Sarah's threat to send Ali out to round me up, when Rosie swings her legs off the bench and turns round properly to face me.

'I don't even know what I'm supposed to call you.'

'Whatever, you like... I answer to most things.'

'Not Dad.'

'That's okay.' I know enough to realise that I need to give her time. 'Even "dickhead" would do for now, as long as you call me something.' And for a heart-lifting moment she grins at me.

'No, that won't work. "Dickhead" is more of a Callum kinda name.'

25

The Morning After

ANNE

THE MORNING brings another conversation with Callum. Considering the volume of alcohol he put away last night he looks remarkably fresh; he's wearing a different well-cut suit with an immaculate white shirt, his one concession being an open neck, no tie. 'Nothing has changed materially. You've met her now, filled in the blanks, so to speak, but I presume we are where we started?' Though he phrases it as a question, it's obvious that he assumes he knows the answer. I pull my robe around me, suddenly conscious of my bare legs. I feel ambushed by him arriving before breakfast, before I've dressed or got myself straight. Apparently he's waiting for an actual answer.

'Yes.'

'I need you to be more explicit, Anne. If you want me to advise you legally you need to be clear.'

Heaven forbid that he should advise me emotionally or morally, like a real friend and confidant. I wonder, not without anxiety, what the bill for these two days will come to. I clarify for him. 'Yes or no

– whatever. Meeting her hasn't changed my initial reactions.' Just wrenched open my heart.

He keeps pushing me. 'My dear Anne, I need you to articulate your thoughts for me. Brutal honesty: you are my client. I'm here to protect your and Rosie's interests in this whole sorry affair, but I need to know exactly how you want me to play it' – he corrects himself – 'approach it. It'll be important when we get to the inevitable nitty-gritty of the "arrangements".' He leans back in his chair and actually steeples his fingers together, the model of an old-school lawyer.

Brutal honesty is what he wants. Honesty, of a sort, is what I give him. 'My priority is keeping Rosie.'

'And by "keeping" you mean…?'

'Just what I said, keeping her. She's still my daughter. Not genetically, but I've raised her, loved her, protected her for all these years. That has to count. I can't face the thought of life without her.'

'And we will make a strong case on those grounds. As you point out, you've raised Rosie in a stable loving home for the past fourteen years – that's obviously going to be pivotal. The close bond between mother and daughter will be central to our position: a single mother and her only daughter.' His pause is stagily dramatic, he's obviously imagining his performance before the Family Court, but he stumbles immediately into awkwardness; his insight into my relationship with Rosie over the past couple of days seems to have called into question the strength of that bond. He hurries on, steering a path away from the murky waters of how Rosie and I feel about one another. 'More complicated are your intentions towards your biological daughter.'

My intentions towards Lauren are… are what?

I look at him sitting smugly opposite me. How Teflon is he really, beneath his well-fitting, expensive clothes and his close shave? 'I don't know.' He's listening properly now. I speak slowly and quietly, making him lean forward so that he can catch every word. 'But I want you to contact Nathan's people and find out what he's planning, with regard to our financial responsibilities, especially in the light of Lauren's needs. He has a role in all this as well, whatever he may think. And he has the wealth. I'm sure he won't object, as long as he can stay away from the actual distress and mess.'

Callum keeps his views on Nathan to himself, as he always has done. Nathan does, after all, pay the bills. 'And' – Callum hesitates – 'with regard to the involvement going forward... for both girls?'

'I think, at least to start with, that it should be limited.' Now he does falter, afraid to ask more, so I lay it out for him, keeping my voice low just in case Rosie can hear through the paper-thin walls. I need to protect what I have, and all I have is her. 'I shall, of course, encourage Rosie to have contact with them, it would be unnatural to deny that. She has a right – a need – to get to know them.' I actually hate the thought of her getting to know them, of her being seduced by their warmth and noise. 'But I would prefer the contact to be, at least initially, by phone and email.'

'But you envisage visits further down the line?'

'Well, it will need careful planning and scheduling, given the distance and Rosie's school work; we have to be careful not to disrupt her life too much at present. It's a critical period.'

'I still think we need to start setting some parameters before the meeting this morning. Frequency, duration, where they will stay on visits. There's also the issue of any unsupervised access.'

'They.' He's factoring in Lauren. The black silt in the pit of my stomach shifts. I need to focus on Rosie. She's my priority in this. I haven't had time to work out my feelings about Lauren. They are too complicated and too painful. 'I feel dreadfully upset about Lauren.' He nods. 'It's a huge shock, the level of her disability.' Another nod. 'I really need time to come to terms with it all.'

'I appreciate that, Anne, but they're going to want to know what your intentions are beyond the financial provision; indeed, if we begin by offering monetary support, they may see that as tantamount to you stepping away from any parental responsibility for her.'

I stand up abruptly and turn away from him, going over to the window for want of anywhere else to remove myself to. 'Callum, stop. Please, for God's sake, just stop for a minute. It's impossible.' I can feel my heartbeat pulsing in my neck. He doesn't move. In my defence, I attack. 'What would you do if it were you? Go on, what the hell would you do in my position?'

And he finally has the good grace to admit, 'I've no idea.'

And so we go into the meeting with very little clear, other than my conviction that the less Rosie sees of them, the better.

Unfortunately everyone else in the room, including Rosie, seems to have the opposite desire. After an unstoppable couple of hours we have somehow agreed protocols for Rosie to communicate directly with the whole Rudak family, and we have pencilled in another get-together, this time unsupervised, in a mere two weeks' time, at their home. *That way, I can see how they've adapted the environment for Lauren and I will have a chance to get to understand her far better in her home setting.* Callum makes ineffective forays into slowing things down, but Daniel frustrates his interventions with the force of a man on a mission. Somehow it's the informality of the meeting that defeats Callum, that and their sheer numbers, because this time the flamboyant sister and the boy join in and, to everyone's surprise, Rosie speaks a few times and each time she does, she agrees with everything that is suggested. I notice, with profound unease, how often she glances at Phil for support.

It's all moving too fast for me. I end up as a bystander in my own life, with decisions being forged and bound together into a firm plan because I simply do not know how to articulate 'no' in the face of such moral and emotional compulsion.

26

The Home Visit

ANNE

A FORTNIGHT later I pull up outside their house and put the handbrake on. I'm just about to warn Rosie about rushing things, when she yanks open the door, hurries round the car and up the path. I have literally delivered her to them. Before she has a chance to knock, the door swings open and I see Phil welcome her in. I sit for a few seconds composing myself, before I realise that he has come out of the house and is waiting to say hello. He takes the bags from the boot. 'Decent trip? You found us okay then? It's great to have you here.' This is what it will be like all weekend, awkward niceties and endless cups of tea.

It's a small terraced house on a nice, tree-lined street. Leading up to the front door is a metal ramp that slices a pretty front garden in half. Phil is still talking. 'Come on through. Sarah's got the kettle on.' As I follow him in, carrying my gift, I wonder what he's really thinking, behind his breezy welcome. We each have our own purgatories to get through over the next two days.

Rosie is here, but within ten minutes of setting foot in our house I can see that the pressure of being trapped under everyone's watchful eye is too much for her. She keeps glancing at the back door as if she's plotting an escape. I feel the same, but as I'm an adult I don't have the option to leg it. When I suggest that I show her up to her/James's room so that she can unpack, she leaps up and follows me. 'You're in here.' I push open the door, and panic. Sarah spent the whole morning trying to make it acceptable, cleaning and polishing and stuffing as much of James's crap out of sight as possible, but it still looks a bit of a pit – a pit made even smaller and more cramped by the addition of a spare mattress on the floor. I'm guessing it's nothing like her room at home. 'Sorry. James has a lot of stuff and, what with the other bed, you and your mum are going to be climbing over each other, I'm afraid.' Rosie's expression is unreadable, which I find quite impressive in the circumstances. 'Anyway, I'll leave you to get settled in. There's no rush to come down, but we're planning on going out later, if you fancy it.'

'Thanks.' She drops her bag on James's bed, which has not been transformed by the addition of a floral duvet and a cushion from the front room, and flops down beside it.

'See you when you're ready.'

I make myself rejoin the welcome party in the kitchen, though there's nothing festive about the atmosphere. Talking to Anne is like pulling teeth. Thankfully, it appears to be Ali's turn to play dentist. When I walk back into the room Ali's trying to get a conversation going, but Anne just smiles and nods and volunteers very little. It turns into a peculiarly dull, one-sided interview, with Anne ever so politely deflecting Ali's questions, and Ali doggedly lobbing more across the table at her. It's like watching someone with a vicious serve, but no groundstrokes, battling against a consummate touch player.

The last fortnight has given me a new appreciation of my sister-in-law. Ali's stubbornness has always irritated me; that, and her constant presence in our lives, forever popping round, having an opinion, always late, always hungry, but I acknowledge that we'd have struggled without her. She's come to our rescue over and over again with Lauren, and with James and, as I watch her bat against Anne, I feel a sneaking admiration for her. Tenacious, with just a hint of mad bitch, it's not such a bad combo in some circumstances.

All three of us jump when the door bangs open and Lauren crawls in, followed by Sarah. If it's possible for Anne to look any more uncomfortable, she does. I stand guard as Lauren awkwardly but effectively levers herself up onto her chair, using the table edge and the chair arm. I know not to help her; she's fiercely independent about the things she can do. Sarah puts a plate of toast, cucumber and small cheese squares in front of Lauren and is rewarded with a big grin that is immediately replaced by a mouth full of cheese. Lauren loves cheese. I catch Sarah's eye and we smile as she scoffs her lunch, but as Sarah turns away to make more tea, I catch sight of Anne, and for an unguarded second, I see the look of distaste on her face, a glimpse of her real feelings behind the fixed, anodyne smile.

Sarah puts the mugs down and joins us at the table, talking quickly like she does when she's nervous. 'It's lovely having you here. Thank you. I know it's a long way.'

'It's not a problem.' Anne can suck the oxygen out of a room faster than anyone I've ever met.

'Will you and Rosie be okay in James's room? I'm sorry, I know it's a bit of a squeeze.'

'I'm sure it'll be fine.'

Another lumpy silence settles at the table. Ali has finally conceded defeat and is texting, furiously. Jess, I'm guessing. I'm in no mood to take over, preferring to watch Lauren stuff bread and cheese into her mouth, at speed, which leaves Sarah to try and resuscitate the conversation. 'We thought we'd maybe take a walk to the park this afternoon. Get some fresh air. It's not far.' Anne nods and smiles. The toaster ticks noisily as it cools on the side. I'm on the verge of talking about the weather when, before I can stop her, Lauren crams the last piece of bread into her already-full mouth, picks up her plate and skims it, Frisbee-style, across the room. The plastic plate bounces off a cabinet door and rattles to the floor. Cucumber slices fly everywhere. Anne flinches.

'You know we don't do that. That's naughty!' Sarah scolds. Lauren's speed-eating and random plate-throwing are habits that Sarah has been trying hard to discourage, but they make me smile; they're a show of will, proof of her personality and her dislike of cucumber. Lauren is unfazed by her telling-off and merely signs for her tablet, or it could be a cake – sometimes it's hard to distinguish her requests. 'No! If you throw things, you can't have it,' Sarah tells her. This is met with a sulky expression and defiance. Lauren then decides that sliding dangerously down in her chair might get her what she wants. Sarah leaps up to intervene and a tussle ensues. I can see that she's struggling, both with Lauren and with embarrassment. Anne's carefully averted eyes do nothing to lessen the tension.

'Lauren.' Ali steps in to help before I do. 'Sit up properly. If you're a good girl and sit nicely you can have my phone, but you have to sit up properly, right this minute.' Ali knows that firmness, repetition and a decent bribe normally work. Lauren pushes herself upright and settles down. The tension ebbs. Ali passes Lauren her phone, relinquishing her lifeline.

'I'm sorry, she's testing her boundaries a bit at the moment,' Sarah says. 'She's normally very well behaved. She's a happy child' – she stumbles – 'teenager.' The correction is for Anne's benefit; before all this started we thought of Lauren as a child because in everything, other than her age, she is.

Anne stirs herself. 'Rosie can have her moments, as well.' But plate-throwing and sliding off chairs aren't, we all suspect, among them. Lauren has obviously found what she wants, because she starts chuckling. Then Sarah does something that surprises me. She pushes her mug aside, reaches across the table and lays her hand over Anne's. 'I know this must be hard for you. We're used to Lauren, it's normal for us, we've had years to get used to how she is; you haven't. You've had to arrive in the middle and it must be difficult. I'm not sure how I would've reacted if I'd known from the beginning what she – what we – were facing. But we didn't. We just brought her home as a baby and went from there.' She keeps her hand over Anne's as she makes her speech.

Anne unbends a little. 'Thank you. I am struggling, if I'm honest. I'm sorry. I don't mean to be insensitive. I just don't know how to be with her. I feel so inadequate, and I'm finding not being able to talk to her so difficult. It's the communication, the not knowing how to...' The sentence trails away. Sarah lifts her hand to push her hair out of her eyes and Anne abruptly stands up. 'If you'll excuse me, I might just go for a lie-down for half an hour, if that's okay? It was a long drive. Let me know if you do decide to go to the park, I'd like to come along.' And she walks out, deftly avoiding the cucumber still stuck to the floor.

'Oh, for God's sake!' Ali's pent-up frustration explodes, the second Anne's out of the room, but, I suspect, not out of earshot. Again a flush of affection for Ali catches me off-guard.

Not so Sarah. 'Ali! Give her a break... And *you* can pack it in as well.' I wasn't conscious I was pulling a face until Sarah chides me.

'I didn't say anything.'

'No, but it's written all over your face.' Ali and I exchange a conspiratorial look.

'Well! Retiring upstairs for a lie-down, like some Victorian lady. And it's ironic that she thinks that communicating with Lauren is the problem, when she barely says anything herself.' Ali humphs.

'She's stressed,' Sarah counters.

'So everybody keeps saying.' Ali's not buying it.

'Please, Ali, not now,' Sarah warns. They stare at each other for a few seconds before Sarah has the last word. 'I'm really not in the mood. We need to make this weekend bearable, so can we please all just *try*. Okay?' Ali backs off, but not down. It's the same old sisterly dynamic of skirmish and truce that they've been playing out for years, but this time it feels different, because this time I'm on Ali's side.

ANNE

There are very few places to escape to in such a small house. I head upstairs to our designated room, James's den. Apparently Rosie and I are sharing. I could tell that Rosie was silently horrified when Sarah explained the sleeping arrangements. It's been a very long time since we shared a room, but I was pleased. Perhaps the enforced proximity will do us good, give us a chance to talk. Maybe, when the light goes out, we'll find a way of getting back to the closeness we used to have. Or maybe not. Because just as I reach the top of the stairs, Rosie appears out of James's room. She brushes past me and heads downstairs, preferring their company to mine. On the landing I pause. Lauren's bedroom is at the back of the house next to the bathroom. The door has one of those plastic plaques that you get at the seaside stuck to it, with *Lauren* picked out in pearly seashells. Depressed by the thought of hiding away in James's room, I venture inside.

Like so many things about Lauren, it's disorientating. It's a child's room for a teenager. There's a pile of soft toys on the floor and a mobile suspended from the ceiling. The slowly rotating grey and black whales drift in the breeze from the open window. There's a star night-light screwed to the wall beside the bed and fairy lights pinned around a mirror. It's pretty, but very childish. There's no make-up, no hair straighteners, no jumble of iPod and phone leads. On a shelf, out of reach, are some medicines and creams and there are wipes and nappies stacked in the bedside cabinet. I sit on the bed, taking in my surroundings. Underneath the bright, patterned duvet it's the type of bed you'd find in an old people's home; it has a remote control for raising and lowering the mattress and sides that can be pulled up. The whole house is full of these reminders of her disabilities.

But at least it's quiet in here and I'm unobserved.

The sister, Ali, is relentless. Sarah and Phil have been careful around me, sensitive to my feelings, but the sister is a bulldozer, digging aggressively into our lives and my intentions. She even asked about Nathan. Sly questions about what he does for a living, when we got divorced and how much contact he has with Rosie. I really don't think I can bear the scrutiny. I catch sight of myself in the mirror, a pale-faced middle-aged woman, hiding in a child's bedroom, and feel a profound sense of shame and weakness. I still can't think of *Lauren* as my child. I reach for my bag and unzip the inside pocket. I allow myself one more pill. I need to stay calm, but I also need to concentrate. I wait for the Fluoxetine to take effect, soothed by the quiet of being alone. From the pile of soft toys on the floor I extract a toy, a rabbit. It's made of some sort of plush velveteen, the colour of brown sugar, with floppy ears and heavy paws. I run my fingers across the fabric, soothing myself. Rosie had a dog that was very similar, a present from me the year she started nursery. She carted it everywhere for a while: to school, in and out of the car, to the shops, into bed every night, even into the bath on one occasion. I used to read to her and her 'puppy' every evening before she settled to sleep. She had a habit of sucking its long ears, making them damp and unpleasant to touch, when she was anxious, which was, sadly, fairly often. She adored Nathan when she was small. Her little soul struggled badly with his sudden disappearance from her life. I didn't handle it well. Not at all. I wasn't in a fit state to cope with her pain as well as mine, though I know that's a poor excuse. A good mother would have put her child first. I'd forgotten about the dog and its importance to Rosie around that awful time. One night, after a particularly bitter conversation with Nathan on the phone, and the subsequent lonely battle to calm myself down, I went up to bed feeling defeated. I lay down on top of the covers fully clothed, too beaten to get undressed and washed. I remember that I pulled the top cover over me and rolled onto my side, wanting nothing more than to disappear; and there, propped between the pillows, was Rosie's dog.

There's so much of the past that has drifted out of my reach. I lean against Lauren's pillows, remembering one daughter and breathing in another. The whales drift slowly above my head.

At the sound of footsteps in the hallway I push myself upright on Lauren's bed, feeling guilty for invading her space. I tuck the rabbit carefully back into its place in the pile, straighten the covers and sneak out of her room, leaving it just as I found it.

PHIL

Rosie appears downstairs just after her mother disappears upstairs. It's a decent trade-off. She avoids the sofa, too high a risk that someone might come and sit next to her, and instead folds herself into the chair in the corner of the lounge. She immediately starts messing about on her phone. James is self-consciously sprawled out on the floor, his long legs taking up most of the space, some territorial thing probably. I perch, like a nervy lifeguard, between the two of them. They both seem to be silently drowning in the sheer awkwardness of it all.

There's a Liverpool v. Arsenal game on the TV; the Liverpool defence is driving James mad, I can tell by all the huffing and puffing and cushion-thumping. I give up on expecting conversation and half-heartedly watch the game. It's scrappy. James grunts in disgust at a particularly poorly defended corner kick, but he's too inhibited by Rosie's presence to swear like he normally does, when Sarah is out of the room. It goes from bad to worse when a defender tackles the latest Liverpool wunderkind, fairly, in midfield, and he flies to the ground clutching his face.

'Dive!' Rosie's voice is clear and adamant.

'Foul!' James decrees, watching the replay.

'Complete and utter dive.'

'Bookable offence.'

And in that instant the course of the afternoon – in fact the whole weekend – changes. It starts with single-syllable exchanges about the game. Neither of them looks at the other, but their comments build and within ten minutes they've taken up their entrenched positions of opposing fans. As the match progresses, they shift into the familiar territory of needling and wind-up. When the game ends and Sarah announces a walk to the park, James counter-offers with *FIFA* on his Xbox, and Rosie immediately agrees. Sarah has the good sense to back off. As much as I'd love to stay and shout encouragement and abuse in the background, I know I'm expected to go on the walk. With Anne. So we leave them to it and take Lauren out for a thoroughly boring three loops of the local park. As we amble along I quiz Anne about Rosie's interest in football.

Anne doesn't sound that enthused. 'She started at junior school, at an after-school club. I thought she'd grow out of it.'

'She's playing with a girls' team?'

'Yes, I wasn't happy with her playing on the boys' team, after junior school. A teacher at her high school recommended Redbourn Girls.'

'What position?'

Anne pauses. 'She was a defender, but I believe she plays in the middle now.'

'Believe' – her lack of involvement with her own daughter is shocking, though her abject ignorance of football is just what I expected. I can't imagine Anne standing on a touchline in the slashing rain, getting mud on her immaculate boots, but I do have a clear image of Rosie, slogging away on the pitch with no one there to support her. No one warning her when there's a 'man on' and shouting, 'Come on, Rosie' when her legs have gone and her lungs are bursting. No one, that is, until now.

'So she's a midfield player?'

'Yes.' Anne obviously isn't certain. She turns away, seeking out Sarah and a change of topic. 'What a pretty park.'

Anne's indifference shocks me, but it does little to puncture my elation. Rosie's passion for the game proves that she *is* my daughter. Somehow a love of football has passed from me to her. Why else would she be interested in it? Anne clearly isn't.

'Was her father into sport?' It's a blurted question that provokes a warning frown from Sarah.

Anne stiffens. 'Nathan wasn't around long enough to influence Rosie's likes or dislikes, sporting or otherwise.' She falls out of step with me and joins Sarah for the last lap of the park.

So it must be genetic. Rosie and James and I have a bond. I feel absurdly happy. I can't wait to get back to the house.

ANNE

On our last lap of the park Sarah asks if I'd like to push Lauren. Of course I say 'yes', though I'm nervous of doing something wrong. I grip the handles of her wheelchair tightly, for fear of letting her go. On the flat it's okay, but up the low rise in front of the bird-house the push makes me breathless and on the slope down the chair drags me forward. The weight of her throws me off-balance. Sarah, seeing me struggle, merely smiles encouragement. 'It gets easier once you're used to it.' It's not until we're following the path through the flowerbeds that I actually relax. The park is pretty, in an old-fashioned kind of way, the beds are formal and very bright, but attractive. Sarah chatters away. The sun shines weakly. Lauren seems content watching the people and the trees. I look down at the exposed pale skin at the nape of her neck and feel protective. She is so vulnerable.

On our way out of the park I misjudge the step and the chair jolts forward. Phil immediately takes over.

27

Together at the Start

SARAH

ON SATURDAY evening, after everyone else has gone to bed, Anne seeks me out and we have a confusing conversation made worse by too much booze. Having drained the dregs of one bottle of red, I open another, wanting the anaesthetising effect. Anne covers her glass with her hand at first, but, without any prompting, changes her mind and joins me. I fill our smeary glasses to the rim and we sit in the kitchen surrounded by the messy aftermath of dinner.

'Thank you.' She takes a drink. I don't try to force a conversation. After a while she says, 'They're a nice idea.' She points at the digital photo frame on the side. We both watch as the pictures change.

It's impossible for me to sit and watch the parade of happy family shots without feeling awkward... guilty. That's what I feel, guilt.

'I'm sorry,' I say, standing up and going to lie the frame face down. 'That was thoughtless. I should've put it away.'

'No – don't. Why should you? It's a lovely record of your life together.'

'It's Ali, she's always liked taking pictures. Something about her not having kids of her own, I think. It was a present from her. We didn't—'

She cuts me off. 'You don't have to keep apologising, Sarah... for the pictures, for the way it is, for any of it. It's not your fault. I can see you're a good mum, and Phil's a good dad. A proper dad. You've both been fantastic with her.' She sounds a bit drunk, rushing her words.

'Photos only show the good times, though.' I respond. 'It's not all holidays and birthdays.' Maybe I'm a little drunk, too, because I can feel a familiar resistance rising in me.

But Anne's not to be shaken in her rose-tinted view of us. 'You're good at it, though, at being parents. James obviously loves you both, he's so at ease with you, and Lauren seems so content.'

Anne's doing what everyone else does. Summing us up on the basis of a quick glance. I push back at her. 'There've been some very tough times.' Tough times that, in a different life, would have been hers. The hospital stays, the unsuccessful physio, the broken nights, the sheer tedium of it. There are no photographs of all that.

'I'm sure, but you have a better relationship with both of them than I have with Rosie.'

I'm not so drunk that I can't recognise a painful admission when I hear one. I force myself to think about her and her life; somehow Anne and I have to build some bridges to support the intolerable. 'It's bound to be rough at the moment. Rosie's kicking out at the person closest to her.' I'm talking in platitudes. I know nothing about their relationship.

She laughs, without humour. 'It's not just at the moment.' She takes another swallow of wine. 'It's been like this for a while. She hates spending time with me.'

'Like any normal teenager.'

'Um.' Compressed into that small noise is a world of disappointment. Neither of us says anything for a while. We both watch the scroll of pictures: a recent one of Dad arm-wrestling with James; Christmas lunch with us all, the year it snowed; Lauren in the baby swing at the park when she was about three; then the one of the four of us on the sofa, me holding a newborn Lauren, a pink helium *Congratulations* balloon in the background.

'I keep thinking about the maternity ward.' Anne blinks and the picture changes to one of James with his football team.

'Me, too.'

'I remember us talking before she was born, in that awful room with all the chairs.' I nod. I remember.

Anne came into the deserted TV room at about two in the morning. I'd been walking loops around it for hours. She had the telltale, shell-shocked look of new mum, but she'd also made an effort, her hair was shiny and brushed and she had some lipstick on; attempts at grooming that looked odd, in the circumstances. 'Oh, sorry.' A soft, educated voice. She turned to leave.

'No, it's fine. Come in. I just can't sleep.'

'Me neither.' She seemed at a loss where to sit, faced with so many empty chairs, and in a very English way she finally chose a seat about as far away from me as possible. I carried on pacing. At first I didn't hear her properly. I caught a question aimed at me, but not what she said. I circled round back to her. 'Sorry?'

'Oh, nothing. I was just commiserating.'

I lowered myself into a chair near her. 'I came in yesterday. I thought it would be over by now. It was all going to plan, then my contractions just stopped. They were supposed to be inducing me tonight, but it seems they can't until tomorrow.'

'They do seem very understaffed.'

We both stared at the darkened glass. It reflected us back at ourselves. 'Do you know what you're having?' she asked.

'A little girl.'

'Ah.' She didn't volunteer any more information about herself. 'Is it your first?'

'No. We already have a little boy, James. That's why I thought it would be easier this time.'

'Are you in pain?'

'No, just fed up and a bit scared.'

'I'm sure you'll be fine, once it starts properly.' She turned to face the blank window again and I studied her profile. She was attractive beneath the post-baby puffiness. I was caught out when she spoke again. She didn't turn to look at me, but talked to the dark night. 'I had a little girl. Today... yesterday. She came early. I was visiting my in-laws. It was quite a shock. I wasn't due until the thirtieth. My husband's not even here.' How awful for her. 'She's asleep in the nursery... my daughter. They've told me I should rest, but I can't. I can't get over that she's here when she shouldn't be.' Then she turned towards me and the intimacy of the past few moments disappeared. 'Shall I go and see if it's possible to fetch us a cup of tea?' And somehow, on a ward with too few staff and too many patients, she managed to rustle up two mugs of hot tea, which we drank sitting together in the depressing, tatty TV room...

'That we talked to each other while you were still carrying her, it's bizarre.' Anne's voice slices through the memory I've been fixated on ever since we found out. She twists the stem of her glass between her fingers. 'I just can't stop thinking about it, the chances... it doesn't seem possible. If I hadn't been up in Harrogate with Nathan's parents, if I hadn't gone into labour early, if they hadn't been put into the nursery.' She's doing the same as me, trying to rethread the past to try and make it make sense. We sit in silence again, our thoughts on the same page: both girls in the nursery, without their mums, both of them in the wrong place at the wrong time.

They still can't establish how the identity bands got switched.

They're claiming that there aren't detailed enough records for them to audit, and that staff 'testimony' hasn't, so far, 'shed any light' on how the impossible became possible. No one is accepting responsibility for it, nor is it likely they ever will. It beggars belief. And yet there's a part of me that almost doesn't care any more, because whatever happened, it doesn't change the massive mess it's caused, a mess that has brought Anne and Rosie into our lives.

Another picture of Lauren as a baby fades up on the screen, this time one of Phil holding her, a classic proud-new-dad photo, a pastel blur of flowers in the background. I look across at Anne and feel such a swirl of emotion that I have to push my palms down hard against the tabletop to root myself. I'm conscious that this woman and her daughter have the power to decide what happens to my family.Whatever the facts, I know that Rosie can never be my daughter. Lauren is, and always will be. We are fused together. Nothing can ever change that. I suddenly feel uncomfortable having Anne in my house, in my kitchen, sleeping in James's room. She's seeing too much of us. Ali is right – we knew nothing about her, not really. In that moment I don't even want Rosie anywhere near us, getting under Phil's skin and turning James's head with her prettiness and sportiness. I drain my glass.

Anne stays quite still, watching the changing glow of the photos, her expression so melancholy that my emotions jerk again in a completely different direction. I feel a sudden rush of pity for her; what has happened has shattered her as well. She's obviously envious of what she can see in the photos. I'm acutely aware that, despite appearances, life can't be easy for Anne. For all our troubles, I have Phil and James and Lauren and Ali and Dad. We are a family, and somehow Anne and Rosie aren't.

And I remember her kindness in the hospital. She kept me company that night, sat with me until my contractions started up again, and afterwards she came to see me to say goodbye. We were together at the start of our daughters' lives. We have both been robbed and we are both guilty. We both took another woman's child home and raised it without question, and that is something both of us will have to bear for the rest of our lives.

But then she confuses me again with a rush of words that I can't immediately make sense of. 'I appreciate that it's none of my business. I'm not sure they'd even want us talking to each other about it, but I wondered if you'd had any news on your claim?'

The bond evaporates. 'I haven't really thought about it. It's in the hands of the lawyers.'

'Ah. Yes. I don't want to overstep the line, but I want you to know that we're trying very hard to get a response from Nathan. He's been estranged from us for so long that it's difficult. It all has to be done in writing, through his legal representatives. I just didn't want you to think we weren't making every effort on that front. I'm thoroughly ashamed of how he's behaving.'

Nathan is irrelevant. I can't see what he has to do with the claim against the hospital. In fact I can't see why she's bringing him up at all, given his absolute indifference to both his daughters. I have no interest in her ex-husband, or the claim or the money. I've had enough of trying to decipher her. 'Anne, if you don't mind, I think I'd better head up to bed. It's getting late, and Lauren tends to wake quite early.'

'Yes, of course. I'm sorry.' She gets to her feet. 'I'm glad we've had a talk. I feel better for it. Thank you. Goodnight, Sarah.' There's a fraction of a hesitation when she seems about to hug me, but she turns away.

After she leaves I don't move, not straight away. Nothing is resolved. Anne might feel better for our conversation, but I don't. I sit and watch the photos change. There's a rare shot of Lauren standing, before her leg surgery and her first wheelchair; James holding a grinning baby Lauren on his lap, both of them wearing light-up Santa hats; one of Phil hanging the whale mobile up in her room just after we'd finished decorating. As I watch I become aware of a heavy, sweet smell filling the room. It takes me a few moments to realise that it's coming from the plant Anne gave us. *A jasmine, just a little thank you for welcoming us into your home.* It sits on the windowsill, a thread of waxy green leaves twisted into a perfect circle around a hoop of thick wire. In the heat of the kitchen the tight white buds have begun to open up into a flush of small, star-shaped flowers. It's these that are perfuming the room, masking the normal smells of food and family.

It takes an age before the shot of me holding Rosie appears within the cycle of photos. As I look at it, I realise that I'm more than a little drunk, more than a little tired and not altogether sure that having Rosie back in our midst is such a good thing after all.

28

Journeys

SARAH

THE FOLLOWING morning the house is full of noise and activity and I'm too busy getting everyone breakfast to speak much to Anne or Rosie. I confess I'm glad that they're setting off early. By the time everything is sorted, Lauren is settled and the kitchen is straight, they're ready for the off. Phil loads their bags into the boot, then there's a pause. We all shuffle around the car, uncertain of the farewell etiquette. 'Let's hope the traffic isn't too bad.' Phil bangs the boot shut. Anne smiles wanly. Phil breaks the awkwardness by shoulder-barging Rosie. She responds by shoving him back into the hedge; both of them laugh. 'You need to use your body more. Less chance of a booking.' Yet more bloody football talk. Somehow his tackle morphs into a bear hug, and this forces us all into brief, much less spontaneous goodbye hugs. Anne is rigid in my arms. She looks shattered; a lot of her surface shine seems to have worn off, a consequence of spending time with us, perhaps? Rosie is equally stiff and unyielding when I hug her. I'm no closer to her now than I was at the start of the visit. She is still resolutely *not* my daughter. Rosie gives James a goodbye thump on the arm, climbs into the front of the car, pulls the door shut and immediately puts in her earbuds. I feel irritation with her and sympathy for Anne. The whole weekend has been on Rosie's terms. It's worked out fine for her and the boys. They've hurdled straight over all the problems and done nothing but talk and play football. The house has been full of noise and thudding about and in-jokes about players I've never heard of. There's even been talk of Phil and James going down to see Rosie play in a tournament in a few weeks' time. Anne and I, and Lauren, have been resolutely excluded from this new alliance, left to try and unpick the snares. We've been forced to watch from the sidelines as they've sailed past the embarrassment and all the spiky, unsaid differences and simply got on with each other. Ali has tried to help, acting as a go-between, talking to Anne – despite her instinctive dislike of her – pitching in with the meals and, as always, helping me with Lauren. It's been scant relief, but I'm grateful she's been around.

All in all, it's been a dispiriting weekend.

As we wave them off, I feel another tug of sympathy for Anne. She has a long drive ahead of her and Rosie looks set to ignore her all the way home. As the car turns at the end of the road and disappears, neither of them waves.

ANNE

On the drive home Rosie sleeps for the first couple of hours, but just before Leicester she wriggles upright, pulls out her earbuds and asks, politely enough, if we could stop for a break. At the services I wait for her outside the Ladies, watching a stream of mothers and daughters coming and going. She takes her time, but when she finally emerges I spot her immediately, my dark, wary, beautiful daughter.

'Do you fancy a drink, there's a Costa?' I say, fully expecting her to say no.

'Yeah, okay.'

I have a black coffee and she orders some iced whipped cream and mint concoction. Watching her dig her spoon into the creamy mess with such pleasure reminds me that she's still a child, at least occasionally.

I risk a question. 'You seemed to get on well with James?'

'Jim? Yeah, he's okay.'

'It's good you have football in common.'

'Yeah. Phil used to play. He's still not bad.' Her focus on Phil is understandable, but troubling. Nathan did so much damage when he left, to her and me. She doesn't look up from her drink. 'Were you all right?'

Her concern catches me off-guard. It's the first time for quite a while that she's expressed any interest in my feelings. Our late-night chat, snuggled in our respective beds, certainly didn't materialise. 'Yes. It was difficult, but like you said the first time we met them, they're nice people.' I am, after all, talking about her parents.

She smiles. 'I said I'd send Phil my fixtures. They might come down for the Watford tournament and we were thinking, if I get picked to play at Aces...' I must look at her blankly. 'The one that's near here, in June. I did tell you about it. Anyway, if I could get a lift up, they could come down, watch and then take me back up to theirs for a few days afterwards. It'd be half-term. I could get the train back.' There's a buzz about her at the thought of it, her face animated and unguarded. I hadn't realised how much they'd talked, while kicking a ball around in the back garden. Again I have the sense of everything accelerating away from me. I reach for the only brake I can think of.

'Would they bring Lauren down with them?'

Her expression immediately becomes guarded. 'I don't know.'

She pushes her drink away. 'Sarah would probably stay and look after her. I can't see them dragging her all the way down south or to Leicester.' 'Her'. I notice how unconsciously Rosie avoids using Lauren's name.

I ignore the rejected drink and the sudden, twitchy desire to leave, and sip my coffee. 'Did you get much of a chance to talk to Sarah?' I immediately know I've pushed things too far.

'You know I didn't. So why are you asking?' She stands up. 'I'm going to look in the shop, I'll see you in there.' And with that, she walks off.

ROSIE

On Monday at school I can't concentrate. At break time I dodge Kennedy and go up to French early, on my own. Luckily the room is unlocked. It's hard to find anywhere quiet around school. I won't go in the girls' loos. They stink.

I emailed Phil my fixtures as soon as I got home, but there's been nothing from him, not last night or this morning. I've checked, loads of times. He normally messages me straight away, or at least faster than this. At last there's something from him in my in-box. He sent it at 10.13 a.m. It's a long email with attachments. I skim-read it. He *is* coming to my tournament, with Jim and Sarah. I feel a bubble of happiness. I can show them what I can do, that I'm good, that it's not all talk, and I can wipe the smirk off Jim's face. For the first time *ever* I will have my dad watching me play football. After years of everyone else having their dads there, I will have someone there for me. What should I say to the girls? I'll have to start telling people now. Now that they're in my life. Despite how screwed up it all is, I think it might feel good saying that my real dad is coming to watch me. And that I have a brother, and an aunt, and a grandfather, and Sarah.

I reread the message. There's lots about how much they enjoyed me staying with them at the weekend, how they loved getting to know me a bit more, that I'm always welcome at theirs, but it doesn't say anything about Leicester. The bubble pops. If they can come all the way down to Watford, why can't they come to Leicester, it has to be closer? And if they don't come to Leicester, then I won't be going back up to theirs for half-term. It's probably something to do with Lauren. Everything revolves around her. I don't know how Jim stands it. Meal times, where they can and can't go, even what time everyone goes to bed. It's like having a baby, except she's not a baby, she's a big lump of a teenager. I click on the attachments. Phil has sent some pictures from the weekend. There's a few with everyone together at the dining table, Mum looking uptight and Sarah fussing over Lauren like she always does, but the best pictures are the ones Ali took in the back garden. There's a great one of me skinning Jim, and a funny one of Phil skying a shot over next door's fence. Ali has even managed to get the ball in the shot. The last one is of the three of us, grinning like idiots. It's a really happy picture: me, Phil and Jim.

I hear shouting outside in the corridor, people starting to move to their next lessons. I save the picture as my new lock screen.

Me, my dad and my brother.

29

Watford

SARAH

ALI AND Jess come over to look after Lauren, as planned. Ali still has pillow creases on her cheek it's so early, but Jess, as always, looks fantastic. They wave us off – the perfect odd couple.

The trip down to Watford feels quite liberating. It's such a break from the routine. The fry-up at Nottingham services takes on a giddy air. It's so long since the three of us did anything without Lauren. There's no trawling for a disabled space in the car park, no division of labour at the food counters, no weight-lifting Lauren in the loo. It's relaxed. With bellies stuffed full, we slide back onto the motorway. Phil drives and bickers happily with James about music, while I sit and watch the fields and pylons whizz by. I know better than to express any opinion about the playlist. My eyelids flutter and close.

'It was never only twenty minutes. You were snoring all the way to Northampton.' James is adamant.

Phil just smiles. 'Leave your mum alone.'

We get slightly lost trying to find the pitches, but, as we set off before the crack of dawn, we still arrive in plenty of time, for a change. Finding Rosie among the sea of ponytailed footballers is less easy. There seems to be hundreds of fit, tall, long-haired teenage girls. Thankfully, Phil and James remember that her football strip is blue-and-white stripes. James spots her team and we head over, threading our way alongside the pitches, past the groups of supporting families with their gazebos and monster picnic boxes, and the piles of girls strewn on the grass, lacing up boots and rooting through kit bags. As we approach, Rosie sees us and starts waving. For the first time I feel a ripple of pleasure at seeing her.

ROSIE

Megan's dad gives us a lift to Watford. There are five of us squashed in his Golf. I make sure it's Holly who's pressed up next to me. Stacey's kit never smells too fresh. We let her have the front seat.

'Are you excited about them coming?' Stacey sticks her head through the gap between the front seats, desperate to get the low-down.

They all look at me, waiting to see my reaction. 'A bit.'

'God, it must be sooo weird! Do you think we'll recognise them – like, you know, do you look like them?'

'Stacey!' Holly bops her on the head. 'You can't say things like that.'

'It's okay. I'm starting to get used to it.'

'Is your brother coming?' Beth asks, trying to change the subject.

'Yeah.'

'How old is he again?'

'Seventeen.'

'Does he *play*?' Beth asks, all fake innocence, and that sets them all off cackling.

Megan's dad pleads, 'Jeez, girls, could you possibly make any more noise?' But he's joking and the mood in the car bubbles round me. He puts on the radio and the girls start screeching along to the music. I lean my head against the car window, happy that my mates are going to meet them. Phil will be okay, friendly with them, but not OTT, nothing creepy. And Beth will bust a gut when she sees Jim, because I suppose he is quite fit. Finally the two bits of my life feel like they're coming together.

SARAH

I needn't have worried about how it would be with Rosie, because we barely have time to talk to her between the matches. The most awkward ten minutes are at the beginning.

She looks different in her football kit, and with her hair pulled back off her face in a simple ponytail, she looks younger. She smiles and hugs Phil, does some kind of awkward arm-slap thing with James, then gives me a brief hug. I feel her bony shoulder blades beneath the slippy material of her football shirt, and the brief pressure of her hands on my arms. Behind us an audience of her blatantly curious teammates look on. Rosie then surprises me by turning to the other girls and, with manners that Anne would be proud of, introduces us as 'My mum and dad, Phil and Sarah, and my brother Jim.' With a curious sweetness, they all chorus back 'Hi' and wave, then Rosie drags Phil off to introduce him to their coach, leaving James and me standing there.

A leggy blonde girl quickly scrambles to her feet. 'Hi, I'm Stacey. Centre-mid. Rosie says you play?' James looks both horrified and flattered, but confirms that he's in a team. One of the other girls toes a ball towards him, which he duly kicks back. Two more girls get to

173

their feet. The pretty brunette says, 'Fancy a kickabout?' He glances at me for permission, but I know I've already lost him. As stealth flirting goes, it's all fairly impressive. By the beginning of the second match James is ensconced as the team mascot, with the more confident girls taking it in turns to laugh at everything he says and share their Haribos with him. He's in his element.

The matches are swift and surprisingly furious. It's very physical. Some of the tackles make me wince. Rosie's team seems to be doing quite well, though their coach spends most of the time yelling and gesticulating wildly at them. The other parents, mostly dads, smile at us, but say very little. There's a tea round mid-morning and I offer to carry supplies back with a bloke who turns out to be someone called 'Megan's dad'. No reference is made to the peculiarity of our situation, but as we walk back, slopping tea out of the overfilled paper cups, he says, 'She's a great little player, your Rosie. Trains hard. Listens, unlike a lot of them.' His kindness is just one of the high points of the day. During the lunch break the sun comes out and some of the parents and girls troop off to the barbecue, and come back with piles of cheeseburgers and cans of Coke. These are wolfed down alongside a selection of random food contributions: iced buns, veggie samosas and Ritz biscuits. How they can eat so much grease then kick a ball amazes me. Rosie drifts between her friends and us, talking tactics to Phil and studying the fixture list. The whole day has an ease and normality that's lovely. I text home more than once. Ali texts straight back to say everything is fine and to quit worrying.

We – that is, Rosie's team – play the last group game fairly soon after lunch. It's a tough match against an opposition that Phil keeps telling me 'are very organised'. My eyes track Rosie as she runs back and forth on the pitch. She's one of the quieter ones on the team, which surprises me. At one point she makes a run down the wing in front of us, and for a split second she catches my eye as she powers past. I'm shouting along with the rest of them, and I can see in her eyes that she's happy.

We scrape a 0–0 draw, then the huddles and arguing start.

'We're out.'

'No, we're not, it'll come down to goal difference.'

Fifteen minutes later we seem to be playing in a semi-final, so it must have gone Rosie's team's way. The match has only been going five minutes when someone smacks a ball really hard. It flies downfield and catches Rosie full in the face, just as she turns round. I hear the sickening thwack and see her neck snap backwards. The referee blows his whistle and for an instant it goes oddly quiet. All the girls stop running. Rosie doesn't fall down, but you can tell that it's nasty. Watching the ref and a few of her teammates gather round her makes my stomach feel watery. When they wave the coach on, I start thinking about concussion and ambulances. The coach walks her off the pitch, his arm around her, shepherding her back to us. There's a deep-red welt on Rosie's face and she's obviously struggling not to cry.

'Just come off for a few minutes.' The coach is already looking past Rosie, summoning her replacement.

'I'm all right.'

'You're not. It's a blow to the head. We have to have you off.' The coach appeals to Phil.

'Rosie. Come here. Let me see.' He holds her face gently in his hands and studies it. She stands perfectly still, her head tilted, sniffing back tears of pain and frustration, but obviously calming down. 'Well, it's a good job you were plug-ugly before you started. No one will ever be able tell the difference.' For a second I think he's completely misjudged it, then she laughs and he drops his hands onto her shoulders. I stand back, uncertain of my role.

The match restarts and attention returns to the game. Even Phil seems to forget Rosie's injury within a few seconds, caught up, as they all are, in the football. But I've lost interest. We score and everyone leaps about a bit, but not Rosie. She looks pale and I can see she's shivering. I remember that somewhere in the mountain of boot bags and kit is her top. I go over and start digging through the pile. Coats, fleeces, hoodies, it's a great stew of discarded clothes, most of it an identical dark blue. I can see Rosie hugging herself on the touchline, her slender back to me. Number 12. I keep pawing through the pile until I find her top. When I pass it to her, she glances down and smiles when she sees her number. She pulls it over her head. As her marked face emerges, she says, 'Thank you.'

'You still look pale.' I can hear that I'm fussing.

'I'll be all right. I've got a hard head.'

'If you feel sick you will say, won't you?'

'Yeah. I'd tell you. Don't worry, I was just a bit cold.'

'Okay.' She turns her attention back to the match. It's a small crumb, but I cherish it, she said she'd tell *me*.

'Maybe Gary'll let me back on in the final.' Another goal goes in. The shouting this time comes from the other side of the pitch.

I get my secret wish. They lose the match, which avoids any possibility of Rosie playing again. One girl on the team bursts into tears, another has a temper tantrum, but the rest seem remarkably sanguine. There's a raid on the tuck shop, more sugar is consumed and the mood immediately lifts. It feels like a team effort as we carry all the stuff back to the car park. As the girls hurl their bags into Megan's dad's car, we stand a little way off, ready for our goodbyes.

'You will tell your mum you had a bang on the head, won't you, Rosie?' She half-nods, but it doesn't fill me with confidence. 'It's been a lovely day. I've really enjoyed it.'

James chips in with, 'You're honoured. She only ever stays for one match – two, max – at my tournaments.'

'You played really well. Well, until that ball nearly took your head off.' Phil hugs her. 'We'll see you soon.'

'When?' It's an abrupt question.

'Well, we need to speak to your' – I don't want to say it any more – 'to Anne, but we'll sort something out really soon.' The other girls are in the car now and Megan's dad is politely looking the other way, pretending they're not all waiting for her. Rosie looks tired and still quite pale. 'I promise, I'll be in touch with her soon,' I say. Rosie's face pinches. 'Okay, tomorrow, I'll call her tomorrow.'

'She'll say I've got lots of school work, but I haven't.'

'Leave it with me.' For an awful moment I think she's going to cry, but she shrugs and seems to decide to trust me. She climbs in next to her friends. They all wave as the car pulls away. We have a tedious trip home ahead of us, but it's been worth it. We've travelled a long way in one day.

30

Overreacting?

ROSIE

AS SOON as I get into school on Monday I can sense that people are talking about me; word has got around about 'my parents' and 'my fit brother' coming to watch me play at the weekend. It doesn't bother me, but I wonder who blabbed. My money's on Stacey. It's kind of exciting being the centre of attention. It even reaches Ms Suri, our head of year, because after lunch she calls me into Red Base and asks awkwardly, 'Is everything all right, Rosie?'

I make her dangle for a bit. 'Yes, miss.'

'Are you sure? You know that we're here for you, if you want to talk about anything – anything at all. That's what we're here for.' She cocks her head on one side, like a bird, as she repeats herself.

'Why, has somebody said something?' That puts her on the spot.

'Well, not directly, but I've heard that you might have had some unsettling news.' God, teachers!

'You mean about my mum not being my mum?'

She blinks twice. 'Oh, Rosie. What a thing to say.'

'What, the truth? It's true. I've already met my real parents and my brother.'

She blinks again. 'Let's sit down and I'll make us a drink.' Which I think is more for her benefit than mine. Actually she's okay. She lets me skip maths and we talk about it all and she doesn't interrupt me once. I suppose she's trained to listen, but it's nice to talk to someone. She keeps patting my hand and saying 'gosh'. I leave with a promise to 'never be afraid to come to her and talk any time I need to'. That's the good bit… What I don't realise, until I get home on Tuesday, is that, as part of her *pastoral responsibilities*, she's going to ring Mum.

Mum's waiting for me in the lounge when I get back. 'Rosie, in here, please.'

'I'm just gonna get changed.'

'I'd like you to come in here first.' I can tell by her voice that I'm in trouble. 'Sit down, please. I had a call from school today. Your head of year.' I say nothing. 'She was very concerned about your welfare.' A pause. 'She went into great detail about what's been happening. She seemed very well informed. You must have had a long conversation with her.'

'People have been talking… she wanted to know if I was okay. It was nice of her.'

'Who's been talking?'

'Just people.'

'The football girls?' The look on her face is a real giveaway.

'I don't see why it's such a big secret.'

'It's not. I'm just very uncomfortable being the subject of school gossip.'

'This isn't about you!'

'Rosie… please.'

'So what if people are talking. They're gonna. It's a mad story. It's me it affects.'

Her neck flushes red and I can see she's struggling to keep her voice down. 'It does affect *me*. Of course it does, deeply. Is that what

179

you said to your teacher: that I'm not supporting you. Is that why she rang?'

I look at her, sitting on the edge of the sofa in our stupidly tidy house with her stupid clock ticking away, her face tight with frustration, and I blow. 'You can't control everything. You want to, but you can't.' She puts her hand up to her forehead, her 'go to' warning that I'm causing her pain. I'm so bloody sick of her being fragile.

'Rosie, please, there's no need to shout.'

There's absolutely no point in me talking to her, she never listens. I walk out of the room, but she follows me. I slam my bedroom door on her, but that still doesn't stop her. I refuse to respond to her questions, but she keeps on at me through the door.

'Rosie, you're fourteen. You can't act like a five-year-old and storm off when anyone says anything that doesn't suit you. Please open the door.' She waits. 'Rosie.' Here it comes. Control queen swings into action. 'Very well. If you choose to behave like a child, you're grounded. I want you straight home after school every day this week: no training tomorrow, and no football on Saturday. We can use the time to talk. We need to sort this out.' With that, she walks away from the door.

I hate her.

PHIL

The doorbell goes as we're eating lunch on Saturday. I open up. 'What the hell!' Rosie is standing outside.

She smiles, nervously. 'Surprise!' She follows me through to the kitchen. I sweep some of the debris from lunch out of the way and take her backpack from her.

'Hey.' James nods a hello. Lauren stays focused on her yoghurt.

'I'm sorry for turning up unannounced. I hope it's okay.' There's a tremor in her voice.

I start to say, 'It's fine, we love—' when Sarah cuts straight across me.

'Does your mum know you're here?'

SARAH

She just turns up. She appears at the kitchen table and Phil reacts as if it's normal for Rosie to be in Leeds, on her own, without any warning. 'Does your mum know you're here?'

'Yes.'

I watch her discomfort with the lie. 'Rosie?'

'I sent her a text from the train.' She proffers me her phone, as if she expects me to check.

'What I mean is: did you arrange this with your mum? Have you her permission to be here?' Her nervy smile wavers and fades.

Phil leaps in.

'Whoa! Let's at least get Rosie a drink, then we'll talk about it.' He rises from the table.

'No!' I surprise myself with my abruptness. I repeat the question. 'Rosie, does your mum know where you are?' The silence that follows is only briefly disturbed by James sliding away from the table and Lauren throwing her yoghurt pot on the floor. Rosie says nothing. 'Right.' My chair scrapes loudly across the tiles as I stand up and fetch my phone.

Anne picks up on the second ring. Her voice sounds hesitant. 'Hello?'

'Anne. She's here. She's safe. She just turned up.'

'She's with you?' I can hear shock in her voice. 'She's in Leeds?'

'Yes. You didn't know?' Rosie and Phil watch me across the room.

'No. I'm sorry.' Anne sounds weary rather than angry. 'We've had a difficult week. When her bed was empty this morning, I was... well, you can imagine. Then I got a text, saying she was with one of her friends. I'm very sorry to drag you into all this.'

'You've no need to apologise. I'll put Rosie on.' Rosie looks startled, but I pass the phone to her, giving her no option but to speak to Anne. 'Phil, let's get Lauren settled in the front room.' We leave the door open so that we can hear the subsequent awkward conversation.

'No... No. I'm not. No. Well, there's not a lot you can do about it... What's the point? No.' Then silence.

Phil makes to go back into the kitchen, but I grab his arm. 'She can't stay.'

'She's travelled all the way up to see us.'

'Without Anne's permission or knowledge, by the sound of it.'

'There must be a reason.'

'We'll talk to her, but we can't reward her for just running off and not telling her mum, or us.'

'Jeez, Sarah, give the kid a break. Let's actually find out what's going on before we make any decisions.' And he shrugs my hand away.

Rosie is flushed and agitated when we go back into the kitchen. She tells us about a row with her mum, something to do with school knowing about what's happened; it doesn't make a huge amount of sense to me. The real trigger seems to have been Anne stopping her playing a football match, hence the sudden flight up north.

'But you can't just leave and not tell your mum where you are.'

'I didn't. Like I said, I texted.' There it is, the defiance and the loose connection with the truth, when it suits her.

'But you're supposed to be grounded.'

Phil is on another tack entirely. 'She actually stopped you playing today – a cup semi-final?' Rosie nods and I feel a surge of irritation with both of them.

'That's not the point. I know it's difficult at the moment, but you have to think about your mum.'

She looks at me for a second with a real spark of anger in her eyes.

'So I have to go back home then, do I?'

'Well, I think you should…'

Phil cuts across me. 'Not straight away.'

'I don't want to go back.' Tough. 'You said I was always welcome. Don't you want me to stay?' This she aims at me, not Phil. She picks up a knife from the table and starts to dig the tip into the breadboard; if she's not careful, she'll stab it straight into her fingers. I'm trapped by a swirl of impulses. I'm concerned about her lack of respect for Anne, and frustrated by Phil's response to her behaviour. He wants Rosie to be here and she's here, so he's glad. He's not thinking about the message we're sending. He and Rosie are bonding, quickly, simply, strongly, but I'm adrift. Do I want her here? Of course I do, but not like this, not this rush and pressure and battle of conflicting needs. It's such hard work. It shouldn't be, but it is. No one should have to get to know their daughter like this, it isn't natural.

They're both staring at me, waiting for me to speak. I decide to compromise. That's what Phil and I have been trying to do. I have to stick to my side of the bargain. 'Let's ring your mum back. Ask her about you staying tonight, but you must go home first thing in the morning. And it depends on what your mum says. It's her call.' But Rosie isn't placated. If anything, she seems to be getting more worked up.

'She'll say "no".'

'You don't know that.'

'She will. She doesn't want me here.' A tear emerges and slides down her cheek. 'And *you* don't really want me here, either, do you?'

183

She keeps playing with the knife – dig, dig, the tip gouges into the board. I reach over and take it out of her hand, trying to calm her agitation, but my attempts to reassure her are obviously not enough. Phil looks at me, waiting for something more. Rosie's voice grows raspy with emotion. 'If you don't want me to stay, I won't. I don't want to be getting in anybody's way.' She stands up and reaches for her backpack, making a show of preparing to leave.

'Whoa! No. Hang on. We do want you here.' Phil stretches to take the bag from her and glares at me to fix this.

Rosie flares. 'I don't fit anywhere. Not here, not there. It's not fair. I never wanted it to be like this. It's not my fault. It's not. I just want a normal family like everyone else. That's all I've ever wanted. It should just be normal.' She's properly crying now, like a small child. She looks so stranded and confused. Out of the corner of my eye I see James slope past the open door.

'Rosie, shush. It's okay.' I go and put my arms round her, genuinely wanting to protect her from the confusion and the hurt. The tension in her shoulders holds for a second, then releases. She leans into me and cries, and I pat her back as if she's a baby. She smells of shampoo and body spray, so different from Lauren. She lets me hug her. As I hold her, I look up across the top of her head and I catch sight of Phil; an odd look of contentment settles on his face as he watches us.

When she's calmed down, we ring Anne. She agrees, without argument, to Rosie staying the night. I'm about to end the call when she says, 'I'm sorry, I didn't ask... how's Lauren?' I tell her she's fine. Anne's 'Good, I'm glad to hear it' is so softly spoken that I nearly miss it.

With everything agreed, Rosie heads to the bathroom to wash her face and I go looking for James, thinking he's upstairs. He's not, he's in the lounge, hunkered down on the carpet next to Lauren, earbuds in, something tinny playing very loudly on his phone, looking at her favourite cookery book with her. They share a love of all things cake.

'You okay?'

He pulls out an earbud. The sizzle of something discordant and thrashy fills the room. 'What?'

'I said, are you okay? It's all calmed down now. Rosie's just going to stay for tonight and she's heading home tomorrow, in the morning. It won't interfere with Dad taking you to your match. Sorry. I know I keep saying that it'll settle down and it doesn't, but it will.'

'We're fine, aren't we, Lauren?' He slings his arm across Lauren's shoulder. She doesn't lift her eyes from the page.

'You can come back in, if you want to.'

'In a bit, we just have to check out the peanut-butter cupcakes first, don't we, Lauren?' He puts his earbud back in.

The two of them sit on the floor, content together, and I feel a surge of pure love and protectiveness for him. I go across, crouch down and hug him. I'm stupidly surprised by how broad and strong his shoulders are beneath his crumpled T-shirt.

ANNE

The house is empty without Rosie. I sit in her bedroom, listen to the quiet and think, *This is what life will be like if I lose her.*

ROSIE

Mum's on the platform when my train pulls in, she's waiting under one of the information boards, scanning the passengers as they pour off the train. I see her before she sees me. She stands out from the crowd. She looks smarter, more glamorous than everyone else, like she has a life that other people might envy. One middle-aged dude definitely checks her out. He slows down as he passes her, one, two backward glances, but she doesn't notice, she never does. She's immune to men. Finally she picks me out in the crowd. She waves and smiles like she's genuinely pleased to see me. I was expecting disapproval, or at least weary disappointment, but she doesn't come at me at all. In fact, in the car she apologises for over-reacting to school ringing, and for making me miss the match. She doesn't even really tell me off for going up to Phil and Sarah's; she just asks what we did and tells me how much she missed me. I guess that she's waiting till we get home to start with the lecture, but even then it doesn't come. Instead she makes us a stir-fry and we watch a film together, she lets me choose which one. It's nice, once I relax; nice not to be fighting for a change, nice to be in the same room without irritating each other, so nice, in fact, that I wait until the closing credits before I mention Dad.

'I forgot to tell you, Dad left me a message yesterday.' She immediately becomes tense and the atmosphere screws back up into a ball. 'He's sounding iffy about my birthday weekend.'

'Iffy?' For once she's not questioning my choice of words.

'He's saying it might clash with a conference he's going to, in Cologne. That he might have to go straight home afterwards because he'll have been away for four days already, so staying up in London to see me might be difficult.' Without meaning to, I realise that I'm sounding exactly like him. He's always hedging his bets, never directly saying 'no', but meaning it all the same. She doesn't say anything, but I can see she's upset and, underneath the upset, really pissed off. She hates it that he puts them before me, though why she's surprised after all these years is beyond me.

'I thought he'd already got tickets for the show.' There it is, the same worry that I'm gonna burst into tears like a baby. She doesn't seem to realise there are only so many times that you can expect something and not get it, before you learn not to expect anything at all – except cash, of course.

'He said he's gonna give the tickets to somebody else to use rather than waste them.' I have to look away from her pained face. She needs to get over him. I have. 'Anyway, I just thought, if I'm not going to London that weekend, maybe we could do something else.' I don't just sound like him.

'What would you like to do?' I can see her rethinking Dad's abandonment of me, seeing an upside, anticipating a spa day or shopping, with lunch somewhere nice, just the two of us.

'I was thinking, on the train, on the way home, that maybe it would be nice to invite the Rudaks down.' Her face collapses like a popped balloon. 'Well, we've been up to theirs; we should invite them back, shouldn't we? It's only polite.'

'Rosie, I'm not sure…'

I head her off. 'But it looks odd, like we don't want them here.'

'You know it's not that.' I can see her wrestling with the logic of what I've said, but it is strange that she hasn't thought to invite them to ours; we're supposed to be getting to know each other, and surely that means them getting to know us, as well as the other way round. At last she says, 'Okay. I'll think about it, but, Rosie, no conversations with the Rudaks about it, not yet. You must promise me? I just want to fathom out how it might work first.'

I know not to push my luck. 'Okay.' I stand up and stretch out my muscles, I feel all bunched up from sitting on my backside all weekend. Before I head upstairs I fold the blanket and drape it over the back of the sofa, positioning it precisely in the middle, just as she likes it. 'Well, I'm going up now. Goodnight, Mum.' I'm nearly out of the room when she stops me.

'Rosie. I will think about what you've said. I know this is really difficult for you… but it is for me, as well.' She's not finished. 'And I'm truly sorry about last week. I'm sorry about all of it. I want things to be better between us. I really do. I love you.'

We never say we love each other, not in actual words. I can't bring myself to say it back because… because… I'm not sure why I can't. Instead I go back into the room and bend down to kiss her goodnight on the cheek. She smells of Arpège, a blast from my childhood that triggers a soft, squirmy feeling inside me. She reaches up and rests her hand on the back of my head for a second, stroking my hair, then lets me go. 'Goodnight, darling.'

31

Different Pages

PHIL

SARAH AND I barely speak to each other after Rosie leaves. We spend the afternoon doing jobs that we've been putting off for weeks, me in the garden, Sarah in the house. I even wash the van. She's cross with me, that much is obvious, but she's reining it in. I can tell. I've been trying to talk more, I really have, but I just don't feel in the mood for yet another in-depth conversation, another microanalysis about what everyone is feeling. So we avoid each other.

In the evening James and I watch TV, an island-survival reality piece of nonsense. Sarah sits with us for the start, but soon disappears. She doesn't return. I resist going to find her. At the ad break James asks, 'What's Mum doing?' Shamed, once again, by my seventeen-year-old son, I go and find her. She's sitting in the kitchen with a bottle of red. One glass. I let that go.

'You all right?'

She says, 'Yes,' but her body language sends out a very different signal. I wait. It doesn't take long. 'I'm worried about the impact all this is having on James... and Lauren.'

I accept the inevitable and pull up a chair. I understand why she'd worry about James, but Lauren? I can't see how any of it is impacting on Lauren. One of the 'benefits' of her RTS is that she never worries, about anything. Life is what it is. 'I think he's doing okay. And Lauren doesn't know there's anything going on. How could she?'

But Sarah is still fixed on James. 'Is he, though? It's not so long ago he was getting drunk and running away from us. We can't just take it for granted that he's okay. The poor sod just has to put up with it all. Christ, we keep kicking him out of his room, out of his own bed. Look at this weekend: no warning, everything being all about Rosie again. All we do is talk and worry about the girls. It's never about him.'

'Sarah, trust me – he's fine. And I know we need to sort the house out. Like we said, when the claim is sorted and we get the money through, we can start looking for somewhere bigger, somewhere that'll be better for all of us. We just have to tough it out in the short term.' She doesn't look reassured. 'It's not just the house and James, is it?' She puts her hand to her cheek, an old gesture that makes her look young and vulnerable.

She studies me. 'You talk with such confidence about the future, about Rosie being with us, like it's all part of the plan, but it's taking me longer to get used to it. I can't just snap into being the mother of three children.'

'I understand that,' I say, though in truth I'm not sure I do. Rosie *is* our child. I already feel like her dad.

'It's easier for you.'

'Meaning?'

'Rosie responds better to you. She wants you to be her dad, because she's never really had one. There's a gap for you to step straight into, but she already has a mum.'

'I get it.'

'You don't.' Maybe I don't, but she's overcomplicating things again, like she always does and she's not finished. 'And you don't ever seem to think about Anne. You're assuming that she'll just roll over and accept whatever we want, whatever Rosie wants. You don't seem to care about what she's going through.'

I notice the distinction she lets slip between our wants and Rosie's. 'I can't see that Anne has a choice.' The look she gives me is despairing, but I don't want to have to think about Anne's feelings in all this. As I'm talking, I feel my phone vibrate in my pocket. I pull it out and see the message is from Rosie. I tap on it.

Hi. TQ for letting me stay. OK with mum, not mad at me, well not TOO mad. Just thinking... r u free 8/9 August? If u r maybe we can do something for my bday? Love R xx

I look up. Sarah's face is stony. 'Sorry, but it's from Rosie.'

'And a text can't wait?'

'I thought it might be important. I wanted to check it went okay with Anne.' I can tell that this doesn't wash with Sarah, by the deep breath she takes. I decide that mentioning birthdays at this point isn't a good idea. Tonight is one of those occasions when the best defence is retreat. 'Let's leave it for now, shall we? Let the dust settle for a few days.' Then I default to the ultimate cop-out. 'I'll just go and check on Lauren.' And I leave Sarah sitting at the table with her untouched wine. The coward in me knows I'm avoiding things. Nothing is clear, but for now all I can concentrate on is that our daughter wants to be with us, and that's what matters.

Her birthday. I start to think about what she might want. It'll be the first present we ever buy her.

SARAH

Phil escapes upstairs. In the solitude of the kitchen, with a glass of red wine, I start to unpack the emotions of the weekend. It's so like Phil to think that the problem is the house! Mr Pragmatic. I wish it were as simple as bricks and mortar. How great would it be, if an extra bedroom was the solution to this sudden expansion of our family? Phil is so confident that we can absorb whatever gets thrown at us, but I'm no longer sure. I'm not sure of anything any more. The pressure of it all – the complexity of it – is too much, and we do have to think about Anne, she has rights and feelings in all this, whatever Phil may think. She's as much a victim of what has happened as anyone else. Rosie can't just pick and choose between us. I'm not going to compete with Anne for the title of 'Mum'. That's not how it should work.

And if the weekend has taught me anything, it's that I'm nervous about how to deal with Rosie. I don't know where the limits and the edges are, precisely because she's *not* our child. She seems to swing from being a composed, self-assured young woman, unreachable, by me at least, to acting like a spoilt kid. She's not like us, she's been shaped and influenced by Anne and Nathan and her very different lifestyle. I feel ill-equipped to deal with her. And I'm ashamed, because deep down inside me, where no one can see, there are times that I'm not even sure I like her. I know I could never love her like I love Lauren.

32

The Birthday Party

TEN DAYS later and, despite all my reservations and objections, we find ourselves driving around St Albans at the end of a long, traffic-clogged journey. For the last leafy leg of it Phil is reduced to muttering about inadequate road signs and cursing at other drivers. We are obviously lost, but he refuses to pull over and ask someone for directions, though even I have to admit that would be quite difficult, as there are very few people around, just a lot of high, well-trimmed hedges and broad driveways. Lauren is very fed up; every time I turn round to check her she tugs at her seatbelt, clearly indicating that she wants out. 'Soon, honey. Very soon.' Another promise I can't guarantee I can keep.

I look at the loveliness of it all and I resent every glimpsed lawn and gabled roof.

This is not how I wanted to spend Lauren's birthday weekend, miles away from home, miles away from James and Ali and Dad. Yet here I am, courtesy of Anne's invitation. Initially, of course, I said 'no' and that should've been the end of it, but I didn't bargain for the pincer movement of Phil and Rosie. They're forming quite a formidable team.

The invitation came, out of the blue, in an email from Anne. She wrote, at length, about the *misunderstanding* that resulted in Rosie turning up in Leeds, and her appreciation of our *forbearance*. It was only after three paragraphs of polite waffle that she asked if we'd like to visit them... *to celebrate the girls' birthdays, if it didn't interfere with any plans we already had. A small house party, nothing elaborate, in the garden perhaps, if the weather was good*. I read between the lines, saw the hand of Rosie in it and Anne's reluctance, and emailed back saying, 'Thank you, we would've loved to come down, but as the Saturday is Lauren's birthday, we can't.' Phil wasn't happy when he found out.

'You should've talked to me before replying to her.'

'But we can't go all that way on Lauren's birthday.'

He was silent for a few moments, but not for long. 'But we never do much on Lauren's birthday anyway, and we've nothing booked. It might be good to make a party of it, with both of them.'

'All the way down in Hertfordshire?'

'I don't see why not.'

I listed the reasons for him. 'The distance; the fact that we've no idea how accessible Anne's house is; the fact that you struggle to speak to her for longer than five minutes without coming out in hives; *and* the fact that it's Lauren's birthday.'

'And Rosie's birthday weekend. She's been looking forward to us coming. She wants to show us around, show us where she plays football, her school, the places that matter to her.' Does she now? And how would Phil know all this. He picks up on the unasked question. 'She's texted me a couple of times, saying how much she's looking forward to seeing us again. And the party is to make up for her dad letting her down. He was supposed to be spending the weekend in London with her, but he cancelled at short notice.'

'Which is tough and cruel, but I still don't want to have to drag Lauren all that way... on her birthday.' We stare mulishly at each other. Phil is the first to turn away.

I think the subject is closed, but I'm wrong.

That night in bed he plays his trump card. 'Sarah, hear me out on this. I've been thinking about this business of going down to St Albans and I can see your reasoning, but I really think it's important that we make the effort to go, for Lauren *and* Rosie. Surely we have to prove that the effort is reciprocal, that we're prepared to put in the hard yards to make it work. We're expected to, as part of the process.' It's ironic that Phil suddenly seems keen to follow the protocols that Mr Brownlee got us to agree to. His next comment really throws me. 'Besides, they're kinda like sisters now – more than sisters, really. I think it would be nice to be together on their birthdays. And...'

'And what?' What else could he have thought up to ensure we trek all that way to see Rosie.

He seems nervous. When he speaks, I can see why. 'Well... I realised something while I was in the shower.'

'What?'

'Lauren's birthday isn't actually on the eighth any more.' He takes hold of my hand. 'Think about it. She was born the day before. Her real birthday is the seventh; it's Rosie whose birthday is on Saturday.'

'Halle-bloody-lujah.' Phil indicates. We drive under an arch of blowsy white roses, coming to stop outside a large 1920s house. Red brick, big bay windows set either side of a solid-looking front door; neatly symmetrical, like a talented child's drawing of the model home. It's lovely.

Rosie appears at the back of the van as we're unstrapping Lauren. 'Hi. You made it. Come in, I'll show you round. Can I carry anything?'

She grabs a bag and tags along beside Phil as he drags Lauren backwards across the sea of pea-shingle on the drive. It's quite a haul, but when we get to the door I'm touched to see that Anne has got hold of a ramp from somewhere, so that it's an easy last push up into the house. Two more trips for all our stuff and we are inside.

Anne welcomes us. She seems unfazed by her hallway being instantly transformed from a stylish, clean white space into a dumping ground for our clutter. 'Coffee... or tea, of course, if you'd prefer?' She slips away to make the drinks, leaving us in Rosie's care. Once we've settled Lauren on a sofa in the corner of the lounge, Rosie is keen to show us around. She takes us up to her room at the very top of the house first. She has the run of the whole top floor. She has her own bathroom and a big, funky, very tidy bedroom. There's a double bed, a wall of fitted wardrobes built into the roof space and a separate sitting area with huge floor cushions. There's also a desk tucked away under the eaves, on which gleams a MacBook. Two big skylights let in the light. God knows what she made of having to bunk down in James's minuscule room. Birthday cards cover most of the available surfaces. Rosie is evidently popular. I can't help but think of the solitary row of Lauren's cards at home on the mantelpiece.

'Happy birthday,' Phil and I chorus together.

'Thanks. I'm glad you could come.'

'So are we.' Phil beams at her. 'Come on, talk us through them, then.' I think for a moment that he means her cards, which seems oddly invasive, but what he's referring to is her collection of football trophies that take pride of place on a set of shelves near her desk. Rosie happily obliges, giving us chapter and verse on each cup, medal and trophy. Phil, of course, is in his element, asking about the different teams she's played for and about the strength of their opposition. I lose interest after the third explanation, make my excuses and head back downstairs. The rest of the house is not what I expected, or what the exterior seemed to indicate. Anne's tastes are not middle-of-the-road. She has a collection of artwork and 'interesting things' scattered throughout the house, some of it quite bizarre, including a series of grotesque face masks that line the staircase, their bulbous eyes and stretched mouths are enough to give anyone nightmares.

Lauren barely looks up as I enter the lounge. She's ensconced, quite happily, gazing around at her stylish new surroundings, her picture books at her side, her iPad on her knee, well and truly at home. Someone – Anne – has put a beaker of juice on a small table within easy reach. In the lounge the furnishings are neutral, understated, but the thing that dominates the room is a huge portrait of an obscured face. It's a disturbing image, a blur of blacks and greys, with one dark-crimson slash of red. The colours seem to shift and re-form as I look at it. Beneath it, on the mantel, is a clock that is at once brutal, but also beautiful. It looks like it's made out of polished Meccano. Behind the bevelled glass face, the inner workings are visible, a complex construction of interlocking cogs and wheels held together by hundreds of tiny silver screws. The front has no hands, so the time is told by the position of the internal clockwork lining up against cuts on the clock face. I'm studying it as Anne comes in with the tea.

'Rosie thinks it's *the* ugliest thing she's ever seen. It's Dutch.' She puts the tray down.

'It's striking,' is my lame response. Then, with a piece of timing that is straight out of a comedy sketch, the innards of the clock start whirring and clicking, announcing the hour in a peculiar echoey chime. We both laugh. 'You have some really unusual things.'

'It's my vice. I used to pick things up when we travelled. Now it's the Internet. I'm always only one click away from something else that I don't really need. Your tea.' She passes me a mug, fine china. 'Thank you for coming this weekend. Rosie was delighted when you said you could. I appreciate that it's a very long way. Was Lauren okay with the journey?' She looks at Lauren and smiles.

'She was. She slept for a good portion of it. Thank you for inviting us.'

Anne then surprises me by choosing to sit next to Lauren. She tentatively reaches out and lightly touches her sleeve. Lauren glances at her and away. Greeting over.

'Thank you for sorting out the ramp.'

Anne smiles. 'I was worried about how it would work with her wheelchair.' There's a pause as we try and re-establish common ground. It's not easy; there are so many unspoken concerns and uncertainties between us. 'Given that she seems content in here for the moment, would you like to come and see the sleeping arrangements?' Anne seems incapable of sitting still. Clutching my tea, I follow her, aware that Phil and Rosie have still not emerged. The back of the house is even lovelier than the front; a big kitchen faces onto a sheltered back garden, which is enormous, lawned and edged with mature trees. The mystery of Phil and Rosie's whereabouts is answered by the view through the wall of windows. They're outside, kicking a ball to each other across the well-mown grass, a stream of banter flowing between them. Anne and I pause on our grand tour and watch them.

'They're getting on well, aren't they?' Anne's tone is neutral.

'Yes,' I answer, equally neutrally.

Anne rouses herself. 'It's through here.' She leads me into the next room. The effort she has made brings a lump to my throat. It's another lovely room, which again faces onto the garden. The floor-to-ceiling windows let light pour in, but in here the shade of a large horse chestnut that's growing close to the house softens the harshness of the sun. Waves of dappled light ripple across the room. I guess that it's normally a study, but for our visit Anne has transformed it into a bedroom. There are two proper single beds, one lower to the ground for Lauren, both made up in pretty, matching linen and there's a chest of drawers on top of which sits a slender glass vase of peonies. There's also a pile of freshly laundered towels and bottled water with drinking glasses.

'Will it do?' Anne enquires anxiously. 'I thought downstairs would be easier. I'm sorry it's not big enough for both of you to sleep down here with her, but there's another guest room made up upstairs. And the cloakroom is just through the door.'

'It's beautiful. Really, thank you for all the effort.'

She waves away my thanks. 'Well, I'll let you settle in. I'll sit with Lauren while you get sorted, if you like. We're aiming for four o'clock for people to start arriving. Sorry, that makes it sound very grand, it's only my sister and her husband and a family friend. See you when you're ready.' And she retreats, leaving me to feel churlish for my initial reluctance to come.

ANNE

I walk back through to the lounge, conscious of the unusual sensation of the house being full of people. Lauren looks up as I enter. She sees me and pats the cushion next to her, beckoning me to come and sit down, which I do.

For a few moments we simply sit there, Lauren watching her video clips, me listening to her breathing and looking at the thick, puckered scars that run along the tops of her thumbs. But suddenly, inexplicably, she starts chuckling. She shuffles around so that she's facing me and she reaches out for my hand, which she tugs. It takes me a moment to realise that she's asking me to do the actions to 'Incy Wincy Spider'. When I self-consciously oblige, she makes a gesture that I've seen her use before, placing the palm of one hand flat on top of the fist of her other hand. She restarts the rhyme and I do the actions again. Next she picks 'Twinkle, Twinkle, Little Star', an old favourite of Rosie's. When I tentatively sing along, the words coming back to me unbidden, she beams. She reaches out again and, for the duration of the song, she holds my hand lightly. Her skin is soft, her fingers short, square-tipped. Her pale, scarred hand in mine feels like a small child's.

We move onto 'Ten Currant Buns', followed by the 'Dingle Dangle Scarecrow', then one I'd forgotten, 'I Hear Thunder'. The song ends and she taps her palm on top of her hand again.

'She's asking for more.' I hadn't realised that Sarah had come back. She stands in the doorway and makes the sign herself. 'I see she's got you doing the full repertoire.'

Suddenly I feel foolish. How long has she been standing there, listening to my terrible warbly voice, watching me put up imaginary umbrellas? 'Yes.' I'm lost for anything else to say. There's an awkward pause before I remember that I have a lot to do. 'Well, I really must go and get the food sorted out.' I stand up and head for the kitchen.

Sarah replaces me on the sofa next to Lauren.

PHIL

When Rosie and I come back inside, Sarah's brow has lifted and the atmosphere seems okay. Anne is in the kitchen, pulling platters of food out of their enormous fridge. Rosie leans across her and grabs two bottles of cold water, which we gulp down in synch. I'm suddenly aware of how sweaty I am, so I make my excuses to go and freshen up.

By the time I'm showered and back downstairs, everything

seems to be geared up for 'the party'. Sarah has changed Lauren into a pretty top and brushed her hair and Rosie has showered and changed. She's wearing skinny jeans and a crop top, and her long hair, which is still damp, is twisted up in a bun. The kitchen is awash with food. Not your average sandwiches, chips and dips, but plates of salmon, sushi and prosciutto, with some tiny vegetable tarts and a spread of amazing-looking salads. And there's a cheese slate with at least six different types of cheese, accompanied not by bog-standard grapes, but by lychees and fresh figs. When Anne's back is turned, Rosie pinches a couple of the handmade cheese straws and throws one to me. I've just finished cramming it in my mouth when Anne asks me if I would be kind enough to take some more ice out to the bucket in the garden. I grunt through a mouthful of flaky, buttery pastry and do as asked.

Outside the sun is shining. I dump the ice onto the beers already chilling on the patio, then turn my face to the sun. All I can hear is the rustle of the trees and the preparations going on inside the house.

Sarah was wrong. This was a good idea.

SARAH

As promised, the party is small and teenager-free; none of Rosie's friends appear to have been invited. It's just us, Anne's sister Clare and her husband Robert, and Anne's friend, Steph. Clare is obviously the elder sibling and her husband is even older, a whole generation, or two, or so it seems once he starts talking. He's an insurance broker and she volunteers for a debt charity. Nice people, but earnest. Steph, in contrast, is a breath of fresh air; she arrives late, clutching a pack of beers, a badly wrapped present and, for reasons that are not immediately apparent, a plastic bag full of cour-gettes. The present gets added to the pile on the kitchen counter and the veg gets stowed in the fridge. The mood lightens consider-ably with Steph's appearance. She asks us all about Lauren, but in a way that's genuinely interested, and her presence seems to relax Anne. Against all the odds, I feel myself starting to enjoy myself. The champagne helps.

An hour later we're all standing in the kitchen chatting quite happily, nibbling at the vast array of food, when the phone rings. Anne reaches out and answers it while topping up her sister's wine glass, but the moment she hears the voice on the other end of the line she stops. Her stillness attracts everyone's attention and, before she has a chance to shield herself from our curiosity, her smile dies. Something akin to panic flits across her features. She turns away abruptly, crashing the bottle down on the kitchen countertop. Unfortunately this only increases my prurient desire to know who's calling.

'Hello.' I've never heard such a cool greeting. 'No, not really, we're having a small get-together for Rosie's birthday.' The atmosphere in the room shifts out of neutral, but I'm conscious of listening more to Anne than to the conversation about possible solutions to the infestation of blackfly at Steph's allotment. 'Now?' Anne's voice is tight. 'Can't she just ring you later, on her mobile.' There's a pause. 'Well, if you must, though in the circumstances it's seems a little unreasonable of you to insist.' A longer pause. 'Very well.' Anne turns and beckons Rosie over to the phone. 'Your father would like a quick word.'

Rosie looks reluctant to take the receiver, but she has little choice. She keeps her voice low, presumably hoping to keep the conversation private, as she has every right to, but this doesn't stop me straining to hear every word of it. 'Um, hi. Yep, thank you. I opened it this morning.' There's a long gap. Rosie twists the phone cord between her fingers. 'Yeah. Okay, yes.' She listens, staring at the floor. Clare asks Phil about our garden in Leeds. Thankfully he responds, keeping the conversation afloat. Rosie's voice drops even lower, almost to a whisper. 'I've already said sorry, what else do you want me to say?' Another gap. 'Okay, bye.' And the receiver goes back onto the wall. For a brief moment she doesn't move, just straightens up and flexes her shoulders. A look passes between her and Anne.

'Right, birthday girl! Are you going to get any of these presents open any time soon?' Steph bounces the atmosphere back up to party mode. 'I insist that you start with this impeccably wrapped offering.' She lobs her gift across the room and Rosie catches it deftly.

Anne recovers her smile and her voice. 'Wait just a minute. If we're doing presents, I've something that I just need to fetch.' It passes through my mind that Rosie has quite enough to be going on with as it is, but when Anne returns, with a small stack of beautifully wrapped parcels, she puts them down on the sofa next to Lauren. This does get a reaction. Lauren loves presents, or rather she loves unwrapping presents. Without waiting, she snatches the top parcel and starts pulling at the ribbon.

In the race to get the wrapping off, Lauren beats Rosie hands down. The first gift is a box of chocolates, which is immediately discarded once she realises that she can't get into it, then she's straight onto the next one. Rosie's present from Steph turns out to be a Rubik's cube, which must be some kind of shared joke, because Rosie looks delighted with it. She laughs and goes to give Steph a hug. Lauren steadily ploughs through her pile, revealing a DVD, a T-shirt and some bubble bath. She moves swiftly onto the last parcel. This she needs some help with. Anne helps her peel the tape free and she pulls out... a hat, a black trilby, shot through with silver thread. This, Lauren does not chuck. We all watch as she turns it round in her hands a few times, getting the feel of it, and then, deciding she approves, plonks it on her head. Anne smiles and I feel touched by her thoughtfulness. I also feel unsettled.

Everyone's attention switches back to Rosie. Her remaining presents include cash from her aunt and uncle, and an iPod from Anne, which comes with the request to *please take better care of this one*. From her friends she gets a selection of make-up and American confectionery. She keeps our presents to the end. She opens the parcel from James and Ali first. A new pair of shin pads, the discounted price-sticker still clearly visible on the pack.

'Thanks. I really needed a new pair, my old ones are knackered.' Her pleasure seems totally genuine. I wish she hadn't left our gift to the very end, thereby ramping up the pressure. As she takes the paper off the box, I look at Phil, who is watching her intently. She slides the lid off and goes quiet. 'Oh, wow, thank you.' She takes a second, then she looks up. 'It's lovely. Thank you so much.' And she comes to give Phil and me a 'thank you' kiss.

PHIL

She loves it. Thank God, she loves it.

I didn't know where to start; how do you buy the first present for your daughter, after fifteen years? It had to be something special. Sarah's suggestions were lame: a football shirt, a school bag, a bloody gift card! All so ordinary and everyday. I was panicking about it quite severely until Jess came to my rescue. She was round with Ali, a barbecue to celebrate the first properly warm days of summer. She crossed her long legs, sipped her beer and really gave it some thought. 'Well, some of the girls at school are obsessed with those charm bracelets, the ones that are hideously expensive. There's a shop in the mall that has a queue of teenagers outside it every weekend. But she's not a "girly" girl, is she?'

'Not girly, no, but she likes clothes and make-up and the usual stuff teenagers are into, I think.'

So one evening after work I drove into town and found the shop she'd mentioned. It was intimidating. Stark white and brightly lit, full of clear glass coffins filled with a bewildering array of different beads and charms. 'Hi, I'm Chantelle, can I help you find what you're looking for?' The young woman looked like one of those heavily made-up assistants you get in posh department stores.

'Um. Probably. I'm a bit clueless about this kind of thing.'

She immediately perked up.

'Who is the gift for?'

'My daughter. She's turning fifteen.'

'Are we starting from scratch?' she asked. If she thought I answered 'yes', a little strangely she didn't let on. Forty-five minutes later I'd chosen a 'sister' bracelet with a rose clasp; with five charms, one each for me, Sarah, James, Lauren and Rosie. Chantelle carefully wrapped it in tissue, nestled it in a box, tied it with ribbon, then rang it through the till. £195. Expensive, but worth it.

Because I can tell by her face that Rosie loves it.

ROSIE

Aunt Clare and Uncle Rob leave after we've eaten, and that means we can all escape from the kitchen. Phil and I go back out into the garden, Phil with another beer and me with a ball.

He doesn't need asking twice for a kickabout. He lobs up high balls so that I can practise my first touch. There's enough light blazing from the back of the house for us to keeping going long after it gets dark. The rhythm of Phil lofting up the ball and me catching it and controlling it is soothing.

Dad was foul to me on the phone, that clipped coldness that he uses when he's angry. I suppose I should've guessed he might ring the house phone, after I didn't respond to his texts. I know it doesn't pay to ignore him. But I'm not going to sweat over it. I'm fairly sure Mum will believe me and not him, so it should be okay. She hasn't said anything. There are some benefits to him behaving like a shit most of the time.

'Watch it!' The ball narrowly misses my head. It bounces high and rolls into the bushes. 'You doughnut!' Phil happily gets on his hands and knees and starts digging about in the border, trying to fish it out. I kneel on the grass beside him and vaguely pretend to help. 'Damn, where the hell is it?' I can tell he's not really cross. He never seems to get properly mad. They are *so* different. 'Whoops!' Phil grins at me as one of Mum's plants gets crushed. He rolls over and flakes out on his back. 'I'm afraid, young lady, that that ball has gone, for ever, to the great football graveyard in the sky.' It occurs to me that he's quite drunk. 'That'll teach you not to take your eye off the ball.'

We lie side by side, saying nothing, watching the bats swoop around the garden, and I love it. It's the best birthday I've ever had, not because of the presents or the party, but because of this, right now: the feeling of being myself, and that being enough.

Phil stirs and stretches his arms out wide across the grass. His hand touches my shoulder. 'Do you know that if you measure from the fingertips on your left hand' – he waggles his fingers – 'to the fingertips on your right hand' – his fingers beat a rhythm against my bare skin – 'that's how tall you'll be as an adult. Not a lot of people know that.'

'Is that true?' I ask, not caring.

He laughs. 'I have no sodding idea.' He doesn't move his hand away. Instead it rests heavily on my shoulder, anchoring me to the grass. I could happily lie there, under the darkening sky, talking rubbish with my dad, for ever.

ANNE

After Clare and Robert depart and Sarah takes Lauren off to bed, Steph makes me sit down. She presses a large glass of wine into my hand, which I sip to keep her happy.

'That went well.' She tucks her legs up beneath her.

'Do you think so?'

'Yeah. The food was great. Everyone was talking. In the circumstances, I think it was a resounding success. And Rosie seemed really happy.'

'Yes.' I obviously fail to disguise my feelings, because Steph senses my disquiet.

'What?'

'Nothing.'

'Come on, Anne, you're not stressing about bloody Nathan, are you? You know it's classic him to choose that precise moment to ring, after all these months. He's got a knack for it. Don't let him get to you. Rosie doesn't.' I go to take another sip of wine, but find I can't because of the tears clotting my throat. 'Aw, Anne.' Steph comes and flumps down next to me, patting my arm. 'He's really not worth it, never has been, never will be.'

But for once I haven't the energy to keep the bad inside. 'Rosie lied.'

That gets her attention. She straightens up. 'What?'

'She lied about Nathan pulling out of seeing her for her birthday.'

Steph loves Rosie. She doesn't want to believe me. 'No. That's low, even for him, blaming Rosie for his failings. What a shit!'

Which he is, but he was telling the truth about the weekend. I knew it the moment Rosie looked at me. 'No, I thought it was odd when she first suggested we invite them down here, and on the phone he told me that she's been blocking his calls. *She* cancelled on *him*, two weeks ago. He's been trying to get in touch with her ever since. That's why he rang the house, risked having to speak to me. She made out it was him, so that I'd feel sorry for her. It was all a ruse to get them here for her birthday.'

Steph clings on to her long-standing disgust with Nathan. 'Are you sure? It sounds more like him covering his arse, to me.'

'No, she lied. She was only happy today because they were here. It wasn't the party or the presents, or all the effort I put in. It's them.' And that's the awful truth. 'Steph, what am I going to do? I'm losing her.'

Steph tuts and pats and fetches me a handful of tissues. The clock strikes 9.30 p.m. 'She's just confused. It's such a massive thing. It's not surprising she's all over the shop. She loves you. You know she does. It's going to take a while to settle, for you all to find your new roles.'

I look at Steph and wish I could buy into her well-meaning platitudes, but I can't.

'I'm not so sure. They have so many things to offer her – things that she wants. They're a proper family.'

'Oh, not this again. A single-parent family *is* a "proper" family. You and Rosie are tight precisely because Nathan left.'

'We were. When she was little. We're not now. And you saw her with Phil. How can I compete with that?'

Steph looks at me kindly, but she really doesn't understand. 'It's not a competition, Anne.' Oh, but it is. I go quiet, giving up on being able to explain. It's sad that our friendship, which I value so much precisely because it is the only true one I have, is so riddled with gaps. When Steph speaks again her tone is cautious. 'Anne?'

'Yes.'

'I hope you don't mind me asking... I know it must be so hard, with all this going on with Rosie, but what are you going to do about Lauren?'

I let the clock fill the void for a few seconds and the sensation of Lauren's small hand in mine returns, bringing with it a sense of peace and a sliver of hope.

'I don't know. But whatever happens, I'm going to have to deal with it on my own, just like with Rosie.' Steph doesn't disagree. I think about Lauren, about her presence in my life, and I try to be honest. 'It breaks my heart every time I look at her. She's so different from Rosie, from anyone I've ever encountered.' Steph waits. 'But I'm beginning to understand her a little more. This weekend has been... calmer. It's given me time to see her. I mean see *her* and not just her disabilities. She is there, inside all her problems.' I can't express myself clearly, because I'm not thinking clearly. 'God, Steph, I honestly don't know what I feel or what I'm going to do.' The clock ticks. 'But at least I now accept that she really is my daughter, she is my child.'

SARAH

I'm becoming a snoop. After I've settled Lauren and switched off the light, I step into the hallway, leaving the door slightly ajar behind me. That's when I hear... *Rosie lied*. I stand very still and listen to their conversation without shame. This is Anne with her guard down, the person we never get to see, and she's hurting: being hurt by Rosie, and by Nathan and, inadvertently, by us. It's a mess of such epic proportions that I have no idea how it's all going to play out, and then Steph asks the most important question of all... *What are you going to do about Lauren?* There is a long, long pause, then Anne says, '*I don't know. It breaks my heart every time I look at her. She's so different from Rosie, from anyone I've ever encountered.*' Her voice changes, growing quieter, more reflective and softer, so soft that I have to strain to hear her as she struggles to put her heartache into words. I creep closer to the door, stealing up on the truth that hides within Anne. I get my just 'reward' for my shameful eavesdropping, because the last thing I hear is Anne saying, '*... she really is my daughter. She is my child.*'

Behind me her child, who is my child, starts to snore.

A door bangs somewhere at the back of the house, startling me so badly that my heart thuds against my chest. The conversation stops dead. There's a clatter of footsteps and I turn abruptly towards the kitchen and come face to face with Phil and Rosie, who have finally come in from the garden.

'Hi there.' From Phil's goofy expression I can tell that he's drunk, blissfully, happily, ignorantly drunk, and beside him stands Rosie, glowing with health and fitness and clear-eyed innocence.

33

Understanding

ANNE

ROSIE BANGS the front door shut behind her, off to spend her birthday money with Holly and Megan. The sound reverberates through the house and my head. I'm free at last; free of Rosie, of the Rudaks and of Steph, who, as much as I love her, is another pressure. She knows me so well. When I'm with her it's so tempting to unburden myself, let fly my real feelings, but it doesn't help. I'm still alone. Still trapped by circumstance. Still vulnerable.

I know that I really should do something to ward off my introspection – tackle the study, clean the kitchen, get the house back in order – but instead I push my bare feet into my old gardening shoes and go outside. Despite the grey sky, the garden offers respite. To prove to myself that I'm doing something useful, I wander along the edges of the lawn picking up stray leaves and pulling out the occasional weed that Stan has missed. I notice that the clump of white anemones in the big side border has been flattened. Rosie and her damn football, no doubt. I try and right the plant, pack soil around the base and snap off the broken stems, but I suspect it's too badly damaged to survive.

The party went well. Steph said so, the Rudaks seemed to enjoy it, my sister texted to say what a nice time they'd had, and Rosie was in her element. Overall it was a success. The weather was good, the food was good, the atmosphere was good and Lauren's reaction to her hat was great. Against all expectations, it was a proper celebration of both their birthdays.

The stain on the day was Nathan's call. Rosie and I haven't spoken about her subterfuge and I have no plans to raise it with her. What good will it do? It will only cause more tension between us, and I already know why she did it. She wanted to be with her new family on her birthday; it's as understandable and as painful as that. Not talking about it is the only course of action I can think of that doesn't bring with it the risk of direct conflict. Instead we'll conspire, as we have so many times before, in blaming Nathan. Us against him. The glue that holds our relationship together. Having a common enemy: is that what our relationship has been reduced to?

The leaves on the horse chestnut rustle in the wind, but apart from that it's quiet. My headache ebbs, withdrawing to the edges, biding its time. I wander round the side of the house and dump the broken stems into the nearest compost bin.

I find myself thinking about Lauren again, drawn to the simplicity of one daughter in preference to the complexities of the other. In the few fleeting moments that I shared with her over the weekend I took a huge step forward. I was tentative at first, but Sarah seemed far more willing to let me in this time. She even trusted me to be alone with Lauren a few times, and I can't imagine she lets many people do that.

It's such a curious experience, unsettling, but I am learning.

I'm learning to look beyond her RTS and see her personality. I've realised that Lauren can 'speak', even without words. That she is adept at communicating what she needs through her signing and her facial expressions. I often don't understand her, but Sarah and

Phil know exactly what she means. They can read her gestures and her unspoken requests. They're able to gauge her level of comfort or discomfort in the angle of her body or the shake of her head, and they know how tired she is by how frequently she blinks. Their instinctive anticipation of her needs and their deftness at managing them, even with an audience, in a strange house, without any of their normal aids and supports, is humbling.

They know the code for unlocking their daughter.

And they can make her laugh. That's been the other revelation of the weekend, the moments of lightness and happiness. I've discovered that Lauren has a good sense of humour and a love of pure silliness. And that she takes real pleasure in her music and her favourite nursery rhymes, and in other people's laughter. I thought her inert, indifferent to her surroundings and to the people in her life, but I was wrong.

And she is no longer indifferent to me. I made her smile and she held my hand.

The wind gusts through the trees and I head back inside my empty house, into the 'study'. Sarah has left it tidy. The beds are made, the towels are folded and the curtains are neatly tied back, letting in the sunshine and the shadows. Instead of stripping the beds, I look around the room. I have a sudden, strong image of it at night, darkness pressing at the window, a single lamp casting a warm, yellow glow. There is Lauren, sitting up in bed, her hair freshly washed and still damp at the hairline, a big picture book open on her knee. And there is me, in bed beside her, the duvet tucked around us. I'm reading to her, pointing out the pictures. As we read together, she grows drowsy and leans into me. We choose one last book, her favourite, then I settle her down to sleep, pulling the covers around her, and kissing her goodnight before switching off the lamp.

Yes, it could work. It would take time and effort and it would cost, a lot, but it's not impossible. I could extend this room out towards the boundary of the property, using the dead area between the house and the hedge. There would definitely be enough space to put in a decent wet room, maybe even a side entrance, with a ramp to the front and back gardens. It would be like a little self-contained unit. Purpose-built. Lauren could come for weekends, in the beginning. I could have help to start with, just during the day, someone with experience of special-needs children. It could work, with some planning. The house would feel full again. It would be a home again. And I would be a mother again. Lauren would need me, in a way that Rosie no longer does. She would never leave me, like Rosie will. The thought of it grows and becomes more defined in my mind, more appealing, more feasible. And if I was a mother again, people might treat me differently. I would have a role, a purpose, a different status. Everything would change.

I realise that I've been looking at it from completely the wrong perspective. Having Lauren in my life might not be the worst thing that could happen; it might be the best.

SARAH

It's a relief to be back home, back into our usual routine, back in my safety zone.

'So, then. Does she live in a mansion?' James is all ears. He's sprawled on the sofa, a bowl of popcorn balancing on his belly in anticipation of a full rerun of the weekend.

'Not quite,' I reply.

'Not far off. It was all very posh. And their garden is *enormous*.' Phil flops into a chair.

'So what was the party like? Did you meet the rest of her family?'

'Her aunt and uncle came.'

'That it?' James misses his mouth, and a handful of popcorn trickles down his T-shirt and disappears down the side of the sofa. He proceeds to dig around, trying to retrieve it. 'No sign of Rosie's mysterious dad then?'

'No.' Phil and I exchange a glance and, by mutual agreement, neither of us mentions the call. I suspect Phil is happy to pretend that Nathan doesn't exist, except as the bogeyman, but for me the call reminds me as much of Rosie's manipulation as of Nathan's peculiar relationship with his ex-wife and daughter.

'Doesn't sound like much of a party.'

'Oh, mate. You'd have loved the food. There was gallons of it. Anne sent us home with a goody bag of leftovers, there's loads of it in the fridge.' James puts the popcorn down, planning an imminent raid on the kitchen, no doubt. We entertain him with tales from the weekend; me, Anne's taste for unusual art and expensive wine; Phil, the number of bathrooms in the house and how dull Rosie's uncle was. It's an anodyne, safe rendition of something far more complicated. Phil is wise enough to rein in his undiluted pleasure at spending more time with Rosie, whether out of deference for James's feelings or mine, I'm not too sure; and I keep quiet about Anne's surprising shift in attitude towards Lauren.

Supper is a pick through the Tupperware boxes that Anne sent us away with. James shamelessly flits between sushi and chocolate cake, then back to olives and cheese.

'You'll be sick.'

'Doubt it.'

Then there's a lull, tiredness catching up with Phil and me, and a full belly catching up with James.

'Chelsea are playing,' James ventures.

'Go on, if you want to. I'll clear up and come through in a while.' They manage to find second gear and disappear to grumble and grouse at the TV, a shared pleasure that bypasses me completely. As I wash up, I reflect on the weekend.

It did go much better than expected – better, in hindsight, than I wanted it to. The effort Anne made for Lauren, and with Lauren, was not what I was expecting. It was good, I suppose, but it was also confusing, and worrying. She's at least beginning to see her as a person in her own right. It obviously demonstrated to Anne that Lauren is loving, and lovable. Perhaps even a child that *she* could imagine loving?

The thought makes me shiver. She wouldn't, surely she wouldn't. Not Anne. Lauren wouldn't fit into her life or her stylish home. Anne wouldn't contemplate it: the commitment Lauren needs, the massive changes it would require. No, she wouldn't. I'm almost certain of it.

But a shard of doubt sticks in my throat. I dry my hands and stare out at the garden. No, the issue is Rosie, not Lauren. That's the battleground. I discipline myself to concentrate on that. What to make of Rosie's lie? Because that's the only way to look at it: she bare-faced lied to us about her dad pulling out of seeing her and, worse, she lied to her mum to engineer the whole weekend. I've not discussed it with Phil, because I know that secretly he'll be pleased. He'll see it as yet more evidence of Rosie's growing bond with us. Which it is, but at what cost…? The truth, and her mother's feelings. Anne's conversation with Steph was never meant for my ears, but it has lodged in my brain. It haunts me. Her sense of betrayal and confusion, and her crushing sense of loneliness. The desolation when she said, '*whatever happens, I'm going to have to deal with it on my own…*' was real.

I hate the stew of empathy and fear that I feel whenever I think about Anne.

Nathan's absence in their lives seems as oppressive as a presence. After all these years, he still seems to have the power to pull their relationship with each other out of shape. And yet he's an enigma. A man with seemingly bottomless reserves of cash but, apparently, no reserves of real affection, or any sense of involvement in or responsibility for what is going on. I feel a wave of powerlessness mixed with restlessness sweep through me – sympathy for Anne, uncertainty about Lauren, confusion about Rosie and, a new feeling, enmity towards Nathan.

My laptop sits on the side. I go and fetch it, and open it up. Perhaps I might feel less out of control if I knew more about what I was dealing with. I start searching, seeking to fill in the blanks from a weekend that has raised more questions than answers.

I begin with Anne.

Anne's public persona is polished and deeply uninteresting. It's an 'old before her time', solidly Middle England existence. There are numerous photos of her at different charity events alongside couples who all look like Clare and Robert; solid, suited, respectable people. I notice that in many of the photos Anne is the only woman without a man at her side. Of her working life, there is virtually nothing. She doesn't appear to work, or certainly hasn't for a long time. I find one biog that mentions her spending time as a medical secretary before her marriage, but nothing recent. In half an hour of searching I find very little to fill in the neat outline that Anne presents to the world: a comfortably off woman with an enviable life, on the surface.

I'm so absorbed in what I'm doing that I don't hear James come into the kitchen. 'It's rubbish. I'm off up. Night, Mum. See you in the morning.'

'Night, love.' I dip the screen half-closed as he leans in to give me a kiss.

Phil follows him into the kitchen. He grabs a beer from the fridge. 'I've just checked Lauren, she's fine. Fast asleep. You okay? Are you gonna come through?'

'In a bit.'

'I can turn it off and we can watch something else.'

'No, it's all right. I was just going to look for a foldaway bed. See if I can't find a decent one, for when Rosie visits.' The ease of the lie should trouble me, but it doesn't.

'Okay.' He opens his beer and ambles out. The search box beckons. I type in 'Nathan Elkan' and a trapdoor onto another world opens up.

Nathan is much more in evidence than Anne, in fact he's quite high profile. There are lots of references to him. He's the Head of Neurology at University College Hospital and a member of the General Medical Council. There are plenty of pictures of him at different stages throughout his career. As I skim through the various links, he jumps back and forth in time, changing his haircut, gaining and losing weight, perfecting his angled-to-camera pose, but always commanding attention with his dark eyes and strong jaw. I catch myself comparing him to Rosie for a second, before I realise how ludicrous that is. He does not look like Lauren, her disability having erased any familial likeness in one fell swoop. This is her biological father and he wants nothing to do with her. Something bitter and nasty twists in my gut.

I keep searching, stoking my escalating hatred of him. In the process I stumble across some society-page photos of his wedding to his second wife, a skeletal blonde beauty called Francesca. He traded up second time around: younger, richer, thinner. There are homes in London and on the Suffolk coast. What shocks, but does not surprise me, is that there's no mention of Anne by name. A couple of the early profiles do reference a daughter, Rosie, from a previous marriage; the later ones merely list his three children as Marcus, Eloise and Freddy. To all intents and purposes, Anne and Rosie have been airbrushed out of his life.

Nathan appears to be precisely what Anne implied: a thoroughly successful, well-respected pillar of society, who is also a total shit.

But even that wouldn't matter to me in the slightest, if this shiny shit weren't also Lauren's father. Hard as it is to comprehend, it is Nathan Elkan's daughter who is asleep upstairs in our house and he is simply not interested.

My bitterness hardens at the injustice of it all. Finally I have someone I can be angry with, someone to blame for Anne's loneliness, for Rosie's behaviour, for my own confusion, for the emotional upheaval that is shaking all our lives, bar one.

Nathan Elkan.

He is escaping scot-free and that cannot be right, and it cannot be allowed.

I go back through my searches until I find the email address for his department at University College Hospital. No one has the right to erase a child from their life. No one. Not even Nathan Elkan.

34

Decisions

ANNE

ROSIE'S BIRTHDAY weekend clarifies two very important things for me.

Lauren needs and deserves unconditional love.

If I lose my daughter, my life will be unbearable.

It also makes me realise that I cannot let things carry on as they are. The lack of clarity is hurting everyone. So at 9 a.m. on Monday morning I ring to make an appointment to see Callum. His secretary makes a show of having to call me back after checking his diary. She claims she's had to move two meetings so that he can 'accommodate me at such short notice'.

Callum's office is on Catherine Street. Presumably it was once a cottage, or rather two cottages; it's been knocked through to form the bijou, brass-plaqued venue inside which Callum roosts, like the provincial solicitor he is.

The secretary, whose name I can't remember, even though I spoke to her not four hours ago, asks me to wait while she checks if Callum is free. He evidently is. I can see straight into his office from the small lobby as she fussily announces my arrival. He shouts through, 'Anne, come along in. Marilyn, if you'd be so kind as to fetch us coffee.' I close the door on her and take my seat in his Dickens-inspired office. His face is carefully composed to indicate concern. 'How was it?'

A small question, but not simple to answer. I remind myself of my decision, and of Callum's well-paid role in ensuring that my decision is acted upon. I force myself to remember that I have some shreds of courage left. I must do what's right, for me, as a mother. 'It went well.'

'Well?'

'It confirmed a number of things for me.'

'Such as?'

Even with Callum I need to be careful how I word my responses. I need to stay in control. 'Phil and Sarah are good people. They're a strong family and they've cared for Lauren unbelievably well, up until now. They understand her needs and are meeting them in a way that's truly admirable.' Callum watches me closely. I swallow and continue. 'Lauren is a very special child. Spending some time with her over the weekend has made me realise that. I couldn't see it before, because of her disabilities. I imagined the problems, but none of the positives.' Callum waits and I can hear my voice start to betray me. 'She draws patience and love out of the people around her in a way that's quite remarkable. When I was with her, my maternal instinct was so strong it was almost overwhelming.' The next bit is so hard to express, but necessary. I need to say it out loud for it to become an instruction, for it to be something that will happen. 'But Lauren is their daughter, not mine. They're caring for her in a way that, sadly, I believe I would never be able to.' Callum blinks. 'I do not intend to apply for a parental role in her life, other than whatever the Rudaks deem appropriate.' Callum's expression of earnest concern doesn't waver and I find myself trying to defend my decision. 'What I mean is, removing Lauren from their care just seems wrong, selfish. She's happy where she is. I can't disturb that, can I?' He neither agrees nor disagrees. 'I feel very conflicted. I've spent so many nights turning this over in my mind.' This is true, I haven't slept properly since this all began, tiredness is stamped through my bones. I'm praying for him to interject, but he stays silent. 'The uncertainty is hurting Sarah and Phil, it's hurting everyone.' I take a breath. 'Removing Lauren doesn't feel like the right thing to do, and I can't see how shared care would work. It would be too much of an upheaval.'

Thankfully, at this point Marilyn knocks and the coffee is brought in, with an unnecessary degree of performance. As she and Callum fuss with cups and saucers and cream jugs, I try to slow my breathing.

I've said it. It will be done. Lauren will never be my child.

I look past them out at the sliver of grey sky visible through the mullioned window.

Yesterday, for three happy, deluded hours, I truly believed it might be possible. I believed that I could unpick the past. And I wanted to, so badly. For those few short hours I believed that I could be Lauren's mother.

Once the idea had taken root, there was no stopping me. I felt stronger, more positive, more full of energy than I had in months. I felt ready for things to change. I whirled around the house, stripping beds, throwing open windows, emptying waste bins, all the while imagining the house and our lives transformed by Lauren. In the kitchen I hauled plates of limp party food out of the fridge and scraped it all away. I wanted a clean slate. Then, armed with a bulging bag of rubbish, I went round to the dustbins and flipped open the lid.

The smell hit me immediately. Half a dozen plastic-bagged, adult-sized nappies, piled on the top of the rest of the normal household rubbish.

*

There will never be a sunny bedroom at the back of the house. There will be no wet room, no ramp into the garden. I will not be reading storybooks by lamplight and holding my freshly bathed child close to me. I will not be loved unconditionally, by a daughter who will never leave me. It was a fantasy. Lauren is not a small child. She is a teenager with profound disabilities, who will become a wholly dependent adult who will need twenty-four-hour care for the rest of her life.

It would not be a life full of love and lightness. It would be a life full of stress and hard work.

'Anne, are you all right?' Callum seems to be crouching beside my chair. I have no idea how long I've been sitting there. 'Do you need a glass of water? You're awfully pale.'

I compose myself, as best I can. 'No. No, thank you. I'm okay. Perhaps a coffee, though.'

'Of course.' He pours me one. 'I know this has been extremely difficult for you, Anne, but having some clarity will allow us to proceed, and that has to be a good thing, for everyone.' I nod and sip my bitter cream-skinned coffee. 'Are you absolutely sure that's how you want me to proceed? You do seem to have wavered over the past few weeks, and I worry that your state of mind at present, your obvious distress—' I cut him off. 'Yes. I'm sure.' It sounds so flatly final. I take another sip.

He nods and becomes brisk. 'Okay. That's good. A clean decision. That's what's needed, in the circumstances. I think it's very brave of you to make it. I'm sure the news will be welcomed by the Rudaks.'

I'm sure it will as well. Sarah and Lauren are inseparable. I know that now. Callum reaches for his pen and notepad. He starts scribbling and I sit numbly, feeling the coffee lying queasily in my stomach. I provide him with the details he needs. After ten minutes he appears to have enough. He recaps his pen. 'I shall get onto this straight away. I'll obviously keep you posted on our progress and we'll talk you through all the paperwork, once it's drawn up.'

He seems a little thrown when I say, 'I want to talk about Rosie, before we finish.'

'Of course.' He turns over a clean page.

'Rosie is getting on well with the Rudaks.' He waits. 'I'm naturally very concerned about the implications of that for my relationship with my daughter.' He nods. 'I'm hoping that my decision regarding Lauren might influence their decision regarding Rosie.' He nods again, but less certainly. I falter, feeling frustration at his obtuseness. Surely it's obvious. 'So I need you to do your very best to fight any parental claims they might make.' He hides behind his note-taking. His writing loops flamboyantly across the paper. 'Callum? I'm saying that you must help me to keep hold of Rosie. She's all I've got.' My distress finally forces him to look up.

But his response isn't human sympathy, it's 'hundreds of pounds an hour' professionalism. 'Anne, I completely understand. Leave it with me. I promise that I'll do my utmost to ensure that the final arrangements are in both your and Rosie's best interests.'

If I had any energy left, I would hate him for his measly caution. Instead we both rise and shake hands. He does not understand, no one does. If I'm not Lauren's mother and if I lose Rosie, I'll not be a mother at all. And if I'm not a mother, then I'll be nobody. Just like Nathan has always said.

35

Relief

I OPEN the door and Sarah bursts into tears; through the hiccuping I make out that there's been a call, a number of calls about the custody arrangements for Lauren. I steer her back through the house and we sit at the kitchen table. It takes a minute of nose-blowing and hiccuping before she's able to tell me properly what's happened. The solicitor apparently called to say that Callum had been in touch to put *on record* Anne's intentions towards Lauren, which boil down to 'doing what is best for her'. By that, he clarified that Anne has – and at this point Sarah digs out a scrap of paper on which she has scribbled his exact words – *expressed her understanding that Lauren is being so well cared for, and is so obviously loved, that she is offering to make no legal claim for parentage.*

'Phil, she's waiving her maternal rights. Completely.' Sarah says it as if she doesn't quite believe it can be true. She starts crying again, prowling around the kitchen, touching the surfaces as if she's reassuring herself of the reality of the situation.

'Wow! Hey, it's okay. Take a breath.' I hug her to me.

'It's just such a relief. Knowing. For certain.' It is. The huge cloud

225

that has been looming over us rolls away, leaving everything clearer. Sarah is fizzing with emotion, unable to settle. 'I'm sorry. James already knows. He was here when I took the call. I know we should have told him together, but he heard some of it and then, by my reaction, well...' She changes tack again. 'I should go and ring Ali, and Dad. Can I, is that all right? I think we should tell them. I know it's not confirmed yet, but Anne's said it officially, so she can't go back on it, can she? Not now the lawyers are involved. Should I ring or leave it?'

'Ring them.'

'Yeah, okay. I will.'

As she dials, I cross the hall and look into the front room, where Lauren is sitting in her regular spot, her head bent over her screen, content as ever, doing her own thing as she always does, and as she will for the rest of her life, and ours.

James thunders down the stairs and comes to stand alongside me in the doorway, his shoulders broad enough to fill the remaining space. 'It's good news, isn't it? Mum went a bit loopy when she came off the phone.'

'She's still a bit loopy, but I think that's fair enough.' Lauren doesn't look up. We stand and watch her, while Sarah's voice hits new heights as she breaks the news to Ali.

After she gets off the phone I open a bottle of champagne and pour three glasses. We chink against Lauren's plastic beaker. There's a pause and they all look at me. 'To family!' Sarah and I sip, as proper grown-ups should, and James gulps. 'To your liking, sir?'

He pulls a face. 'I'd prefer a beer.'

'You have no refinement.'

'Not my fault – I'm your child.' The moment he says it, he flushes red.

Sarah smiles at him. 'It's okay. We can stop dancing around things now.'

'Sorry.' James gulps another big mouthful and winces as if it's battery acid.

I sprawl out on the sofa, Sarah sits on the floor next to Lauren, and James drapes himself over the armchair. I feel the alcohol nosing steadily into my bloodstream; to be gently drunk on a Wednesday night feels like a good plan. A Chinese takeaway might fill out the celebrations nicely: chicken and black bean, some Singapore noodles, a big bag of greasy prawn crackers. We could send James to fetch it. I stretch out my legs, feeling content. 'Don't drink it, if you don't want it.'

James smiles. 'If you've taught me anything, it's not to waste free alcohol.'

'That it, then?' I adjust the cushion behind my head. 'The sum total of your inheritance from me?'

James makes a show of thinking it through. 'That, and maybe how to slide-tackle, badly.'

'Cheers for that.' I raise my glass to him.

He raises his in a mock salute and we both take a swig. 'Any time, Dad.'

SARAH

I'm just checking that the back door is locked before we go up to bed when Phil comes into the kitchen. I flick the lights off, but he stays there, getting in the way, a funny look on his face. 'Come here.' He puts his arms round me and pulls me to him, kissing me, open-mouthed and urgent. We break apart. His breathing is uneven.

'I love you.'

I'm about to say it back, but I don't get the chance.

36

Consequences

THERE HAVE been so many phone calls over the past few days – from Callum, from the social-work team, from the Trust, and two from Sarah, they were the only ones that have offered me any comfort – that I'm unprepared. The first thing he says is, 'Is Rosie there?'

'No.' It's not a lie. She's not back from school, though I would've lied to keep him from speaking to her.

'Good. We need to have a conversation.' Emphasis on the *we*. Finally he wants to talk to me, after more than a decade of trying his utmost to avoid anything more than the most stripped-bare exchange of information.

Perversely, I try to derail it. I want to deny him, frustrate him, block whatever it is he wants, whatever it is he is about to demand of me. 'You've made your position perfectly clear through your lawyers, Nathan. So why call now?'

'I received a photograph.'

'Of?'

'The girl.'

228

I immediately know he means Lauren. 'You mean our daughter.' I imagine his smooth, unyielding face masking his cold fury at my insistence on the truth.

'Anne, be very careful.' He pauses, waiting for me to heed his warning, then he continues in the same tight, measured tone. 'Sarah Rudak contacted my PA and emailed a picture to my offices at University College.' That would not have gone down well. I admire her audacity. 'It gave me pause for thought.' For a second I wonder what he's going to say, what impact seeing Lauren has had on him. He draws a deep breath. 'You need to make sure that she never contacts me again – her or any of the family.' Nothing. It has had no impact on him at all.

'I've notified them that I'm not pursuing any maternal claim on Lauren. What else can I do?'

'I don't know, but I simply cannot tolerate any further attempts to link me to this child. You need to ensure these people grasp that.' He enunciates each word as if I'm an idiot.

'How am I supposed to ensure that, Nathan?'

'Again, I don't know. That's not my concern, but you're the one who seems to have been cosying up to them. Inviting them to the house!'

'I had no choice. It's a two-way street. They have rights as well... to Rosie. They could try and take her away from me – from you. Have you even stopped to think about that? And there's what Rosie wants. She's—'

He slices me off. 'Anne, as her primary carer, that's for you to sort out. I'm paying for the best legal advice to resolve things to your satisfaction. I'm sure some accommodation will be agreed in the end that's mutually acceptable.'

'How can you—'

Again he doesn't let me finish. 'I refuse to go down this road with you. You need to listen to me. This cannot... is not... going to touch me. And believe me, Anne, it's in your best interests that it doesn't.' He pauses again, making sure that he has my full attention. 'I will honour my financial responsibilities towards the child. That's in hand. And I will cover the legal costs of this whole mess, above and beyond whatever compensation is paid. I think, in the circumstances, that is more than generous. But it might be salutary for you to bear in mind that this fundamentally changes our relationship as well.' Again he waits, drawing out the moment. 'Should I choose to make it an issue, there could be ramifications for *our* current arrangements. After all… Rosie is no longer my child, in the eyes of the law, as well as in reality. Though I know that you struggle with that concept, don't you, Anne? Reality.' The bastard! 'Any further support – and I'd remind you that it is a considerable sum you receive from me every month, for the house, for Rosie's schooling and for the maintenance of your comfortable lifestyle, for all your expensive knick-knacks – it could all be back on the table, *if* there are any further attempts to involve me directly. Do you understand?'

'Yes.'

'Good.' I'm about to be dispensed with. His tone changes back to the smooth, impersonal politeness of the past twelve years. 'Tell Rosie I called and asked after her. Have a good evening.' The phone clicks and he's gone.

I feel the warning throb of pain behind my eyes.

The migraine hits during the night. Rosie, used to my withdrawals, ignores me, beyond checking that I'm still breathing before she sets off for school in the morning. I didn't think it was possible, but the pain is even worse than normal. I can't separate out the physical symptoms from the panic. The nausea rolls up and over me every time I contemplate my next move. It seems easier not to move at all. Nathan's threat – for that's what it is, a direct threat – preys on me.

I wonder if he's really capable of such cruelty, capable of completely disowning Rosie. I suspect he is. I lie with the curtains drawn, and reopen old scars pinned down by the pain and by memories of my life with Nathan.

To begin with, our marriage was good. Being with Nathan was exciting, romantic, so much better than anything I'd ever experienced before, better than I deserved. I was dazzled by him and by the life I had, as his wife. I loved all the travelling: the conferences in Paris and Amsterdam, the lovely hotels, the amazing service, the pampered existence. And I was proud of the respect and deference shown to him, which were, in turn, extended to me. Nathan was exceptional and passionate, and that was exhilarating to be around. When he talked about his work it was inspiring, a heady mix of genuine zeal to treat and heal and a driving ambition to 'best' his colleagues, especially his old mentors and professors. Yes, for those first couple of years it was genuinely good. I had the type of marriage that I'd always dreamt of, with a man I idolised.

Then we decided to start a family. I was, after all, twenty-nine. There was no point in waiting. I'd given up my job. We had enough money. We already had a beautiful home with plenty of space. We agreed that the time was right. We used to talk about it over dinner, in the evenings, after Nathan got home from work, sipping wine by candlelight, mapping out our future. The 'plan' was for three children, two boys and a girl, his preference. We were going to have them close together, so they would always have each other to play with and compete with (that was Nathan's little joke). We both agreed that it would make their education easier to organise as well. Nathan already knew which schools would be best. We wanted them to be robust, outdoorsy children, who liked sports and riding. They'd be the type of kids who could cope with a bit of rough and tumble. We even talked about moving further out into the countryside.

Nathan said he could always commute into London. We assumed they'd be intelligent – their birthright from their father. We didn't discuss what their inheritance from me would be. They would be lucky children who would grow up with the world at their feet. Who knew what they might achieve in life.

But I didn't get pregnant. Not the first month or the second, or any of the subsequent months, and as time crawled by, my failure to conceive cast a lengthening shadow over our marriage. It was a wearying cycle of expectation and disappointment that took its toll on both of us. Not that Nathan ever said anything, directly, that was not his way. He remained polite, deferential, solicitous, which made me feel worse. The arrival of my period every month felt like an indictment. I was his wife. He desperately wanted a child. I wanted a child. Yet I was failing to provide one.

One morning I woke up next to him, conscious that I'd started bleeding during the night. Trying hard not to wake him, I slipped quietly out of bed and, hunched over to stem the flow, hobbled into the en-suite bathroom. No sooner had I taken off my soiled nightie and knickers, and started running the shower, than he knocked at the door. Softly, but insistently.

'Anne?'

I froze. 'Yes?'

'Are you going to be long in there, darling?'

'No. I'm just going to have a quick shower. I'll be out of your way in five minutes.'

There was a pause, then he said. 'Can't you shower later?'

I looked down at myself. 'Well… '

'I'm sorry, darling, but I really need to be away by seven-thirty. I'm due in theatre at ten.' There was no arguing with the needs of his patients, or with Nathan. I turned off the water, grabbed my robe and covered myself up. The minute I unlocked the door, he strode into the bathroom. 'Thank you.' He shut the door on me. It was only as he turned the lock that I remembered the pile of nightclothes on the floor.

That night Nathan was a little later home than usual, but he brought me flowers, creamy-white Calla lilies, elegant and fragile. As I cut the stems and put them into a vase he talked, at length, about his new schedule and how he was going to be busier than ever, due to a trial that he'd been asked to work on with a colleague over at Guy's. Apparently it was going to necessitate quite a few very early starts. He was worried about disturbing me, especially given how much I needed my rest.

I moved into the guest bedroom and used the house bathroom that night, and for the duration of every period from thereon in, allowing both of us to avoid the messy evidence of my failure to conceive.

Fourteen long months later I finally fell pregnant and Nathan fell in love with me and my body again. He would lie pressed against my back, his fingers stroking my non-existent bump, adapting and embellishing our plans. He was loving and protective, and very pleased. And I felt safe and happy and hopeful, for a little while.

But my happiness faded quickly. It became infused with the anxiety that I was going to fail at being a mother. I began to worry that, given I'd taken so long to *get pregnant*, somehow I wasn't designed to *be pregnant*. And as the weeks went by and I expanded to accommodate our child, my worries worsened and darkened. They spread to encompass every problem that was possible, at every stage of pregnancy. At first I was terrified of miscarrying the baby, losing the child that we both wanted so much. When I voiced my fears, Nathan would smile, lay his hand on my stomach and say it was only natural to be concerned. And he was right. Everything proceeded quite normally. I passed the twelve-week landmark, my sickness abated, my belly grew, it was all going to plan, but inside I was increasingly tormented by anxiety about the development of the baby. I had no faith in my body to deliver what Nathan wanted. When I braved talking to him about my worries, he was initially supportive and reassuring, but it became obvious, very quickly, that my concerns were beginning to irritate him. Before long he began to discount everything I said as hysterical nonsense. He claimed that my old job had given me a morbid fascination with *birth anomalies*. He told me I just needed to calm down.

The irony of his response still doesn't mean anything to him.

And as the months went by, he started staying up in London more and more and I stayed home, alone. By the end of my pregnancy I found myself saying very little to him at all, certainly nothing about my persisting fears, and he seemed pleased with my silence. In hindsight, it was the beginning of a separation that was only ever going to end one way.

It was fitting, I suppose, that he was halfway round the world when I went into labour.

I can't bear to think about that week. How frightened I was. How utterly alone I felt during the birth. How shocked afterwards. Nathan simply was not there. At the most difficult time in my life he was absent.

Of course he expressed delight at the birth of his daughter, when I finally got hold of him; he sent a bouquet of exquisite flowers, which were not allowed on the ward; he caught the next plane home, after he'd delivered his keynote speech, and drove straight up to fetch me, after he'd slept off his jet lag. All actions that made the right impression, but revealed his real priorities. I remember him coming into the room when he finally made it up to Leeds. He bent down to embrace me, smelling of aftershave and cold air, and of the world of importance and normality outside the hospital. The nurse who had shown him in glanced back at us before she left, curious and perhaps envious. Then he turned to Rosie. He lifted her out of her crib and examined her, silently, before lightly pressing his lips against her downy little head. My heart contracted. I felt balanced on the cusp of two lives, neither of which I could envisage, both of which I was unsure I would cope with.

Nathan professed love at first sight and promised me, faithfully, that things would be better now that we were a family, and I wanted to believe him.

We travelled home in silence, save for the snuffles of our new daughter.

But he was too impatient to be a good father, and too frustrated with me to make the effort to be a good husband. Despite having a newborn in the house, everything still had to fit in with his priorities and his schedule. His home life was supposed to be a calming backdrop to his career, there to sustain and enhance him. I let him down badly there. I knew that the sight of me, in my dressing gown, in a kitchen littered with baby paraphernalia and milk-crusted muslins, was not how he wanted to start and end his days. As Rosie fed and cried and grew fat and healthy, latched onto me like a limpet, he retreated further and further into his work and I withdrew, once again, with my daughter, to my separate bedroom.

Then came his effortless lies about working away, and his mounting frustration with what he saw as my leaky, emotional needs. He never understood how trapped I felt. He believed in resilience and, when I failed to deliver that, he advocated – strongly – medication. Quiet was better than vocal, in his book. And I went along with it because the tablets did help, at least a little; they made me realise that I had to do better.

So I tried. By a sheer act of will, I set about hauling myself back up to his exacting standards. And I did it. By the time Rosie turned one, the house, Rosie and I were always 'Nathan-ready', neat, clean, perfect at all times. It was such hard work and it was, ultimately, pointless.

I did try, but it was never enough.

I gave him the child he wanted, the life he wanted, and still it was not enough.

The pain blots me out.

I hear Rosie come in from school, but as much as I want to get up and go down to her, I can't. Yet again I can't. There've been so many times when I haven't been there for her. I listen to her footsteps.

When she was very little and I was ill, she used to come and play on the end of the bed, whispering to her toys while I lay there, out of reach. When the pain started to lift, she'd sense it and wriggle up inside the covers for a cuddle. The comfort of her small body used to be enough to bring me back to myself.

There's a tap at the open door. I struggle upright. 'Come in.'

'Here!' She passes me a flannel, warm to the touch. 'Is it a bad one? I know nothing really helps, but...' She shrugs.

'Thank you, darling.' I rest my head back against the pillow and lay the cloth across my forehead. It smells of lavender oil. The heat and the gesture touch the sharp edges of the pain, which recedes slightly. 'Have you time to sit and talk to me for a while? Tell me about your day.'

'Maybe later. You rest. I've got homework to do.' And she flees.

37

Support

ROSIE

MUM LASTS till Wednesday before she flakes out. I leave her to it. She does look crap, proper ill, the worst she's been for a while, but it's still classic Mum. She can only keep up the pretence for a few days at a time before she collapses. The weekend was her grandest performance for quite a while. Hiring ramps and beds for her, all the fuss about trying to get the 'right' presents for her, turning the house upside down for her. It was completely OTT. And I noticed that she kept sitting with her, trying to get a response. I had to look away, it was so awkward. I didn't know what she was playing at – playing at being her mum. Lauren is Sarah's, always will be... end of.

With Mum in bed, the house feels like it used to when I was little. The same silence, the same hollow feeling in my belly. Course, it's not the same, not really, not now I'm grown-up. It's not like I need her fussing around me. I go to school like normal. I'm not the hot topic any more. Lou Mabbot has been suspended for something they found in her locker. The top theory is drugs, but the bitch-queens are trying to get a rumour going that it was a pregnancy test, a positive one. I'm old news.

Period three is history with the sub-teacher Mr Omiduran. He's having a 'mare arriving this late in the term. He's made the fatal error of thinking that a top set, full of 'nice' girls, is going to be okay. Wrong. We've had four lessons with him so far and the behaviour has been getting worse. It's not helped when he moves Marcus Hill next to Emma C! We all wait for them to start. It doesn't take long. She claims he's drawn on her shirt, he says that she's kicking him under the desk, she moans that he won't keep his elbows on his side, and so on and so on. Petty stuff designed to make sure we don't get any work done. He's stupid enough to keep talking to them, pleading with them to settle down. Then Emma C pushes Marcus and he falls off his chair with a massive clatter. Something inside Mr Omiduran just snaps. He yells, proper yells, and once he's started he doesn't seem to be able to stop. He starts ranting on about how we're wasting his time. Wasting our time. How we should be ashamed of ourselves. That we have a world of opportunities and privileges. That we could do what we want with our lives, but that we're too stupid to make the most of what we have. He's furious, out of control, his words loud and nasty and personal, shouting that we're all a waste of space. I'm a waste of space, useless. Ugly and useless.

It surprises me when Indira puts up her hand and keeps it up, trying to attract his attention. At last he notices her, the quietest, best-behaved girl in the class braving his rant. It stops him in his tracks. His voice drops from raging to tired. 'Yes, Indira. Sorry. What is it?'

'Mr Omiduran. Rosie!' Everyone swivels round to stare at me and I become aware of a choking noise in the room.

He nominates Indira to take me to Red Base. She looks horrified, but does as she's told, walking alongside me down the thankfully empty corridors, which seem to amplify the noise coming out of me. She deposits me outside the office and scuttles off. And I just stand there until Mrs Boyd comes out.

'Lord, Rosie, you gave me a fright. Whatever's wrong?' There's no way I'm going to talk to Mrs Boyd. Small, big boobs, dressed too young for her age, thinks that students like her because she's popular with the naughty kids, which she is, but only because they know she's such a pushover. 'Come in. Here.' She passes me a handful of tissues; there are always plenty of tissues in Red Base. I wipe the tears off my face, but I don't say a word. Mrs Boyd gives up after ten minutes and we stare at each other. She cracks first. 'Shall I ring your mum?'

'No!'

She jumps.

'I want to talk to Ms Suri.'

Half an hour later Ms Suri arrives, takes me by the arm and pulls me into the side office. 'Now then? What's the matter?'

So I tell her. About the weekend and the party, and about the ramp and Mum making such a fuss, and about the bracelet and the bats, and about all the food and Lauren wearing her hat and Phil playing football with me. I don't tell her about Dad. Even I can tell it sounds mental. Like a really nice weekend. And it was, but it wasn't. She listens, then she says, 'So you're worried about keeping everyone happy and finding it impossible?'

And it seems like kinda almost the right reason for why I'm so upset, so I nod and she makes a sympathetic noise and passes me some more tissues. Because in a way she's right: what am I supposed to do with them all? There's Dad, who doesn't really care about seeing me, he just likes pulling me out of a drawer when it suits him, showing me off for a bit, then shutting me away. And there's Mum, who's all over the shop, making a huge effort at the weekend when everyone was around, but completely withdrawing into herself now it's just the two of us. She always wants me to talk, to tell her things, but she never tells me anything. And there's Sarah, who likes me one minute, then doesn't the next. I can tell, I can see it in her face.

She finds me hard work. And my friends think I'm really moody and weird and they're not interested in what's going on any more, because nothing really is. Nothing is getting any easier or any better or any clearer. The only person I want to be with is Phil. He's the only one who likes me as I am.

I ramble on about it all to Ms Suri, talking crap, because that's what it is: crap, confusing crap; and she's sympathetic and patient and doesn't look at her watch once, which is nice of her because she's always busy, always running around sorting out people's problems, but even she goes and stuffs it up by suggesting, after about half an hour of me talking, that maybe she should call Mum. I stupidly say, 'No, she's ill in bed' and that seems to worry Ms Suri even more, and she starts talking about counselling services and I realise that me spilling my guts at school, even with Ms Suri, is a really bad idea. So I backtrack and say I'm just tired and then – and this is mean – I say that Mr Omiduran lost his temper in class and it was that that had set me off. That really I'm okay. That I'm just tired after the weekend, and that me and Mum are getting on well really. It takes me another twenty minutes of this kind of stuff before she's convinced I'm not going to run off and do something stupid. In the end she shrugs, pats my arm and promises that she'll check in with me every couple of days and then she lets me go. I walk back to my last lesson feeling stupid and genuinely tired.

That'll teach me to confide in teachers.

ANNE

In the morning the migraine is gone, leaving me exhausted, but functioning. I make myself open the curtains, shower and fix my hair and make-up. In the afternoon I even manage a little bit of shopping. I contrive to be chopping fresh basil for a home-made pasta sauce when Rosie thumps into the kitchen after school.

'Hi. You feeling better?' She slings her school bag on the floor.

'Yes, thank you. Pasta okay for tea?'

She glances at the pans and my efforts. ''Kay. Nice. I'll just go up and get changed.'

We eat early in the kitchen, together for a change, with the radio on in the background, her choice of channel, but she's mindful enough to keep the volume low. We talk about school and about my plans for the garden. In truth, I've not thought about it. We avoid talking about the Rudaks. It's such a pity that I have to spoil the little oasis of calm that we've achieved; the call from Nathan was a warning that I can't ignore. As I watch Rosie eating her pasta and chatting, I feel a chill at the thought of the havoc that Nathan being dragged into it could cause. I need to warn Sarah off.

'I was thinking, I might come up to the tournament in Leicester.' Rosie stops forking pasta into her mouth. I persevere. 'It sounded like a nice day out, from the way Sarah was talking about the one in Watford. I could maybe make us all a picnic.'

Her response is not encouraging. 'You never come to watch me play. You hate football.'

'I don't. Anyway, that's not the point. I should support you more.'

She looks at me so sceptically that I feel ashamed. 'But it's all planned. I'm going with the girls. Phil and Sarah are meeting me there and taking me up to Leeds. You said it was all right. You said that I could stay with them for some of half-term.' Her fork clatters into her bowl and I can see the flare of rebellion in her eyes.

I need to placate her, quickly. 'I know. I'm not going to interfere with you staying with them. But I need to speak to Sarah. Things have... moved on – at least they have regarding Lauren.' She makes a gesture that is so dismissive that, even in the midst of my turmoil, it shocks me. Her self-absorption is absolute. I plough on. 'I've been meaning to tell you, but with being under the weather I haven't had a chance. Anyway, what I mean is, I've formally agreed to Lauren staying with Phil and Sarah. I'm not making any legal claims to shared maternity or regular access, just to staying in her life, but only in as far as Phil and Sarah feel comfortable.' Precisely the arrangement I can only dream of them agreeing to, in relation to Rosie. I watch her processing this information and wait for her questions.

'Right.' Nothing. She has no interest in Lauren. Then. 'What about me?'

'You?'

'Yeah, me.' She studies me with her pale grey eyes and I feel breathless in the face of such a direct question.

'Oh, Rosie. Please. One thing at a time.' I see her brace herself. I step in swiftly to head her off.

'I know we need to sort things out, but it's so important. I don't want us to rush into anything. With Lauren, it's simpler. The solution. What's best for her, and for the Rudaks... and for us. But we still need to work out what's best for you... for us. Properly. Don't we? And we will. I promise. I'm not sure we, or you, or they really know what that is yet, do we?' I've never been so inarticulate.

She slowly twists the rings on her fingers, then she says bitterly, 'So Lauren is the priority, is she?'

This is going so badly wrong. 'That's not what I meant.' Though she's right to doubt me. My motives are muddy. For an unnerving moment I wonder if she can see into my soul.

'But that's why you want to come to Leicester... to sort out stuff about Lauren. It's not really to watch me play, is it, Mum?'

Our truce is well and truly over.

For the next ten minutes I attempt to convince Rosie that she *is* my priority and that what I want, more than anything, is to get back some of the closeness we once had. I desperately need her to see how much I love her. But she can't. She isn't listening. Her beautiful face is stiff with disbelief. She has had enough of me.

She pushes her chair away from the table and stands up. 'Forget it, Mum. I'm going with the girls.' And with that, she walks out of the kitchen.

38

Home and Dry

PHIL

THE TOURNAMENT is tough and Rosie's team doesn't perform very well, but I don't care. It's another day with my daughter, precious hours of watching her play, witnessing her resilience, cheering her on, being there for her. When she grabs my hand to steady herself as she pulls off her boots at the end of a long, unsuccessful day, my heart lifts. Her tired silence on the journey home is a gift.

Time together, that's what we need. Not words or actions or decisions, just time.

We get home, eventually, and Rosie calls first dibs on the bath, limping upstairs on her stiff legs to soak away her disappointment. I fill Sarah in on everything that happened. I don't want her to feel left out. When Rosie comes back down, she's in her pyjamas, her face scrubbed clean of muck and make-up. Another small step on the road to normal. She sits at the table and eyes the pile of bread. 'Have some, if you're hungry, I think tea's going to be another ten minutes or so.' It makes me smile to see her take a big hunk and spread a thick slick of butter on it. Lauren, sitting across from her, immediately signs for some as well. Mid-chew, Rosie hesitates and looks at me, I nod and she tears off a lump and puts it on the table in front of Lauren. We eat dinner, then all decamp to the front room and watch rubbishy Saturday-night TV. Lauren claps and rocks along to the crappiest bands, happy as a clam, and James stays in and makes an effort to participate by mocking each sobby backstory. It's nothing we haven't done a thousand times before, just an average night in, but this time it's all of us together under one roof and that's what's special. Sunday is the same. Good, relaxed, a normal family weekend, which is all I've ever wanted.

ROSIE

For a few seconds when I wake up on Sunday morning I'm confused; everything smells, sounds and looks different. I stretch out under the thin duvet, and pain shoots up my calves. My foot touches Dog at the bottom of the bed. I curl my toes into his fur. I need a wee, but I can't be bothered to get out of bed. Jim's room is a tip, there are clothes piled high on the chair and there's a mountain of crap on what I'm guessing is his desk. The wardrobe door doesn't shut properly because there's a sleeping bag spewing off the top. And I guess this is the tidied-up version of it. I'd never be allowed to let my room get like this. I sit up and press my heels down into the rug, easing my Achilles. The radio's playing downstairs and someone's clonking about in the bathroom. I wait, not sure what to do, but I really need a wee. The toilet flushes, then I hear Sarah's voice and an odd swishing sound moving across the landing. 'Good girl, let's get you dressed.' It's Lauren, crawling back to her room. I stay put, listening to Sarah's voice through the wall. 'That's it. Lift up. Good girl. Good girl, all done. Trousers on, now your top. A blue top today, yes, blue, good girl. Now what do you need? Socks. One sock, two socks. All done. There, you look lovely.' The swishing sound passes across the landing and down the stairs. 'Go careful. Good girl.' Sarah's voice follows her down each step.

I wait another minute, making sure it's safe, then rush to the bathroom. When I get downstairs, Sarah's in the kitchen encouraging Lauren to eat her breakfast nicely. She's not. She's cramming pieces of toast into her mouth as fast as she can without chewing. 'Help yourself.' Sarah gestures at the loaf of bread and the toaster. 'Are you a bit stiff?'

'Yeah. It's just first thing. It'll ease off.' I don't know where they keep the jam and stuff.

Sarah must be telepathic because, without taking her eyes off Lauren, she says, 'Top left. There's Marmite as well, if you prefer. I hate the stuff, but Phil's addicted.'

'No, thanks, I think it smells rank.'

She laughs. 'He'll be back in a bit. He's just gone to get some petrol. I thought we could maybe have a wander around the shops later. If you fancied it.'

'All of us?'

Sarah wipes Lauren's face and hands. 'No, James would rather poke his eyes out with a stick than go clothes shopping.' Which isn't the answer I wanted.

We drive into Leeds. I sit up front with Phil, so that he can point out all the local landmarks. We leave the van in a disabled parking space and walk into the shopping area. It's busy, better shops than I was expecting, lots of buzzy cafés and some really cool arcades with some good boutiques. Phil pushes Lauren as we wander around among the crowds. He waits outside a lot of the shops because they're too cramped to get her inside. There's a really awkward moment when we're in one of the malls and Phil points out the store he got my bracelet from. I'm suddenly very conscious that

I'm not wearing it, but Sarah helps by chattering on about mind-less stuff and keeping us walking. When we do go into some of the shops, I feel quite self-conscious looking at stuff with her. I can tell she's following me around, not sure where I want to go or what I like. She doesn't pick anything up or suggest what might suit me, like Mum always does. She seems totally disinterested in buying anything for herself. Besides, I don't have any money with me and I can't really expect them to pay. It's nice, but it's all a bit pointless.

As we walk through the crowds I notice how many people openly stare at Lauren, not just kids, but adults as well. One fat woman actually stops talking to her equally fat friend and cranes her lardy neck round as we pass. Rude cow! Again Sarah must have some sixth sense thing going on because she says, 'You get used to it.'

'She didn't even pretend not to stare.'

'I just wish people would smile more.' Sarah seems relaxed about it. 'Shall we find somewhere to eat?'

I look at the waves of people and just know that everywhere will be packed. I think of Lauren with her snotty nose, speed-eating, cramming food in her mouth with her fingers, and I feel a bit sick. 'It looks really busy, I'm fine just going back to the house.'

'Okay, if you're sure.'

Once Phil has fastened all the complicated straps onto Lauren's wheelchair in the back of the van we're ready to head home. 'Hop in.' He slams the boot shut. The side door is open, but no one tells me where I'm supposed to sit. It's like this in the house as well. I don't know where my spot is, not yet. I can't just climb in the front again without being asked, so after a second or two I get in next to Lauren and we set off home.

It's really unnerving the way she looks at me. She breathes heavily through her bunged-up nose and blinks a lot. It's impos-sible to know what she's thinking. I look out of the window. A few seconds later I feel her fingers grab my top and pull. I try to ignore her. She pulls harder. I shuffle further away from her, but there's not much space for me to go anywhere. She yanks even harder. By now I'm sweating. I can't face reaching down and unpeeling her fingers from my sweatshirt. She tugs again. Finally I turn round and see that she's grinning, her face very close to mine. Another tug. She waits for my response. I tug back and she grins some more.

It's a game.

Sarah does her psychic thing again from the front seat. 'Lauren, you'd better not be making a nuisance of yourself' and, as if she understands, Lauren looks me directly in the eye and gives an almighty tug. It catches me off-balance and I half-fall into her, it's only the seatbelt that saves me from slipping right off my seat. That makes her laugh out loud. Sarah looks back at us. 'Are you sure you're all right, Rosie?'

'I'm fine,' I say. 'She's just messing about.' Sarah looks relieved.

We spend the whole trip home doing this weird Lauren version of tug-of-war, but it seems to make her happy. It's nice to see her smile. It changes her face completely.

We don't go far for the next couple of days: the park, the local shops, Phil takes me and Jim for a game of pool at the local pub, but mostly it's around the house, talking, helping Sarah cook and just watching TV. There's also lots of hanging around while we wait for Lauren to be ready or fed or changed or entertained. It's very different from being at home. It's almost boring. I would normally be with Kennedy and Holly most days during the holidays. They keep messaging, asking me what I'm doing. There's not much to say, we're not really doing much, but still.

Mum texts every five minutes asking how it's going.

On Monday teatime Jim challenges me to a match on his Xbox. It feels okay when we're alone together now, less awkward. He's actually the source of most of my information about their lives. I feel I can ask him things that I can't ask Sarah, because he's not judging me, deciding about me. He seems so placid, so 'whatever' about life, so okay about having me around. I'm grateful. I'm not sure what I'd be like in his situation, if Mum really had been mad enough to try and get custody of Lauren. We set up a game and he starts his usual showboating, which means I score, twice, in the first couple of minutes. We play in silence apart from the odd insult after that, but as always, I can't resist picking his brains, catching up on the years of family history that I've missed.

'Are you hanging around cos I'm here?'

Jim's eyes don't leave the screen. 'Don't flatter yourself.'

'You don't have to babysit me, you know.'

'I'm not. This is where I live.'

I know he doesn't mean anything by it, but it reminds me that I'm still just a guest in their house. I'm not really one of them. My being here is an inconvenience, especially for him. This is his bedroom, not mine. I'm screwing up his life, invading his space. 'I'm sorry you're having to sleep on the sofa.'

He just shrugs. 'It doesn't bother me. I can sleep anywhere.' Across the landing we can hear Phil and Sarah bathing Lauren – it takes two of them. Jim shoots and scores. 'Mum and Dad said they're gonna use the money, when it comes through, to sort something out. Maybe convert the loft. Or we might move.'

'Oh.' I feel a jolt. I like their house. It's the place I picture, when I try to imagine living with them.

'It would help with Lauren, having somewhere bigger.' The clock ticks down on the second half. We both try hard to score in the last twenty seconds. I shoot and miss. Game over. He immediately starts scrolling through, setting up another game. 'Street match?'

'Okay.'

The sound effects of the ball thwacking around the indoor court on the Xbox mix in with the splashing coming from the bathroom. Phil's doing some really crap singing. Lauren likes his singing.

'Now, lie down for your hair wash, good girl.' There's a loud slosh of water. I suppose in a bigger house you would at least be able to get away from hearing every single thing. There's no getting away from Lauren here.

I sneak a look at Jim. He needs a haircut, his fringe is flopping in his eyes. Side on, I can't tell whether his nose and his neat lips are anything like mine. He scores another easy goal. 'So much for your defensive prowess!' He pushes his hair out of his eyes.

'Does it ever drive you mad?'

'What?'

'How much time they spend with Lauren?'

He doesn't even seem to think about it. 'No. I'm used to it.'

'Even now, now that... you know.' I don't know how to say it.

Again he answers me without hesitating. 'She still feels like my sister.' I'm not sure what that makes me. 'Besides, sometimes it's good that they're not always looking my way. Yes!' Another goal slams in. He celebrates by rolling over onto his back and waving his legs in the air like a little kid. I give up and toss the control on the bed and flop backwards next to him. For reasons I'm not sure of, I feel like crying.

'One, two, three. Out you come.' Through the wall there's a grunt from Phil and another swoosh of water – him lifting her out, I guess.

Jim sits up and pokes me with his foot. 'Hey. You can't bail just cos you're getting thrashed.' I ignore him and stare at the ceiling. 'Rosie? Rosie? I didn't mean anything. Come on, don't sulk. We're getting on okay, aren't we?' I don't answer him, which I know is mean. I feel the bed bounce as he gets off it. 'Suit yourself.'

I lie on his bed for a few more minutes, not crying, listening to the sounds of the house, then sit up. I'm not going to behave like Mum, hiding away when things get tough. I go down and offer to help with tea.

39

Home Alone

ANNE

I TALK to no one for two days, except Stan. I know he hates having to speak directly to me; our normal mode of communication is a note tacked to the shed door, yet I hurry out to greet him as soon as he arrives. I keep him talking about the garden for as long as I can, about the moss in the lawn and the blight on the pear tree. I even ask about the latch on the back gate, which has been broken for years and really isn't his responsibility. As I rattle on at him, he keeps looking past me towards the shed with a silent yearning. Later on in the morning, when I take him out his second cup of coffee, he literally tries to hide from me by burrowing himself into the wisteria. He shouts at me to leave his mug on the wall as he tries to blend into the foliage. I step back inside the house and the silence is just where I left it. The emptiness seems to expand and grow heavier with every hour that she's absent. I check my phone again; still no reply to my last three texts, nothing since yesterday. I scroll back through what little she's told me over the past two days. *She's been shopping. She's been to play pool. She's fine.* I sit in the lounge and listen to the clock clicking slowly through the seconds and torment myself by wondering what they're doing, what I'm missing and what I'm failing so abjectly to compete against.

It will be noisy. James's music will be thudding from upstairs, Lauren's pre-school tunes will be trundling along on a loop, and in the kitchen the radio will be playing. Where will Rosie be? In the garden with Phil kicking a ball around, their banter cementing their growing bond, or in the kitchen, helping Sarah to cook, learning another version of a mum. A better one. Or, worse, they'll be out together somewhere, a day trip, maybe to the coast. Was it Scarborough or Sandsend that they *always* go to? A classic family day trip to the seaside, ice creams and beach cricket, with a granddad thrown in for good measure. Because that's what I'm up against: a whole family, not just Sarah and Phil, but a sporty brother, a doting grandparent and a wacky aunt. There's Lauren as well, she's the one ingredient in the mix that I'm fairly sure Rosie is less enamoured with, but it's still an unfair fight.

Against my better instincts I phone her. It goes to voicemail. I leave a nice, bright, cheery message.

When my phone finally pings, mid-afternoon, I snatch it up, but it's not from Rosie, it's from Steph, scarily intuitive as ever.

I've bashed together a lamb casserole for tonight. See you at about 6.30? S x I'm about to text my apologies when another message appears: White rather than red by preference. But you know me, I'll drink anything. See you soon. S xxx

As always, I let myself in; no one ever answers the door at Steph's. 'Hi,' Steph shouts. She's at the sink washing new potatoes, muddy water sloshing around in the bowl and onto her T-shirt. Her passion for her allotment is unabated by a year of backache, rain and veg-nibbling bugs. 'The corkscrew's in the drawer. I'll be with you in a minute.' It's not, it's in the draining rack, where it always is. I fetch three glasses. 'He's in the study – Tokyo. All hours. Grumpy as sin.'

Steph's casual, staccato rudeness towards her husband, Matt, masks a lot; a lot of love and mutual respect. They've been married for longer than I've been divorced, for the most part happily, despite Steph's perpetual grumbling and the occasional explosive argument. I've always envied them, deeply, not just for the obvious strength of their family, but for the atmosphere that prevails in their house. It's relaxed, easy-come, easy-go. They're always so uninhibited, irrespective of whether they're bickering or laughing or full-on arguing. Without asking, I pour a third glass and take it through to Matt, tapping lightly on the study door before entering. He smiles and beckons me in, not missing a beat in his conversation. I put his wine on his desk and glance at his computer screen, which is awash with stats and graphs. How he can do business dressed in baggy shorts and flip-flops, with half an eye on the cricket scores, is beyond me. I wander back through to the kitchen and start laying the table. I've never felt anything other than completely welcome at Steph's house. One of the family, even though I'm patently not.

When Matt gets off the phone we eat. Ellie and Greg are both around, so there's five of us, plus the dog. We drink wine and chat, and after the plates have been cleared away, we play cards. The kids seem happy to hang out with us. There's lots of good-natured banter and loud accusations of cheating. I don't manage to find a way of making my excuses until after 10.30 p.m.

When I get home I check my phone for the twentieth time. Still nothing from Rosie. I call her.

She picks up. 'Hi.'

'It's Mum.'

'Hi.'

'Did you get my messages?'

'Yeah.'

'I thought you might have had a chance to call me back.'

'We've been busy.'

'Doing something nice?'

'Yeah.' But she gives me no insight into what. Then her tone softens and she asks, 'Are you okay? Have you been doing much?' I fabricate a trip to Luton Hoo for lunch, and I try and make my trustee meeting sound funny, and I tell her about the meal with Steph and how badly Greg was cheating. She's silent as I babble away. Then she says, 'Given you're quite busy with stuff this week, would you mind if I stayed here a bit longer?' It's the calculation that hurts, almost as much as her desire to stay with them.

'Rosie, I really don't think that's a good idea. We said Wednesday.'

'Please.'

'Rosie, you don't want to overstay your welcome.'

There's silence on the line. When she speaks her voice is tight. 'I'm not. I *am* welcome here.'

'That wasn't what I meant, you know it wasn't.'

'But it's what you said.'

'Rosie, please?'

'Please what? I want to stay here.' She's like a child, defiant, petulant.

But I can't let her escape without a fight. I won't. 'Well, I'm sorry, but you can't. I'm picking you up, as planned.'

'I'm going to ask them if I can stay.'

'Rosie—' She hangs up on my objections.

I stare at my phone, willing her to call back, but she doesn't and after four, five, six minutes of hopeless waiting I decide not to call her. I know she'll not answer, and I can't face trying and being rejected for a second time. As I sit cradling my phone in my hand, I notice that I have new email from Nathan's solicitor that I've not opened. I click on it, knowing before I read it that it won't be anything good. It's not.

Dear Ms Elkan,

Nathan has asked us to get in touch with you to set up a review meeting to assess your financial settlement. Nathan would like to discuss the existing terms of reference and the schedule of payments. I believe there are also some issues relating to the maintenance arrangements that may need to be amended.

In light of the range of issues under consideration, a face-to-face meeting with yourself and legal representative[s] is required. If you could call my PA, Jackie Peyton, on 020 6780 1471, or email her on jackie.peyton@hamiltonandreynard.com, to let us know which dates you are available, that would be greatly appreciated.

We look forward to hearing from you very soon.

Yours sincerely,

Chris Marfleet

Another warning shot.

40

What's Right?

SARAH

PHIL GOES back into work on the Tuesday, Lauren goes off to holiday club, James heads over to Ryan's – allegedly to study, more likely just to chill out – and Rosie lies in for most of the morning. The house is blissfully quiet. I actually manage to get a few hours of work done. It's not until lunchtime that Rosie finally appears, her face creased from sleep and her hair a shaggy mess. She offers to get us both something to eat. I watch as she opens cupboards and drawers, retrieving plates and cutlery. She knows where everything 'lives' now. It's relaxed, almost normal. We listen to the radio, I work and she stirs beans in a pan. It's only for the sake of something to say that I ask her what she's got planned when she gets home. I immediately sense the atmosphere shift.

'Nothing.'

'Aren't you going to meet up with your friends? You must've missed seeing them this holiday.' I close down my laptop.

She studies me, then out of nowhere she asks, 'Can I stay? Until the weekend? I don't have to go home.'

I'm thrown. 'But your mum's coming to pick you up tomorrow.'

'Please?'

Again the sudden shift to small child unnerves me. I feel the familiar, uncomfortable rush of contradictory emotions; there's the pleasure that she wants to be with us and the relief that we're getting somewhere, but stronger by far is the fear that it's all moving too fast. 'I know it's hard, Rosie. And I know we need to agree something more definite about how often we see you, but that's going to take some time to sort out.'

She isn't listening. 'But I want to stay here.'

'What about your mum?'

'You don't understand. I can't talk to her. I've never been able to.'

'Rosie, you have to have some patience.' That ignites her.

'Please!' Her ferocity has an edge of hysteria to it. 'Please. Ask Phil. Please, ring him and ask him. Just for the rest of this week. There's nothing for me to go home for.' It's such a stark statement.

For the lack of any other solution, I do. I step into the garden to make the call, conscious that she's watching me, pretending to wash up at the sink. I turn away to avoid her gaze. The dial tone buzzes in my ear, but Phil doesn't answer. I leave him a message expressing Rosie's wishes, glossed with my uncertainty. When I finish I don't hang up; I keep the phone to my ear, faking the call, to buy myself some time. Again the sense of being pressurised by Rosie swamps me. I watch next door's cat pick its way delicately across the weed-choked flowerbeds at the bottom of the garden and, as I stand there, the certainty grows within me that she needs to go home, that we have to stick to some sort of rules. Her life is there, our life is here, we can't just smash the two together and expect it all to work out fine, whatever Phil thinks. It's chilly in the shade of the house, but still I stand there, unable to face my daughter and tell her that I want to send her away because I need some space to breathe.

When I step back into the kitchen, Rosie immediately drops whatever she's washing in the sink and comes towards me. 'Well?'

'He's in an office full of people, so we couldn't really talk, but we will tonight when he gets home, I promise.' It's enough to placate her.

She comes closer and reaches out towards me, putting her hand palm-flat against my sleeve. It's an odd, awkward gesture. 'Thank you,' she mumbles. When she steps away, I look down and see the faint print of her hand outlined on my shirt.

Our 'talk' that evening is an uneven, unresolved thing. Rosie grows increasingly adamant. 'But I can't think of her as my real mum any more, so why do I have to live with her?'

We acknowledge all her arguments and listen to her confused emotions, and I ache for the loneliness that lies behind everything she says, but I still try and get her to think about her life and how she can't just walk away from all the things that support her, without there being a cost. Phil keeps talking about it in terms of the end goal. 'It can't all be straight away, Rosie. Like Sarah said, school – especially this year – is important. And there's your football and all your friends.' There's the implication, however, in everything that he says that she will, eventually, somehow, be with us.

As we stumble around what could or might be possible, I'm conscious of the empty seat at the table. Anne. The presence of three unanswered texts on my phone from her is a reminder, should I need one, that she has as much riding on this conversation as anyone. It seems wrong that we're even talking about this without her having a voice, but when I mention her, Rosie grows even more emotional and irrational, and Phil is brutally indifferent. But it nags at me. We can't just take Rosie away from Anne. It's too cruel. I can't let it go. I push for us trying to arrange things in agreement with her and I stress, over and over again, how much better it will be if we can sort things out amicably and fairly. It's only when I argue that it will be much quicker to deal direct with Anne, rather than having to go through the lawyers, that I get a more conciliatory response. The threat of Callum getting involved seems to hit home. Phil and Rosie share a deep dislike of him, but my motives are complex and conflicting. We finally agree to start by asking Anne for regular, scheduled weekend visits across term time, and longer stays in the holidays, and Phil promises Rosie that we will raise the possibility of joint custody.

By 8.30 p.m. we've talked ourselves out of words and compromises and emotions. Phil takes Lauren up to bed, late, and I take the house phone out into the garden. I sit on the bench and try and compose myself before I make the call. The sound of my mobile vibrating rattles me. I stare at it, acutely conscious that Anne is on the line, no doubt wondering why we've left it so late to contact her about the arrangements for tomorrow. I listen to her message. She sounds understandably anxious about the lack of contact from us, and from Rosie. I steel myself and call her back.

And it goes okay, or at least as well as it could have, given that I'm effectively telling her that her daughter is refusing to go home, for now. I expect anger, but when Anne eventually speaks, her voice is thick with sadness, not bitterness. I apologise, more than once, and I try and make amends. I try and reassure her that we're not encouraging Rosie, that we are trying to get her to take things slowly, think things through, not rush into any big changes when everything is still so raw and new and confusing. How much that is true, I'm not sure, and how much these are my feelings rather than Rosie's, I'm not ready to acknowledge, but somehow the empathy between us is enough to help us stumble our way around the mess.

'When can I come and fetch her, then?' I can hear the hurt in Anne's voice.

'Friday, maybe?' Rosie can't have everything that she wants.

There's a long pause. 'Well, if you can cope with her being with you, I suppose it's okay. I can't force her to come home, can I?'

I don't know what to respond. I just want the conversation to end. Then Anne asks meekly, 'Sarah, do you think we could perhaps meet up? To talk? Just the two of us?'

'Of course,' I say, though there's no 'of course' about it.

'Thank you. I think it would help. Perhaps if I came up to Leeds, on Thursday? I'll book into a hotel. I wouldn't want to impose on you. We could try and see if we can agree how to handle Rosie. Sorry, I don't mean "handle", but you know what I mean. Maybe we can work something out between us.'

Perhaps we can. Because whatever Phil feels, and whatever Rosie thinks she wants, Anne is a mother struggling with her daughter, and that I can identify with. In the end we agree to meet at her hotel to talk properly. Disloyal as it is, I know it will be better if Phil and Rosie aren't there. I say goodbye and end the call, feeling hollow, but at least we now have a plan.

We go to bed late and tired. I'm relieved to switch off the light, welcoming the thought of sleep or at least a respite from thinking, but Phil isn't finished. 'Do you think that joint custody is enough?'

I'm so tired of it. 'Do we have to talk about this now?'

'Well, you can't sit down with Anne unless we're clear about what we want.'

'Precisely,' I snap.

'What do you mean?'

'I mean, yes, *I* will need to be clear before *I* sit down and talk with her. Before *I* try and come up with some sort of compromise that is bearable for all of us.' He's silent for a few seconds and I regret my sharp tone. 'Phil, please. I just think it's too much to tackle Anne with, all at once.'

'I don't understand you sometimes, Sarah.' His voice contains genuine bewilderment.

I don't think I can make him fully understand, but he's waiting, so I try. 'I just don't know what's right.' I push myself up against the pillows, accepting that I'm not going to sleep anytime soon, and we whisper to each other in the dark.

'What do you mean, "right"?'

'I mean right for us, and for Anne, and for Rosie. And that means I don't think we should just agree to everything Rosie wants. We're her parents. It's up to us to make the right decisions for her. She's not really in a stable enough frame of mind to know what's in her own best interests at the moment, is she? She's a teenage girl, a very confused teenage girl, with so many conflicting desires and emotions running through her. We don't want her deciding something that she later regrets.'

'But she's our daughter and she's unhappy.' It's that simple to Phil.

'I know. And I want her to be happy, but that can't be at the cost of everyone else. We owe Anne that much, at least. She has let us keep Lauren without a fight. That has to count for something. We can't take Rosie from her as well.'

I wait for his response, but it doesn't come. We sit in the dark, separated by our differences, while the house creaks and shifts around us, our battered old house that is having to stretch and expand to accommodate so much. Loneliness seeps into me, a faint but frightening echo of the bad days when the chasm between Phil and me was too wide to breach. I can feel us straining apart again and it scares me. Phil shifts position, away not towards me, and the gap tugs wider.

41

Talking

ANNE

THERE'S NOWHERE lonelier than a big hotel, if you're checking in alone. The lobby of the place I've booked in Leeds is big and flashy and full of the twanging voices of a group of American tourists. The receptionist doesn't pause in tapping away at her keyboard as she takes my credit card, checks me in and exhorts me, above the cacophony, to *Enjoy your stay*. My room, on the sixth floor, is perfectly nice, perfectly bland and imperfectly quiet. It takes me four minutes to unpack and three to freshen up. By 12.24 p.m. I'm sitting on the bed listening to the muted sounds of the city beyond my double-glazed window, wondering what I can do to occupy myself until 6.30 p.m., the agreed time for Sarah's visit. I click on the TV and watch a fruitless antique hunt and the news. By 1.30 p.m. I can't face it any more. I grab my bag and my jacket and I head back downstairs. The lobby is now empty, the sound of piped harp music audible alongside the relentless tap-tap of the receptionist. Through the revolving doors I can see the rush and blur of people on the streets. I consider joining them, but the effort is beyond me.

The barman is polite as he pushes a single glass of red wine across the counter to me. The bar itself is quiet, just me and a scatter of businessmen. They glance up from their phones and laptops as I pass, but their cool scrutiny quickly turns to disinterest. I retreat into a corner, place my solitary drink and my phone on the table in front of me and bide my time. My phone doesn't make a sound. I'm not in demand, not required to mutter urgent instructions to some colleague in the US or bash out terse emails to keep the wheels of commerce turning. I take slow sips of my thin wine and hope that the alcohol will relax me.

I've received nothing from Rosie since our row. I've texted her, repeatedly, and have left her a number of messages, all of them light and airy and non-demanding, letting her know that I love her and that I understand. That's all I can do: hide my own feelings, tiptoe around her and pray that the bond between us is stronger than it looks. Just like the old days with Nathan... and I'm fully aware of how that played out. I take another sip. The wine tastes metallic and sour in my mouth. I know that she's drawn to their sloppy warmth, that she likes that there are five of them reflecting and deflecting each other's energy. I know our lovely, large, but empty house is no competition. And there is Phil, the real prize for her, a fully functioning, loving father. The opposite of Nathan.

Nathan and I were together for seven years. That's all. But his mark is imprinted on me. I'm still a version of the woman that he wanted, moulded, then discarded. My actions are still being dictated by his desires. He still has control. Why else would I be here, alone in a hotel, cringing and placating the Rudaks, for fear of what they might do or say? Why aren't I fighting, screaming and shouting that Rosie is mine and they cannot have her.

It's because I know the truth about myself. I don't deserve her. I am not enough on my own. I never have been and I never will be. Rosie, like Nathan, can see through me and she knows there's something missing.

I am not a good mother.

I drain the dregs of my wine, run the gauntlet of male eyes and go back up to my room, where I lie on the bed and await Sarah and my fate.

SARAH

I'm anxious about my meeting with Anne, it hangs over me, a dark shadow that chills only me. Phil sees Anne as nothing more than an obstacle. I see her as my mirror.

I call Phil. It's a short conversation. He's driving, it's not a good time to talk. I hang up, feeling adrift. I ask Rosie to keep an eye on Lauren and go out into the garden, where I ring Ali, feeling the need for some moral support. She's her usual brutal, uncompromising, loving self. 'Don't let the Wicked Witch of the South screw with you. Remember she's the one who's turned her back on Lauren, so you don't owe her any favours over Rosie.' It's odd how the same deed can be judged so differently, depending on your point of view. Ali asks, 'When are you seeing her?' When I tell her, she immediately insists on meeting me at the hotel. 'It's round the corner from work. We can go for a drink afterwards, to celebrate the slaying of the witch.' I barely protest; the thought of having Ali as my wingman is reassuring.

Phil comes home early and follows me around as I get ready to go, reminding me about what *we* want to get out of the conversation. In the end it's a relief to get out of the house, away from his instructions and from Rosie's imploring silence.

The Metropole has been done up since I was last inside it. It's now all polished wood, new upholstery and huge flower arrangements, the upmarket ambience is completed by the plinking of harp music. The lacquered receptionist rings up to Anne's room. 'I have a guest at reception for you, Ms Elkan.' Pause. 'Yes, of course.' She puts the phone down, with her immaculate talons. 'She asks that you go up. Room six-four-nine. Sixth floor. The lifts are just to your left through the doors.' She smiles for a fraction of a second, then returns to tapping at her keyboard. Ali says she'll go into the bar and wait for me. It's a comfort to know she's there.

It's a quiet walk down the corridor. I don't see any other guests. I knock and wait, feeling uncomfortable; it's like the setting for an assignation rather than an awkward, impossible conversation about the fate of a child. The door opens quickly, almost as if Anne's been standing right behind it, and she gestures me in. She points me towards the only chair. The room is unnaturally tidy. She seems to have eradicated all evidence that she's staying there. There are no clothes in sight, nothing on the bedside tables, I can't even see her handbag. The bed is pristine. Anne herself looks as smart as ever, overdressed for the occasion, in a skirt and a silk top, but on a closer look I can see that her make-up is a little too heavy. It gives her face an oddly rigid look. The powder has gathered in the creases at the corners of her mouth, and her colour is sickly beneath her blusher. As she settles herself on the edge of the bed and crosses her ankles, I see that her hair at the back is flattened, as if she's been lying down. But she seems as composed as ever. 'Thank you so much for coming. I think you were right to suggest that we got together, on our own, to talk things through.' I remember it being Anne's suggestion, but I let it go.

I'm nervous. The connection between us seems loose and faulty again. 'Yes. I'm sorry that Rosie has been so… upset and uncommunicative. I have tried to get her to call you.' I feel awkward apologising for her daughter, but Anne doesn't appear to notice.

She clears her throat before she speaks. 'I know we need to talk about how we're going to handle things with Rosie, but before we do that, I really want to try and explain my decision regarding Lauren. Would that be all right?'

'Of course.' I was right not to come with Phil. He'd have no patience with this.

She composes herself. 'I feel I owe you a proper explanation. It was such a big decision.' But then she dries. I wait. 'I was trying to do what was best for Lauren. That's what motivated me – doing what seemed right for her.'

'I understand that, Anne, I really do, and as you've known all along, I just couldn't imagine a life without Lauren. The thought of any big changes was very unsettling for me, and Phil, and for James.'

'Yes, but it's important that I'm honest with you. It wasn't just Lauren, it was me.' She swallows. 'The problem is me. I just don't believe that I have the skills to cope. You and Phil are so good with her; what you do for her, it's so admirable, so impressive. I wouldn't be able to come close, not on my own.'

'I understand.' I truly do.

She makes an odd, fluttering gesture with her hand. 'No, I don't think you do. You have a good marriage, a good husband.' It sounds like an accusation rather than an acknowledgement. 'Nathan has never been that. I've never had that. I've had to raise Rosie on my own. He pays, but that's it. He's always been very insistent on what he will and will not tolerate, in terms of any demands on his time or his attention.' I keep silent, for fear of offending her. 'And that's something I need to speak with you about.' I wait. 'I gather you've been in touch with my ex-husband.'

That pulls me up short. I've been trying to forget that I did such a stupid thing. I don't know what I was hoping to achieve, but there's no denying that I did it, as she obviously knows. 'Yes. I sent him a picture of Lauren.'

'So I gather.' She swallows again. 'Sarah, I understand why you can't comprehend his actions, or his motives. I'm sure most people wouldn't, but it really was pointless getting in touch with him. He won't get involved. He has another life. Rosie and I, and Lauren, we don't fit into it. You mustn't take it personally.' Anne ploughs on. 'He's adamant that he wants no direct contact with Lauren. He isn't capable of caring, Sarah – it's not in his nature.'

Which, in hindsight, is exactly what I want. We look at each other for a moment, both of us, I suspect, reflecting on the shittiness of her ex-husband. Then a thought occurs to me. 'When did you talk to him?' I ask. 'You said that you never spoke.' I'm not sure why I'm bothered. Maybe it's something to do with Anne and Rosie's shared comfort with half-truths.

She blinks. 'I don't normally, but he rang me after you emailed him.'

'Why did he ring you? Why not contact me?'

Her face stiffens. 'I've just told you, he doesn't want to get involved.' There's a brittle edge to her voice now, which grates on me. I wasn't prepared for all this. I was expecting to talk about Rosie, not Lauren, and certainly not about Nathan. Her focus on him after all these years seems out of proportion, almost obsessive. Watching her, I can see that she's getting agitated. She stands up and starts pacing around the room, avoiding looking at me. 'I can't answer for him, Sarah. He's a cold man and he can be cruel. Trust me, you're better off not having any contact with him. Truly you are. I'm not denying Lauren is my child. I'm not. I know she's my daughter.' She seems to think that I'm accusing her of something. I'm not, but it makes no difference to her mounting distress. Her voice becomes high and breathy and she pulls at the skin of her throat. 'But I just can't cope with it any more, I can't. I'm sorry, but I can't. It's not just having to decide about Lauren – it's Rosie. I'm losing Rosie and she's all I've got. And now there's Nathan.' She starts scratching at her neck, raising red lines on the pale skin. 'He's absolutely furious, again. He's threatening to make life very difficult for me, for us, maybe even for you. Please, Sarah.' She suddenly rushes across the room and leans over me, her face unnervingly close to mine. 'You mustn't make it worse. You must promise me that you won't try to contact him again.' I'm alarmed. Her breathing is snatched and noisy. 'I can't.' She starts rasping, clawing at her throat. 'Sarah, I can't breathe.'

I know it's a panic attack. She can breathe, she is breathing, that's what all the gasping is, but the look of terror in her eyes is genuine. She thinks she's choking. I try to calm her down.

'Anne, listen to me.' I place my hands on hers and gently pull them away from her throat, revealing the lattice of scratch marks on her neck. 'You're having a panic attack. You just need to get a bit more oxygen into your lungs.' Her grip on my fingers is vice-like. She fixes her eyes on me and nods, but if anything her breathing gets worse, shorter and shallower. It sounds horribly loud. I inject as much calmness into my voice as possible. 'Anne, listen to me, you need to try and breathe more slowly. No, Anne, slowly.' But she doesn't; her breaths become more snatched and ineffective. I'm having no effect on her at all. Her colour is dreadful. 'Wait here.' She looks panic-stricken as I leave, assuming, I suppose, that I'm abandoning her. I wedge my bag in the door to keep it open and hurry downstairs.

The receptionist is no use whatsoever. Eventually the manager finds a big brown envelope in the back office. It's probably fifteen minutes before I get back up to her room. She's still struggling. I can hear her rasping breaths as the lift doors open. She is kneeling on the floor, clutching at the bed covers. She looks very frightened.

'Anne, breathe into this.' She grabs my hand and I guide the scrunched-up envelope to her lips. 'Now, breathe. Slowly. There you go. Keep going. Good. That's better.'

It's an old trick, but it works. Her breathing gradually slows and she grows less frantic. In and out, in and out, each breath gets deeper and less snatched, until at long last her breathing steadies. We sit on the floor side by side as she slowly calms down. After a few minutes I take my hands away and she holds the envelope in place herself. In and out, in and out. Without thinking, I stroke her back to soothe her. After another few minutes she lowers the envelope from her blue-tinged lips and breathes normally.

'Thank you.' Her voice is soft and colourless. She shuffles around and leans her head back against the bed. She looks wrecked. The room settles back into silence. As much as I know she's exhausted and in no fit state to have a rational conversation about anything, some of Ali's steel enters my soul. This is my one chance to speak truthfully with Anne. I can't let it slip by, just because she's had a meltdown. There is something here that doesn't add up.

I ask gently, but firmly, 'Anne, why is Nathan furious with you? You said he was furious with you, *again*.' When she doesn't respond I stroke her hand, trying to draw her back into the room. I'm surprised at how kind and concerned I sound. She rolls her head against the edge of the bed and closes her eyes. I try one more time. 'Anne, it's okay, you can tell me. What did you do?'

42

What's True

ANNE

OXYGEN BEGINS to creep back into my lungs. It hurts, but I can breathe again. Sarah sits quietly, holding my hand. I close my eyes. Everything grows still.

Sarah's voice is quiet and calm. It reaches inside me. 'Anne...' she says, 'it's okay, you can tell me. What did you do?'

And because I can't bear it any more, because I simply cannot endure the loneliness of it for one more day, I tell her. I tell her every tiny detail that I've replayed in my head a thousand times before...

'It was the day you were discharged from hospital. Do you remember, we sat together and waited for Phil?' It sounds odd to finally hear the words out loud. 'You were packed, ready to go, sitting on your bed. So very pale, your lips chapped and flaky. We talked in fits and starts about nothing and, as we talked, I watched your baby sleeping, her little chest rising and falling with each breath.'

I feel Sarah let go of my hand.

'One of the nurses came by and cut off her identification labels, and yours, with those weird scissors they have, the ones with the blades that bend upwards. Right there, right in front of me, precise little snips, taking care not to nick the skin. You put your own labels on the side table. I remember you made a joke about having your price tag cut off. You put the baby ones in your bag, a memento. Then the nurse checked the discharge paperwork and your tablets. There was something wrong with the dose they'd given you. She cursed under her breath and bustled off to sort it out.

'You started talking about the future, about trying to get back to normal and how hard it was going to be. You were worrying about James and how you'd manage once you went back to work – the travelling, childcare, stuff like that. You were already trying to map it all out. You kept looking at your watch. You started stressing about your meds not being ready. I suggested you went and asked. You left it for another five minutes, then you decided you would go and see where the nurse had got to. You eased yourself off the bed, very carefully, and looked into the crib. She was fast asleep.

'It was a genuine offer. I said I'd watch her.'

Sarah makes a choked noise and draws in a sharp, shallow breath.

'You did hesitate. You glanced back at us before you left the ward.' I pause, then go on, because I have to. 'I picked her up and I walked along to my room, just another mum with her baby. I put Rosie on the bed and lifted Lauren out of her crib. I laid them side by side. They were the same size. They had the same dark, soft, tufty hair. I unpopped Rosie's Babygro and vest, then Lauren's. I noticed their nappies were different, so I swapped them. I remember the tabs didn't stick very well. I was careful getting Lauren's name-tags off. The ankle one I managed to ease off without too much trouble, but not the one on her wrist. I had to use my nail scissors.

'I was very careful not to hurt her.

'Then I swapped their clothes, quickly. Neither of them got cold. I put Rosie in the crib in my room. She didn't cry. And before I could change my mind I picked Lauren up and carried her "back" to the ward.'

Sarah says nothing, but I can feel the tension pulsing through her.

'You weren't back. I sat with her on my knee until you returned and, when you did, you simply lifted her away from me and we waited quietly. You stroked Lauren's downy little head. I watched you stroke my baby's head and it was almost as if I hadn't done anything.'

I hear Sarah's breathing grow faster and shallower.

'Phil arrived. He was flustered, he'd had to leave the car somewhere he shouldn't. You tried to put Lauren into the car seat. You struggled with the straps and Phil got agitated. I offered to hold her, one last time. Then the nurse checked your medicines, again, and finally it was all sorted. You hugged me goodbye. I kept my hands in my dressing-gown pockets, gripping onto a little tin of lip balm. I gave it to you as a parting gift. The nurse escorted you off the ward and you left and took her away. And it was done and couldn't be undone.'

I have to get to the end.

'I went and sat in my room. I didn't pick her up. She lay with her eyes fluttering open and shut, and I waited. I waited for you to realise and come back. I knew it couldn't work. I resigned myself to the anger and the drama and the punishment. I just sat there and waited for the inevitable chaos.

'But you didn't come back.

'It grew dark. Lights went on. A nurse looked in on us. I said we were fine. Rosie started snuffling, then crying. That broke the spell. I picked her up and tried to comfort her, but she needed milk, not soothing. Her crying built and spiralled: angry, demanding, hungry wailing. I was worried a nurse might come to see what was happening. So I fed her. My milk flowed into her, making her mine.'

I stop.

There is no screaming, no rending of the heavens, no swift summary justice. The room is silent and still.

What I feel is relief, a great, powerful, cleansing flood of relief.

I want to curl up right there, on the floor, close my eyes and go to sleep.

SARAH

I don't interrupt her. I daren't, in case she stops. She gets to the end. After a long silence she says quietly, 'I'm so tired.'

I'm numb. Any other response is beyond me. Bizarrely, I still feel the need to help her somehow. A residue of caring. 'Why don't you lie down?' Like a child instructed to take a nap, she clambers up onto the bed and lies down, facing away from me. I retreat to the chair. The pale soles of her stockinged feet snag my attention, reminding me, for reasons I can't even begin to fathom, of my Mum.

When she speaks her voice is hypnotically calm. 'That has been eating away at me for the past fifteen years.'

It's quiet in the room. The ping of the lift arriving and departing punctuates the silence. Inertia overwhelms me. Her confession sinks in, slowly, heavily; the weight of it, the enormity of what she did. I sit on the chair looking at her and she lies on the bed looking away. Neither of us moves.

The buzz of an incoming text startles me. It's Ali: Are u ok? You've been up there ages. Do you want me to come up?

I can't face Ali. I can't leave this room, where Anne and I are suspended, in purgatory. Not yet.

I text Ali back: No. I'll come down. Wait there for me.

Anne hasn't moved. She's so still I don't know whether she's even awake. The thought that she could sleep stirs an ember of rage. 'Anne!' My voice is sharp and loud. It cracks the atmosphere. She rolls over and pushes herself upright on the bed. I stare at her and see a delicate, opaque image of Anne, the woman I've grown so familiar with over the past few weeks, the woman I've allowed into our lives, who I've defended, felt sympathy for and whose pain I've shared; and inside her, I see something black and ugly and hard. The truth.

'Why? Why did you do it?'

She looks straight at me and says quietly, but very clearly, 'I knew there was something wrong with her.' It's as simple and awful as that.

I feel punched. She carried Lauren for nine months, gave birth to her, held her in her arms, then she rejected her. Words fail me, but Anne can speak. She can voice the unconscionable. 'My job, before I was married. That's what I did all day. I typed up the consultants' notes. I used to collate all the medical assessments for the paediatric team. Down's syndrome, cerebral palsy, cleft palates, the whole gamut of things that can go wrong with a baby, if you're one of the unlucky ones.' She keeps talking, words spilling out of her, in some sort of compulsive confession. 'I spent my whole pregnancy having nightmares that my child would have something wrong with it, that my baby wasn't going to be healthy. Nathan said I was being ridiculous, but I knew... I knew as soon as I saw her thumbs, and the mark on her forehead, that I was one of the unlucky ones.' Her self-obsession is breathtaking.

'So you got rid of her?'

'I didn't plan it.'

'But you did it.'

'Yes.' The word hangs in the air.

My brain is scrambling to catch up with what she's saying, to regain some degree of equity with her. 'Does Nathan know what you did?'

'Yes.' Again her newfound compulsion to be honest knocks me back.

'From the beginning?'

Her voice is monotone. 'No. He found out when Rosie was three.' At last she drops her gaze.

'How?' I want to know. I need to know it all.

She's no longer really talking to me. 'He would have left me anyway. He wanted rid of me by then. I told him to hurt him. He was appalled, furious. He couldn't believe that I'd done something so stupid, so reckless.'

I look at her bowed head and struggle to accept that this nightmare is a by-product of Anne's warped relationship with a man who left her more than a decade ago. She's still talking, to herself. 'He's worried it will all come out and he'll be under suspicion. It will damage him, professionally, very badly.' Finally she falls silent. Her hands lie lifeless in her lap.

'Fuck him!'

She flinches. I'm struggling for control. She sits on the bed, passive, awaiting judgement, and I hate her. I hate her self-obsession. I hate her calmness. I hate the fury that she has stirred inside me. And I hate that I have no idea what I'm going to do with the bitter, black truth she's just spewed out. The adrenaline that's been building up inside my body pumps through me, smashing into nerves and skin, finding no release.

'What are you going to do?' She isn't pleading. She asks as if she no longer cares.

I don't answer. I suddenly, violently, want to get as far away from her as possible. I stand up, grab my bag and walk out. As I pull the door shut, she doesn't move. My last glimpse is of a dishevelled, passive, broken woman who is not the victim of chaos. She's the cause.

*

I'm outside, stumbling down the street, when I hear my name. 'Sarah! Sarah! Wait.' But I don't. I want to put as much space between Anne and me as I can, so I keep moving, running across one road, then another, blind to my surroundings. I have no idea where I'm heading, nor do I care. Ali eventually catches up with me at the big intersection when I step back onto the pavement just in time to avoid getting flattened by a truck. She grabs hold of my wrist. 'Sarah! Calm down. What the hell's happened?' She pulls me away from the edge of the kerb and keeps tugging me along after her, until we find a bench. 'Sit down. What is it? What's wrong?'

'Sorry.' That's all I can manage. She releases her grip and instead takes hold of my hand. 'Sorry,' I mumble again. I feel sweaty and cold. Hot and breathless from running, but at the same time chilled to the bone by Anne's awful truth.

'Wait here. Don't you dare move,' Ali barks at me. She slips off her jacket and drapes it across my shoulders before dashing across the road. A few minutes later she forces a paper cup in my hands: tea. The heat leaks through the ridged cardboard into my stiff fingers. 'Sip it. It's hot.' I do as I'm told.

I sit next to her, anchoring myself to her, and she waits patiently for me to explain why I'm behaving like a lunatic. As the rush-hour traffic stop-starts past us, I tell her, 'It was her. From the moment she started talking, I knew. It wasn't the hospital. It was Anne. It was never a mistake.' And out it pours: Anne's confession, her pathetic justification and her self-pity. As I'm talking Ali puts her arm around me and swears softly and repeatedly. 'The bitch. The fucking, evil bitch!'

A welter of thoughts coil and spiral in my brain. Everything I thought I knew is wrong. Every reaction I've had has been mis-directed. Everything she said was a lie. And I believed her.

Ali is white with rage. 'You need to ring the police. Do it, ring them. I'd do it, right now. She stole Rosie. She stole your life. I can't get my head round it. All this time. Seriously, I can't. It's unbeliev-able.' She goes quiet for a second, but I can still feel the energy vibrating through her. Then she says, 'Jesus! Phil is going to go crazy.'

The thought of telling Phil makes me feel sick; of telling Rosie… of telling James. I go blank. I can't. The thought of walking into the house and lobbing this at them – another bomb blast, more carnage, more wreckage – I can't. I won't.

I straighten up, crushing the cup into a tight, hard wad in my fist, and ask what time it is. My voice sounds remarkably normal. Ali scrambles her phone out of her pocket. 'Ten to eight.'

It's late. I'm late.

'I need to go home.' I stand up, hand Ali her jacket and set off in the direction of the car. 'I want to say goodnight to Lauren before she settles.'

Ali chases after me, clearly bemused by my sudden shift of focus. 'Sarah, wait!'

But I keep going. 'Ali. I need to go home. That's what I'm going to do, just go home. And that's all I'm going to do tonight.' She starts to remonstrate, but I hold up my hand, stopping her. 'No, Ali. This is my call. I'm not going to say anything tonight, and you mustn't either, to anyone.' And I speed up, making her hurry to stay with me as we race back to the car.

She insists on coming back with me. She won't take no for an answer and I haven't the strength to argue. I can feel her staring at me as I drive. We barely speak. There's too much to process. After twenty minutes of cautious, careful driving I pull up outside the house. Most of the windows are open, lights blazing from each room, and I can see the TV flickering in the lounge. Another normal night at home. I brace myself. Nothing feels like it will ever be normal again.

'Sarah. Seriously. You can maybe get through tonight without saying anything, but what are you going to do after that?' Ali asks.

'I honestly don't know.' It's such an inadequate response, but it's the truth. She's seems about to say something more, but checks herself. I pull down the sunshade and look at myself in the mirror, scrubbing my finger across the thin, crêpey skin under my eyes to get rid of the mascara smudges. 'Do I look all right?' I ask, turning to her. What I mean is… *Do I look normal?*

'Yes,' she declares loyally.

'Good.' I snap the mirror back up. 'But, Ali, not a word when we go in. I don't want you to say anything about any of this. Not yet. And nothing to Jess, when you get home. You must promise me.' I stare at her, knowing full well that I'm extracting a dreadful, almost impossible promise from her. Eventually she nods. We climb out of the car and head inside, united by a truth that's so awful I have no idea what to do with it.

ANNE

After Sarah's gone, I doze. The rumble of the shower in the next-door bathroom is soothing. I don't move from the bed. The room darkens. I think about the pack of pills in the bedside drawer, but even that seems too much effort. The knot has been untied and it will unravel of its own accord. I don't need to hold it tight any longer. I reach down and untuck the covers from the end of the bed, pull them up to my neck and go to sleep.

PHIL

Sarah is late back and, for reasons I can't fathom, she has Ali with her. They both seem subdued. Ali only stays for about an hour, and most of that she spends upstairs, 'reading' with Lauren. While she's up there, Sarah and I grab ten minutes alone in the kitchen. I'm anxious to know how it went with Anne.

Sarah says that it was difficult, but she thinks we'll be able to get things resolved. She is, however, reluctant to go into the details of what they actually agreed. She keeps batting away my questions with vague reassurances and her familiar mantra that 'These things take time'. I feel frustration begin to fizz in my gut.

'But do you think she's going to put up a fight over us having shared custody?'

Sarah grows still. She looks smaller, paler than usual; in fact she looks completely done in. 'It's early days. There's a lot to sort out.' I decide to leave off badgering her. She's bearing the brunt of this, and me chipping away at her isn't helpful. I step forward, intending to give her a hug, but she avoids my embrace. When she speaks again her voice is surprisingly firm and resolute. 'Phil, I promise you. We will get what we want. We'll get what's right. For us and for Rosie… in the end.'

It's the first time I've heard such certainty from her. Despite my best intentions, I push a little harder, testing her resolve. 'What about what Anne wants?' Sarah's empathy with Anne has always been the stumbling block.

She looks past me for a moment, out at the garden, her expression stony. 'She'll just have to accept that Rosie wants to be with us. We're her family now.'

That really throws me. I'm pleased and impressed, but I'm also slightly stunned. Sarah appears to have travelled a very long way in one conversation. I wonder what Anne said, or did, to provoke such a response. It can't have been good. Sarah then adds, almost as if it's not newsworthy, that Rosie is definitely staying until Sunday. Rosie will be delighted. I'm delighted. Christ, what did Anne say? I'm just about to find out when Ali comes downstairs to say 'goodbye'; she's followed into the kitchen by Rosie, her hair wet from her shower, then by James, who starts rummaging around for snacks in the cupboards. Then Sarah chooses that precise moment to remember that it's bin collection day tomorrow. And so family life swallows up the end of our conversation, and whatever Anne did or said goes untold.

I whistle as I haul the dustbins out to the kerb. Rosie is staying, Sarah and I are finally on the same page and Anne is relegated to the margins, exactly where she should be. Things are looking up.

When I come back into the lounge. James is eating a bag of tortillas and Rosie is sitting on the floor, with Sarah on the sofa behind, brushing her hair. It strikes me that we look like a family from a TV ad, which makes me smile. I sit and enjoy the simple pleasure of having us all together.

We don't go up until nearly midnight. In the bedroom Sarah shrugs out of her clothes slowly, like an old woman. The itch to know about what went on with Anne is strong, but far stronger is my faith in my wife and my concern about what all this stress is doing to her. She climbs into bed, lies down and pulls the duvet up around her. I know there's more to come out. Something went on between her and Anne tonight, something that changed the dynamic between the two of them dramatically, but it can wait. Sarah will tell me in her own time. I know she will. Sarah is not a keeper of secrets.

After I switch off the light, Sarah rolls towards me, wordlessly seeking me out. I put my arms around her and she buries into my embrace.

ROSIE

I lie in Jim's room listening to the house creak. I'm so happy that I can stay. I need to, because the more time I spend with them, the more normal it feels. And I want it to feel normal. I want it to feel like home. I hear Lauren shuffle around in her bed through our adjoining wall. She settles and starts snoring. Even Lauren is beginning to seem normal to me now. Because she is. Lauren is Lauren. She's their daughter, and James's sister, and me being here is never going to change that. I thought it needed to, but it doesn't.

I am fitting in. They are fitting me in.

Tonight when Sarah said, 'Do you want me to brush your hair for you?' I was thrown. I hate anyone touching my hair. I have done ever since I was little and Mum used to spend hours yanking knots out of it, trying to tame it into the perfect bun for ballet. But I said 'yes' because I knew I needed to. To start with, I felt self-conscious sitting so close to her, but after a while I relaxed. She was gentle, holding the tangled hair away from my head as she brushed so that it didn't pull at the roots, and easing out the knots with her fingers, patiently. Once it was smooth she brushed it slowly, rhythmically, keeping going long after she needed to.

I didn't want to destroy the nice, relaxed mood, but I had to ask how it went with Mum. It made it easier that she was sitting behind me. She answered me quietly, as if she didn't want Phil and James listening. 'It wasn't easy.' She stroked the brush through my hair again. 'But we will work it out. I know you need clarity about the future. And I know I've not always been… very sure about how things should be arranged. But I absolutely, faithfully promise you that I'm going to do everything I can to make it right.'

Something about the way she said it made me believe her. I said, 'Thank you' and for a moment I leant back against her legs and we had a curious kind of hands-free hug. The warmth of her body pressed against mine felt good. Then she went back to brushing my hair.

I roll onto my front and search around in the bed, but Dog's not there, so I hang over the edge of the mattress and sweep my hands around among James's assortment of crap. Eventually I find Dog lying next to a pair of Jim's trainers, under the bed. I shake the fluff balls off him, then hug him to my chest, running my fingers through his tatty fur. Here in this cramped little house, in Jim's cluttered room, without a bed or a drawer or a corner to call my own, I feel safe – safer than I have done for ages, safer than I ever did when I was little. I'm sorry. But it's true. The Rudaks make me feel safe. I can't change that, not that I want to.

I roll onto my side and face the wall, glad that in the dark I can't see Jim's awful taste in wallpaper. I don't want it to be true, but it is: the Rudaks make me feel better about myself, more okay with life, more loved, than Mum ever has done. Where that leaves her, I don't know. Of course, in reality I do, but I don't want to have to keep thinking about her. It shouldn't be my responsibility. She's got to find her own way to live, to be happy, to have a purpose in life. I can't do that for her. I never have been able to. I can't live my life her way any more, not now that I have an alternative.

I roll back onto my front, holding Dog to my cheek.

I listen to Lauren snoring softly, and imagine Phil and Sarah asleep across the hall and Jim crashed out downstairs on the lounge sofa. The house shifts and settles. And despite myself, I think about Mum, alone in a hotel room, feeling rejected and unloved, by me.

I take for ever to go to sleep.

43

Congratulations

SARAH

I JERK awake, unconscious to conscious in a second. It must be early as the house is silent. Phil is fast asleep, his face pressed into the pillow, so close that I can feel the little puffs of air as he breathes. He and James look so alike when they sleep, the same bony nose, the same dark brows and smooth forehead, the same utter stillness. I slide out of bed, wrap myself in my dressing gown and creep downstairs, staying close to the edge to stop the floorboards creaking. I need time to think, on my own, before they all get up and fill my day with their needs and wants.

The stark truth is that Anne discarded Lauren because she wasn't perfect. She gave away her own child because she didn't meet her and Nathan's expectations, but another woman's child did: mine. She stole Rosie from us and, in the process, she stole away the family we should have had. And then, and this is the worst part, despite it all – the years of me making my peace with the challenges of Lauren's disability, after we'd learnt to accept and survive, even thrive – she comes back into our lives and lies and lies and lies. I reach for my phone and scroll through my contacts, looking for Jeremy Orr's number. I pause on it. One message and I can rip Anne's life apart, just as she has ours.

I think back to her slow, deliberate voice telling me that everything I've believed about this whole sorry mess is a fiction. It was never a mistake or fate or misadventure or human error. It was a deliberate act. I touch the screen, bringing Jeremy's number to life. One phone call. Nothing less than she deserves.

But there's another stark truth that I have to face. My own culpability. Because Anne didn't swap them straight away. It wasn't immediately after the birth, when I was unconscious, it wasn't during those first few days when Rosie was in and out of the nursery and I was ill; it was the day I was discharged. For five days I fed my real daughter, I held my real daughter, I nursed my real daughter. For five days I had Rosie, then I let her go.

What Anne did was wrong, unnatural and wicked beyond words, but what is also very, very wrong is that I didn't even notice.

I put my phone aside and go and fetch the photos. They're where Phil left them, propped at the end of the bookshelf, but when I look through them, the one I want is missing. I search around, pull out the books, root behind all the shelves in case it's slipped down the back, but after ten minutes of fruitless searching it's clear that it's gone.

Frustrated, I head back upstairs into Lauren's room. She stirs as I enter and I stand completely still, watching her. She sighs, scratches her nose and resettles. I cross to the chest of drawers, pick up the baby box and creep back downstairs.

I sit down and draw the box towards me, the last remaining arte-facts of our five short days as Rosie's parents. The Babygro is folded on the top, impossibly tiny, the pattern still bright and cheery, as befits the first outfit for a newborn. The tiny Scotty dogs are actually a dark red, not the insipid pink they look in the photo. I sit with it in my hands, threading it between my fingers, feeling the softness and the give of the fabric. I move the cards aside. And there, tucked in the very bottom, are the name-tags from the hospital. The cloudy plastic bands are still soft and pliable between my fingers, the words clearly legible. Lauren's name, date of birth, weight and my name as her mother. All wrong. All Rosie's. Holding the bands and the Babygro to my chest, I rock back and forth, trying to soothe the baby I never loved. I wasn't mum enough for Rosie then. The question is: can I be mum enough now?

PHIL

I wake to a lovely, sunny day and with a bubble of happiness in my chest. Sarah and I on the same team, wanting exactly the same things, at last. Nothing can beat that. Nothing. Music drifts up from the kitchen along with the smell of toast. I roll onto my back and starfish across the bed for a couple of minutes, relishing the space and the cool sheets until I hear Lauren shuffle out onto the landing, my cue to get my lazy arse out of bed.

Sarah is in the kitchen, drinking tea, silhouetted against the window when we get downstairs. She turns and smiles as Lauren and I come in. A proper smile that reaches her eyes. I brush my fingertips across the small of her back as we wait for the kettle to re-boil, wishing she could come upstairs with me. She leans back against me and we watch as Lauren does her worst with her bowl of cereal. It's unusual nowadays for it just to be the three of us around the table for breakfast. We eat with the sun streaming in through the window and discuss what we're going to do with Rosie's last few, bonus days. Lunch out, maybe a swim, the cinema?

For the first time in a long while I'm able to set off for work without a nagging anxiety about Sarah, or Rosie, or Lauren, or James, and it continues to be a good day. It's the same boring routine at work, but I'm buoyed up by the thought that we're getting closer to resolving things. I'm out at the plant extension that we're overseeing near Halifax by mid-morning, reviewing the schematics, when my phone pings, a text from Rosie. I'm guessing that she's just got up.

Morning. Hope the world of sewage is flowing well!!! Sarah says can u pick up some milk on yr way home. And some more tortillas. R xxxx

Out of such mundanity can come happiness. After three more hours of trying to resolve the pumping problem I set off back to the office, sunroof open, radio on loud. On a whim I swing left, deciding that a slight detour is excusable.

The same grubby white plastic chairs await, as does the same seductive smell of overcooked onions. I order a cheeseburger and watch the swifts dart around the sky as Mrs Chu slaps two frozen burgers down on the hot plate. As my portion of grease and heart attack cooks, I ask after Mrs Chu's family. She updates me on her over-achieving daughter, at Cardiff Uni studying chemistry, and her under-performing son, running orders for his uncle's takeaway in Hebden Bridge. My interest is purely selfish because, as she flips my burger, Mrs Chu reciprocates by asking, as she always does, after my family; she especially likes to hear how Lauren is getting on. When I tell her we have a new daughter, she smiles and I try and explain about how we were separated from Rosie, but how she is back with us now. Mrs Chu nods and smiles even more broadly than normal, as she layers cheese onto my burger and wraps it in a napkin. In exchange, I pull the photo out of my wallet and pass it across the counter to her. She wipes her hands on a cloth, meticulously, before she takes it from me.

'Your new daughter?' She studies it.

'Yes. She's called Rosie.'

'Congratulations.' She passes it back to me. 'And your wife, she is okay?'

It takes me a second to realise that she's not understood a word of the complicated tale I've just told her, seeing only a mother and newborn. I grin back at her. 'Yes, they're both doing fine.'

ANNE

On Friday morning there's a knock at the door. I assume it's the maid trying to get in to clean the room. 'Not today, thank you,' I shout, expecting a pause then the sound of the housekeeping cart being pushed along to the next room, but instead a male voice responds. 'Ms Elkan, if I might have a quick word?' I open up to find what looks like a fifteen-year-old, with acne scars and an ill-fitting suit, standing on the threshold. He extends his hand. 'Danny Carver. I'm the deputy manager here at the Metropole. I was hoping to have a word with you about your booking, if that's okay? I thought we'd see you in the lobby this morning but...' I keep the door ajar and make no move to invite him in. He flusters. 'I just wanted to confirm when you might be checking out?'

Having not been able to conceive what happens next in my life, I certainly haven't thought about what I am supposed to do with myself for the next few days. It all hinges on Sarah. It's Sarah who is in control of my life now. The young man blinks and the awkwardness thickens. 'I plan to stay a few more days now. That's not a problem, is it?'

'No.' He swallows. 'Not as such. You did originally book for just the one night and it's, well... room allocations, we've a busy weekend coming up. Do you know how long you will be needing the room for?' he trails off weakly.

'I really don't know. Another couple of days, maybe more. I shall come down and confirm with you later.' I bully him with my grammar.

'Okay. Thank you, Ms Elkan. That would be very helpful.'

I close the door on him. As I turn round I catch sight of myself in the mirror. I don't blame him for being suspicious. I pull back the curtains, revealing the unmade bed. The room is stuffy and I'm still wearing my clothes from yesterday. Everything is crumpled and stale and thoroughly depressing. On the bedside table lies my watch. It's nearly midday. As I'm trying to make myself look respectable my phone beeps, a text. It's from Sarah. I hold the phone tightly, trying to concentrate on getting air into my lungs. The message is short and specific and terse. It instructs me that *Rosie is staying with them until Sunday*. And that *I'm not to ring or go to the house. I'm not to say ANYTHING to Rosie. I'm not to say anything to anyone. I'm to wait for Sarah to contact me.* I sit and contemplate the consequences of my revelation.

My life is over. The life I've had will fall apart. Nathan will disassociate himself from us completely. The house will go. It will all crumble. And the Rudaks will have the whip hand. Whatever they want will be sanctioned. How could it not be? They are the innocent party. Prosecution? It's possible. And…

And Rosie is not coming home. She may never come home. When they tell her what I did, she will hate me. I am going to lose my daughter. I am truly on my own.

Panic licks around me and I force myself to breathe. In and out, in and out. Just like Sarah told me. I know I should really go back to St Albans, but I can't face the drive or the distance or the empty house. My only option is to stay close as I wait for Sarah to light the touchpaper and blow it all up.

In fresh clothes, with my make-up done and my hair brushed, I lie back down on the straightened bed, swallow a pill and stare at the ceiling.

44

Limbo

SARAH

IT'S A strange, strained feeling, a kind of intense limbo, at least it is for me. I watch life go on inside our house as if through a pane of glass, with me on both sides, participating and observing. I look after Lauren, I cook meals, I talk to Rosie, I nag James, I even fabricate some story about Anne mentioning something about going to see friends for a couple of days, to reassure Rosie that her mum is not just sitting in a hotel room with a broken heart. And God help me, I smile and laugh and put on a credible performance of genuine happiness for Phil, to keep him at bay.

And so one lie begets another.

I also text Ali, repeatedly, secretly, begging her to say nothing until I've decided what I'm going to do. And inside all this activity curls my conversation with Anne. I can feel her hand in mine and see the pale soles of her feet and I can hear her voice slowly, calmly telling me the awful truth. Her confession is wedged within me, a hard, black, indigestible mass that I cannot shift.

In stark contrast to my ill ease, Rosie is happy. She's more smiley, more relaxed, more affectionate, especially towards me. It's as if she can sense my turmoil and the enormity of the decisions to be made about her future. She's helpful around the house and she makes much more of an effort with Lauren, asking questions, trying to get involved. Late on Friday afternoon, after we get back from swimming, I catch her sitting with Lauren going through the characters in a picture book. She sits there for more than an hour, reading each page over and over again, at Lauren's insistence. The sight of the two of them together opens and closes a painful place in my heart. And at some point on Friday evening she must have hunted out the linen cupboard, because when we head up to bed, she announces that she wants to sleep in the lounge. We begin to argue, but she points out that she's already changed James's bed and that she's perfectly happy sleeping downstairs.

As Phil and I undress for bed I ask him for the photo. He doesn't need to ask which one. He takes it out of his wallet and passes it to me. He's had to fold it to fit and there's a deep crease down the middle. I smooth it flat on the palm of my hand.

'What do you want it for?'

When I explain he goes quiet, thoughtful. He watches me wrap everything in the sheets of pink tissue paper, placing his finger on the ribbon as I tie the bow. 'Do you want to come down with me?' I ask. He has every right to be part of this. I know that.

But he smiles and shakes his head. 'No, this is from you – you should give it to her.' And he looks at me steadily, understanding.

It's dark downstairs and I worry that I've left it too late and Rosie's asleep, but when I get to the doorway I can see the white glow of a light. She's lying on the foldout bed with her phone held close to her face, connecting with her other life, the one that I'm about to shatter. The screen illuminates her face, a bright spot in a dark room. She has a beautiful face, even more lovely tonight, stripped, as it is, of the make-up and the defensiveness that guards it most of the time. I must make a noise because she suddenly starts and looks up, fumbling her phone away. 'Sorry, I was going to sleep, it's just that Megan messaged me.'

'It's fine. Sorry, I didn't mean to snoop on you. Can I come in?'

'Course, it's your house.' I hunker down on the floor beside her low bed. She tosses her phone away onto the hearth where there's a little pile of her possessions, including her bracelet. She turns her full attention to me.

I feel nervous, but sure. 'Rosie, there's something I want to give you, something we really should've given you on your birthday.' She props herself upright, expectant. 'I hope you like it, maybe more than that awful bracelet we got you.' She starts to disagree, but I stop her. 'It's okay. We bought you that because we didn't know you. We do now.' I place the parcel on her lap, where we both stare at it. 'Go on. Open it.' I reach behind me and click on the lamp, causing us both to blink blindly for a few seconds. When we've acclimatised to the brightness, she slides off the ribbon and unfolds the tissue paper, one layer at a time, revealing the Babygro. She looks up, uncertain. I pull the photo out from underneath it and pass it to her. As she dips her head to study it, I feel something hard break inside me. 'It's you, and me, and Phil.'

She draws the photo closer to her face. 'Are you sure?'

'Yes, I'm certain.' Because for the first time since this began, I am certain, I'm certain that she's mine.

'Oh.' She sucks the word up with a short, sharp breath. 'And this is the same outfit?' I nod and she carefully lifts the tiny Babygro up, and as she does the ID tag falls out onto her lap, she recoils, giving a little yelp, and flicks it onto the floor. She must catch sight of my face because she immediately apologises. 'Oh, sorry, what was it?'

'It's okay. I should've explained.' I reach down and retrieve it. 'It's your name-tag, from the hospital. It belongs to you. It should've always belonged to you.' She takes it from me gingerly, reluctant to touch the yellowed plastic. She still isn't grasping its significance. 'Every newborn has two hospital ID tags. They have the baby's name, NHS number, time and date of birth and the mother's name printed on them. This is yours.'

'Oh.' She squints at the tiny printed label and finally she sees it… next to *Lauren*, in the small space remaining, I've written *Rosie* in thick black biro. I could never wipe out one child, but I know now that it's possible to add another. 'I hope it's okay, I've kept the other one.'

She nods and her face flickers with such a swirl of emotions. She's too young to bear so much. Even my love is painful for her. She lays the tag on the palm of her hand and studies it. 'It's so small.' Her voice wobbles. 'It's hard to think that it fitted round my wrist once.' We both stare at her wrist, the trace of slim blue veins beneath her skin.

'You were small, but you were perfect.' She was, and I never saw that, I never got to cherish that. 'I'm so sorry.' My voice cracks.

She lays the band carefully down on the covers and takes hold of my hand. She's the first to compose herself. She smiles at me bravely and says, 'It's okay. It wasn't your fault. It wasn't anyone's fault.'

45

Saturday

SARAH

I CAN'T lie next to Phil. I can't bear to do nothing any longer. I've only had about two hours' sleep and I'm grainy with fatigue, but I'm full of restless emotion. It's 6.30 a.m. I have one day left to decide, one day to talk this through with Phil. But still I can't.

I get out of bed as quietly as I can, but Phil must sense me moving because he stirs and mutters, 'Is everything all right?'

'Yeah, fine,' I lie. 'I just can't sleep. I thought I might go for a swim.'

'Really?' He still hasn't opened his eyes. 'What time is it?'

'It's early. You go back to sleep.' I creep around the room, collecting my clothes. Phil dozes. 'I won't be long.'

'Okay, if you're sure…' His voice is still clogged with sleep. I kiss the top of his head and flee.

The pool is, unsurprisingly, virtually empty. *Lane swimming, 7 a.m. to 9 a.m.* appears not to be over-patronised at the weekend. There are only three other swimmers: a white-haired elderly couple who are doing stately lengths of breaststroke in the slow lane, and a teenage girl, with broad swimmer's shoulders and flawless technique, who is powering up and down the fast lane, seemingly without taking a breath. The middle lane it is, then.

I haven't been swimming on my own, without Lauren, for years. This morning the thought of mindless exertion appeals to me – anything to distract me – but as I lower myself into the pool there's no welcoming shock of purging cold water. The pool is tepid and heavily chlorinated. A sense of pointlessness hits me, but I'm determined not to let it swamp me. I push off from the side and begin my inelegant lengths, feeling the water slick against my skin. Arm over arm, a controlled leg kick, trying to minimise the splash, a breath on every second stroke; the same freestyle technique taught to me by Mrs Wilson when I was nine. I touch the wall in the deep end, turn and set off back, finding, if not elegance, then at least enough coordination to pick up speed. By the second turn it's beginning to feel natural, a blind rhythm of air, water, effort and movement. But as muscle memory takes hold, my brain returns to my impossible dilemma.

Anne hasn't gone away; she's near, waiting, counting down the hours. Just one more day, then she will pack her bag, check out of her hotel and drive the short distance to our house. Anne is coming, and there is nothing I can do to prevent it. I take a deep breath and plough on through the water. Twenty-eight hours. That's all the time I have left to decide.

Her confession is poison. She's infected me with it. Even now, as I swim, my heart is pumping it around my body, spreading its bitterness through my veins. And that's precisely what she wants.

She wanted me to share her guilt. She wanted to pass its destructive power on to someone else. She wanted to abdicate responsibility, yet again, for her actions. And what Anne wants, Anne gets.

When she was talking, in that dreadful, claustrophobic hotel room, the thing that appalled me the most was her self-pity, her willingness to blame others, to blame Nathan, to blame me. But the truth is the truth. She cold-heartedly looked at Lauren, saw her flaws and rejected her. Then she cold-bloodedly took our child. She stole Rosie and gave us Lauren. She took away the life we should've had.

I cannot conceive of how you can live with doing something like that. And yet Anne has, for years. Everything she's ever said has been a lie, every emotion faked, every expression a charade. I swim faster, trying to exorcise my fury.

I don't know what to do. I'm choking on anger so sharp and big that it frightens me. I want to expose her, to shame her, to tell everyone. I want to keep Rosie away from her, for ever, banish her from our lives and make her pay for what she did.

Suddenly my mouth and nose are full of water and I'm sinking, not swimming. My arms whirl and my legs thrash. My throat burns. Scorched skin blocks my airways, as the water forces its way up my nose and into my lungs. I'm drowning. The world blurs, and for a second all I can see are white tiles and blue water, then my face breaks the surface and I'm sucking in air. I can see the edge of the pool and the skylights overhead, and I see the lifeguard readying himself to dive in. 'I'm okay,' I croak. I force myself to calm down, to breathe, to stop panicking. Gradually the world rights itself and I swim slowly to the end of the pool, where I catch hold of the rail. I cling onto it as my chest heaves. The lifeguard runs around the pool and kneels down, reaching out for me. 'Here' – he stretches out his hand – 'I'll help you out.'

I manage to speak, despite the searing in my throat. 'No. I'm okay. Sorry if I gave you a fright. I just lost control for a minute.'

He doesn't look reassured. 'I really think you should get out of the pool, for your own safety.'

'I will. I'll just give myself a minute or two to calm down.' He looks doubtful. I'm now embarrassed as well as breathless. 'Really. I just panicked for a second. I'm fine.' I even smile to prove it. At last he stands up and walks to his post, glancing back as he goes. As I watch him retreat, I see the old couple, white heads bobbing like seals, treading water six feet away from me. There's a look of real concern on both their faces. I shout, 'I'm fine' and wave cheerily at them. The young girl continues to swim her lengths, unperturbed.

The changing room is busy. A throng of older women in Lycra and sports bras are getting ready for a class. There's a lot of laughter and cruel anecdotes about useless husbands. I have to edge past a sea of creased flesh to get to my locker. I dig out my clothes and go and hide in one of the cubicles. The energy and good humour of their voices batter against the thin curtain that separates me from them. As I attempt to struggle out of my swimming costume, the straps stick to my wet skin and become tangled. Half-naked, I twist and yank, trying to get free. The small space hems me in. I crash my elbow against the wall.

It's too much.

I give up.

I sit down on the ledge, still trapped in my swimsuit, feeling chilled and shaky. Their voices bounce around the room. I bury my face in my towel, trying to block it all out: them, Anne, it, everything. Only when the door bangs shut behind the last of them and the changing room falls silent do I raise my head.

46

The Party

ROSIE

IT'S A going-away party. No one says it, but it is, because Mum is coming to get me tomorrow. The 'old me' would've sulked and stropped, spoilt it for everyone, including myself, but I don't, because I'm learning. Sarah is right. Things take time. I apply another layer of mascara and stand back to look at myself: not at my make-up, but at me. I've changed. For the better. I know who I am. I'm their daughter.

The bell goes as I'm coming downstairs. I open up and Jess and Ali bundle into the hall, their arms full of carrier bags and foil-covered plates: drinks and snacks from Ali, home-made buns and brownies from Jess. As I help lay things out in the kitchen, James hovers around nicking food and Phil puts on the radio. The house vibrates with voices and loud music. It's going to be a good night. I can feel it.

We all eat too much, Lauren included. It takes three wet wipes to get rid of all the chocolate frosting on her face and hands. She's excited by all the noise and bustle. After we've eaten, we take our drinks and all go through to the lounge, groaning about our bursting bellies. Lauren sits quite happily with us, looking at her books, until we start playing games – James's suggestion. It's no surprise that it gets out of hand within minutes. We're all so competitive, apart from Jess, who seems to get more fun out of cheating than playing. A slanging match kicks off when Ali accuses Phil of moving an extra square. He denies it, insisting that he threw a six, not a five. It matters. There's Monopoly money riding on it. Everyone joins in with an opinion. It's Jess who finally notices Lauren. Unseen by us, she must have climbed down off the sofa and crawled to the door, opened it and taken herself off into the hall, where she sits with her hands covering her ears, waiting to be taken up to bed.

Phil goes to her. 'Are we being too loud for you, honey?' She lowers her hands and signs 'bed', two hands to her cheek. 'Someone else play my go for me, while I take Lauren up to bed, will you?' Lauren makes for the stairs. 'But not Ali!' They disappear upstairs and the battle for Marylebone Station kicks off again.

SARAH

They arrive at 6.30 p.m., armed with home-made cakes and brownies, all Jess's handiwork, and the house expands to absorb them. Music and laughter fill the rooms. Rosie is buzzing, shiny-haired, bright-eyed, happy to have the family together. She flits from Ali to Phil to Jess to James to me and Lauren, embroidering on the thread that connects her to each of us. It's a proper celebration of family... that I could do without. Because despite the easy atmosphere and the sense of real affection, I feel profoundly uneasy. Ali's repeated glances are understandable, but they only serve to remind me that I'm deceiving them. I eat, smile, laugh and watch them banter and bond, from what feels like a great height.

With Lauren settled in bed and a third bottle of wine opened, the mood gets even more hyper. They bicker their way through Monopoly for what feels like hours until, with great hilarity, they bankrupt Phil. When James brings out a pack of cards and suggests 'Cheat', I excuse myself.

I slip out into the back garden, hoping that the fierce competition of their card game will buy me at least a few minutes on my own. I only get five, because Ali follows me out. She passes me a fleece and I put it on, grateful for the warmth and the consideration, but she brings with her questions as well as comfort.

'You okay?'

'Yeah.'

'You sure?'

'Yeah.'

'And?'

'I've thought about nothing else.'

'And?'

'I still don't know what to do for the best.' There's a beat, a moment of pale darkness filled with the sound of laughter from inside the house.

'You can't seriously be thinking of keeping quiet about it?' Ali's indignation fills the garden.

'But if I reveal what she did, what good will it do?'

'She'll get what she deserves.' Ali is so sure. I'm so unsure. I say nothing. She makes a despairing gesture. 'It will eat you up, if you don't say anything.'

'It won't – not if I don't let it.' I can only hope that's true.

Ali doesn't offer me any comfort. 'It will. And it will let Anne off the hook. She'll get away with it.' She pushes harder. 'And you'll have to let her see Rosie. You do get that, don't you? She'll still have rights. Can you live with that?'

'I don't know.'

We're silent for a moment. 'So... I do it for revenge?'

Ali hesitates. 'No. Yes. Sod it! Yes!'

She doesn't understand why I'm so conflicted, so trapped by the truth of what Anne did. But I know that whatever I decide, it will lead to more pain. Ali's voice is still sharp when she says, 'What about Phil? What about his right to know? Are you going to lie to him about it for the rest of your life?'

'I don't know.' The thought hurts too much.

She shakes her head. I reach out and pull her towards me. There is only one certainty in all of this. It's me who must decide what happens next. No one else. Me. 'Ali, you must keep your promise. I'm sorry, but you must.' She catches the firmness in my voice. I can see the impulse to argue bubbling within her, but I don't let her interrupt. 'Ali. This isn't yours to share. I'm asking you to trust me to know what's best for my family.'

She looks me in the eye and, after an age, she nods. I feel some of the resistance in her body give slightly. I know how much it's costing her to quell her rage, but I also know that I believe her. She will not say anything, because I have asked her not to.

'Thank you.' We stand there for another few seconds, so far apart and yet so united, then we go back into the house.

PHIL

I have to tell them to shush, they're making so much noise. They're both red in the face from exertion. Who knew a game of 'Cheat' could be so full-on? I'm benched, thrown out of the game for sitting on my 'impossible to get rid of' set of fours. Jess, with the coolness of the lovely cucumber that she is, managed to get rid of her cards early on, by slow, stealthy, under-the-radar cheating that none of us spotted, which leaves Rosie and James duelling it out. They both seem to have a lot of cards left.

Jess and I chat about work. She's passionate, me less so, but after a while we lapse into a comfortable wine-induced silence. The bang makes us both jump. The back door? A sudden gust of wind? From somewhere in my 'pre-programmed, good parent' brain, I remember that Lauren's window is still open. With an effort I haul myself up.

As expected, Lauren is fast asleep, despite the shouting and carrying-on downstairs. The curtain is billowing. I reach up to pull her window shut and hear, 'What about Phil?'

It's hard to enjoy the party after that.

I wait until Sarah and I are upstairs and the house is quiet. I close the bedroom door behind me. That gets her attention. I switch the main light on. I want to see her face.

'What is it that you're not telling me?' She pulls her T-shirt up over her head, obscuring her face for a second. 'Sarah, I heard you in the garden with Ali.' Her face re-emerges. I can't read the emotion that ripples across it. 'Sarah, tell me. Whatever it is, just tell me.' Something changes in her demeanour, a tiny adjustment; again I can't decipher its meaning.

Then she says, 'I did something that I shouldn't have.'

'What?'

There's another uncomfortably long pause. She looks down at the carpet. 'I sent a photo of Lauren to Nathan Elkan.'

It's not what I was expecting, though I don't know what I *was* expecting. 'Sorry, I don't understand.'

She meets my eye. 'Neither do I. Not really.' She sits down on the bed. 'I was angry. I hated how he was rejecting Lauren, as if she didn't matter. I did it to shame him.' I'm stunned at her rashness. It's *so* not Sarah. 'I hated that he was ignoring the whole thing as if he wasn't involved. I wanted him to have to accept that his child had a disability, but that she still had value. I did it on principle.'

'But if he'd got involved, it would have been a nightmare.'

She nods. 'I know. I'm sorry. I know that nothing about this has anything to do with principle, does it?'

'That's what I've being telling you all along.'

She looks down. 'I know. And you're right.'

I go and sit next to her. She says 'Sorry' again. 'And you never heard back from him?' She shakes her head. 'So we dodged a bullet.' She nods. 'And that's what you've been keeping from me?' She nods again, very slowly. 'Okay.'

She looks up, her face still clouded by anxiety. 'Okay?'

'Yep, okay.' I kiss her on the cheek, and for an awful moment I think she's going to burst into tears. She tries to smile. 'Come on, it's late, let's get some sleep. We've got Anne to face down tomorrow.' I'm relieved. It was stupid and very unlike Sarah, but no harm's been done. From the way Ali was talking, I thought it was something serious.

47

The Last Day

ANNE

I'VE BEEN summoned to appear before them.

After days of nothing, I receive a message from Sarah on Saturday morning. It is brief and brutal: Arrive on Sunday afternoon, after 1 p.m., not before. That's it. A clear instruction, but no indication of what she's planning.

As I pack my few belongings I feel anxiety building in my chest. This hotel room has been my sanctuary for the past few days, the world outside has shrunk away. I've barely had contact with anyone. I've received a couple of chatty messages from Steph that have required me to lie, and another polite, insistent enquiry from Nathan's solicitors. That hardly seems to matter now. Nathan hardly matters. It's to my shame that it's taken me this long to realise that. He has always stood between me and my capacity to love my child. From Rosie herself I've had a few normal, uninformative texts. I've read them again and again, cherishing their bland ordinariness. They've given me a fragile thread of hope to hold on to. They cannot have told her, yet.

At reception I settle my account. The girl is clipped, efficient, impersonal. She processes the payment, passes me back my credit card, and wishes me *a nice day*. If she's curious about my hermit-like stay, she does a good job of pretending otherwise. Perhaps she simply doesn't care. As I walk through the revolving door I have to discipline myself not to keep pushing and merely emerge back into the lobby. How ridiculous have I become? At the multi-storey car park it takes me fifteen minutes to find my car and to the pay the huge sum for four days. Driving down the ramp and straight into the city-centre traffic is a baptism of fire. I'm honked at twice as I switch lanes, struggling to find the road that leads to the west of the city. I'm anxious about being late, but I'm even more fearful of arriving. I know that at long last I'm about to pay the real price for stealing Rosie away from them. My suffering up until now has merely been a precursor. Rosie has wriggled and struggled for years and now she's about to rip free, back to where she was always supposed to be. When Sarah tells her what I did, she will hate me. I took her away from parents who would have loved her properly, naturally and unconditionally. That is unforgivable.

48

Us

SARAH

AFTER TEN minutes of crashing about, fetching coats and shoes, the door bangs shut and the house falls quiet. Lauren glances up from her iPad. She pats the carpet, requesting my presence, and I settle down beside her.

Anne is on her way.

I sit on the floor and we watch a stream of happy, sunny children's TV. The time edges by.

Phil and I haven't really talked any more, beyond reassuring each other that it's going to be all right. He still thinks that today is little more than an uncomfortable formality, a simple step on the path to a bright future. And I've let him think that. He's looking forward, confident that the good times will roll, gathering pace and momentum, sweeping any obstacles out of the way.

But there is an obstacle: Anne's confession.

I know in my bones that keeping it from him is wrong. Last night I lied to his face and he believed me, and the strongest emotion I felt was relief. I was relieved that he only heard the end of Ali's conversation and that he accepted my tale about Nathan Elkan and the photo. But it also reminded me that to keep a secret for ever I'm going to have to lie to him, for ever. Which is wrong. It's a betrayal of our marriage. Phil and I do not lie to each other. We have never lied to each other. Yet now I am, because I'm paralysed by the thought of telling him the truth. When I tell them what Anne did, it will shatter, yet again, the fragile equilibrium we've managed to re-establish in our lives.

But I'm going to have to do something, because the time is up. Anne is on her way.

Lauren nudges me and signs for a drink, reminding me that I have responsibilities in the present. She drinks noisily, a full beaker of juice, straight down. I feel bad that she was thirsty and I didn't realise. After she's finished, she hesitates and I wait for her to fling the cup across the room, but she doesn't, she passes it back to me, politely. I return the beaker to the kitchen. On the side the photo frame scrolls through its endless loop: me, Phil, James and Lauren, Dad, Ali and Jess, different combinations of our family across the years. Only a couple of photos of Rosie so far, but there'll be more. When Rosie finds out that it was Anne who robbed her of her place in her real family, it will destroy their relationship. And what else will it smash in the process? Her faith in adults, in the truth, in ever feeling secure enough to grow up into a confident and positive young woman? How will she survive finding out that both Nathan and Anne put their needs and desires before her? That she was little more than a pawn in their weird, twisted marriage. What good will that truth do Rosie?

Back in the lounge, Lauren pats the floor next to her again, demanding my company. I rejoin her and watch the clock inch slowly round as the rain patters down the window, drawing comfort from being close to the child who has had my heart for fifteen years, but who was never supposed to be my daughter.

It would've been so different without Lauren.

There'd have been a whole other life. A career for me, options for Phil, more travelling, more money, more excitement and choice, more time and space. There'd have been less stress, less anxiety, less clinging to what was safe and predictable, in the face of what was uncertain and fragile. And there'd have been no surgeries, no grey dawns after sleepless nights, no watching my child in pain, no leaving my other child to fend for himself, no specialists, no social workers, no endless forms and relentless appointments. There'd have been no slow realisation of the gap between our expectations and our future. No acceptance of the loss.

Something on the screen amuses Lauren and she laughs and pokes me, requiring me to pay attention. It's a clip that she's seen a thousand times before, but she laughs, delighted by the simple silliness of it. I stroke her cheek.

Yes, it would've been so different without Lauren.

There'd have been no unequivocal love. No Dad with his reserved, concerned affection; and no Ali, supporting us through it all, going way beyond what it's reasonable to expect from a sister. There'd have been no James, my kind, unselfish, resilient son, who has grown into a strong, decent young man full of empathy and compassion. And, above all, there'd have been no Phil and I, locked together by our love for them all.

Because, if there'd have been no Lauren, there'd have been no us.

I put my arm around my daughter and hold her tight, but only for a moment, because she unceremoniously wriggles free and signs 'rain', demanding that I sing to her.

I hear the van arriving back. When I open the door they flood in, all noise and energy and wet, cold air. 'Whoa, you're not traipsing all that upstairs.' James halts on the step and grins at me, he's plastered in mud. They obviously won. He bends and starts untying his laces with dirty, clumsy fingers. Ali comes in, shaking raindrops off her jacket, followed by Phil and Rosie, both of them soaked.

Rosie bounds upstairs. 'I'll run a bath.' James, free of his boots, steps into the hall, dripping wet. His big feet and curiously manly toes are white and wrinkled. His shins are clean up to his knees, filthy above, his kit streaked with mud and grass stains. As he tries to pull off his soaking football shirt he gets himself into a tangle, the wet fabric sticking to his back. I step forward to help. As I tug the shirt over his head, a shape appears on the other side of the door. Silhouetted in the frosted glass is Anne. The hall falls silent. She doesn't reach for the bell. She simply stands there, an ill-defined presence awaiting admission. We all freeze, like cartoon characters: James mid-strip, Phil halfway out of his coat, Ali on the bottom stair, unzipping her boots. Anne must be able to see us through the glass. James recovers first. He scoops up his stuff and pelts upstairs. Phil shakes himself out of his inactivity and goes to open the door. I turn away, clutching James's wet football shirt to my chest, and escape into the kitchen.

ANNE

I see their van pull up, followed by a small white car. Ali climbs out of it. Phil, James and Rosie emerge from the van. The boy is covered in mud. There's a flurry of voices and activity, the front door opens and the house swallows them up. I have to get this over with. I climb out of the car, pull on my coat and walk up the ramp towards the house, listening to their voices bouncing off one another inside. Through the frosted glass I can see their outlines moving around, a blur of colour and shapes. I stop and wait; inside, they stop and wait. As I stand there, I notice the jasmine that I brought up for Sarah all those weeks ago. It's dumped outside the front door, no flowers any more, just a few leaves clinging to the twisted stem and a scatter of unopened fallen buds around the base of the pot. The pause stretches out, then there's a flash of movement across the hall, followed by Phil coming forward to let me in. 'Come through to the kitchen. We've just got back.' No anger, just dismissal. She cannot have told him yet.

I step inside. 'I can wait in the car if you'd prefer.' My voice wavers. Perhaps if I prostrate myself before them, they'll have pity on me.

'No. Don't be ridiculous.' Phil is brusque. 'Come through.'

I follow him into the kitchen. It's painfully bright, the overhead lights have been switched on to combat the gloom of the day outside. Sarah is over by the sink and Lauren is sitting at the table, a plate of toast in front of her.

Ali has her back to me, but she turns around and glares as I walk into the room. 'Hello, Anne.' The coldness reveals that she knows.

'Hello.' For a second they all stare at me, even Lauren. The eyes that are missing are Rosie's.

Sarah picks up on my unspoken question. 'She's upstairs, getting changed; she'll be down in a minute, then we'll talk. I'm making tea, would you like one?' Sarah's voice is colourless, deliberately so. 'Yes, please.' My own voice sounds small and pathetically polite. My only option is to sit down and await my fate. Sarah and Ali make forced small talk about the unseasonal weather and the football, and about how nicely Lauren is eating, while I sit dumbly in their midst waiting for Rosie to come downstairs. It's a conversation designed to exclude me. I can't bring myself to look at Lauren in Sarah's presence. Ali, however, has no problem meeting my eye. She stares at me, plainly outraged. As I go to take a sip of tea, my hands shake so much that I have to put my mug down. Rosie has still not appeared. Phil goes to the foot of the stairs and calls her. 'Rosie! Anne's here. Can you come down, love?' His voice is so normal, so at ease, as he strips me of my role. There's a thud and footsteps and, finally, she enters the kitchen. I twist round at the sound of her.

'Hi.' She stops on the threshold, glances at me, then looks at Sarah and Phil, seeking reassurance. Sarah beckons her in. 'Come and sit down. It's going to be all right. We're just going to have a talk, like we discussed, about the future. Isn't that right, Anne?'

Rosie does not come to me, there's no welcoming hug or kiss. She slides into the seat next to Lauren. Phil pulls up a chair at one end of the table and Sarah sits down at the other. We're ready.

PHIL

I'm glad we're finally getting down to it. Rosie wants to be with us. It's her decision. Not ours. Not Anne's. I can't see what Sarah is so anxious about. It's going to be okay, once we get past this bit.

ROSIE

Mum looks awful, really poorly. I feel bad. I shouldn't have spoken to her like that on the phone. I shouldn't have ignored her messages. She looks so out of place. Suddenly it doesn't feel so simple.

ANNE

Sarah starts talking, staring at a point just past my head. Her restrained politeness contains no warmth. 'Thank you for agreeing to let Rosie stay with us these past few days, it's given us time to get to know each other properly. I think we all feel much closer.' Rosie looks at Sarah as she says this and I can see that it's true. She belongs to them now. Another strut collapses within me. 'It's also brought home to us the importance of getting things in place, going forward.' Going forward. I can't imagine it. 'Our conversation on Thursday made things much clearer to me.' A look passes between Sarah and Ali that Phil picks up, but can't decipher. I can, all too clearly. Sarah's face searches mine, checking that I've grasped her meaning. She continues, her voice growing stronger by the second. 'It helped me realise something important. What we might want – me, Phil, you – is not the issue. We are the parents. Rosie is the child. We must do what's best for her, not us.' She hesitates, perhaps waiting to see if I'll object. I don't, how can I? Rosie is not mine. I have no rights. 'Anne, do you agree?' Sarah is demanding my consent.

I nod. I feel light-headed. Braced, but still not ready. The kitchen feels too small. The chair presses me into the hard edge of the table. There's so little space. I can feel panic rising inside me. 'Sorry. Might I have a glass of water?' Phil fetches one. I take a tiny sip. There's silence while I drink.

'Mum?' Rosie's voice is soft, concerned. She is so beautiful. A flicker of hope stirs inside me, but it dies when I look at Sarah. There can be no future until I've dealt with the past. Sarah will not allow it. I place the glass carefully down on the table and stretch my hand out towards Rosie. I want to touch her one last time before she despises me for ever. My hand looks exposed under the harsh light, blue-veined, old, but she reaches out across the table and takes it. Her slender fingers are warm. 'Are you sure you're all right, Mum? Is it another migraine? Are your tablets in your bag?' We did have a life together. I love her and she loved me, however, imperfectly. But I'm about to lose her.

'I'm okay.' My voice sounds distant. The pause can't last for ever, as much as I might want it to. I straighten up. 'You're right. We must do what's best for Rosie.' Rosie squeezes my fingers and I falter. 'But first there's something I need to say.'

SARAH

Anne looks shocking, dishevelled, ill. Poor Rosie, I can see her struggling to take in how much her mum has changed. Is this what the loss of her child for a week has done to Anne? What will happen when it's for a lifetime? The reserve and control are gone, leaving in their place a defeated passivity. She just sits there, accepting the blows. There's no fight in her any more. It's heartless to go on, but I have to. Rosie and Phil are expecting me to sort this out, and Ali is on the edge of her chair, waiting. I feel the truth pressing down on me, demanding to come out.

Then Anne reaches across the table for Rosie.

She's hanging on by her fingertips to the last thing she has – her daughter, a daughter who is no longer hers and never was. She draws a deep breath and says, 'We must do what's best for Rosie. But first there's something I need to say.'

I push my chair back so hard that it smacks into the wall, making everyone jump.

'No!' I look around the table at the people I love most in the world, and at Anne, who has both destroyed and created us. They all stare back at me, waiting.

I shake my head. Anne looks at me, uncomprehending.

This is my life.

This is my family.

Rosie and Lauren are my daughters.

I bear the responsibility for what happens next, and for the rest of our lives.

I know what I have to do.

The truth cannot help, it will only cause more harm and pain, and there's been too much of that already. Rosie needs protecting, we need protecting, even Anne needs protecting. Her confession must stay a secret, a burden borne by two mothers. That is the only way that we can love our daughter, unconditionally.

We will both have to pay the price.

Anne's penance is that she must bear her guilt alone; mine that I must keep the truth from Phil. But it will be worth it.

They are still waiting.

I take a breath, trying desperately to find the words that will haul us back from the brink.

It's Lauren who saves me.

She suddenly decides that she's had enough of the silence and the long faces. She picks up her plate, flings it across the kitchen and laughs as it clatters to the floor. Then she reaches out to the person nearest her, Rosie.

I AM SAFE.
I AM LOVED.
I AM LAUREN.

RTS

The Second Child depicts one family's experience of disability. Rubinstein-Taybi Syndrome is a real condition that affects individuals very differently and to very different degrees. Lauren's character is but one version. I want to acknowledge the sterling work of The RTS Support Group (rtsuk.org). They are an invaluable source of information, advice and support for those who live, cope and thrive with RTS.

Acknowledgements

THIS BOOK started life in an unsolicited submissions inbox, so my first 'thank you' must go to my agent, Judith Murray, at Greene & Heaton, for seeing something in the writing and the story. Her valuable advice has helped to shape and sharpen *The Second Child*, making it a much better book. Also I want to express my appreciation to Sara O'Keeffe, my editor at Corvus, for her faith in the novel. Her guidance has been insightful and instructive. She is a pleasure to work with, as are all the team at Corvus.

But this book really only exists because of the small number of people who supported my writing when the prospect of publication was a long way off, on a seemingly distant horizon. Foremost among these people, is Kath Burrow, my very own voracious reader. She has 'lived' this book almost as much as I have. Thank you, Kath, for your advice, support and belief. Thanks are also due to Martyn Bedford, who was the first professional writer to ever give me confidence in my writing, alongside plenty of specific and very useful criticism.

Then there are the important, everyday people in my life, the people who provide the counterbalance to the long hours of staring into space and keyboard bashing. Namely, my family. They are the bedrock of everything, especially my husband Chris, who never once doubted that all the effort would be worthwhile, and Alex and Rachel, who also played their part, which they may or may not recognise. Also thanks must go to Sam, Kath S and Joss, my running buddies, for stopping me seizing up!

Finally, I want to say thank you to Geena Blythe and Anne Bond, who will never read this book, but who inspired it.

A note from the author

IN MY first ever interview about *The Second Child*, a book blogger asked me how much research I'd had to do into the issue of disability to inform the story. The honest answer, and the one I finally gave, was '—very little', not because I'm shockingly lazy and unbelievably arrogant, but because I didn't have to. My eldest daughter has RTS, the condition that affects Lauren in the novel.

The hesitation and the answer are both worth reflecting on.

I paused before divulging that I have personal experience of disability because I was, and still am, concerned that an awareness of my daughter's condition might lead readers to expect an autobiographical novel. And that it might cause others to avoid it completely.

The Second Child is not about me, nor about my daughter. It's not a memoir, nor is it a study of the impact of disability, nor an examination of 'difference'. It is, I hope, a twisty exploration of parental expectation, adversity and resilience, with a cast of characters who have very different approaches to life, loving and change. My aim was to write an engaging page-turner of a book, not an exercise in self-help or reflection.

That said, the book is obviously informed by our experiences as a family. To deny that would be ludicrous. Lauren shares many traits and behaviours with my daughter. It would have been perverse to have chosen a different disability to the one I know, inside and out. And there is no doubt that some of the emotions expressed in the course of the book, especially Sarah's, chime with my own.

The blogger's question did, however, make me think more deeply than I ever have before about what impact having a disabled child has had on my writing.

Here is what I concluded.

Firstly, and very practically, writing is a good 'job' for someone who has to be at home a good deal and who has additional caring responsibilities. It can fit around and in between other commitments. A lot of the creative process doesn't actually involve touching a keyboard. It lies in the hours and hours of speculation and thinking that go into a character and plot... and you can think while washing, half-watching kids' TV and being awake in the early hours of the morning. Using your imagination in the pursuit of a story is the best antidote to worrying that I've ever found... much better than red wine.

Secondly, there has been the long-term impact of our daughter's disability on our attitude to life. We had our normal parental expectations snatched away when she was diagnosed as a baby. And ever since then we have had to make substantial changes, emotionally and practically. There's that word again, practicality! I believe that that process has given me an awareness of the precariousness of life and an insight into what it feels like when God laughs... best laid plans and all that! Disability forces a huge, on-going readjustment on everyone involved, and those changes help you to reassess what really matters.

But the biggest revelation for me, when I stopped to really think about it, is the contrast between *writing about disability* and *actually living with it*.

When your child is diagnosed with a life-changing condition and their disabilities start to emerge – through their inabilities and their differences – you have to make a conscious decision to let go of the life you had imagined. You slam a lid down on 'what if' and live with 'what is'. It's a useful and effective technique. It means that you can accept and adapt, and, with time and support, you learn to survive and thrive.

320

But writing requires the exact opposite discipline; its lifeblood is 'what if'. That's where the challenge and the excitement, the plot-lines and the characters, the drama and the tension come from.

If I'm honest with myself, and it's an uncomfortable thought, it was the question 'what if my daughter was not disabled' that motivated me to write *The Second Child*. In fiction I found the freedom to imagine a different world – one full of alternative choices, actions, emotions and outcomes. A world unimaginable in real life.

And so, though I hope I have risen to the challenge of portraying a disabled character well and shown how those with no voice and little capacity can have huge influence on others, the story of *The Second Child* is not my story.

It is Sarah and Anne's, Phil and James', even Nathan's. And, of course, it is Lauren's.

It is a book about dads as much as mums, sons as much as daughters, about real love and distorted love, and whether truth matters more than what's right.

I have my daughter to thank for the inspiration for *The Second Child*, but not for the resulting novel!

And one final thought. It occurred to me, on re-reading my own book, that I'm not sure I'd be as strong, as resilient or as forgiving as Sarah given the same choices and dilemmas. Thankfully, as my life sure as hell doesn't imitate art, I will never have to find out.